Advance P[...]
A RAIN OF N[...]

A Rain of Night Birds is beautiful, courageous, [...] d deeply thoughtful exploration of the living fro[...] [...]us and colonial perception. As a powerful and complex cross-cultural love story, set within the urgency of rapid climate change, with its conceptual causes and tremendous consequences, the novel asks us to listen carefully and respectfully across personal, social, scientific, and historical borders. It asks us to intellectually engage with, and feel at the core, both the inherited divisions and the potentials for resolution of the most crucial issues of our time. It gives no easy answers, but immerses us in an intimate and far-reaching world that requires one of the most difficult challenges we'll ever face, a profound shift of intention toward all that lives. It does so with eloquence, dignity, grace, and passion.

—Stan Rushworth, author of *Going to Water*

In clear and elegant prose, Deena Metzger yet again explores the most important issues of our time, in yet another profound and compelling way. *A Rain of Night Birds* is a beautiful and important novel.

—Derrick Jensen, author of *A Language Older Than Words, Endgame* and *The Culture of Make Believe*

Now more than ever, we need to read, and then read again, Deena Metzger's new novel, a thrilling exploration of the dilemmas we face as a species beset with extinction and as individuals beset by doubts as to how that threat to our loved ones and the Earth can be avoided in our age of confusion. The four complex protagonists take us on a journey into the depths of their despair and the lightening of their hopes, and by its end we are left trembling with grief and wisdom, challenged to leap into the arduous self-understanding of ourselves and the indigenous past that alone can guide us through the turmoil and the fire and, perhaps, who knows, save the Earth.

—Ariel Dorfman, author of the play *Death and the Maiden* and the forthcoming novel *Darwin's Ghosts*

This book blew me away! I loved the characters, the writing, the unfolding of it. As a longtime environmentalist with strong Indigenous and racial justice leanings, I found it riveting, compelling and resonant. The story and characters drew me in deeply, in ways that reached my intuition, my dream time and my empathic, embodied sense of self. I immersed myself in it, reading it in several sittings as I was so engrossed. It's rare that a writer can convey so much that spans from the deeply personal to the transpersonal or universal levels, but Deena does it, masterfully. I highly recommend this book for anyone who loves Mother Earth, who resonates with Indigenous Wisdom, and who wishes to fulfill their own greatest destiny at this transformative moment for all life on Earth.

—Nina Simons
Co-Founder, Bioneers; Co-Founder, Cultivating Women's Leadership

A Rain of Night Birds is an extraordinary story in which love and compassion create a field where the deep knowing of the Indigenous Soul can grow and the truest relationship with the natural world has real possibilities.

—Cheryl Potts, Alutiiq, Kodiak Island, Alaska

When I finished reading *A Rain of Night Birds*, words immediately entered my mind: Deena has written a creation story. A creation story that does not soften the reality of where we find ourselves, one that asks us to know the devastating and fatal harm our way of life inflicts on our Mother Earth and all Her beings. To know Her suffering viscerally. To know that we are Her. And to know that creation speaks to us in so many ways. *A Rain of Night Birds* is a beautifully written story of witness and sacrifice, of the fundamental questions we must ask, of the necessary and possible alliances we must make with each other, the earth, the spirits, the elementals and the Mystery.

—Nora L. Jamieson, author of *Deranged*

Deena Metzger is a force of nature, and so is her latest novel, *A Rain of Night Birds*. Master storyteller Metzger conjures lives of awareness in a world of changing climate as no other writer before her. "Take the opportunity to know wind, rather than know about it," says a character early in the book. The novel's endearing and complex characters begin to trust one another, and the possibility of listening to the land in its own language, not in translation. As they do, so might we. Whether Deena Metzger is writing and healing from her high mountain perch in Topanga Canyon, listening to elephants in Africa, or bearing witness at Standing Rock, she is a teacher for our times. If you don't know her work, begin with *A Rain of Night Birds*.

—Susan Cerulean, author of *Coming to Pass: Florida's Coastal Islands in a Gulf of Change*

It took great courage and a fierce spirit to write *A Rain of Night Birds*. Deena Metzger's uncompromising honesty penetrates the core reality of climate change, its causes, and its implications for all of us. And she does this while exploring the power of love on all levels: between woman and man, father and daughter, indigenous people and white people, the human species and the natural world. Written with passion and clarity, this astonishing story never ducks the truth, yet brings the reader into the fullness of life on our beautiful blue planet.

—Anne Batterson, author of *The Black Swan: Memory, Midlife and Migration*

A Rain of Night Birds is urgent, mythic and beautiful. Deena's words take us through an unflinching experience of deep repair as great story is meant to do. Our hearts are torn open with blade-like revelation. Few novels today reach beneath the roots of our human and Earth dilemma with such poignant grace and compassion.

—Laura Simms, author of *Our Secret Territory: The Robe of Love*

The story told by Deena Metzger has deep and mysterious meanings. I believe that what is being told here is the elemental interplay of masculine and feminine energy as these interact in what we call reality. Understanding of the natural world through different worldviews and sciencing are dealt with in the relationship between Terrence and Sandra. They are both trained in a science that at its root is patriarchal. Yet, underneath there is a matriarchal call from the Earth herself for healing the split between these powerful forces that created the universe. Deena gives us the prescription for healing our personal and collective split through becoming conscious of these forces and their interplay in the human ceremony called relationship.

—Eduardo Duran, author of *Native American Postcolonial Psychology*

This book is an offering to our own reconciliation with our shared past and history, both its beauty and suffering. A steadfast marriage of fact, fiction and possibility. A sincere prayer, reliable and patient, bridging the spectrums between science, belief systems and traditional Native ways. If you have ever wondered if you can listen to the wind, the plants, the animals, rather than just know about them, this book is for you. If you have ever dared to question the human cultural narrative, this book is for you. As we each strive to meet the challenges of our times, *A Rain of Night Birds* allows faith to know that something more exists than what we have so far considered as possible.

—Krystyna Jurzykowski
Council Carrier and Wilderness Guide
Co-founder of Fossil Rim Wildlife Center and High Hope, a Sanctuary for Retreat

Deena Metzger's *A Rain of Night Birds* is a masterfully written story that simultaneously speaks to restoration of the environment, the institution of medicine, and the role of right relationships. It is a true love story: love of the Earth and Spirit, love of the Native people and Indigenous ways, love for the sake of and at the heart of healing. Metzger's writing, rich with prescient wisdom, not only engages and entertains, but also provides important and timely guidance to help navigate these tenuous times.

—Karen L. Mutter, D.O.,
(Founder) Integrative Medicine Healing Center, Clearwater, FL

If our way of life as humans is making the planet sick, isn't it making us sick as well? What would it take to heal us, to heal the Earth? Do we have any idea what healing truly is? These questions reverberate through this difficult and deeply necessary book. Sandra Birdswell is a climatologist who understands climate change as "a euphemism for extinction by human hands." Terrence Green, Chair of the Department of Earth and Environmental Sciences, has had to adopt the methods of Western science at the expense of the traditional knowledge he, a native man, was raised with. When Terrence and Sandra fall in love, each of them is thrust into a deep and almost unbearable knowing about the suffering of the Earth and their complicity in the culture of disconnection that is responsible for it. The knowing changes them both from the ground up. What is required of each of us, colonized and colonizer, in order to preserve this precious earth? This profound and beautiful love story has the timeless power of myth – but it is also a metaphor for our time. "What have we done? What are we doing?" is Sandra's anguished cry midway through *A Rain of Night Birds*. By the end of the book, it has become the reader's as well.

—Lise Weil, editor, *Dark Matter: Women Witnessing*

A Rain of Night Birds is an unforgettable, life-altering novel. It carries a love story to open your soul, the beauty of longtime friendship, and the deepest love – of Earth, weather, wind, birds, lightning, ancestors and the great, vibrant hum of the land. The characters will charm you and teach you in their raw undoing and the wisdom they ultimately receive. The novel is a momentous and needed confrontation between Indigenous knowledge and the modern scientific mind. At this historical moment of heartbreak and maximum peril, Deena Metzger offers a roadmap to dismantle old assumptions and habits in our own ways of thinking. "We can't go back to our old lives," says Sandra Birdswell after an encounter with the Earth's mysterious forces. After reading this novel, I felt located, clarified, made true. With gratitude I will pass this book along to everyone I know.

—Carolyn Brigit Flynn, author of *Communion: In Praise of the Sacred Earth*

A Rain of Night Birds is a love story regarding the interconnectedness of human beings placed within the boundaries of science. Today when words wear disguises and can be used as barriers to what we really mean, Deena Metzger provides her characters the courage to be still and listen and discover mysteries trapped in the past that must be woven into present solutions. Encased in a cocoon of quiet, truth-telling information patiently waits to be revealed and with clear headed guidance Metzger invites us to trust what's imbedded in the gift of silent communication. To know what we already know, what's already in us is a pathway to save all living things including the planet and each other.

—Joan Tewkesbury, writer of Robert Altman's *Nashville,* author of
Ebba and the Green Dresses of Olivia Gomez In a Time of Conflict and War

In *A Rain of Night Birds,* Deena Metzger's voice is big true medicine – for our last-chance human sickness. Indigenous mind, ceremonial mind, gathers force in us through Sandra and Terrence's missteps and unpredictable harmonies. Old and new ways begin to flow together, out of the labyrinth of human-Nature apartheid. *Night Birds* is a warning. It's almost too late for the wisdom-poetry of this book. Or any book. The soul moves slowly and in a serpentine manner. *Night Birds* is a call: it's too late not to become one who is given to another understanding on the mountain and (therefore) asked to live accordingly: dancer, collaborator in the turning-returning dream music of Life.

—Maia, author of *The Spirit Life of Birds*

Deena Metzger's *A Rain of Night Birds* is a beautiful and provocative story of remembrance and forgetting, of reclamation and loss, and of deep listening, not only from one beloved to another, but across time and space, across generations, and across the great divide between humanity and the earth. It carries the power both to disturb and to confer the blessing that comes of sitting with what is true.

—Allan G. Johnson, author of *Not from Here: A Memoir*

Deena lives her life navigating and negotiating many worlds, just as her protagonist, Sandra, in *A Rain of Night Birds* also lives her life. Exploring what is mysterious and liminal, the experience of reading and studying with Deena challenges me to pray for help, to reach far beyond what is easy and familiar, to plumb the depths of my potential to create and serve compassionately in these demanding times. Bringing forth her love and respect for Native lifeways, she offers a unique quality of creative wisdom through her spiritual and artistic teachings. Whether one has a one-to-one exchange, participates in a council experience, or joins an interactive retreat with Deena, her deep questioning and guidance opens hearts and minds to new possibilities and pathways of love and service to Mother Earth and All The Ancestors.

—Jaune Evans, writer and photographer of "Collecting Fog," Everyday Soto Zen Priest

In Deena Metzger's new book, we are given a fierce and passionate gift, a book that opens us to the deep healing presence of silence and the elements – sun, wind, storm, and lightning, imparted by singular and vital voices. Terrence – a Tsalagi university professor of climatology struggles between Indigenous wisdom and science. Sandra – his lover and a climatologist in her own right seeks to claim her own astonishing intuitive gifts in tending the earth. Hosteen – her friend and a Diné elder speaks from the far-reaching ground of his tradition. And John – her father and a doctor, longs to bridge their differences. They have entrusted their stories to Deena and there could be no more reverent guardian of these gifts. Every step of the way Deena keeps faith with the soul-work that must be done, with the heartbreaking questions of climate change and devastation, with the vital Diné/Navajo and Tsalagi/Cherokee relations to Earth and Sky, and with the essential healing imperative of Western medicine, Do no harm. In the end, we are all connected to these voices that link worlds and also suffer the terrible divisions of our time. We must read this book and listen well, for the wind speaks, the land shudders, the animals attend and so must we. Earth demands this kind of vision, and we can no longer pretend that we are separate from her.

—Regina O'Melveny, author of *The Book of Madness and Cures*

I doubt if there has ever been a time when a book is more needed than Deena Metzger's, *A Rain of Night Birds*. Its searing journey insists that we face complex and difficult truths about climate change, its causes and the enormity of what is required to meet the challenge. Yes, it is a love story but with dimensions that are both mythic and prophetic. The lovers, two climatologists, a white woman and an Indigenous man, love the Earth as much, or more, than they love each other. They will not let themselves escape into their personal love until they face how each has contributed to environmental devastation. It takes nothing less than life threatening encounters with elemental forces to shock and transform them at the deepest levels. Clearly the writer of this book has asked no less of her self. We know as we read that our guide has traveled this arduous path. And so we allow her to help us strip away our habits of mind, and our attachments to comfort, that stand in the way of our rescuing all life from extinction.

—Naomi Newman, director, writer, the Traveling Jewish Theatre, playwright, *Snake Talk*

With lyrical grace and truth, Deena Metzger's *A Rain of Night Birds* crosses the border from Western into Indigenous ways of knowing and asks: how shall we heal the wounds we've inflicted upon Mother Earth? Sandra, Terrence, John, and Hosteen manifest the human struggle to transcend a dominant scientific myopia and deepen our relationship with the Great Mystery. Their story is the dream within our own dream of the crucial quest we'll each need to make while there's still time.

—David Edward Walker, author of *Tessa's Dance* and *Signal Peak*

Deena Metzger knows how to light a fire in the heart with only one match. In *A Rain of Night Birds* she gives us a literature of restoration, an act of moral witness and great creative purpose that challenges us towards deeper aliveness in the face of a wounded earth. She is showing what it is for words, or, more exactly a story, to carry medicine. Those who fear losing purpose will find a lifetime's worth of it in this gritty, wise, loving and rigorously beautiful novel.

—Amnon Buchbinder, author of *Mortal Coil*, writer-director of *The Biology of Story*

I am grateful to everyone who has stepped forth to endorse this book. In my mind, we constitute a Council of Elders gathering to protect the Earth and to honor spirit-based, Earth-centered Indigenous wisdom. As we go to press, the world is moving into a shadow of great darkness. Despite these tragic circumstances, there is the light of the undeniable presence of the elementals, the spirits and the hearts of all those committed to the planet. We are called to so much more than protest. We are called to fundamentally change our thinking, systems and lives, to divest from all forms and activities that lead to genocide and the ravages of pollution and climate change for humans and non-humans alike. The devastation we call Climate Change and the barbaric ruins of the Anthropocene began in North America in 1492 with the brutal Conquest and Colonization. Paradoxically, the Lakota prayer, *mitakuye oyasin*, provides all of us with the essential guidance needed to transform and sustain life. Please join us and enter the conversation.

Deena Metzger, February 2017

A
RAIN
OF
NIGHT
BIRDS

Other Works by Deena Metzger

Fiction

La Negra y Blanca
Feral
Doors: A Fiction for Jazz Horn
The Other Hand
What Dinah Thought
The Woman Who Slept With Men to Take the War Out of Them
Skin: Shadows/Silence

Non-Fiction

From Grief Into Vision: A Council
Entering the Ghost River: Meditations on
the Theory and Practice of Healing
Intimate Nature: The Bond Between Women and Animals
(with Brenda Peterson and Linda Hogan)
Writing For Your Life: A Guide and Companion to the Inner Worlds
Tree: Essays and Pieces

Poetry

Ruin and Beauty: New and Selected Poems
Dark Milk
The Axis Mundi Poems
Looking for the Faces of God
A Sabbath Among the Ruins

Drama

Dreams Against the State
Not As Sleepwalkers
Book of Hags

A
RAIN
OF
NIGHT
BIRDS

To Colleen
The spirits have
always called you
in love,
Blessings

Deena Metzger

HAND TO HAND

Hand to Hand is a community based endeavor that supports independently published works and public events, free of the restrictions that arise from commercial and political concerns. It is a forum for artists who are in dynamic and reciprocal relationship with their communities for the sake of peacemaking, restoring culture and the planet. For further information regarding Hand to Hand please write to us at: P.O. Box 186, Topanga, CA, 90290, USA. Or visit us on the web at:

www.handtohandpublishing.com

Donations to organizations have been made to replenish the trees that were used to create the paper in this book. We also wish to acknowledge the RSF Social Finance AnJel Donor Advised Fund for their support. 50% of the profits from the sale of this book will be donated to support Indigenous environmental efforts.

References to quoted materials are at the end of this book.

Book and Cover Design: Stephan David Hewitt
Author Photo by Jay Roberts

    Publisher's Cataloging-in-Publication

        Metzger, Deena, author.
            A rain of night birds / Deena Metzger.
            pages cm
            Includes bibliographical references.
            ISBN 978-0-9983443-0-0

            1. Climatic changes--Fiction. 2. Indians of North
        America--History--Fiction. 3. Geology, Stratigraphic--
        Anthropocene--Fiction. 4. Spirituality--Fiction.
        5. Ecofiction, American.   I. Title.

    PS3563.E864R35 2017   813'.6
                QBI17-900024

Acknowledgements

F irst, I acknowledge the spirits who have guided me every step along the
   way of writing this book. A Voice came and introduced Sandra. Then
her father, John Birdswell, his friend and elder, Hosteen Tseda, and finally,
Terrence Green appeared. They have taken on their own lives; I am grateful
for their presence and willingness to reveal themselves to me and to us. What
good companions they are for these difficult times. Their stories, as they
have permitted to know them, have been told and now they are finding their
ways among us. I wouldn't say they offer hope; I would say they offer a broad
and complex path that can be followed on behalf of all beings. The future,
if there will be one, is theirs. We are in their hands, if they will have us.

Next, I acknowledge the land, the generous and storied land here in
Topanga which has held me as I struggled to bring this text into existence.
And the Wind which has been with me for so many years and suddenly
blasts through the trees as I write these words. Then, Joshua Tree National
Park, which in its spare winter beauty invited me onto it so that I could hear
the Voice in February 2011. And then the incomparable beauty of the Four
Corners Reservation and Canyon de Chelly, the dark birds and the horses.
The anguish that these lands experience from our cruel experiments in
power that are paralleled at the Columbia Gorge in the monstrous activities
at Hanford Nuclear Reservation that has devastated the Yakama Reservation
and the sacred waters. Awareness of the global nightmare that is Los Alamos.
In return, gratitude to the salmon who endure and continue to nourish us
and to Michael Ortiz Hill who introduced me to Canyon de Chelly.

In the realm of the inexplicable, gratitude for and wonder at the happy
intrusion of Neil Young's songs as if Young were an invisible and silent
partner in the writing of the text. As if the music wanted to support the
book's devotion to drastically healing the environment and honoring the
Native people who have remembered what is essential despite five hundred
years of genocide, an understanding which we, it appears, both share though
we do not know each other.

My sons, Marc and Greg, their wives, Kris and Becky, their children,
Jamie, Sarah, Finn and Cole, are a constant reminder of the preciousness of

life and the need to protect it. And equally the companionship of the four-leggeds, Cherokee, Shoonaq' and Cheyenne who have accompanied this writing.

My father was a Yiddish writer and my mother supported his work and guarded the little time he had to write on weekends and occasional evenings when he was not preoccupied by and exhausted from the effort of supporting a family and a community devastated by World War II. So I thank my parents for their example, and my friends and community who encourage me and hold to the need to revision our culture entirely, to step out of imperial mind, to try to understand and live by the great Lakota wisdom – *mitakuye oyasin*, all my relations.

Gratitude to the Elders who have taught and guided me, to the Lodges that I have had the privilege of attending, to the prayers that have entered with the heat and the drum into my consciousness, to the gift of the daily awareness of the sacred, to the offerings that being made transform us. To Stan Rushworth, Cheryl Potts and Terry Delehanty, who have heartfully shared their wisdom and histories with me. To K who would like to remain anonymous but with whom I came to know Four Corners in an entirely different way as several of us made a pilgrimage there together. To Lora Matz, who traveled with me to the Hanford Nuclear Reservation and suffered, as I did, the consequences of an accidental release of radioactivity. To Valerie Wolf, Lawrie Hartt, Muz (Richenel Ansano,) Sharon Simone, and Nora Jamieson with whom I have walked the sacred paths to the ancestors. To all those who walk in Indigenous ways who have gifted me with their friendship and to those who are returning to or rediscovering these Paths and have shared that journey with me, and to the myriad friends, companions, colleagues, mentees, students who are also devoted to revisioning Western mind, to Indigenous Wisdom and spirit-based, Earth-centered lives.

To F. David Peat whose book, *Blackfoot Physics*, accompanied me and sustained me as I was simultaneously undone by traveling to Hanford. To Yakama Elder, Russell Jim, head of the Confederated Tribes and Bands of the Yakama Indian Nation's Environmental Restoration and Waste Management Program who spoke from a true place, as elders do and who perseveres, though heartbroken.

To the artistry of the Diné and other Native American peoples, whose weavings, carvings, sand paintings, sacred objects speak eloquently in languages more powerful than words. To the writers of the scores of books I have read by Native people, and non-Natives, who have imparted the wisdom they have gathered and the beauty of their ways, so that the Earth and Her peoples, non-human and human, might survive.

Thankfulness for the transmission of the 19 Ways to the 5th World, to the dreams that have educated my soul. For those who have accompanied me all these years, for those who have become part of Daré, of ReVisioning Medicine – including Karen Mutter, Kjersten Gmeiner, Marc Weigensberg, Tobi Fishel, Danelia Wild – for the Training Circle for the 5th World, the Tuesday night, Wednesday night Writing Circles, for Called Together and the various writing and healing circles and intensives here in Topanga and everywhere we have gathered. For Africa and the elephants and the other non-humans whose consciousness, intelligence and agency infiltrates every thought and every word I write.

Deep appreciation to Stan Rushworth, Ariel Dorfman, Carolyn Flynn and Regina O'Melveny for your ongoing reading and deep engagement with the text as it developed year after year. Needless to say, all the errors – all the errors – are the responsibility of the writer who hopes there are not too many. Appreciation for David Edward Walker who reminded me of a crucial reference and for Kejsa Cedar who graciously shared her story of being struck by lightning.

Thank you Leanne Hunt and Jude Weber, your efforts, labor, conscientiousness and kindness are helping to make this book a reality.

Gratitude to Cynthia Travis of everyday gandhis, and Krystyna Jurzykowski, Claude Pepin and Mark Finser of the AnJel Fund of the Rudolph Steiner Foundation that has supported this writer and her work with love, wisdom and financial support; without any of these, the book would not exist.

Deep appreciation that Hand to Hand exists as a community based endeavor that supports independently published works and public events – books, plays, music, performances, films etc. – free of the restrictions that arise from commercial and political concerns. It is a forum for artists who are in dynamic and reciprocal relationship with their communities for the sake of healing, peacemaking, and restoring culture and the planet.

Very special thanks to Stephan Hewitt, the publisher, whose untiring efforts sustain it. Additionally, we must speak of the gifts Stephan offers as artist, designer, reader, editor and friend. When Stephan showed me his design for the cover of the book, I knew that, once again, we were collaborating in a sacred realm.

Gratitude to Earth, Air, Water, Fire and to the Great Heart from which all Creation emerges. How grateful I am that I have had glimpses of the Awesome Presence and the opportunity to serve the future.

And at the moment when the book is finished and I am writing the acknowledgements, it is essential to recognize the Water Protectors of Standing Rock who are, by offering their lives, showing all of us what matters and how to act, resist and live in these difficult times. May this book be a way of standing with them on behalf of the ancestors and the Water.

Mni Wiconi – Water is sacred.

To my sons,
Marc and Gregory,
our kin descendants and ancestors,
so there may be a future
for all beings.

At last Sweet Medicine said to the people: "I shall not be with you long now. I am getting to be old and have lived as long as I want to: but before I die I have something to tell you. ... Soon you will find among you a people who have hair all over their faces, and whose skin is white. They will be looking for a certain stone; they will be people who do not get tired, but who will keep pushing forward, going all the time. They will keep coming, coming. They will travel everywhere, looking for this stone, which our great-grandfather put on the Earth in many places. These people will not listen to what you say; what they are going to do, they will do. You people will change; in the end of your life in those days you will not get up early in the morning, you will not know when day comes. They will try to change you from your way of living to theirs. They will tear up the earth, and at last you will do it with them. When you do, you will become crazy and will forget all that I am teaching you. The white people will be all over the land and at last you will disappear. I am sorry to say these things, but I have seen them, and you will find they will come true.

The Prophecy of Sweet Medicine to the Cheyenne People

Sickness that sweeps through a population has its origins
not so much in viruses as in ideas.

F. David Peat, <u>Blackfoot Physics</u>

PREFACE

The Mystery

This book began when I heard a voice speaking to me. The voice identified a character by name and occupation.

"You know ..." the voice began.

I shuddered. I didn't know and hearing a voice speaking so clearly and precisely overwhelmed me. It was not only what the voice said. It was that there was a voice speaking to me, a voice that was real, coherent and external.

It was February 2011. I had just published another novel and was hoping to be inspired to write the next. Walking in Joshua Tree National Park, I found myself preoccupied by picking up garbage until my pockets and hands were full and yet there was no end to it.

"I'm sorry."

The words surprised me. I had said them aloud.

"I'm sorry," I repeated.

That's when I heard the voice.

"You know," the voice said, "her name is Sandra Birdswell and she is a meteorologist."

The voice spoke with authority; I couldn't dismiss it. Authority and insistence. I had been longing for a novel and now it was being given to me, so I could not refuse even though I knew nothing about the character. I had no choice but to accept the challenge that would take me far beyond myself. I did not understand where I was being led, but I had to commit myself and write what was called for.

At the moment of this book's inception in Joshua Tree, Terrence Green didn't exist. Then a year later, he came to be. To me as the writer, Terrence Green is a greater mystery than Sandra Birdswell who introduced him. Once manifest, Sandra determined the Story that is being told and Terrence, she revealed, was at the core.

At that first moment in Joshua Tree, I didn't know anything about Sandra

3

Birdswell, except her name, her profession, but not what followed from that, a vast terrain both entirely unknown and completely mystifying. I knew less about Terrence Green.

The process of writing seems simple, but it isn't. Write a character into a story, press Save. He or she exists. Highlight his or her name and the surrounding paragraph, press the scissor icon on the toolbar, one or the other or both die, then press Save to insure the demise.

Theoretically Terrence Green can be entirely disappeared from the text. I could paste the words that describe him into a file labeled Outtakes and he would only exist in limbo waiting to know if he will ever have a real life. That possibility is only theoretical.

Sandra appeared and then Terrence appeared. I had great trepidation about writing about him. I didn't know if I have the right to write about a Native man inasmuch as cultural appropriation is an ongoing violation. But I didn't have the right to refuse him either. Finally I had to accept what negative consequences might come to me from my limitations and hope to have the skill to record his true self, to honor and respect him as is his due. I had to yield to him. He wanted to live. Sandra insisted and then he insisted. He asserted that the text cannot exist without him. He carries wisdom.

When Terrence came forth, Hosteen Tseda began to speak more forthrightly. He is an elder and certainly a wisdom keeper. The time for this wisdom has come. They will not be erased.

PART 1

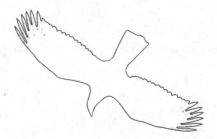

1

The Whirl of Everything

It was very early, long before dawn when light awakened Sandra Birdswell. The broken cloud cover was shimmering with a red glow. It reminded her of the full moon turning red a year and a half before on August 12th, 2003 when proximate to Mars at its perigee to Earth. The radiance was unnerving as the moon had been then – a blood tide. She propped herself up on pillows and stared out the window, almost eye to eye with the clouds themselves. She waited. Listened. Could this shimmer be caused by red waves similar to those she had seen several times in her life as they rose from the imminently vibrating Earth before extended earthquakes? But no, everything on the land seemed unmoving. The red persisted.

She sensed that deep in space, a flare from the body of the sun was rising up, perhaps already streaming out through the sun's surface toward Earth, across the 93 million miles that is the exact distance that makes life possible. She was sure that she wasn't seeing an aurora borealis, though on occasion such has been viewed far south in California, and once, in the Caribbean, in 1859. She had seen auroras when she was in the Arctic, but this was different. Glimmering clouds, perhaps the entire night sky, luminous waves of color, sensation and light had awakened her, were coming in, as if beneath the radar. They could have created Northern Lights, but they hadn't, except, apparently, in her. She continued listening. She had no stories of her own to speak of this to herself. However, the coexistence of different forms of perception in a single pulse of sight, color, sound and sensation was familiar to her. Phenomena were more than phenomena. Something was morphing into something else and back again. It hummed or shimmered or vibrated, burned like amber. It resonated, it was like a metal gong, a bell, a light ignited in the universe and fading out.

Over the years, she had learned to translate these odd perceptions into mathematical or technological languages that her colleagues could grok, but they didn't serve her and she didn't want to be distracted by translation now.

For her, the common language of science, which she spoke fluently, undercut awe though she knew that her colleagues marveled at the order and complexity of the Earth and the universe. But when they started speaking, writing … where was awe? Somehow the technical language that had developed to meet the infinitely large or small, a language that required training and study, and asserted the speaker's command of the circumstances, took focus away from the thing-in-itself, the astounding and incomprehensible beauty that was revealing itself to her.

At such a moment, she had almost fallen into the trap; she could be sidetracked so quickly. Sandra roused herself from the repetitive inner argument and the thrall of finding language and explanations in order to pay attention to what was so mysterious –the incandescent pulse of blood and fire that was pervading the sky.

She rose from bed and went out onto the circular deck surrounding her house and then mounted the wooden stairs to the roof that she had converted into a viewing area so there was no impediment to immersing herself in the hymn of color in the dark light. She opened her pores to it, allowed it to enter her, and she, to enter it, to the extent that dissolve was possible. The tones and colors persisted in their metal harmonies of copper and bronze. She turned to view it in all directions and then turned faster and faster as she had as a child, spinning and spinning, faster and faster, until she experienced the whirl of everything around her and she fought to stand upright, to be steady "at the still point in a turning world."

She was spinning and the Earth was spinning. The sun spinning too. Planets and meteors circling the spinning sun. Our Milky Way turning. Andromeda turning. Spiral galaxies revolving. All the galaxies turning and the universe spinning as well. Everything in motion. As above, so below, the macrocosm and the microcosm. All of it, red and magenta, in her body too. This was not physical sensation alone. It was the whirl of everything turning in relationship to everything else. It was the essential, sacred activity of creation.

She wasn't simply remembering spinning this way as a child in similar woods behind the house where she had lived with her father, but she was somehow back there in a clearing among the trees and here as well on the roof of her own house on January 20, 2005, in the way she saw, felt, heard the toning of the red, this moment on the roof.

Turning and turning, she tried to understand and give up understanding simultaneously, as words spun up from the surface of her mind in the way she felt herself whirling up into whatever mystery was swirling around her. She wanted to stop but she couldn't without stepping away from what was occurring around her, as if she could twirl herself into the ruddy world that was beckoning. That world did not communicate with her in English or any other human speech.

Without language, she was empty inside and yet filled with what was outside. Maybe she wasn't spinning into it, maybe it was spinning into her. Breathe, don't think, she cautioned herself. Listen. It was important to listen without putting words in her own mouth or mind. Listen! She cautioned.

Then she couldn't maintain herself any longer. A bit wobbly, she climbed down the ladder that was fastened to the wall, arms extended, holding on to the rails but refusing the urge to let herself fall backwards until she was standing firmly on the earth, allowing the inner whirligig to run its course as she came to a standstill. She made her way to the nearest pine to lean against it, pitch be damned. In time, the glimmer faded entirely, a burnished shadow shortening in retreat to deep rose, to fire opal and finally to sunstone, to ocher, then sandy colored, the exact color, she imagined of her name, and then, gone. The dark reappeared though diminished by the waxing gibbous moon.

The physical affect of the flare had evoked a analogous attunement to global events that concerned her, a visceral experience of the twist of tornadoes, thunderstorms, cyclones, hurricanes spinning across land and oceans. A familiar vertigo seized her, not from the motion, but from the alteration of beauty and distress. Her gut knowing. She had sensed this since childhood. But lately the sensations were accompanied with grim understanding. These were no mere natural events. The Anthropocene, she thought. We are responsible.

She accepted the painful knowing that was hammering her. She lay down, her knees up, her arms stretched out, palms on the earth. Maybe she felt a pulse, maybe she didn't. She usually knew, but at this moment, she couldn't tell.

Back in her house, Sandra expected that the instruments in various laboratories that viewed and recorded eruptions on the sun would soon start humming with measurements, and confirmations. If it were a CME, a Coronal Mass Ejection, it would have greater consequences and would trigger power grid alerts, announcements of electronic interference, computers going down, astronauts taking cover; this was a big one. She never thought such premonitions or perceptions were warnings for her to take care of herself. But why not? Was this her arrogance? Or was it that concerned with its possible ill effects, few would focus on its beauty first and foremost. Maybe this was her task.

It could take two hours, more or less for such a flare to stream from sun to Earth, or a few days for a CME. Sandra wasn't certain which or where it was in the process, but given the cloud and the way the color and its speed were one, not an equation but a single event, which had started on the sun and was already here, she assumed it would be identified as a flare. She had seen a red glow that probably no one else had seen in this way or that others would dismiss as an inversion layer causing an unusual reflection from the city lights. This, however, was no reflection of urban density, industry or technology. The belly of a cloud, a great whale in the sky, had been secretly glowing internally with the extremity of a celestial event, definitely not of our making. And, she had been in it.

After color, intensity, astonishment and nausea subsided and she was steady, Sandra telephoned a friend working at NASA – night shift this month on sun watch.

"You name it," her colleague sighed. It was nearing the end of a long night. She was weary. And maybe wary without knowing why.

"Solar Flare, X class at 2:31 a.m.," Sandra announced with, perhaps, too much bravado.

"How do you know, Sandra?" Colleen didn't really want to know and Sandra didn't want to say.

Sandra hung up the phone as soon as the woman's coolness entered the room the way breezes come up at the exact second of sunset. Then she felt bad and called back.

"Let me tell you what color it was, Colleen. Wonder, Colleen. The red glow in the clouds was the color of wonder."

"Is it still there, Sandra?"

"No. I wouldn't have called yet if it were. I was mesmerized. After a while, it turned … a faint … amber. And then it disappeared or lost interest in me. Everything returned to its night state."

Colleen called back and confirmed, "Yes, an X3.2 class flare. You probably saw it because it is a really big one. Lucky no one was on the moon." She hesitated, "You were watching it, weren't you?"

"Watching what, Colleen?"

"Watching sunspot NOAA720. We've been watching it. You must have known."

"No, I didn't know. I haven't been following the sun's weather." The information was disturbing to Sandra. Confirmation was disturbing. She had been ambivalent when she called, she had wanted to know and she didn't. Now her knowing had a dark tone to it. Why did she know what she knew?

"Local auroras?" Sandra asked to ease her mind.

"None," Colleen conceded reluctantly. "But wait about thirty-six hours for the CME that may follow."

Yes, Sandra had just seen an invisible sun flare. Individual sun flares, probably have only minimal if any impact on weather and global warming, despite the great heat and force that generates them and sends them shooting toward Earth. While it is implicitly assumed that they are invisible, that humans can't perceive them without instruments, it is generally admitted that the pattern of solar cycles might well affect ozone layers and ocean temperature over time and these, in turn, are involved in climate change. She had just seen a sun flare and this mystery challenged the scientific assumptions that were fundamental to her training.

She had just seen a sun flare. She was certain of this. Colleen had verified it. But disbelief arose in her. Had this happened? Truly? She went out of her office onto the deck. Turning to the east, she closed her eyes. "Did this happen?" she demanded to know.

She was in a mystery. She hadn't sought this out, yet here she was, entirely responsible to her experience. Sun flares have impact. The activity of the sun, the dynamic of its essential form and nature, must affect us, subtly and also directly. This understanding did not contradict her certainty that she and all humans are fully responsible for the current shift in weather, the grave expansion of deserts, and the deadly consequences of climate change. The mystery did not relieve or diminish her concerns for the world. Her distress was a constant buzz, a ceaseless irritation, a drone of white and ambient noise that kept her honest. She would not relinquish it.

What connected Sandra to the universe, disconnected her from her colleagues who familiarized themselves with the invisible through equations and instruments to which they were wedded. Sandra's peculiar gift was knowing through her own body. Her sensations were irrefutable. Not for others. Her work was scrutinized by others to be certain that she came to her conclusions in the right way. She had to be careful when writing papers or consulting that she corroborated her thinking and observations in the conventional manner – according to the exactness of Western science. Her colleagues might be interested in the phenomenon of her witnessing, but would ascribe no authority to it. Contrarily, she had to respect the event itself and consider its implications, not that it had happened to her, but that it had happened at all, to anyone. This was as intriguing as the sensate phenomenon of the event itself.

The mystery of her perceptions was beyond her; it could not be dismissed even though it couldn't be explained. Reality, as she was coming to know it, was so much greater than what was postulated to exist within the realm of reproducible experiments, coherent models and recurring events. There were myriad, complex, interactions between distinct beings, organic and inorganic, human and non-human that weren't easily recognized or explained but that had to be acknowledged. She had just experienced one.

Sandra had been teaching at the local college for a semester. She hadn't found the work she had imagined when she started out on the path toward climatology. She had taken this job to give herself a break – doing something of value, earning a little money, creating time to think about the relationship of her future to the future of Earth, both becoming increasingly precarious.

"Climatology or climate science is the study of climate, scientifically defined as weather conditions averaged over a period of time. This modern field of study is regarded as a branch of the atmospheric sciences and a subfield of physical geography, which is one of the Earth sciences." That's how Wikipedia defines climatology and Sandra, "respecting" such a "national authority" had immersed herself as deeply as possible in the field of the atmospheric sciences, and the earth sciences, so that she might be competent before the challenge that climatology presented to her. In 2000, when she was deep into research for her dissertation, Paul Crutzen, (five years after receiving the Nobel Prize for ozone layer depletion caused by chlorofluorocarbons, CFCs), with Eugene Stoermer, identified the Anthropocene geological time interval as an epoch. They suggested the Anthropocene could be said to have started at the time of the steam engine, in the latter part of the eighteenth century, when analyses of air trapped in polar ice showed the beginning of growing global concentrations of carbon dioxide and methane.

She had been just starting out, was researching her dissertation. The Anthropocene was not a fact, it was a threat. The Wikipedia definition did not mention saving the Earth in the time of climate change and the Anthropocene, but that was all that interested her or ever had. Someone who had known her from birth might say that she had come in with such an obsession.

She lay down in bed again. There was not yet any hint of dawn in the eastern sky. The dark rocked her back to sleep until the faintest intimation of light awakened her two hours later, the light rising and spreading itself out everywhere. Branches on the nearby plum tree were becoming rosy with the paint of dawn and then dimming into their own dark bodies in the light of day. Steady light revealing intrinsic darkness. One limb was reaching up and out of the canopy as if the entire world hinged on this living shaft of light and dark. She observed this almost every morning that she was living in the house, and it was always magical. Like the sun flare, the light on the plum tree made the world intimate for Sandra. Incomprehensible vastness was gathered here on point, which, like every point in the universe, is the very center of all being.

She was trying to fathom it. The sun had been flaring; its own fiery braids had swirled out from deep within with the force of its spin as if seeking her out. With the proper welder's glasses or shields, you could even see a sunspot. Today, she had been in the dark, literally, that is, asleep, and so without instruments, scopes, screens, dials, data, printouts, and then catapulted awake toward the great fire that was light not heat. She was perceiving an intelligence, an energy far beyond her for which she had no language. An intelligence and a great mystery.

Nothing she had studied was going to meet the mystery. Soon the sun that was extending itself to Earth would rise, or, more precisely, the Earth would turn and dip toward it, in a deep unending bow. Rising and falling depend on perspective. For Sandra, the night did not fall nor did the sun rise though she would use that language not having found any other. The Earth spun toward the sun, bowed, spun, centering its own darkness in order to see the other stars that were eclipsed, in turn, by the blinding light of the sun. After dawn, it would be impossible without instruments, to note the sun's precise turning, the exact speed or direction of its spin, for the naked eye cannot look at it. Face to face with such wild brilliance, one needs to cover one's eyes.

Indigenous people recognized such spirits and honored them. It was good to be humble before a divine nature that sustained the universe, and could take it down in any moment. It was important to maintain respect for forces beyond her control that demanded she be alert.

That night, she told her father, John Birdswell, "The sky turned red and then red was inside my body. The same red. You know that red, don't you? It's a red at the edge of platinum. You know what I mean?"

"I don't, Sandra," he answered. "As it happened, I was up for no good reason and so I was looking out the window, but I didn't see anything. This afternoon, I read about the flare. I'm impressed that something awakened me."

2

You're My Girl

When Sandra's mother, John's wife, died on the delivery table, the baby was lifted from her body onto his chest in one motion. He knew enough as a physician to tear open his shirt and place the baby on his body even as he knew he would never hold his wife again. This intimacy as instant as his grief. The nurses offered to take the baby and put her in an incubator for a few hours so he could absorb the blow, but he refused, and, however awkwardly, he held the infant while they tested, prodded, washed her to be sure she was healthy. He didn't want to let her go for a moment as she had not only come through birth trauma but had lost her mother in the same instant.

A few hours later, standing confused in the niche they had prepared for the child in their bedroom, he wondered about the stories he had heard of desperate situations when a man had put an infant to his nipple and milk had come in. He couldn't cross that barrier. Instead he stared at the bottles they had purchased to supplement nursing or to hold the extra milk Samantha might pump for midnight feedings when he would get up to relieve her. That had been his plan, though he had suspected that Samantha would not yield to it. She probably would have preferred a wet nurse if such were needed and existed, but now there was no mother, no one to consult, and only some bottles and ready to feed formula. He had wrapped Sandra loosely in a blanket over her diaper and was holding the tiny life against his naked body. He did not want to put her down even to fill the bottle though, ultimately, he had to do so. He didn't know where the sling was that would have held her across Samantha's chest. The cradleboard that his friend, Hosteen Tseda, had given him was propped up in a corner. Samantha would have used it; Hosteen would have to teach him how. The tools were there to take care of the baby, but he had to invent fatherhood and motherhood. In his office it was second hand to remain fully in conversation while picking up the tools with which he cared for patients. But alone in the bedroom, the light from the glass paned doors fading across the bed that Samantha had, despite labor pains, meticulously made up before they had gone to the hospital, he was awkward and divided. The bottles, the baby, the bed all existed, distinct from each other, as if sterilized, wrapped and sealed. He had to warm a bottle, he knew that much. He had knowledge but it was far different from experience. He had not carried the child within his body for nine months and, he was so quickly learning that being outside, even if alongside, was not the same as the blood knowing that had seeped into mother and child but had been spilled in the massive hemorrhage that had taken the mother's life.

He saw the ghost of Samantha as she had been just hours earlier, bending over, fluffing the white feather pillows, smoothing the ivory satin feather quilt. Her touch, tender across the bed where they had made the child. He did not, in this moment, know what to reach for, what to do. So he stood there, stunned, holding the child, rocking to an echo of Samantha's voice playing through him. The baby stirred, a gurgle of need. Startled, he lay the child down in the middle of their bed, now his bed alone, and prepared the formula. The phone rang. He placed the baby in the crook of his left arm, balanced the bottle in her mouth against his chest, by raising his left arm to tip her toward him and reached for the telephone. It was not the best beginning. He had not said her name to her or himself. He stopped to cohere himself. He knew what Samantha would do. He sat down in the rocking chair that he didn't think he would ever dare sit in, gently offering the nipple. "Here, Sandra," he whispered and began singing from Neil Young's song "You're My Girl." He would be singing that song for many years. A new life of impossible and exquisite balance began.

From then on, first as a papoose and then in her aluminum and green canvas seat slung on his back, Sandra was carried by him wherever he went, sometimes even on a bicycle, in and out of his new home medical office and, when necessary, to his patient's homes. She even went to the small community hospital where he worked, at times leaving her with a nurse and other times bringing her with him on his rounds. She was his version of a therapy dog. His patients smiled and reached out to her. Sometimes the nurses prepped the patients and he changed diapers, or the opposite. It all, so quickly, became natural to him and the community he served, and remained so for years; no one objected.

As soon as Sandra was walking, she climbed down from her father's back and followed him. Everyone laughed when they saw them together as their gaits were so similar; he loped and she loped.

3

What She Knew

Early on, Sandra learned to live in, to negotiate two worlds. Her intuitions were admired when she was a child. Her father always respected them. But when she went to school, she was directed to set her perceptions aside.

"Your dream is interesting, Sandra, but it is not proof." But how could she ignore her dreams or her intuitions? Didn't she tell the medical office manager that her lost cat was in the crawl hole under the neighbor's house hiding out before it was verified that the cat was missing? Her dreams were real. She became skillful in balancing the two realities, the one that was intrinsic to her and the one she was pressured to accept.

Sandra was certain she would never learn as much in class as she learned from her father. She was able to skip kindergarten; she could read. She could do math. These skills had been necessary to understand what her father was doing. She had been in his jet stream. He had navigated while she looked around. School separated them and it bewildered her. He was unable to explain convincingly why she couldn't go to work with him, learning from him and everyone around them which she had been doing all her life, rather than attending school. She had picked up some Spanish from some of his patients and staff. She saw how respectfully he treated his patients and so she assumed they had the capacity to teach her too. If their skills were sufficient for basics, she could learn what else was needed from a book. In first grade, she discovered she already knew everything they planned to teach her and beyond. She argued that she could learn geography from his friend, her uncle, Hosteen when they visited him on the reservation, also a lot about the plants and animals because that is what Uncle talked about, if he talked when they were sitting in a circle together or when she was stepping on the heels of Hosteen's lumbering shadow as they walked on the land. He would teach her American Indian history she argued; Hosteen was an expert.

"Why?" she demanded to know.

John Birdswell wanted to indulge, "Because," as his answer, which he had sworn he would never use. He was daunted. "Because it's the law," was not any better. He agreed with her, he would have loved to educate her as he worked and she "assisted." He couldn't find the way.

Their lives together had been characterized by unity; they both felt the split. Their alliance was being reduced to separateness. She quickly learned that there were two distinct categories – what she desired and what she had to endure. At the university, she accepted that she had been trained to tolerate the contradictions she felt in her own profession, its forms and limitations, opportunities and constrictions. She had hoped and expected to feel the same wholehearted passion for her work that she saw in her father day in and day out. After all, she was as devoted to her goals as he was to his. There were grave illnesses and great injuries – how might they be healed? He never doubted the choice he had made. One of the first things she had learned from her father that stood her in good stead was what might be changed and what could not be changed. How things are. Like her mother's death.

Everyone asked her the same question: "Are you going to be a doctor when you grow up?"

"No," she would say, showing them a pail and shovel which substituted for his stethoscope, "I am going to take care of the Earth."

This didn't mean that she didn't watch him carefully and that she didn't enter the consulting rooms when she was home from school, or that she didn't tell him, afterwards, who, by her lights, was going to get better and who was going to die.

She knew when people were ill or troubled or hungry. She told him. He tracked it. She was an intuitive. Medicine was deep within her. Neither of them wanted to consider the evidence that she was close to infallible. Once a week, she identified a local need and they stealthily dropped off packages at people's houses – clothing, food or medicine. Did he indulge her or did he trust her assessments? He trusted her. He didn't know how she knew what he often didn't know without data or a battery of tests. She knew. She didn't know how she knew either. She never expected it; an insight always surprised her. She was delighted when she learned there was an expression, "out of the blue." "That's how it is, Poppa. It comes to me out of the blue." Did she point at the sky? Maybe she did. From then on, "Blue," was her default response.

She had walked home from school, speaking Spanish with one of her classmates from fourth grade. Then she returned to her father's office with the boy's father, reluctantly, in tow. "How did you know that Edmundo's father, Sr. Padilla was ill when Edmundo didn't know, when Sr. Padilla didn't want to own up to it?" the admitting nurse asked and then her father repeated the question. To the nurse, she shrugged her shoulders and ran from the room, mimicking the behavior of a giggling ten-year-old girl that did not come easily to her. To her father, she said, "Blue." To herself? She tried to set aside the moment she woke up in the night with a sense of foreboding. Had she had a dream? She could remember only feeling crushed by a mountain of strawberries and the pall left by the dream. She happened to see Sr. Padilla dropping Edmundo off at school. At first she couldn't see who was driving the pickup because there was a gray cloud in the cab that blurred the figure at the wheel. When Edmundo said he was walking home, she said, "Let's race," inviting herself along. She had a mission.

Pail in hand, she went into her father's office. "Poppa, please ask Sr. Padilla about the strawberries," she said. John Birdswell looked at her, wary and curious. She shrugged her shoulders to say she didn't know more. The doctor looked at his patient and waited. Sr. Padilla also waited until the silence in the room was excruciating for all of them.

"*Por favor*, doctor," the man said, meaning he didn't want to speak about it.

John understood. "Do you have relatives in Watsonville that you visit in the summer?"

The man nodded. "Sometimes, the family goes on a picnic and picks strawberries, is that right?" John Birdswell continued, watching the man closely. "You just had a celebration and it lasted a few weeks and …" Until the picking season was over or until he couldn't breathe anymore. He didn't need to go on. "Methyl bromide," John Birdswell whispered under his breath. "Damn." Sr. Padilla had heard and nodded. The doctor ordered oxygen for the moment and some medications and asked him to come back. Whether Sr. Padilla would or not, John Birdswell couldn't predict. He wrote up the bill very carefully so that it could be used with Padilla's employers though he knew it wouldn't be. "Sra. Padilla sometimes goes with you to the family, but Edmundo stays home with *abuela*, is that right?" Padilla nodded. "Please tell Senora she can come to see me if she needs." The only thing John Birdswell could do was to give him the treatment and medications he needed without charging. He expected that Sandra would invite him to a midnight package drop at the Padilla's house the next Thursday night.

Sandra knew who was ailing and needy just as she knew the side effects of the medicines John Birdswell prescribed for his patients. It was easy to see the side effects of medicines but harder to see the side effects of physics, chemistry, other sciences. In medicine, the side effects were apparent to those not in denial, and the patients often able and sometimes willing to testify. But the Earth? The short and long term harm done was known to some who profited from them and hid them so that much of the harm was not visible to those who preferred to look away.

Although Sandra was clear she was not going to be a doctor, she could by age ten, engage him in medical conversations:

"Sra. Rosa Delgado is nauseous from the chemo you prescribed for her."

"How do you know?" He wanted to distract her by pretending to be totally absorbed by the patient's chart.

"Because she looks green, her eyes are half shut, her mouth is open and her lower lip is thrust up in case she vomits. And she is saying *"Dios mio. Dios mio."*

Sandra's accent was pretty good. Having started learning in his office, she continued to study Spanish at school – one of the only benefits she acknowledged – and conversed regularly with her Xicano schoolmates and the hospital staff. She felt it gave her a secret language. Her father didn't have a chance. That was clear when she raised her pail filled with earth and stirred its contents. "The Earth, you see, is nauseated too. It's going to have a convulsion. What can we give her?"

"We can give her …" Wait a minute. How did she determine … ? He panicked. The chemo. Had she touched it, gotten access to it, somehow? He quickly realized his alarm was ludicrous, but it served to draw attention to her unique perceptions.

"The Earth feels everything we feel. So if I hold my pail by Sra. Rosa Delgado's arm, the earth inside my pail gets nauseous." She felt his alarm. How did she know this?

"How do I know?" She knew what he was thinking. "How did I know this, Poppa?" How could he not know? "Blue!" The word exploded from her but it didn't satisfy him. She acquiesced to his questioning stare. "I can feel everything in me that it feels inside my pail," as if such identity were the most natural. "Don't you feel it?" As if everyone did. As if she could reassure him by being casual and continuing quickly. "And angry. It knows it's being attacked. Sra. Rosa Delgado is taking pills for nausea but what are you going to give the Earth? And when she pees out the chemo, where it is it going to go? And where can the Earth pee? The Earth gets really nauseous and then she buckles."

He had heard Sandra explaining earthquakes, volcanoes, floods and drought to a few Zuni fetishes he had given her – deer, badger and wolf. He had heard her explain arctic melt to polar bear and forest fires to mountain lion. He did not want to pursue this further.

It had been easier for him when she was young, before she was walking. Before she had learned to read and practiced by picking up everything he was reading. Before she somehow understood everything that was said in his office to his staff or to his patients. Before she went to school and came home entirely discontented each day. Before she carried the pail of earth with her wherever she went, leaving it in a hollow between the planted area and the school wall while in class, by the nurse's station in the hospital, in the alcove that served as a patients' waiting room in their house and always picking it up afterwards to take to her bedroom at night – she never forgot it though she misplaced many things as a child will.

He had given her the pail on her fifth birthday when they had driven to the beach on the Pacific coast and John had the naive idea that she would make sand piles or build castles all day. She did briefly, until she was satisfied with her intuitive skill at combining sand, water and mud in the right proportions to put up a structure. She built some tepees and square houses by the water line so the tide could take them and others further up in the hot, dry sand. For awhile she was content to watch them, noticing the dribble in response to a little creature moving somewhere within, or how the wind began to shape the buildings more to its liking. People walking by did their own unconscious damage along with dogs and a few little children, all oblivious to her. The beach took her structures back. It was time for lunch. She tore every slice of the loaf of bread he had brought for themselves to make sandwiches —

"Every slice, Sandra?"

"Every slice, Poppa," she was adamant,

— into bits to feed the sea gulls who flew in and surrounded her in a flurry of feathers, strutting up to her feet, almost ready to take the bread from her hands, and equally happy to dive down when she threw it, or happier still when she got John to stand up and throw it high into the air so that they could snatch pieces in flight. Then he helped her stand still, one arm straight up, holding bread so that they swooped and cavorted around her, in a swirl of wings and feathers seeming as much a retinue as a different species. Then the bread was gone and the gulls as well.

She began to examine the sand, coming to John to ask him what seemed an infinite number of questions about the composition of each shovelful, about each shell, pebble, glitter, glimmer, grain, speck, that together composed sand.

"Almost as if you're trying to find out what you're made of, Sandy," he teased her.

She glowered at him and sat down apart from him, letting the sand slip through her fingers into the pail. At the end of the day, he wanted to protest when she brought the pail with a layer of sand in it into the car and placed her feet around it to steady it as they drove, but he saw that she was considering something important to her and he let her follow her own thoughts.

The metal sand pail was not a toy. She started carrying it with her, filling it with dirt from places she visited. At night after she had been put to bed, she slipped out of the sheets and sat on the floor and ate some of the earth that was in her pail. This is what she created to substitute for her mother's milk. When she became adept at writing, she labeled the different colored and various textured thin layers of sand and soil in glass mason jars that lined up on shelves anywhere in the house that she could find, primarily alongside her books, as they were themselves forms of books, and on her kitchen shelves when she left home and bought her own house. The contents of the jars resembled the tiers of sedimentary and volcanic rocks of the canyons of the southwest. As an adult, the pail and sometimes the mason jars, traveled with her: evidence, memory, icon, ritual object, prayer.

Sand, stones, rock carry the history of the Earth. Sandra wanted to know her origins. She wasn't convinced that everything had a beginning and an end. While challenging finality, she still asked to know her story, her beginnings. This is what John Birdswell did not want to discuss. This is what drove her. He tried to fabricate a story when she was very young, one that mimicked folk tales: "I found you in a walnut shell." Or "Two eagles brought you to me." Or, "I dreamed you and when I woke up, there you were and I had to change your diaper immediately." Make it light. Distract her. Sandra was more likely to believe the dream story than the others. "Tell me my story," she insisted. He relented.

"Your mother died in childbirth and the doctor, lifted you out of her belly into my arms."

John Birdswell was desperate and lonely. He was a physician. It was the substance of his being. As he watched, helpless, his wife had died on the delivery table. The obstetrician did everything she could to stanch the bleeding as the staff rushed to save the baby. It was completely unprecedented. There had been no warning. John repeated these words to Sandra again and again to reassure her. "Your mother died in childbirth. It was completely unexpected. We did everything and it was not enough. The doctor lifted you out of her belly into my arms." What he wanted her to hear and remember was that she was placed in his arms.

"You knew I was coming," she said in a tone that was soon to hold accusation. "You knew I was coming, why did you name me Sandra?"

She hated her name.

"Tell me my story," she insisted. Not as if she wanted to hear it again, but as if it had never been told to her. John went to other stories. It was so common, he had lots to choose from. The Queen died, the Prime Minister's wife died, the Chief's wife died and the King, the Minister, the Chief …. That wasn't what interested Sandra. "What," she asked repeatedly, "did they name the child?"

"Why are you asking?"

"It's not my name. It's the wrong name."

"Why do you keep saying that?"

"Blue," she sometimes answered. More often she said, "I feel it." Or, "I know it."

Sandra's name was the wedge between her and John Birdswell. The first day at school she saw the gray brick-like erasers by the blackboard. "My name is an eraser," she accused him.

"What do you mean?" He asked because he was afraid to ask.

At first she couldn't say more. Her name was her obsession. Her story meant her name. Many times he made the mistake of reading a story to her without having read it first himself. When he came to the part in Grimm's Goose Girl story when the servant girl stole the princess' handkerchief and took her name and identity, Sandra cried inconsolably. When he read about the entire tribe deliberating together to find the newborn child's name, she strode out of the house to the small woods behind where she spent the day making herself a shelter of broken twigs and branches, covering it with leaves. As a teenager she could argue that a name determined one's future.

"Your name, Sandra," he argued, "is as plain and anonymous as it can be. Make it what you will." What he didn't say, what he hoped would be true, was: "You're a motherless child, you can become anyone or anything you wish, Sandra." How could he explain? He had not expected to raise a child. He didn't want to impose anything on her. He had imagined her mother guiding her. He was determined to leave her to her own intelligence.

Sandra was adamant in her disappointment; he was frustrated in not being understood. Reproach sat between them. A boulder. A seawall. An impasse. His name was as plain as hers. Her name had been inevitable, given his upbringing. A circumstance she couldn't accept.

The subject was always between them. It arose whenever he said her name. He tried pet names but she didn't allow that. "Why 'honey?'" "Why 'pup'?" She couldn't abide the diminutive.

"Sandra." Was John Birdswell calling her or invoking her? In order for her to respond, he had to call her Sandra, never Sandy, although this didn't improve her moodiness. At least, she answered.

Whenever he said her name, called her, she felt that John was doing more than seeking her attention or whereabouts, but was calling her to a life that her name couldn't contain.

"Sandra."

"What do you want of me?"

He would never have considered himself spiritually ambitious. Certainly not for his daughter, but every interaction implied something for which they were not prepared

True to himself, unwilling to saddle her with his own ambitions and attitudes, he gave her free rein as much as he was able. They visited Hosteen at least once a year. Uncle Hosteen taught her to ride bareback with only a rope. But with a rope, John noted to himself.

As she matured, her resentment and disorientation continued. She saw herself as a woman without a name and a woman without a mother. The two were intrinsically related. She wanted lineage, she wanted a place to stand. The Earth was shaky and the atmosphere seemingly spinning away. Where was the breath of life going? The air was poisoned, the rains erratic. The winds blew wildly, dust storms and hurricanes. Everything she loved was falling apart or splitting apart, earthquakes first, then glaciers melting into the sea while a photographic team was catching it on video, elated by their "scoop," making it another spectacle, like war had become.

Despite Sandra's complaint, John liked to think that he had a lineage even if it didn't come from his adopted parents or birth parents whoever they had been. He wanted to pass it on to her. As a physician, John had held the thinking of Hippocrates dear and was constantly meditating on what it might imply. Being a single father and working full time as a doctor left him little time and so Sandra was not only his child, but his companion. He often thought aloud, murmuring his concerns as if in conversation, and she was the one by his side, she assumed the commentary was meant for her. His parents had been Quakers with a secular edge. John's liturgy was equally quasi religious. He passed it on the way he lived it to Sandra. By the time Sandra was ten, she could recite certain sections of the Hippocratic Oath with him. When he heard Sandra, the words sounded ultra formal but no more formal than religious liturgy. So they chanted it together as he wanted to keep it fresh in his mind. It was his way, when he wasn't with Hosteen, of keeping himself honest in the midst of the turmoil of patients, administrative details and child rearing.

"The physician must be able to tell the antecedents, know the present, and foretell the future – must mediate these things, and have two special objects in view with regard to disease, namely, to do good or to do no harm. The art consists in three things – the disease, the patient, and the physician. The physician is the servant of the art, and the patient must combat the disease along with the physician."

John changed the text to do good AND do no harm. He wanted her to know the original and wrestle with the distinction herself. The conclusion she came to was that trying to do good, what one thought was good, that is, what one thought was good for self or other, was not necessarily so. "Like someone thinking they are doing good by making me go to school when, actually, they are doing me harm," she asserted to her father and her teachers whenever she had the opportunity.

John's take on the Oath was that "knowing the present and foretelling the future" had to do with more than testing and statistics and he often said "meditate these things" instead of mediate. A slip of a letter changing the field entirely. This is why he would ask her when she was young and accompanied him on his rounds, with the utmost seriousness, what she thought about the patient. He saw that she could see into the present, and could often foretell the future, or the best future, or the best future outcome, if ....

Finally, "then the patient must combat the disease along with the physician." He always made an alliance with the patient whom he questioned closely to see what each one understood about their suffering or affliction. He even asked the children, or especially the children – out of the mouths of babes.... Whenever issues came up between Sandra and himself he was never inclined to dominate and wanted to avoid conflict and so he was likely to listen to her deeply. If there were to be combat between them, it would have the quality of aikido. Much later in her life, when she was trying so hard to listen to the Earth, she saw that this was his legacy to her. She did not want to do harm, she questioned everything and listened to her patient as he had listened to his patients and to her.

4

Medical Ways Or Medicine Ways

John had met Hosteen Tseda when he had agreed to work with the Indian Health Service at Chinle, Arizona, instead of being drafted. 1966. It was long before he had met his wife, before she had died and so before he was raising Sandra.

John had been running when he was startled by a man staring at him from outside a homesite, his arms folded across his chest. He realized he had been trespassing.

He stopped and waited to see how he would be greeted. When the man didn't respond, he said, "*Ya at eeh*," tentatively, looking down at the ground, kicking at a stone with his toe.

"What are you doing here?"

"I was running and seem to have gotten lost."

"You don't seem to have a running uniform on," he was noting John's loose old khakis and his tennis shoes. "What are you running away from?"

"I am actually hoping to get to the IHS and a shower before noon."

"You will certainly need a doctor if you run that distance."

"Well," John answered, "I did park my car at one of the lower outlooks. I'm only running about ten miles."

"What do you want with the Indian Health Service?" the man continued the interrogation undaunted.

"Well, actually I'm a physician, testing my medicine in the old ways – on my self."

"Going to prescribe running?"

The man kept his hands folded across his chest, scrutinizing him. John was definitely going to be late and the man knew that. John didn't know if the man recognized him.

"My name is John Birdswell," John waited not knowing how deeply he had offended.

The man also waited what seemed like an unending interval, and then said he was Gad. "Gad Tseda." He followed the introduction with a question: "What kind of doc are you?"

"What do you need?" John spoke quietly, putting his backpack down on the ground.

"I put my shoulder out."

"May I?" John nodded to a bench, indicating that Gad sit down.

Gad hesitated, then sat down. The invisible, unspoken challenge that had arisen when John was trespassing remained, taking another form.

John, the younger, white man was not to win. Gad Tseda, the Native older man, though by appearances not much older than John, was to win, that is retain control. This was the setup and John was to play well. He put his hands out slowly, tentatively, as if asking if could touch the man. Silent and motionless permission was given and John placed his hands on the man's shoulder, moving gently and confidently and without turning Gad into a patient. This was John's skill. He could not work successfully on the reservation if he didn't have such sensitivity. His fingers had to find the injury and ease it while also communicating respect.

John asked quietly, "You drive a lot?"

"Who doesn't?"

"Your arms have gotten used to a forward position."

John placed one hand on Gad's chest and another under his shoulder blade and pressed forward so that Gad's chest expanded. "I was going in the other direction," Gad said.

After a few stretches, both men pulled back. John reached into his backpack, which served as his doctor's bag, and pulled out a small bottle of aspirin and a tobacco pouch. He handed them both to Gad without any fanfare.

"Funny what the best medicine for you might be," he said cautiously then paused to sense an opening before he said, "juniper berries." He was looking at the tree by the house. "Boil some in water for twenty minutes and sip the tea."

Gad scrutinized John and saw by the smile John couldn't contain that John knew that the name, Gad, meant juniper tree.

"You can also put your hand against the tree, stretch your arm out and pull forward away from the tree to stretch your pectorals." John waited. "Your tree, your medicine," he dared.

Gad glanced at the tree and asked, "Where did you learn this?"

"From Old Man at Spider Rock. He said it was Bear medicine." John was betting that the somewhat growing ease he was feeling was mutual. "I could stop by tomorrow as I circle around and see how you are doing and bring you some celery to optimize it."

"Do you use juniper berries yourself?"

Damn, the exchange was challenging. John had to indicate he understood the question – that was probably more important than his answer. "I used to drink gin, but have mostly given it up since I've been on the reservation."

"How long have you been here?" Gad was definitely interrogating him.

"Not long. Couple weeks."

"And how long are you staying, Doc?"

"Two years, I guess." John said.

"Hmm." It was quiet grunt. "Draft dodger?"

"Reckon so." John saw that Gad was assessing him but he couldn't discern what the man was thinking.

"Two years. That's a long time," Gad's tone was enigmatic. John had been on course with the juniper berries and bear medicine and although he didn't want to undo whatever connection might have been made, he decided to go ahead with the one more thing he had to say. Although Native people had very high enlistment numbers in the military and the prestige of the Navajo Code-talkers ran very high on the Four Corners Reservation, his heart insisted that he speak without calculating Gad's response beforehand. "There is no way I could work with the vets coming back if I were drinking a lot, even if I do get lonely," John said as if reasserting his commitment. "Many of them are broken."

Gad nodded. John felt easy.

"I could meet you tonight at the hospital. I have a patient there whom I'm doctoring," Gad's voice was steady and without emotion. "Late, after visiting hours."

Gad was reaching out to him and John was embarrassed when he realized who he was. "Oh, you're Hosteen Tseda! Several members of the staff told me about you." Hosteen seemed young to carry medicine in the ways that were attributed to him. John had expected the elder healer to be a much older man. He realized he didn't know a lot about life on the reservation. Much less than he assumed he did. He continued, quickly, "Sorry, I didn't come to meet you formally."

Hosteen shrugged it off and went into the house. The invitation and John's acceptance had been considered one action.

John did not run past the house again unless Hosteen explicitly invited him. Signs on the reservation said, The Navajo Nation, and he was slowly recognizing that he was in another country, with a distinct culture, and he would do well to learn the etiquette that allowed for respectful relationships. This would affect everything in his life, his medical practice as well as daily interactions. Every exchange was charged in the beginning until John became fluent in the difference between the two worlds. He had thought of himself as tolerant and without prejudice because he always assumed that everyone was the same in fundamental ways. He thought differences were interesting but of negligible importance. He had not considered that other people might have entirely different values, interests, concerns, beliefs and desires. Having finished medical school and a residency in family medicine, a new specialty, he had mistakenly thought he was qualified to practice medicine anywhere, particularly on a reservation. Yes, he would have to be sensitive to social interactions, but he had never considered that the way he practiced medicine, the medicine itself might have to be adjusted. For example, he had not understood that the pharmaceutical painkiller Darvon and juniper berries were medicines that emerged from distinct and, perhaps, irreconcilable cosmologies. He had not ever thought that Darvon might not be superior to juniper berries or that the reasons for taking a medication might be different for different people from different cultures.

The connection with Hosteen Tseda helped. The two men regularly met for the two years that John was at the IHS hospital in Chinle and came to trust each other, or Hosteen came to trust John as John would say he slowly became trustworthy. Right fist to the ribs. Blocked. Laughter. It was good between them.

As soon as they knew each other somewhat better, Hosteen began advising John. "Best thing you could do," Hosteen said, "is learn how to set a bone without x-rays, or cure an infection without antibiotics. We could do all of that once, before you came, before you declared most of what we value superstition and made a lot of what is sacred to us, illegal. So we have to buy pharmaceuticals and go to your hospitals. We don't like them and we can't afford them. Your food, your way of life and your medicine makes us sick — like it does everyone else."

John listened. He didn't doubt anything Hosteen was saying but it wasn't his habit to think this way though he had taken the residency in family medicine the first year it was given because he was interested in community, not a particular part of the body. He had questioned the way medicine was compartmentalized, and the lack of access to medical care for the poor — he had not questioned the medical assumptions themselves.

"Don't speak to me or us about diet and don't tell me I will be healthier if I don't eat this fry bread," Hosteen sallied. They were in the cafeteria and

Hosteen was digging into a Navajo taco. On another plate, he had a large portion of fry bread that wasn't covered with ground beef, salsa, lettuce, avocado and cheese. He was going to drizzle it with honey, cinnamon and sugar to accompany his coffee. John didn't know if this was his preference or if he was testing John who was eating a turkey sandwich, which he had thought was a more modest choice.

"We didn't invent white bread," Hosteen flicked his head toward John, "we just try to make it palatable. I am going to eat what the people eat, or have to eat, no matter what. If you have anything to say about diabetes or alcoholism that isn't patronizing that will help as well. You brought these illnesses, so don't blame us; it would be helpful if you could take them back." He paused to continue eating then continued. "What can you offer us to make amends?"

John understood that Hosteen was asking more than what John would or could do in the hospital. "I like making house calls," John said without being offended, actually with a little bit of pride. "I can change a diaper, treat diaper rash and allergies, discern a temperature within .1 of a degree with the back of my wrist, diagnose strep infections by looking at the patient's tongue, identify a host of imbalances by taking a pulse, and I can make some diagnoses by just looking at the irises and the whites of your eyes. I can do a Heimlich maneuver if I'm there in time, perform an emergency tracheotomy, teach first aid, lance a boil, design the right support for a sprain, help a hunter deal with chilblains, deliver a baby at home – what else?" – he paused, thinking, "and my car can serve as an ambulance. I can mostly diagnose a heart attack without a bunch of tests, and also diabetes and often cancer, and several other diseases, but I only know the diseases my people have identified in the ways they catalogue them, and that's where someone like you has to come in." John stopped, his expression grave. "This is where you come in Hosteen."

"Hosteen" he emphasized, he wanted his new friend to know this, "I have a nose for battle fatigue, or whatever the hell they call it, soldier's heart, what happened to some of the men in Nam – where as you know, I wasn't willing to go." They both nodded.

"Maybe, Hosteen, there's some other unexplained illness they're bringing back from there, and I don't know its nature or the cause." John paused emphatically, "I have been looking around the reservation, something else is going on, and there are a lot of illness, among the animals too, and it makes me uncomfortable."

"Shall we bring the goats to you?"

"We may have to resort to that," John answered, subdued by his concerns.

Hosteen did not respond. There was no change in expression and John recognized that he knew exactly what concerned John. He had considered it. He would continue to do so.

So John continued, "That's some of it, except that, again, I know when I am out of my element and, as I said before, need to call a medicine man. That's probably my range within, 'First, do no harm.' "

They picked up their trays, sorted their dirty dishes into the gray plastic containers by the kitchen wall and walked to the patients' area. When they got to a room on the cardiology unit, they could see the woman who looked old but wasn't, staring out the window as if the two men weren't standing opposite at the open door.

John took the chart, and read aloud to Hosteen. Heart failure was indicated.

"If you are careful not to talk too much white man talk to her that will serve us all well," Hosteen spoke brusquely wanting John to lower his voice and be less officious. "Illness not disease," he continued. That the patient's heart had failed had a different meaning for Hosteen.

"Maybe I should leave," John said, not wanting to interfere with Hosteen's work.

"That's what I was trying to explain the other day," Hosteen said, "ceremony brings everything and everyone together. But you can't be here primarily as a doc. You have to be here as a person, then your prayers become part of the medicine." John stepped back, making himself as invisible as possible in a corner of the room, but not before Hosteen greeted Margaret Zah formally, asked about all her close relatives and introduced John as his friend. She looked skeptical, given John's white coat and the stethoscope, until Hosteen explained that although he was a doctor at the hospital, it didn't make him less a friend. John was forced to come out of his corner and speak about himself and also to inquire about Margaret Zah's health without any reference to what he knew, or didn't know yet, from her chart. He answered her questions about where he had lived before he came to Chinle. He spoke about his parents. He saw what mattered to her, and that it would affect her healing while she did not regard any information in the chart as relevant. When the exchange was made to Margaret's satisfaction, Hosteen switched to Navajo to speak to her about her losses and disappointments and to do ceremony.

"What happened in there?" John asked as they left the room.

"Nothing you can write in a chart," Hosteen answered.

"You gave her something to drink. Was that tea you brought with you from the cafeteria?" John asked.

"Yeah, it was tea," Hosteen answered as they strolled toward the hospital lobby.

"What kind?"

"Hard to say. Thank you for not noticing, John."

"Right, Hosteen, I didn't see anything. But if I had, what would I have seen? She looked better when we left. Was it the chanting, the tea, what you said to each other? Should I learn Navajo so I can understand?"

"Absolutely, John, you should learn Navajo. They say it's one of the most difficult languages in the world. And, yes, if you learn it, really learn it, you will understand everything. The language will teach you.

"My teacher told me this story, John, about his own experience. He had had a cough for months. Nothing worked. Sometimes it was so bad he lost his voice. One day, he had to speak at a tribal council and he couldn't. An old man who had a reputation as an herbalist came over to him and said he could heal him that night at his home but my teacher would have to get the herb first. After the council, my teacher was instructed to follow very elaborate directions up and down unmarked dirt roads until he came to a particular rock with a bush his height growing by it, five steps to the north. He was to say prayers before picking an exact number of branches of a certain length, no less and no more, and then to make his way back to the road and to the teacher's house which was several hours away. He arrived at the teacher's house after midnight. He was exhausted. As he stumbled through the door, he saw the same plant growing very close to the house. When he came in, the old man made a tea from the leaves and my teacher drank it."

"And what happened? Was he healed?"

"My teacher stayed and studied with the old man."

"So the tea healed him, Hosteen?"

"If it was just the tea, John, the two of them could have gone out into the yard early in the evening and picked the leaves. It was the leaves, the drive, the chant, the prayer, the ordeal, the willingness, devotion ... all of it. Maybe the cough was to get him to study with the teacher and pass it on to me so I can pass it on – when it's right – to you. You can't package medicine, John."

Hosteen had become his teacher, a relationship he had not expected. When he was stymied by a case or saw that the healing he expected wasn't occurring, John looked for Hosteen before he went to his medical colleagues at the hospital. A few months into his service, John encountered Hosteen at the nurse's station. It was a fortuitous meeting. John was bewildered and agitated. "I had a patient who came in with headache and other pains, intermittent dizziness, weakness in his limbs. We gave him some medication for his symptoms and were ruling out various possibilities. I thought we had made him fairly comfortable and that he was glad we were doing a full workup. I'm gaining a good reputation, I think, for pulling out all the stops, getting every test I possibly can.

"When I came back an hour ago, he had left. Just like that. I had just seen him. He didn't ask permission. He didn't sign himself out. I asked the nurses what happened," John looked around to see if they were listening – the two women had blank expressions as if they had both been stricken with acute deafness, "but they said," John was raising his voice, "they had no idea why he had left."

Hosteen's smile was confusing to John. "That's how it happens here," Hosteen deliberately lowered his voice. "The patient comes in because someone in the family has been at him until he can't resist anymore. But the medicine doesn't make sense. He can't imagine how any healing can happen here. He doesn't know what's in the pills or IVs and he doesn't like the machines or the tests, he doesn't think anyone should take blood from him and he doesn't feel better. Or he only feels better when he's taking the medication – which tells him he isn't getting well and that the pills are blocking the symptoms which are very important to him because they point to what he still doesn't understand and it's not about his body. There's a lot of pressure on him to stay and accept your regime. Your every four hour regime. And when he objects, what are the words you use? Non-compliant. You make a medical diagnosis, pathology, out of his belief system and philosophy. Non-compliant. So he waits for an opportunity to sneak out." Hosteen stopped abruptly. "He's certainly not going to ask for permission." Hosteen was emphatic. "You understand that, don't you?"

John heard something under Hosteen's words, "It's about time you understand that, John!" There was the omnipresent edge. Yes, it must be something John needed to understand.

"He'll make a telephone call at the Conoco station or flag down someone who'll take him home to a medicine man. That's the medicine he believes in."

"Does he have to believe in the medicine to get better, Hosteen?"

"Oh yes, John. Like you believe in your medicine. It's the same."

"I don't believe in my medicine. That's faith healing." He was annoyed with Hosteen for the first time or the first time he was aware of it "There's evidence, testing, statistics, you know, all of that."

"Oh yes, John, you do believe in your medicine. You are a true believer."

John turned away and strode down the hall, glancing into the patient's rooms. It was all familiar – a hospital bed, an over-bed table with a plastic cup and a pitcher for water, a chair for a visitor, blood pressure cuff attached to the wall, an IV pole, a white board with the nurse's name and other information for the staff. A chart holder outside each room. Each patient tucked neatly into his or her bed. It was meant to be reassuring. It reassured him. He had been relieved when he first came to find a standard hospital with the basic equipment he needed to do his work. How could it not be comforting?

Hosteen was still at the nurse's station when he returned. "I don't fully understand," John admitted. "Why are you here? The Office of Native and Spiritual Medicine? Do you work for them, Hosteen?"

"No, John, actually I don't. It's a little too organized for me and you have to sign in and sign out and keep yourself busy for the appointed time. So when someone calls me, I come in. When the patient sees me, he can trust a little. We're not used to being so confined. You saw the desert out there when you came in. That's where we live, far from everyone and everything. You know how I live. If he sees me, he may be willing to stay somewhat longer."

"I don't understand," John repeated, clearly flustered and concerned. "What about my patient? What if he has anemia, or high blood pressure, or a tumor? He came in with dizziness, headache, fatigue and weakness. We didn't get a diagnosis."

"You're taught that it's so simple. Get the right diagnosis, check the protocol, prescribe the authorized medications, watch for side-effects, expect healing."

"Yes, that's right, Hosteen. And the trick is the diagnosis. Getting that right. That's why he came to the hospital. That's why I ordered all those tests. That's why it took so long…." He was infuriated.

"I agree, John. The trick is the diagnosis. Getting that right. That's why we go to a Diviner for a diagnosis. Diviners spend a long time with the patient, listening to his story, listening to the spirits. Then when they think they know what harm, what imbalance exists, what spiritual offense occurred, they send him to a Singer to perform a healing ceremony. A particular Singer who has learned a particular Healing Way. We also have our specialists." This amused Hosteen. Then he continued, "They don't focus on a part of the body. They learn a ceremony; it could take nine days. That is, the ceremony takes nine days. Learning a single ceremony takes years. Just like becoming a doc. The *hataali* have to know each ceremony perfectly. No mistakes. No mistakes," Hosteen emphasized the No and John knew he was referring to rampant medical errors that occurred everywhere on the reservation and on Federal land. "Everybody comes to the ceremony. It's about making everything whole again. The community needs to heal too."

John couldn't encompass what Hosteen was communicating. "And what, Hosteen, if he doesn't get well? If it turns out he's got an infection and he needs antibiotics or has asthma and he can't breathe, or a heart condition and needs digitalis?"

"Well, if you want to argue the point, what if your standardized and packaged medicine for asthma doesn't have the sacred wind in it anymore, or the digitalis wasn't picked at the right time, and the patient takes it and doesn't improve? What do you do? You say, it's the patient's fault, he isn't responding well to the medication. Maybe it's the medication's fault; maybe it isn't a medicine any longer if it is manufactured in a lab to exact but impersonal physical specifications. All the individual medicinal qualities are left out. It no longer has a soul."

Aware he was on a rant, Hosteen moved John to a plain small room off the main hallway available to staff or guests. No one was there and they could sit down and speak without having to modulate their words or tone.

"When I'm going to give an herb to a patient, I go out to the right place at the right time on the right day to gather it for that patient. Because her story tells me what to do. Not the story of what's happening in her body, but the story that led to those symptoms. The story that includes the ancestors, the spirits, the place, what happened there, not only recently but way back. Maybe something that happened to her great, great grandmother wants healing. Maybe my patient has asthma because her great, great grandmother collapsed on the forced Long Walk to Fort Sumner and the pain of that has taken my patient's breath away. My patient is going to have to figure out how to help her great-great-grandmother. That story wants a healing and that's how we heal – it's all connected. You can't contain that. You can't package it.

"Your pharmaceuticals come from the same source as your diseases. When you make us go to your hospitals and undergo your treatments, you're sending us diseases in the same package. You don't understand contamination the way we do, you don't know what you're sending with your IVs and little pills. You're sending disconnection, disrespect and domination and these, more than anything, make us ill. Your hospitals are inhospitable. When you sent smallpox in those blankets you started a process and it has never ended. You have never stopped."

John knew he had to listen deeply. He could see the pain on Hosteen's face. Perhaps he had never had the opportunity to talk to a white man about this so openly and without any apparent moderation. It hurt John to hear it. It didn't hurt because Hosteen was saying it to him. It hurt because it might be true and Hosteen was living it.

"You want to know what illness is caused by disconnection, John? I could tell you depression. You would accept that. Not enough to change your system, but enough to agree. But I won't tell you that. I will tell you all diseases come from disconnection and the rest. All diseases but old age. Domination makes all of us ill. Maybe it doesn't make you ill –I think it does – but it makes us sick."

John both understood what Hosteen was saying and was also confounded by it. One phrase in particular – "When you make us …" had gotten to him and he countered, "We don't force you to participate in our medicine." The moment he said it, he knew he was wrong. How often had Hosteen or another Native person said they could lose their child if the social worker decided the child wasn't getting proper medical care, by which was meant Western medicine. Anything was an excuse to steal the children.

So John started another track. "What do you mean about contagion?" He had the sense not to speak about sterilization and high standards. He even corrected his own thoughts and substituted hygiene for sterilization because he knew the tragedy of Native women being sterilized without their knowledge by doctors who didn't want Indian children in the world.

"What do I mean about contagion? I mean the way you practice medicine, the way you package it, the way you wrap up every illness in a nice little neat room, one room next to the other down the corridor, the way you wrap every pill, infusion, examination, every consult and conversation, the way you separate each thing from every other thing, transmits more than you know. Your medicine makes me sick."

"I don't understand."

"That's at least four times you've said that." Hosteen looked and sounded as tired as the patient they had just seen. "Maybe you're not to understand. Maybe your patient will come back and ask you for medication. John, there is an idea, an attitude, a belief system, embedded in every wrapping, package, medicine, medical interaction. Just because it is everywhere, it is only there because of money and power, because someone will make money from the treatment. Not because the ideas or procedures are good or true. Listen John," Hosteen changed his tone, lowered his voice, "your patient made a prison break and I need to do the same. There's a long empty desert out there with nothing but miles between here and the mountains. If you must continue the conversation, we have to go outside."

Clearly, John didn't understand yet, but followed. Hosteen sat down on a concrete bench looking out toward the hills, stretching his legs, hooking one of his leather boots over the other. John sat down next to him. Night had come, the moon had not risen yet, but it was possible by starlight to make out the waves of the hills, slightly darker than the sky.

The wind came up in dust devils. John asked tentatively, "Are we seeing the same sky?"

"I don't think so," Hosteen answered looking at the constellations he had been shown by his elders as a child rather than those he had been taught to see in the government school. "I don't think so," he reiterated.

"The same sky?" The different figures twinkled in and out of their distinct shapes. "I don't think so."

5

There Are Illnesses And There Are Plagues

John Birdswell had wanted to be a good doctor and a good father and he wanted his friend Hosteen and his people to thrive. He wanted to avoid iatrogenesis. He wanted to do no harm. See no evil, hear no evil, speak no evil – do no evil …. He wanted this to be sufficient. It never occurred to him that his daughter might have to carry more than he did. It was as much as he could bear that his beloved had died in childbirth, his end of the world.

John Birdswell was dogged in his treatment of his patients even though he was raising Sandra. He transferred his medical practice from an office building near the hospital to his home. He and Samantha had considered that possibility and he acted on it immediately when she died. He added another staff member, so there was always someone to attend Sandra if need be.

As if from birth, Sandra loved Earth the way her father loved the body, admiring its dynamic and complex mechanisms, wanting to be a catalyst for setting it right when something went wrong. Having learned what she did from her father, she feared by the time she got to the University that what she would learn there would increasingly entangle her in doing more harm than good. She watched John agonize over protocols he didn't accept as necessary and valid. She watched his confidence in healing diminish as he was less and less able to act on what he instinctively knew and trusted or what he had learned during his years on the Four Corners Reservation. When his colleagues asked him why he kept returning to the reservation, he said it had been his parallel medical school and residency.

Hosteen saw that Sandra was ardent in her connection to the natural world. He didn't want to influence her, but he did watch her to assist if it were required. Sometimes it was enough to praise her so that John would be free from anxiety and this would free her to follow whatever called her.

"She's going to make you proud," he told John outside of Sandra's hearing. He asserted that she was going to redeem John's ancestors, the ones that came to him through his adoptive parents, each one, back to the first ones who had colonized this country, and according to Hosteen had from the beginning to the present day attacked the Earth. John's adoptive parents had been Quakers by choice, their blood ancestry vaguely traced to England or Wales. John thought that being a Quaker, or rather, coming from a Quaker household, might redeem him, get him off the hook for having been born a white man, though, as he explained to Hosteen his ancestry hadn't been his idea or his preference. But it didn't absolve him.

"I get it about the quiet, but why would your people sit inside a church and listen?" Hosteen like to tease John when they were walking on the land "when you could hear so much more listening outside."

"Because we're listening inside ourselves," John answered, anticipating Hosteen's laugh, even though he didn't go to church, or Friend's meetings, nor had he since his parents' death.

"You think God is a little voice inside you," Hosteen continued, "The spirits I know would hate being so confined."

Since John had been working on the reservation and then afterward when he came regularly, they developed a rare and blessed friendship, good-natured and robust. That was in itself a miracle, if either of them believed in such.

One year when Sandra and John were visiting, John addressed a question to Hosteen in a way he never had before. "The few people I know, some are even patients, who seem to really believe, whether they go to church or not, sometimes speak in a common language about what they call 'the dark night of the soul.' They're believers, they say," he stretched his long legs out toward the fire while glancing over to the mat next to him to see if eight-year-old Sandra was asleep, "and I 'believe' they are, but it's as if their faith is connected to their doubt or disconnection. Like you can't have one without the other."

John hesitated before he continued, he was about to ask something intimate and he didn't want to offend Hosteen. He was asking for himself but really he was asking for Sandra because she was, in some ways, not like him, was so unlike him, that he feared his failure to understand might do harm. What that might be, he didn't know, but still, he worried.

"Hosteen," he began again, tentatively, lowering his voice as if there were anyone about but the crickets that were making an outcry, "do you ever wonder about the spirits? Are you ever so disconnected from them that you don't know if they exist?"

John looked toward Sandra tucked close to the fire into a dark green sleeping bag. She was too deeply asleep to hear what he was asking. He turned to Hosteen, who was huddled close toward the flames that cast shadows of light across his features. Hosteen's face registered puzzlement, an expression John had not seen in the seventeen years they had known each other. Because Hosteen recognized John's tone and the sincerity with which he was addressing him, Hosteen had to answer spontaneously without intermediate thoughts. How would he communicate what was inexplicable?

"We don't think about believing or not believing." If he were speaking in Navajo, the words that would explain this to Hosteen would have a rhythm and song to them through which the meaning could enter. He spoke slowly, hoping to echo the natural pulses of his Native language so John might understand what meanings were under the words. Hosteen did not know how to speak over the historic and cultural divide that had just risen and cracked open between them. Hosteen could not explain what he meant in English. The language hadn't incorporated this way of being into itself. "We don't think about belief." The divide. It was there. Difference by its nature did not create a rift – male and female induced magnetism – but this split was real.

Hosteen had had to learn English to survive while seeing that every sentence spoken was a reduction, like putting blinders on a horse before racing or stuffing his ears when his elder was teaching. Natives who communicated in English knew they were receiving only part of what was there. But that's how their traditional culture was saved, how the secrets were preserved – the non-Natives thought they understood, but the sacred was sequestered, inaccessibly, in the old languages. The white man's way unwittingly saved as it destroyed.

"You don't think about believing or not believing?" John repeated the words as slowly as Hosteen had spoken them even if they didn't sound the same to his ear. Hosteen seemed to have disappeared. Maybe John was to try to understand this on his own. What could Hosteen possibly mean when he said he didn't think about belief? Hosteen did ceremony for the spirits, John assumed. What could he possibly mean by denying that he believed? Had he denied it? John decided to be silent too.

John's retort called Hosteen back into the conversation, into the dark night. Hosteen stretched and went for wood and laid some logs beside the fire for later, prepared to stoke the fire when necessary while keeping it small. In that interlude, he also decided he wouldn't speak to John in Navajo. He had considered that as an option, but John was not ready to grasp the embedded meanings. To teach in that way, Hosteen would have to repeat the words over and over, for days. It was the way the young who hadn't spoken Navajo from birth learned it from their elders. Just listening. Day after day. Or for years. And then, they understood!

"I don't worry about belief or faith. I don't understand why you people do." He continued speaking in English but kept to the rhythm of Navajo, consciously, deliberately, so that he didn't undermine the slim possibility that the knowing could enter John if he didn't block it.

"The fire is here," Hosteen began, pointing at it as if John might not be seeing it. "And the sky," he continued with hand gestures, "Father Sky. You can hear Owl in the tree, she has something to say." He pointed down, "The Earth is here." Had he said enough? "And you're here. I don't need proof of that."

John nodded, meaning he heard but not that he understood. The words weren't diminishing his concern. Something was being transmitted but not enough for him to become someone else for his daughter. He knew what they denoted but he didn't comprehend Hosteen's intention. He didn't know the way Sandra did and he didn't know how to support her if she was ridiculed or embarrassed. Or worse, if what she experienced or believed was pronounced to be superstition or untrue.

"We wouldn't have to worry about this, if she lived here," John muttered.

"Really?" Hosteen countered, his voice unexpectedly shrill. He had not expected John to be oblivious. "What about the Mormons, the Catholics and the Christians with their kidnapping and adoptions and what about the government schools? I thought you were worried about them. We still don't have our children back. What about the violence against our children and the spirits? What about the children who are tortured and killed, John? Right here. Not over there in that war you didn't fight. What about here? Are you draft dodging here?"

As if slapped awake, John realized he had privileged Sandra. He welcomed the blow, shook himself like a wet dog and focused. It came just in time or he might have been blindsided by his innocence or ignorance, he wasn't sure which.

"We all want to protect our children," Hosteen said with acrimony, "some of us have the power to do so and some of us don't." John's inquiry had opened him up to this brother and he felt betrayed. He hadn't seen it coming from this white man.

It looked to John like Hosteen was going to slam the log he had just picked up into the fire, but in the end, Hosteen placed it precisely where it would be most effective. The fire dimmed and flared. "You don't want to know," Hosteen said, morosely.

"I do. I do want to know," John was ashamed. He had been concerned for his patients, for the people on the reservation, he hadn't been concerned for his teacher, his brother as himself. He hadn't taken it in as his own. He should have understood in his own body and soul after all these years.

"We'll talk about it at the hospital, then," Hosteen said. There was no way to palliate the truth. "It's a health issue." He was asking John to leave.

"I get that," John's tone was even. "I get it."

John picked up Sandra in her sleeping bag and put her in the back of the car, shushing her when she stirred. He took a package of tobacco from the front compartment and walked back to Hosteen seated so close to the fire, John worried that his blanket might catch. "I don't know how sincere apologies are made among your people, Hosteen, but I am deeply sorry." He lowered his head while speaking so that Hosteen would not see the tears in his eyes. He did not want to solicit sympathy or be the focus of concern as had happened with Sandra and he could not postpone this moment. "I apologize. You are my brother and my uncle. I hope to learn from you, if you will have me."

Hosteen tapped his shoulder. A quick acknowledgement. He, also, had not wanted to lose such kin.

John was grateful to be included in medicine circles on the reservation where he could sit with everyone else and speak when he felt invited both by the community and by his heart. Being with Hosteen was succor for him in the way his concern alongside his knowledge and skill was succor for his own patients.

When Sandra was born, he devoted himself full time to raising her and to his medical practice. Though he returned to the reservation to visit, he was not practicing there. Amnesia set in. He practiced good medicine at home, with more caution than if he had never been on the reservation, but he followed the conventional protocols. He did not have the time or the camaraderie of his colleagues to make the changes that his time on the reservation suggested. He would have liked to practice like a Native doctor in a conventional setting rather than a white doctor sometimes offering medical care on Native land.

Everything was set right for him on the rare occasions that he was visiting Hosteen at the time of a healing. Sometimes he could find common ground between his professional understanding and the community's. Then he felt legitimate as a healer. When Sandra was with him, he liked to speak of her gifts. Telling the story of her intervention with the Padillas gave him pleasure. He could not fully support her intuitions because such didn't come to him. But the community accepted them quietly and so she was sustained.

For himself, his license and all its obligations drifted away from him in the cool breeze that he wished had no toxins in it, only dust, the tang of horse manure, a bite of skunk, various pollens blowing through the dwelling where they sat around the patient who seemed to rally from the company and the stories. After some time, the medicine man or woman would tell a story of the time they had seen this condition before and what was done and what occurred. Somehow a decision had been made. The ancestors appeared. John never understood exactly how it had happened.

Visiting Hosteen over the years, Sandra had been able to observe him and his friends engage "doctoring" an entirely different approach to health and healing than the medical way. Her father's office and the hogan were her places of learning. She didn't have to choose one over another, both extended mystery and wonder.

But the first time she saw a medicine man extend his hand to scan a patient's body, she felt a shiver of recognition. She wanted to meet the Earth the way he approached the man or woman lying on carefully folded blankets on the ground. He moved with quiet attention, deftly tracing every energetic current and flow in the field, both discerning and easing in one gesture with his sure understanding, after years of apprenticeship, training and prayer, that the restoration of the patient's body and soul could occur just so. His hand moved, like weather does, in waves and eddies, restoring the patterns. Sometimes a hand. Sometimes a feather. Common sights took on new meanings. Sometimes she saw that the bird passing overhead, its wings stirring the air was bringing relief to the Earth beneath as She cooled for an instant from the inflammation, the fevers, a world on fire. Sandra paid attention. Hosteen's example taught her to be aware of assumptions or judgments. Not knowing what something meant, not interpreting, became a habit. If her mind was still, it seemed the non-humans could be heard. As with her father, it was easier to respond this way in Hosteen's presence, not easy at home, increasingly more difficult the older she became, the more intense and focused her studies. But during the crucial years before university, it became second nature to live the analogy between healing mammalian bodies, humans and non-humans, and healing the Earth, that body. A murmuration of starlings, the soughing of crows' wings might bring relief; why not? She did not know about shapeshifting, but longed to become one of those birds.

Between watching Hosteen and his daughter, John's thinking shifted.

He had not expected to feel more possibility for healing on the reservation than he did at home. Towards the end of his two-year commitment, he had engaged in a different kind of differential diagnosis: was this a condition he should treat medically or should he encourage the patient to go home to his or her own healers? The lesson of his first escapee patient stayed with him. He saw that most often the adult patients made the treatment judgment themselves, sometimes came in when native ways had failed, but more likely when overwhelmed, as Hosteen had said, by the fear generated by Western medicines' authoritarian assumption that people will die if they didn't get conventional Western medical treatment. Sometimes, he told Hosteen, he felt as if they were hypnotized or, worse, brainwashed.

"And you?" Hosteen asked.

"Well, I made it my profession. And I am not ready to leave it. I think it still does some good." The litany was familiar, ready to be recited: antibiotics, early diagnosis, surgery. It wasn't a long list and he wasn't sure of its purity. He didn't want to be challenged here. He did not want to account for the good or the dangers. Maybe a patient would die without the Western medicine, and also, maybe a patient would die from Western medicine itself. He could hear Sandra speaking *sotto voce*: "What about the Earth?"

"I helped your shoulder, didn't I, Hosteen?"

"You helped," Hosteen laughed. "You gave me bear medicine." They both laughed.

Diabetes challenged him. It was increasing in geometric proportions on the reservation but similarly among non-Natives – a white man's illness, Hosteen asserted. "Are you sure diabetes isn't contagious?" Hosteen asked sardonically. "Don't you think we're catching it from you guys?"

John disliked prescribing meds, particularly for young people who hated regimens, were increasingly confined by them and, as was said too often, were "non-compliant." Having learned that lesson, John wouldn't dare use those words around Hosteen, but that didn't solve his dilemma.

At home, John was hogtied. He had nothing to offer the teenagers but the standard formula: diabetes – meds. It was a two-step. But on the reservation he had options. Hosteen's way added another effective medicine. John started the young people on medications, but required they go to Lodge as well. The dark, the great heat emanating from the stones Hosteen called Grandfathers, the even greater heat as water and herbs were poured on them, the four doors of prayers from the heart, the songs and drumming, all of this shifted them. Not only emotionally, but sometimes physically. John saw that with or without corroboration from medical literature, many youngsters attending Lodge and engaging in council were able to regulate their condition without meds.

There were illnesses he couldn't begin to heal. The best he could do, he had told himself, was to offer what he could and close his mind to the rest. At the time of Hosteen's challenge he should have been more aware of the unremitting problems on the reservation. A physician's distance was not serving him here. He needed a broken heart to be a better doctor though the Board of Medical Examiners might not agree. Children were taken from their homes by social workers who claimed the parents or grandparents or conditions were inadequate, the veterans came home lost and depressed, glassy-eyed. Alcoholism and meth use was on the rise, employment was scarce, depression became a common illness not a rare condition of the soul. The elders tried to warn the people against increasing their reliance on medicines that did more harm than good, but they couldn't keep the young people from their desperate exodus to the cities.

Hosteen was caught by the plague. When his two daughters, who were some years older than Sandra, moved away from the reservation to Winslow, Hosteen thought that was far enough. When they couldn't sustain themselves in Winslow they moved to Tucson and Hosteen seemed defeated. He knew they needed jobs and who knew better than he that the original vibrant, Indigenous life systems were being undermined and survival was threatened. For a few weeks, he refused to eat in his own house alone. Although he wouldn't let Sandra or John cook for him when they drove out to check on him, he did agree to go to the pizza joint next to Basha's grocery store. Sandra didn't argue when he ordered a large coke and she was grateful that he ate most of the pizza, unaware that she was only picking at hers, hoping he would take whatever was left home.

His daughters would be working in a government supported medical clinic. "Health," Hosteen growled, "has become a commodity." John understood his bitterness at the irony of their situation. "Small pox blankets, guns and whiskey is what they brought us in the beginning and their gifts haven't improved any." He looked away as he spoke these words so John and Sandra wouldn't feel personally accused of being part of the "they." But by now, John and Sandra knew they weren't innocent.

The three were seated outside at Pizza Edge, sharing a nicked metal table on a narrow walkway bordering the parking lot that served Basha's market and other shops. A Shell gas station with a convenience store was across the main street. Their conversation was punctuated by the drone of cars, motorcycles and pickups. "They took the land in exchange and ruined that too." Hosteen finished his lament. The loss of his daughters' presence was a great wound. John had brought Sandra here, but Hosteen's daughters were gone. Privilege was at the table with them. Buying pizza and groceries did not make amends.

6

When The Wind Blows

"The Holy Wind." With these words, Dr. Terrence Green, Chair of the Department of Climatology, opened his introductory lecture.

"We have come here to study wind. Remember, however, that wind is always invisible and ungraspable. 'Holy Wind' say the original people of this land. In your way, you will forget this again and again. Wind is ungraspable in all meanings of the word. You will think you see it, think you have it pinned. But you won't.

"Different peoples refer to wind as spirit. Spirit and breath. *Ních'i*, the Holy Wind, the Diné say. In Hebrew – wind, breath, *ruach*, Spirit – similar. As atmospheric scientists, as climatologists, you will have to study and understand wind and apply your knowledge and observations to follow its different, most common and most erratic courses. However, whatever you learn, do not forget that the Holy Wind is always beyond you. You may see its imprint, you may see evidence of its landing, you may fly into it as a hurricane hunter, spy on it as a tornado chaser, you may think you can measure and predict it, and to accomplish this will be your work, but it will always be beyond you. Buddhists say, 'The finger pointing at the moon, is not the moon.' If only scientists would know that numbers are not the thing-in-itself. To understand that you will never see and never understand wind, is the first step to knowledge."

Dr. Terrence Green turned on a fan and said, "Because you can make this wind blow, don't think you can control the forces of nature; know that trying to control them can do life great injury. You may be able to turn the fan on and off, but you aren't able to turn wind on or off."

He chuckled, "Also be careful not to let the wind out of the bag. Every culture, from the ancient Greek to the living Maya, warns us about this. See if you can become both a Western scientist and a devoted guardian of the winds."

Twelve students were seated in a circle around a vintage wooden table he had probably purchased in a used furniture store. She had come in early, assessed the room, knew she didn't want to sit opposite him and took a seat at 45 degrees, but like him, facing the north wall of windows. Few of his students credited this introduction as more than theater. But she had been watching the wind sweep into the walnut trees and she heard what he was saying. Their branches were swaying, the leaves shifting color from dark to pale as they twisted in and away from the light. The early autumn light was already more golden than high summer. She would be seated here for several months, as the leaves would begin to fall, marking the transitions, the limbs becoming bare and dark against a sky moving toward chill and rain. As if everything before her were moving north. If she managed to come in early in the beginning and establish this seat at the table, then she would watch the night arrive stealthily, by a minute or two longer each day, enough so that it would overtake the last hours of the last classes. A few cumulus clouds were coming in. Maybe they had been moving through before but she hadn't noticed. A southwest wind, so familiar it had been invisible. A little ripple in the grass. Maybe rain. No, too early in the season. Of course, she had checked the weather report in the morning but she hadn't checked the weather. Then it struck her like a blast of cold – the class, everything they were to study and explore – was outside the room. The entire curriculum was outside. The bare floor to ceiling windows were the book. She turned toward Dr. G, as his graduate students called him, had he arranged it so? His simple preference or a careful design?

He was looking around the circle and looking out the window at the same time. He caught her eye and reflexively she shuttled her chair back from his line of sight though she did not escape his glance of easy curiosity about who had come to share his table. His last words were echoing in her mind, "See if you can become both a Western scientist and a devoted guardian of the winds."

Someone asked a question. She didn't hear it. The young man was voicing familiar concerns. He wanted the book list, the overview of the course, deadlines, what they would be expected to know by the end of the semester. Instead of paying attention to the exchange, Sandra kept looking around the circle, examining each face – they would be spending the next years with each other – wondering who had chosen, like Dr. G had, to watch the outside and who had chosen to stare at Dr. G himself and the row of books behind him, and would their choices ever matter to her? Had those who had chosen to sit with their backs to the windows feared they might be distracted by the play of light and shadow, by movement and change? Or did their academic ambitions demand they watch the Chair of the Department carefully? When she looked up from their faces, Dr. G was watching her. Repositioning had not obscured her. He had caught her wandering. Wandering where? Wandering away from the window, away from the wind, away from what concerned them most. She had fallen into the trap.

Dr. G was speaking. She changed her focus, listening to him but looking to another place. This required concentration. It was not easy to hear what he and the others where saying while being attentive to outside. To hear and see as distinct and coexistent experiences. She would have to develop this skill as well as everything else graduate school would demand.

"You think you are here to learn about wind." Dr. G continued. "My grandfather introduced me to wind when I was young." Neither she nor any of the other students had expected him to reveal anything of his lineage.

"What do you mean?" asked a man whose graduate work, she had learned earlier in the day in another seminar, was leading him toward offshore wind turbines as a future source of energy. Sandra thought her fellow student's tone held a subtle hope he could learn to manage wind and so become a successful player in the necessary conversion to sustainable energy.

"What do I mean? What I mean is harder to understand than quantum physics," Terrence met his question with an unanticipated rebuke. Terrence Green had been the Chair of Climatology, which had been subsumed within a larger field of study, Earth and Environmental Studies in 1997. It was his range as a scientist, teacher and human being that defined the Department and had drawn Sandra to it. It was as if Earth had been speaking in her, leading her to an imagined future without denying the disaster that was looming. A future that could only come out of bearing witness, not looking away. Increasingly, she felt that everything was arbitrary, even existence itself. So many exact factors coming together that needed always to be considered and were not being considered, without which life would not exist. She hadn't known his name before she enrolled, but she was hopeful that she might learn what would matter to her when she had read the curriculum he had created. Now she was hearing something beneath the words that he was saying aloud.

Everyone in the room was startled by what he said and also by the fleeting instant of transformation, a rare openness followed by the shock of irritability, two qualities they would probably never see again in him. For a split second, he had responded as the Native man he was. Then he had readjusted the collar of his blue denim shirt and straightened his shirt inside his jeans held smooth by a leather belt with a bear embossed on the silver buckle that could have been purchased by any tourist in Santa Fe, and returned to being Dr. Terrence Green, Chair of EE&S. The plastic lining in his shirt pocket protecting against ink stains was the essential component of a disguise that somehow obscured his features, his dark braid, and his unique consideration of conventional assumptions. "Well," he responded as was his way to any certainty, "let us consider this from different perspectives …."

Dr. G spoke a few words to each person as they left the class. When she came up to him, he asked her, "What did you consider noteworthy, Ms. Birdswell?"

"I'm Sandra, Dr. G." He nodded. The question literally threw her off balance and her name steadied her. That realization was enough to make her smile, which he took kindly. "What did I consider noteworthy? I would say the wind is from the southwest at 11 miles an hour and the temperature approximately 66 degrees. I can't estimate the barometric pressure – maybe 29.75 and I think the weather is going to be the same tomorrow. Maybe, based on the intermittent clouds, a degree cooler."

"I'll make a note of that myself, Ms … uh, Sandra," he said as he turned to the man behind her. "Hello Mr. Wú…."

She understood immediately, she had failed the test. The numbers she had cited hadn't revealed the nature of the weather. She had a lot to learn.

None of her classes had ever met in such a circle until she studied with Dr. G. though his preferences were not adopted by his colleagues. She was relieved by the informality and respect for each person that it implied. Predictably, she hadn't liked the more common, conventional forms of study, but that didn't mean she hadn't acquiesced to learn everything there was to learn, in whatever forms, so that she might help in setting everything right. Setting it all right and setting the system right that she was studying. She understood that each system seemed to require its own medicine. She wondered if her fate would be to attempt to set science right, since Earth did well enough when humans behaved themselves. She had an intuition that Dr. G would direct her well, wherever she was going.

Sandra was engaged with what Dr. G said about wind because her father had also introduced her to wind, but she hadn't thought of it that way until she heard Dr. G speak. John Birdswell had told her stories of Mr. Wind knocking at the doors, bowing out the windows. Their household myth was that Mr. Wind took her out of her bed on stormy nights, returning her in the morning, and that is why she became a climatologist.

When they had lived at the summit of local hills, there was nothing between them and the far desert. The wind came roaring across miles of dry land, increasing desertification resulting from lumbering, ranching and urban water acquisition. Lying in bed, she would wait for signs of the wind coming up and imagine outracing him, leaping to wherever the wind was going. When she was seven, the window in her bedroom had filled with wind like a spinnaker and shattered before the house could sail with it across the earthen seas. Glass over the floor like shards of light shining on the waves. That day, she had asked her father the origin of the word, window. He said it was an eye through which one looked at the wind. Then he stopped, looked, quizzically, and continued, "Maybe the window is the eye through which we show ourselves to the wind." Mr. Wind. A spirit? What had John Birdswell intuited?

She had started with meteorology, because she loved the Earth and she loved wind. Having spent much of her childhood alone, she appreciated wind's companionship. It had never been her intent to pursue meteorology in order to predict weather, but to know clouds and wind, water, earth and fire. Soon this wasn't a large enough field to satisfy her. By twelve, she had known that weather was current and climate extensive and that climate depended on the ongoing patterns of wind, water, earth, light, heat and that she had to know all of it. And as indicated by the onset of the Anthropocene, she had to know as much, or even more about the activity of humans than the activity of solar flares. If she worked from a patient-centered, or in this case, Earth-centered perspective, she might do less harm.

Sandra shifted her emphasis from meteorology to climatology after meeting a professor for whom climate was not abstract, and climate change was not merely an opportunity for an academic position, a dissertation, employment or investment. Her father had always been a hands-on physician; Sandra was determined to be a hands-on scientist.

Environmental studies and climatology were increasing in importance and funding – their focuses broadening and deepening. She was encouraged to create her own program, to be sure it was extensive enough to understand the Earth's entire interconnected living system, its history and resources and the processes of change, a program that embraced geology, oceanography and the atmosphere to or beyond the edge of space, even as far as the sun, and included all forms of human impact. Daunting. OK, Sandra accepted it. She wanted wisdom not merely information. She wanted science but she also wanted what she believed was in the growing adjunct curriculum referred to as TEK, Traditional Ecological Knowledge, what Native people had understood after eons of intimate observation and interaction. TEK was the old, old way of understanding change and living systems, but regarded as if new by many of her faculty who were less than enthusiastic about it. Some even considered such studies politically motivated and undermining of scientific rigor and hegemony.

Her own inclinations and the rising need and alarm over the rapid and extreme climate changes coincided. What she wanted was a program that recognized Earth as a living being. Indigenous sciences, Sandra argued with her other professors and colleagues, were based on deeper relationships with the elements that supported life. She didn't have words for what seemed so evident to her. "It's simple," she maintained. "We have to change everything, including our assumptions. Or the Earth will go down."

James Lovelock's Gaia theory intrigued her, but the ongoing scorn, leveled as much toward Gaia herself as toward the "self-employed scientist" who had, however, invented the means to trace CFCs in the atmosphere, unsettled her. He also claimed the microwave oven. Would she have to invent something or work as Lovelock did at NASA before setting out on her own? And would that be to gain a substantial income or to gain sufficient prestige to be acknowledged? She had a goal she didn't find echoed in the school catalogue: to be a self-appointed physician to the patient Earth. Every aspect of dealing with a living form that might even feel pain instead of a manipulating a dead field, required a systemic shift. Hadn't people insisted, even most recently, that animals and human infants didn't feel pain, and so subjected them to procedures without the immediate and ongoing trauma being considered? And then there was the growing pattern of inflicting pain for the pleasure of it. Sandra feared that torture was primarily instigated to satisfy sadistic urges rather than to acquire information. Her head reeled from the global chaos in every direction. Recognition of a sentient Earth would not mitigate all harm, but it might make some difference. The task before her was huge but she had a hard core feeling in her belly that she wouldn't have been graced with such anguish for the world if there weren't some way that she would find to approach it. She trusted her belly.

"Why don't you study biology?" her father asked hoping to move her interests closer to his. "The Anthropocene, Poppa, refers to the time human beings affect the environment. When nature disappears as we increasingly manipulate and control it. I'm not here to focus on people. You do that. I have only one concern: Her."

Dr. G had become Chair when the world crises began to loom large. He adamantly insisted that the narrow focus of specialization had to yield to wider latitudes, greater range of knowledge, connectivity and experience. The necessity to see the whole was not arbitrary. He sent his students on a scavenger hunt to find all the missing parts to any problem.

What was missing from his evident position in the department? The evidence, Sandra answered, of the University's equivalent of cap and trade. The University had hired a Native American scholar as Department Chair. There was something for each of them to be accomplished or gained from their association, but he had to appear to be one of them, generally supportive of their policies and curricula. The pressures from the Board, corporations, funders, private and public were obvious to Sandra and her fellow students. It wasn't hard to monitor the PhD theses, which were hailed, the prizes won, the grants funded, the list of public speakers and presentations, and see which way the winds were blowing.

Sandra had expected everyone in the department, faculty, students and staff to be climate activists. And some were, of course. For almost everyone the weight of what they knew was overwhelming. Despair, Sandra felt, was often leading to a kind of hedonism she didn't understand. Carpe diem. Her professors seemed preoccupied by their own personal projects and grants while the larger issue of the Earth's survival was left for individual contemplation. Even as Sandra felt compelled to acquire all the skills and learning she could to meet the challenges, she was disheartened by the ongoing refrain: cost. The cost for any project from meeting the Kyoto accords to cleaning up toxic sites, from implementing early warning systems to building levees, from cyclone relief to protecting agriculture worldwide; there was never enough money, not for the individual projects nor for global relief. The cost was always too great, too daunting, impossible to meet. No matter whether private monies or public monies, or a combination, financing was unavailable to the extent necessary to make the changes required on behalf of all life. Everywhere around her, she saw ravenous hunger for a certain kind of life and an increasing gloom about the cost and sustainability of it. Her early concerns with career and profession were rapidly dimming with her mounting understanding of the rapid and systemic decline of the environment. She saw few positions listed which met the gravity she recognized. She didn't know if was possible in her lifetime to acquire the knowledge equal to the tragedy. The knowledge equal to the heartbreak.

Her concerns were not generally mirrored. No one in her peer group could imagine the world shifting its reliance on energy. Developing countries, they noted, would need more energy, not less – and they deserved it – to meet poverty and civil unrest. Developed countries were not going to give up the lifestyle they had worked to develop or the goods upon which their economies depended. No one in her class was living off the grid, nor was she. Sometimes she came home at night and challenged herself to live without lights or electricity. It was useless. She couldn't do her work without the computer. She tried to assess her value or potential in relationship to the resources she used. When her associates saw her eyes fill with tears or her hands clench in frustration, they moved to reassure her that science would solve the problem in time, only more effort, devotion and funds were needed. Wasn't this what the department was training students to accomplish?

Sandra had regular conferences with herself, reminding herself of her commitment. "You were born," she said, to the mirror, "when we humans began to understand the terrible impact of human life on the Earth. You were born into the Anthropocene," she scolded. It was a little theater piece she engaged in that amused and sobered her. Or she walked out to the trees behind her father's house and asked, "What am I, what are we going to do?" It was her manner of prayer. She didn't know any other so she used this form of interrogation to anchor her to a spiritual life. It didn't matter any longer what she wanted to do or be. Her original passions and enthusiasm for her studies might be diminishing but the need to know something to meet the dread consequences of climate change was escalating. She persisted in the ways that her profession encouraged inquiry. Behind every unknown, a known must be waiting.

During winter break in her second year of graduate school when she was equally engaged in taking classes and pursuing independent studies, she went to the reservation to rest. They were sitting outside on a log, warming themselves in a patch of sunlight when Sandra asked Hosteen what he thought of TEK. He couldn't refrain from speaking angrily even though he was speaking to her as he always did, as her uncle. He had suddenly become another academic course, he snorted bitterly, something else to be studied and integrated as needed into the curriculum, when its value was verified by Western scientific observation – the gold standard for a so-called civilization that believed in gold. But nothing was going to change. The academics would take what suited them but weren't going to give up their ways.

Sandra had not seen him angry in this way before. Hosteen did not hold back what he thought and he did not direct it at her. This was not a fist or a club. This was a storm. A fact of nature. It built, swirled and passed, leaving an imprint on the Earth. It was to be noted and respected but it was not directed at Sandra. It was not to be taken personally, and most importantly, it was not to be argued with.

"I thought it was a good idea. I thought it meant progress," she said meekly. Not meekly, respectfully. The way she responded, the way she asked a question, was as important as the statement itself. Hosteen's perception of the field that was established through inquiry was as subtle and complex as her father's intuitive attention to every nuance in a patient's body and demeanor.

"Progress," Hosteen shouted, "is a device used to turn our people against each other." The weather was turning bad. They would need to take shelter soon. "Traditional knowledge is traditional knowledge. Should we be grateful that a few academics are interested in considering it when it suits their purposes? Does this mean they will see the light and set their destructive ways aside?

"Bunch of fire bearing witches invaded this country five hundred years ago," he continued, "and kept coming and reproducing. Now the land is dying." He didn't pause his tirade when he turned directly to her. "Do you have some tobacco?" Sandra knew he had some in his pocket, but he wanted her to make the offering. Despite his request, Hosteen didn't wait for her to respond, but strode toward his house and emerged with his pipe wrapped in red cloth and tramped toward the nearby cairn where he did ceremony. The tenderness with which he always held the pipe began to undo his fury. Anger was a friend to no one. When he returned, nothing more would be said. She had learned what she needed to learn. He had fulfilled his duties to her as her uncle.

7

The Riddle Of Knowing

Dr. G received Sandra's dissertation proposal: Meteorological Seasonal Climate Forecasts (SCF) and Indigenous Knowledge-Based Seasonal Forecasts (IKF) Can Complement In The Face of Climate Change and Desertification.

He had always observed her carefully from his distant position as chairman, intrigued by her privileging Indigenous knowing rather than placing Western science exclusively in the center. It was a bold gesture and she would have a hard time getting support for her investigations, but this university claimed to be open to meeting the current global crisis by all means possible. He could not tell yet whether she was a very naive student or very canny. He hoped that she was smart enough to write an irrefutable paper.

She had made the requisite appointment with the chairman. She was confident and she felt shy, didn't quite know where to sit. Dr. G pointed her to a chair across from his desk and he took another to her side. Before them was the unimpeded view to the north and the foothills. They were both facing it though also looking at each other. With a certain narrow focus, she could imagine that they were outside of human habitation. Books lined every inch of wall that had no windows as if they were in an outside library.

"You want to undermine Western science even as you are gaining its expertise," Dr. G observed, but without refusing her. She didn't notice his irony. "TEK isn't a recognized scientific method. It isn't a field, an organized body of knowledge, an academic major, a department. It isn't an authority," he was lecturing her.

Despite Hosteen's reaction, she had expected his full support. It hadn't occurred to her that he wouldn't offer it exactly because he was a Native man. She was caught between being polite to the man who had her life, that is her career, in his hands, and the desire to assert that she understood exactly what she was doing. Permission to pursue such a subject would determine whether she would stay in graduate school or not. She tempered her response and proceeded as if he was ignorant of its growing authority. "It can't be an academic field validated by peer review, by its very nature. It emerges from other cultures and cultural values entirely and it has been with us since the beginning. When we couldn't destroy it, we decided to see if it had anything to offer us. That's TEK, I guess." As soon as she heard herself say "us" she saw she hadn't learned much in two years. She was speaking TEK and wanted to use it, "use" it for her own purposes – she confronted herself in her mind. She had committed the very crime Hosteen had described. "First do no harm," she cautioned herself. Co-option was harm. Privilege was harmful. This was going badly. Looking over at Dr. G, she saw that he was waiting, patiently. Could she forgo strategy and speak about why this mattered to her so much? Truly?

"Still," she paused, "all those articles being written in conjunction with Native informants, aren't they creating a body of knowledge? Isn't that a good thing? If I interview Native people about the weather they think is coming and why they think so, and then interview some non-Native people about their predictions and what they are based on, and then wait and see what occurs and compare the data might that not be useful? Or at least interesting? Well, let's say, informative. And if I asked the Native people what they would do to remedy climate change if they could do whatever made sense to them, might that not be interesting too? It might give us a new direction since we seem have to run out of remedies." Interesting was the wrong word. "Might this not be important? Beneficial?" There was no right word.

She was going to stop there when her repressed alarm rose to the surface. "And artificial rainmaking seems to be headed toward unacknowledged global warfare. Indigenous input could modify the way we're going." She was scared and angry and didn't hide it.

For a moment it seemed to her that he was grinning despite his placid expression. Or he was silently challenging or rebuking her: "Do you really believe we're going to change?" He hadn't said anything.

He's going to let me hang myself, she thought but didn't know how to get out of the noose she was creating.

"I am not wanting to undermine anything. I just want to know," she persisted.

"That's the problem," he continued, "because knowing in the way you may want to know, may distort both ways of knowing – the developed world's and the Indigenous'. From one perspective, that's the problem with TEK. It isn't about knowing, it isn't just another reference or footnote, or bit of evidence. No matter how it is cited or presented, what it reveals is not as potent as it would be if the reader were sitting with an elder, without a computer, without having ever known a computer and was just listening as a world, not information, came into view. You won't be able to duplicate the understanding that can come when living with an elder and without a narrow question to be addressed. An elder isn't just an informant, you know." Maybe she didn't know. Maybe she was naïve. Naïve and good hearted – the worst of his students. But maybe she wasn't so naïve.

"Did you come here to combine the two, Western and Native, heal the divisions that undermine the whole? Can they be healed, Ms. Birdswell?" Why had he called her Ms. Birdswell? She felt her cheeks redden as if he had slapped her but maybe he wasn't critiquing her topic, only trying to awaken her. She listened with more attention as he continued. "Will their interminable and unavoidable interchanges destroy them both? Reduce one even further and inflate the other?"

He wasn't only challenging her, but was directing very serious questions to her, ones she had not fully considered. She would have to take them on. She would have to listen more deeply, outside of what she presumed he was saying. Outside of what she thought she would say, if she were him.

"So what do you want to know, Sandra?"

Finally, he had called her Sandra. "Thank you for those questions, Dr. G. No, I mean it. I am not being rude. Just awkward."

His eyes met hers fleetingly in response to her honesty. She had recovered her ground. He met her eyes and they both looked away. Her childhood had trained her to be very aware of people's responses. They matched each other in this exchange. She decided to continue, as if trusting him. "What do I want to know?"

She did not know him well, nor did any of the students. He had a reputation for being reserved. He also had the habit of stopping to think before answering a challenging question and might take a long time, long enough to make students and colleagues uncomfortable, though he rarely, if ever, disappointed with his final response. Others learned to be patient with him as patient as he was with others. As everyone in the department seemed to be running out of time, it was assumed that it had been allocated to him, for he never hurried anyone or seemed to hurry himself while whatever he needed to do, got done. Reliable and patient. And solitary.

Gambling on all of this, she dared an answer even though she was in dangerous territory, understanding that the adamant and thoughtless desire to know, central to Western science, was wreaking havoc with all life. She was sure that Indigenous thinking included inquiry but she didn't know its forms.

"I want to know why there is such a great gap between scientific thought and non-scientific understanding. I want to know why the cave painters didn't see the world the way it is seen by contributors to the journal, Nature, for example. We're the same species. What did they see? Why the enormous difference? Is it only a matter of time? Would the cave painters have caught up to us inevitably? Did they? Are we them? And, then why are we so hostile to what they saw and thought?"

"I don't think that is a suitable dissertation topic," he had gotten up from his chair and was leaning against the file cabinet, looking out his office window. "I think you will be better off returning to your interests in desertification, science and TEK." She followed his glance to the dark shadows on the rounded hills and the white clouds sweeping across the sky toward them.

"What else?" He didn't look at her, yet his attention to the shadows comforted her.

"I want to know if there is a way to predict in the morning whether there will be a spectacular sunset at night and where I should place myself to see it. Red sky at morning … doesn't quite do it. It hints that I might be better off staying inside and checking my instruments, but …."

"What do you think?"

"I think that I would be better off developing the discipline to go outside and watch for it before dawn and at twilight."

"I agree with you, Ms. Birdswell." He had removed himself from her once again. But maybe because he was amused. She couldn't tell. Or because she had crossed one of the invisible boundaries that were integral to the department. She got up to leave, throwing her backpack over one shoulder as he continued, "I look forward to hearing about your progress on your dissertation. I don't imagine that sunset watching will cause you much delay. It will only be a minor diversion in relationship to time."

"Dr. Salazar will be happy to chair your committee, why don't you contact her?" he pronounced. In a sentence, he withdrew from direct supervision of her thesis, handing it over to a colleague more expert in Sandra's field of investigation. "As you know from your classes and independent study with her, she is very capable." Again, Sandra couldn't discern if his statement was an observation, an acknowledgement or an assignment. Sandra recovered by smiling to herself; she was becoming expert in ambiguity, another skill that could serve her well in the future.

Though Dr. G was not her faculty advisor or mentor, she attended his lectures when she could because of the environment he created around himself. In his presence, words resonated and so it seemed to her that was a harmonic continuum under the general subject he was discussing. When Dr. G did the math, provided the calculations, presented the data from climate models, Sandra heard the wind moving in the algorithms, she heard whether it was dry or wet in the way she assumed his original language would have distinguished these most carefully. She heard it moving over the earth and the earth it was moving over, she heard it brush against her bare calves, she heard it whistle in her ears, she heard it whistle to her; she heard it. This more than anything else consoled her.

Sandra wanted to listen to the land and the weather in its own language, not in translation. English had a remove, saw the land as object; this, alone, accounted for many of the troubles that were arising. She came to this understanding through frustration. Not being able to say what she wanted to say. English wasn't deeply enough acquainted with the elements of the natural world so she could speak of them. At best, it offered a translation of their nature. How then, she wondered, was change going to occur without intimate understanding of the other?

Sometimes, she thought Earth and weather were speaking to her in their own vernacular, but as she and they didn't have language in common, she heard but couldn't grasp or retain what was transmitted. So when Dr. G spoke of the ways of the Earth, she listened and tried to retain the full essence of his words. It would be easier to learn from someone, to trust his interpretations and opinions, the subjects he chose to present, the reading materials he found relevant, if they looked at the world from a similar perspective.

Sometimes she thought she heard the Earth call out in pain. She wondered if concrete and macadam, metal towers or steeples bruised the wind while the spikes of trees did not. Cities, buildings, architecture, affect weather, even if it isn't exactly known yet why or how. Tornados seemed to like the path between towns and large open fields like farm land, like so many other species, Sandra explained to herself, that thrive in the rich diversity of an ecotone.

Sandra was looking to work with architects to consider how their structures in any given place might affect the weather. They were already interested in how weather might affect their constructions. The intensification of floods, landslides, hurricanes, the frequency of earthquakes in unexpected areas of the country necessitated such concern. However, how human configurations, urbanization, for example, might affect the weather was an entirely new perspective for consideration. It was not difficult for Sandra to see the dynamic between human invention and construction and the elements.

While working on her dissertation, she was asked to consult on a joint HUD and BIA housing project in the desert and while there, she took advantage of whatever she could learn from the crew who spent so much time in the area. Discovering that one of the engineers was a Native man, she asked him to tell her how he would approach the project if he were completely free to follow his tradition's knowledge and values. He was amused by her question and studied her face carefully to see her motivation. She let him scrutinize her, trying not to hide or convey anything.

"What advantage will it give you to know?" That much he decided to trust or test her by asking.

"I don't know." She was sincere. "Maybe it will help the project. But probably not. The likelihood that any changes will be accepted is minimum. But I will have learned something that could be important to me and, hopefully, others, down the road."

"Good enough," he agreed and suggested they take their lunches and drive to a nearby rise to see the site from above. From the vantage of a full landscape, she saw how one might think differently about placement. An eagle's perspective as well as the prairie dog's.

They felt the same inclination to sit quietly eating their lunch. Sandra poured ice coffee for them from her thermos and gazed down at the broad, flat vista between hills and stony rises shimmering with heat waves in color variations of sand, reddish orange to gray, faint dabs of yellow and pale green with glints of quartz. When she looked away, she added blue to the sandscape, but it disappeared when she looked back. She didn't know where the blue came from except she would have to introduce it here and there if she were painting the scene to make it right. The invisible had to be included with the visible.

"From here," Jack Bekis said when they had finished eating, "I can see where the wind mainly enters from the southwest, but occasionally from the north. I need to see where the wind wants to go before I put anything in its way."

In January, 2001, she was attending a graduate seminar with other PhD candidates. Though Dr. G was not speaking, she found she still learned, as she had the first day, by observing what he was watching. She thought she saw him look away suddenly as if something extraneous to the discussion had momentarily caught his attention. Just a blink. At the same time, she felt physically, disquieted, faintly tremulous and even nauseated, but suppressed the impulse to shout, "Earthquake." She couldn't situate it — it wasn't anywhere near them. She didn't feel endangered, only unsettled. What was there to say? If she were correct, she would be open to teasing. And if she were wrong, then ridicule was inevitable.

To meet the earthquake, she remained still. However, when she checked her computer later, her perception was verified: a 7.9 quake in northwestern India. Ultimately, it would leave 20,000 dead. This confirmation left her with aftershocks. What she was studying, what she read and learned every day was sufficient to unnerve her. She didn't want information pouring in uncontrollably from a secret source, a fissure in her own system, a deep well of knowing, extending down to her core.

8

What Vanishes

Her dissertation was accepted. She got her PhD. An opportunity came her way and she went to the Arctic to study ice. She would be there long enough to fully experience the winter, which meant darkness. The night, like the cold, called her to silence.

To know the Earth, she would have even gone down to the bottom of the deepest ocean if she'd had the opportunity. The Arctic was one way. Studying ice ultimately meant studying oceans, current wind and water patterns and their history, bird and animal populations, listening to Native stories, being attentive to Native knowledge and beliefs, accompanying hunters and trappers, worrying about a range of concerns from teenage alcoholism, unemployment, depression and suicide to the fate of glaciers, polar bears, and the release of methane gas from the melting permafrost into the atmosphere. All of these and the steadily decreasing, diminishing, retreating ice fields that had sustained a teeming life of beautiful interdependence for thousands of years.

She was studying ice because it was vanishing. She had to learn why it was vanishing in ways that would convince her colleagues and the world at large of the tragedy. There were climate change deniers everywhere, even in her department. Were they sincere or strategic? She didn't know. Why it was vanishing was obvious to her and needed awareness, not proof. It was vanishing because of the impact of all that was being created and imposed from the rapid multiplication and metastasis of extraction and excavation of resources and the manufacture and buildup of goods and weaponry. The garbage and toxic waste of contemporary life. The Anthropocene.

Since the ice was vanishing, she felt compelled to see what was beneath it. Was it scientific interest, or mere curiosity? At moments her interest felt prurient. She knew she did not want to mine the Arctic, or exploit the innards of the Earth body. To understand? To understand, to what purpose?

The sun might not be directly affecting climate change, but melting ice certainly did. For weeks, she watched the great translucent ice beings, the glaciers, calve, but in this case the progeny meant death not life. Sometimes she went out with various researchers in the area, other times she went out with Native people. The skill she had developed through her thesis transferred to this project. Her Native colleagues were always interested in what their Western counterparts concluded although they didn't trust their assessments entirely. The myriad research papers that studied one aspect or another of the area each month were very narrow in focus and Native science was rooted in collaboration. It would have amused them, if circumstances were not so dire, to see so many individuals studying an area they couldn't possibly know well as they didn't live there, hadn't grown up there, didn't have ancestors there. The Western scientists trusted their instruments more than they trusted their own powers of observation or those of the Indigenous. The researchers that Sandra met did not trust the Native assessments, their understanding or explanation of the changes that were occurring. The Native people were quick to point out that they had lived in the area for thousands of years without fouling the nest. Their judgments were based on long periods of observation, compared to the scientists', who had even challenged how long they had lived there. They noted that the truths of Western science fluctuated, and what was axiomatic one day, might be replaced the next. However, science maintained certainty about its methodology and was casual about its shifting conclusions. Maybe the methodology and response of Western science was a factor in the rapidly disintegrating situation. Sandra found herself moving from ambiguity to complexity. In order to write the paper she envisioned, she had to weave all the positions in their entirety into a cohesive whole.

Standing on the increasingly precarious ice in the brief light of winter day, she would not assert, despite ice's knife-white brilliance, that the sun's flares affected the Earth in critical ways, but at night, under the terrifying splendor of the aurora borealis, she wondered, how could it not? She was further split between the observations of the laboratory and what internal certainties overtook her, which she could not deny when she was alone with her own perceptions in the light and in the dark.

Then she was overwhelmed with uncomfortable thoughts. If vibrations, waves and particles from beyond the Earth might be affecting the planet, then, might not the manufactured, contrived constructed increasing radiation, toxic emanations, explosions, earthquakes affect the atmosphere and beyond, even more intensely or create a feedback system from which Earth might not be able to escape? With every new discovery, she descended into dread instead of hope. What might be the unexpected consequences?

The Earth was one body, climatology was revealing this reality. How much more of the universe could or should be understood in this way?

"Why did you go to the Arctic, of all places, Sandra?" her father, John Birdswell, had asked her, on her return. They were standing in the house she had purchased before she had left, an act that seemed to him as impulsive as her postgraduate studies, but he had not commented, nor would he ever.

They had routines. When she traveled, he would come over as soon as she came home. He knew that she needed someone to hear the stories of her experience, someone who could listen deeply. This time there was something odd about her stance, as if she had been frozen. Maybe that is why he asked her about the Arctic instead of waiting for what she might say.

"I'm trying to break the ice," he said; she grimaced at the pun. Had he been able to offer her hope, he could have warmed her. But he could not reassure her about the world that was melting away.

Why had she gone to study the Arctic, which seemed so far from her field of study?

"The Arctic could become a desert," she had answered. "Global warming. Climate change. The melt goes into the sea. It is not returning."

"Maybe trees will grow there then."

"Not in our lifetimes, I'm afraid.

"And," she continued morosely," there are people just waiting for enough ice to melt to begin drilling; they will turn the emerging deserts into waste dumps. They will sully the pristine with new trade routes that will pollute the waters."

"Are you afraid?"

"I am."

"That's not the only reason I went, Poppa. A sub-theme of my dissertation was to find the common ground between science and TEK or to show how they might inform each other. It seems to be a nano-niche of expertise I have developed. Do you know how I got to it?"

He didn't and looked to her for an explanation.

"From you, Poppa. Watching you and Hosteen."

He had brought vanilla and dark chocolate gelato. Wild salmon and yellow tail sashimi. Uni and giant clam. Rice, though he knew she wouldn't eat it, and two quarts of miso soup from a Japanese restaurant they both liked. They sat down on the sunny side of the patio. Late afternoon. It was warm enough, except it was still winter. He poured hot sake for both of them. She ate from the gelato to the soup just as she had as a child. He had stopped worrying about her strange proclivities. They always worked out. Now he just wondered at them while he ate in a more conventional order. The sun began to set and the cold followed it. They went inside.

"I worked in tandem with a local conservation group. Their goal was the best available science modestly informed by TEK on the status and trends of Arctic biodiversity and accompanying policy. I wanted to be a part of the best available science." Shadow crossed her face. "At that time, I wanted to be part of the best available science," she repeated as if hearing herself say it for the first time.

There was something she wasn't saying.

"Like you, Poppa, I go where the emergencies are."

He waited. He had learned waiting as a physician though most of his colleagues were trained by economic and corporate pressures to be impatient. If he started questioning, he would be leading and would not get anything he hadn't anticipated. He always worked for himself, or as he put it, he worked for his patients. When he was waiting, he was working with his patients. He was waiting for them to say something that would reveal a story or a cause neither of them knew how to look for. His trust that they knew something. Their trust that he would listen. Trust took time. He did not feel things in his body the way Sandra could. But he had learned enough from watching Sandra to assume that his patients felt what they said they did. He even asked his patients about their dreams. He thought the dreams might help him understand their condition.

"I have been having a reoccurring dream," Sandra stated flatly. She had experienced intimacy from her father who raised her in an atmosphere of trust and respect, but still it was difficult to speak so openly to him about what meant so much to her and distinguished her from most of her colleagues and acquaintances. She could not say she had friends, or rather, deep friendships.

"The dream never seems disturbing enough to merit coming back. What am I unable to see that causes it to return, again and again?

"A lecture hall," she began. "It resembled a small amphitheater. I was at the podium and my colleagues were in their raked seats before me. I had notes to guide me and they had yellow pads of paper. I was speaking about what we can learn from studying Arctic ice. I wanted to call the lecture:

'What the Ice Knows.' But that wouldn't fly. My task was to translate what the ice knows, what the ice told me, into a language that would assert what I thought I knew or had discovered.

"I put my left hand out, cupped palm up." She was in the dream now, her left hand extended, her palm curled as if containing something, an offering she was making. "Too late, I realized I was mimicking a respectful gesture of an older colleague, who would sometimes extend his hand in that way before beginning to speak. He would close his eyes as if to see what he was holding, what he would present. I was copying him but I couldn't feel anything in my hand. I wanted to feel the ice and offer it to the audience. But, I was making the wrong gesture to the wrong culture. Wrong language. I had no right to do that. I was using it. I was co-opting it.

"I had to pull myself back quickly. Instinctively, I opened my hand flatter, bending my fingers back, as if to say, 'Here they are. The facts. Let's be clear.' I began talking about the Arctic Oscillation, thinning Arctic ice cover, glacier melt, permafrost, methane, global warming. At the end of the dream, I was reading icicles and babbling numbers, formulae, algorithms. It was terrifying.

"Poppa, I am not sure I want to be part of the best available science anymore. It's all funded by the government, the military or the corporations. Like medicine, I guess. You only get to ask certain questions that will lead to certain answers. What science has invented, what it assumes is essential, what it does not question, has brought us to this melt. Deviate from this and you're met with scorn. It's very effective. But, from the long view, it's obvious that creating a life of instruments and technology diminishes the people living on the ice –living with the ice – who know so much more than we do. Or know what we need to stop doing. How are the same methods and methodology going to fix it? Einstein said, "Problems can not be solved at the level at which they were created."

He was concerned, but didn't respond, only nodded as if he understood. But he hadn't understood. She was just starting out and already questioning her field. He had expected her to be a physician, had even imagined a common practice. Climatology had seemed a significant choice instead, a larger field than he had ever considered. The times demanded such a stretch, she had maintained. But he didn't expect her to be unsteady. He would not have followed her lead even if he were younger. He needed the intimacy of working with each patient. Somehow she had that intimacy with Earth itself. What he could do was raise one child, heal one patient at a time.

"Why science, then? You could have …" he stopped, flustered. John couldn't imagine another way for her. He refrained from his pat retort,

"You could become anyone, could do anything you want." He had to face the truth, he hadn't ever imagined anything else for her.

"I don't know if I am up for what is needed," Sandra frowned and tossed her long hair around her, trying to shake off despondency. He picked up his sake cup, stumbled into the living room, set it down on the wooden table and threw himself down on the leather couch. There were no shades or curtains on any of the windows or glass doors of the house that faced in all directions. There were no other houses or roads around. Where the sun had been, the dark was entering, coming in through every window. Their long history told him that he could not reassure her.

She wanted him to listen, not to comment. She would find her way by hearing herself talk. "Maybe I went into science in order to make a name for myself." Her lips were pressed together as if to suppress the sarcasm. Was she smiling or grimacing? Were they going toward humor or bitterness?

"You didn't give me a name to stand on," she continued. "I need a foundation. You didn't give me a foundation. You might have equally named me Mary Smith. How would you expect me to become anyone, to accomplish anything, to do what I am called to do?"

She was at it again. He hadn't seen it coming. He didn't see the connection that was so clear to her. He wanted to dismiss her talk as crazy but looking closely, he saw she was more likely crazed. Like she was being bandied about by the winds. Just as she said, as if she had nothing to hold on to. She was standing at due north and the north pole was shifting, from climate change, from the ice melt.

She flung the wide living room doors open. The wind entered, rattled the papers she had been reading the night before that had been left on the small table. He had hoped she would sit down too but she was standing over him, so he got up and they went back into the kitchen where they were always most comfortable, both standing around the central counter, or perched on bar stools. Whatever his intentions, she had turned the discussion of the Arctic into a device to return to her obsession, her name. As if speaking about it could change it. As if speaking about global warming would cool it down.

"Sometimes I was honored by an invitation to visit a Native family and they would ask my name. I never understood why they stared at me when I gave my name until I realized they were looking for another name, they were looking for my mother in me, or an ancestor. But mostly I think they were looking for my mother and when I said you had given me the name because you liked it or some other neutral reason they seemed puzzled in the way they were puzzled and defeated when they themselves were forced to take on a non-Native name. When they introduced themselves as John or Mary, extending their hand, as I took it, saying, Sandra, I knew we were in a ruse. They thought my mother's soul was loose somewhere with no place to land. It made them uneasy. The way white people make them uneasy. Our souls are flying around aimlessly. Maybe that's why we take so much, to weigh ourselves down. No lineage line to the dead, to a tradition or to the Earth." She stopped to take a breath. Her next question was plaintive, "How am I going to survive?

"When I was out in the field or when we met at the field office our exchanges were perfunctory. But like I said, Poppa, sometimes they liked me and invited me home. At the threshold, so there would be truth between us, they sometimes told me their Native names and what they implied and I couldn't reciprocate. I couldn't offer them the same glimpse into who I really am. Who am I, Poppa?

"If you don't know who you are, Poppa, who am I?"

It was that old argument. She was tired and dispirited. It could happen any time, like a volcano erupting. This was their personal North Atlantic rift at their common core. The conflict continued, threatened to rise up at any moment, as it was doing now, as if she were one plate moving toward North America, he another moving toward Eurasia. Between them the fire coming up in great plumes on land and the magma flow along the oceanic tear that separated them further.

He was a physician, he looked at fissures such as this and went for an ointment to soothe and ease the pain. She was a scientist, trained to observe. It did no good. He wanted to heal the rift but didn't know how. She had been trained, with his encouragement, to look steadily, to try to comprehend, to bear witness, to acquaint herself with the deep reality before her whatever it turned out to be. Her training did not provide her with a way to act except to look further, as far as Iceland, where the rift rose up in fire and separated the two continents that were a single country. Fire and ice — two of the extremes that engaged her. She knew the sun in her body and she had studied ice. A discrepancy he, though her father, could not fathom.

She walked to the kitchen window and opened it to the dark and wind. The cross currents eased her. She always wanted to be outdoors though she wasn't always comfortable there. So she invited the outside in. She also always wanted to be living within her own interior. But, ironically, her work required her to be indoors and her colleagues rejected the inner life as a source of knowledge.

It was fairly cold outside and the open windows created a stronger breeze. She went to the wooden clothing pole at the entrance to the living room and put on her sweater that was hanging there and handed him his jacket. He understood it was going to be a long night.

They would have to talk about her name once again. She was anguished still and again about it. Secretly her obsession embarrassed her, but she couldn't relinquish it. Like the Native people she had met, she believed that names and history and lineage were of a single territory. That they went back in time and carried the bearers forward. She believed that people grew from or into their names. A name matters, she insisted. It determines fate. It perplexed her that she would be deprived of this base, given her concerns for the world.

She was berating him, "My name, Poppa?" He was recalling how the subject had come up when she had signed the papers for the house a few years earlier. Then she couldn't fully accept that ownership would align with such a name, she felt like she was signing with an alias while he was marveling that she was decisive enough to make such a purchase without a quaver of doubt. When he saw her signature on the deed, her name seemed solid as earth to him.

Her PhD behind her, she had found a house with a lease purchase agreement with a kitchen facing south, a bedroom facing north, and a living room with a niche for late afternoon reading and viewing the sunset; she signed the contract immediately.

"Tell me about the light," was the first request she had made to the real estate agent.

"It's perched on a hill, with a 360° view. Isolated."

The details that would make it a hard sell for most anyone, were exactly what she had dreamed. Early morning eastern light entered through what would become her office and also through the entryway.

The other details washed over her. She insisted on seeing it the next day just before dawn with permission to stay past dusk. It was a simple but un-usual house, built, she could tell, by someone as idiosyncratic as she was. It was entirely circular, with a central fireplace. The unknown woman had been a bookish type who lived alone. The bookshelves which were also room dividers, were filled with world literature and there was a pair of binoculars standing in front of the Buddhist texts. Looking out, looking in; looking. Similarly alone, Sandra watched the light rise and set, explored the chaparral, confirmed the privacy; it was hers.

The seller had been flexible because she wanted out by any means —

sale, rental or lease, or any combination thereof. Another life was calling her. Sandra bought it in order to acquire some certainty in her life, even if such was delusional. Her few certainties were far more abstract. She could not live with her father, nor he with her, because they were so close and had separate lives and commitments. They wanted all their contacts to be voluntary. She was not going to live in a neighborhood or an apartment. This was not an acquisition. She was not thinking of investments or status. She needed to be alone. She needed land or land needed her. Lodging and land were not readily available in the ways she thought were right. Based on the design, the furniture and artifacts, she trusted the seller. How the land had come to be for sale would not reveal how it had passed originally into non-Native hands. She hoped the spirits of the land would welcome her, that she would live in ways that did not disturb them further than the original transfer had unquestionably done.

When she was born, John had found a small house that served both them and his patients backing onto a patch of woods, opening to the desert, near enough to town for his patients to come to him and no great distance from the hospital. She wanted the simple equivalent with a view – a home among all the elements aligned with each other.

She had wanted a home. No, a house. Not a house, really, but land. Not land, either, but a place to stand from which she could see all around her. She knew that what she would see each day would become her foundation. The dynamic Earth, the constantly shifting sky, all their creatures and the stories that accompany the land, all the way back to the beginning of human and geologic time, these were her periodic table of elements, her personal building blocks of creation. She turned the roof above the house into a viewing area to see the weather come in from all directions. On the hill to the north, she put the weather station she couldn't live without. She went from the weather station to the roof deck and looked around. "The world is round!" Obvious, it always surprised her. "The four directions form a wheel." Dr. G had taught her that when she was a graduate student.

Here they were, a few years later, with the perpetual problem of her name. The house had not eased it, was not supporting her in the ways John Birdswell had hoped. It was not lineage or ancestors.

He determined to try to settle things. She shivered with the cold, but wouldn't relent and close the windows. He went to the white kitchen cabinet to the side of the kitchen sink and took out a bottle of brandy, pouring a shot into his cup and then hers. To succeed this time would have to mean they both succeeded. He was determined to relieve her chronic discomfort. He felt beleaguered but she was his daughter and his responsibility was to ease her first.

"I understand, I think, what the Native people said. But this has been going on forever. Why do names matter to you so?" John Birdswell asked, allowing himself to be truly perplexed.

"Not names. Not anyone's name. My name!"

"It was the best I could do," he admitted drinking down the shot.

Her mother had had other ideas. She had chosen a name but in the moment of naming he was afraid it would bind his daughter to a history and a tradition, foreign to him, without a mother to support it. He had never told Sandra the name that her mother had chosen. And even now, he couldn't tell her. He was paralyzed in the way he had been then when he gave Sandra the first, most neutral name that came into his head. He remembered the moment.

He had been holding the baby. His wife had just died and was there in front of him. Dead. He was afraid he would faint and drop the baby. He was entirely present and entirely absent. The nurse asked, "The name?" The two words flew out of his mouth without his even understanding them. "Sandra Birdswell," he whispered, turning his face away from the baby so that she wouldn't hear the lie. He had never thought of that name before. He couldn't think. He had been focused completely on his beloved expecting that she would focus on the child. He had always assumed that his parenting would be from a distance. Then the mother was gone.

There were very few thoughts he allowed himself on the subject. How had his wife known she would die of what turned out to be an unpredictable event? When he saw her prophecy coming to life, he unwittingly snatched her only gift away from his daughter as he took the infant into his arms.

He was a doctor; preventive medicine was not on the curriculum when he was in medical school, except in theory. He knew how to meet affliction after the fact. He had not been able to save his wife's life and he could not save Sandra from the pain she experienced being without a mother. His ruminations were not easing the conflict.

Sandra persisted. "I am not disturbed that I didn't have a mother. You were and are a splendid parent. But you do have a tragic flaw. You refuse to understand my dilemma. I wasn't lacking a mother; I am lacking a tradition. If you had named me properly, I would have a past to count on."

"My dear," he said, smiling the wry smile that came from thinking he might still get a tentative handle on the situation, even if it didn't fully reassure his daughter. "Not having a tradition is how it is in America. The tradition here is … emptiness. You were born exactly into your time.

"I would never presume to give you a false anchor," he continued feigning confidence. "You will have to find place yourself."

She pretended to sulk while pushing her long, straight light brown hair back behind her ears, and then, as if it were a new idea, did what he expected her to do. She strode to her rescued oak desk and searched out the paper she kept at the bottom of the incoming mail basket, which meant that she saw it every time the basket was emptied, which, depending on her mood or persona, could be frequently, or seemingly never at all.

Sandra means, "Helper of mankind," she read. "Another way of saying it is, Helper of the People. I don't mind that. Sandra Birdswell means the helper of the people lives by a spring where there are lots of birds. Not bad in terms of meaning, Poppa, but did you ever think of what it meant that you also named me for a conqueror, Alexander and a woman who was conquered, Cassandra."

"I didn't name you for Cassandra. I gave you the plainest name I could think of. Still, an earth name. Clay. Creation. Create yourself, my dear daughter."

She knew what was coming, they had gone through this routine so many times. He sang the line from "Cowgirl in the Sand"… "Old enough now to change your name …" It always came together between them through the songs he'd been listening to then. Neil Young was their unlikely mediator. Young had kept to his values and her father had kept to his. Sandra remembered this when he began singing.

She waited and waited and waited and then he began to speak. Neil Young had opened the way. It wouldn't be the full truth, but, still, an approach.

"Your mother had a premonition she would die. I didn't believe her. There were no signs. So when your partner has a vision that she's dying and she's carrying your baby, who do you listen to? You live in denial and insist on your own hope. But, she was right. I should have known when she started singing "Birds" to me, that it was a warning that she would fly away without me.

"She went into labor, delivered you into my hands and left! I was living the future as my world was coming to an end." He had never quite told it to her that way.

He had sung her birth and their loss to her. But he wouldn't ever speak about Sandra's mother because he had to reverse everything. Instead of

Sandra belonging entirely to her mother, she had to have been born of him without being conceived or gestated elsewhere. As if she had been his idea and as if he had known what was coming and that she would be his salvation against intolerable loneliness. As if he had to name her in order to have her for himself.

He did not know what he was going to say when he finished singing and began speaking.

"I was adopted. My adoptive parents wouldn't tell me anything about my origins, or they didn't know, which is what they claimed. I guess I am passing it on. My adoptive parents were as white and non-denominational as the Friend's meeting we sometimes attended. Francis and Raymond Birdswell. I was their only child. In my second year of medical school, as far from my adoptive parent's home as I could get, I was called out of class to be informed that my parents had been killed in a head-on collision on the highway. Someone pulled across the white line from the other direction, stepped on the gas, and slam! You know all of this why do you want me to repeat it?

"My parents had been shopping for groceries. It was that mundane. Instant death for both of them – and the driver too. You can't argue with that. They'd never felt like my parents, though they had been kind. They cared most about my grades and graduating with honors. As if I were a charity case. Respecting them in the most sincere way I could, I went home for 48 hours, returned to school, finished the term – it was two weeks before finals – with the highest possible grades before attending to the homely details of closing up their lives. My inheritance and the sale of the house kept me out of medical school debt.

"We did a Sunday service for my folks at the Meeting House. Our next door neighbor read a poem by William Penn. I remember a few lines." he began declaiming the poem so that he could distance himself from this moment. He hadn't felt it then, so why should it affect him now?

"They that love beyond the world cannot be separated by it, death cannot kill what never dies...."

"I appreciated it because it told me that they would be as present, or not present, as they had always been. I did not hold them responsible for the loneliness they could not meet. It was done. Short and sweet. Well, short."

He thought he had told her most of this before. He hadn't.

"Instant death!" The words blurted from her. "It prepared you for my mother."

74

He'd been standing in the kitchen, as had she, but he collapsed onto the kitchen stool like a sheet of aluminum being crushed by an invisible fist.

She put her hand on his shoulder. "I'm sorry."

"Just make up your history," he said desperately. "Tell anyone who asks that your mother's mother was from the yellow earth people and your father's mother was from the water bird people. Tell them your father was raised without religion because of a war between his parents that no one could win. They went to Quaker meetings so they wouldn't have to talk. Your mother died in childbirth and your grandparents on all sides were dead by then. Tell them your mother's people, whosoever they were, had been angry with your mother for the life she had been living and marrying a Quaker would not have redeemed her. She left home early and that was that. Maybe they died before your mother died. There was no evidence of their presence when she died. You had no aunts, uncles or cousins. Your closest living relative when you were born was a German shepherd, but his lineage back to the old country was cloudy."

His humor revived him and soon he was standing again. "His name was Question Mark. He was a German shepherd. We sent him to live with a nurse at the hospital when I became a single father, and he remained there. I couldn't handle both." In retrospect he wondered if this was true. Couldn't he have handled both of them? He saw questions arise in Sandra too, like a river about to overflow its banks and he had to be quick to act. "Don't get your back up again, he didn't have papers either."

She watched as he put this cup in the sink, hurriedly gathered up his things, made his way to the door. "Someday you'll tell me everything," she looked him in the eye. "Someday. Right?"

There was nothing he was capable of saying or doing except waving his hand goodbye.

PART II

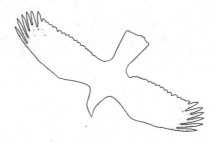

In this war morality... the ideals of freedom, justice and human dignity had all slid off man like a rotten rag. We said there is no crime that a man will not commit in order to save himself. And, having saved himself, he will commit crimes for increasingly trivial reasons... first out of duty, then from habit, and finally — for pleasure.

Tadeusz Borowski, from *This Way for the Gas, Ladies and Gentlemen*

9

An Unexpected Phone Call

Graduate school led to postgraduate school, led to research projects, teaching assignments, various consultations, a range of opportunities to be pursued while sometimes earning a salary. Sandra followed where she was led, staying in the erstwhile community. As she had feared, she did not find a path that engaged and eased her heart. The chances to bridge one culture to another were few and, little, if anything, seemed to come of it.

Dr. G remained Dr. G. They re-encountered each other at a conference. While the proceedings were going on, they were, independently of each other, escaping, making their dedicated way to a small grove of aspen by the lake behind the conference center. He saw her coming up the trail, stopped, waited for her, and laughed. His invitation. She laughed back. Her response. They didn't act on the laughter.

He waited a long time after their meeting at the conference, following professional decorum as one would wait to contact a psychiatrist after a long analysis, to announce he was interested in her as a human being. She thought that was an unusual statement, but she did not hang up the telephone, simply commented that it was an odd interest he had. He responded that he had many odd interests and hoped she would join him on a walk in the desert to explore some of them, or at the least, to observe the clouds and the sunset.

When the call was over, she went out on the platform above her house. Cumulus from the north spread across the wide skyline filling the bowl of the surrounding mountains. These were the foothills of the greater stone majesty that rose up inland. From her vantage point, perched at the summit of a rise, the clouds seemed close and familiar, assuming one shape after another, which she tried to read to make sense of his call and of the unexpected excitement she felt anticipating their meeting.

The clouds were speaking, forming phrases, sentences stretching across the sky, though in a foreign language she, as a child, had thought she would someday master. She hadn't. It wasn't what they were saying to her, but what was awakened in her, by their presence, or by his sudden appearance in her life.

Standing there, confused and excited, she yielded to a great longing for rain. Such longing had been the original impetus for her dissertation. She would have liked to include such longing as part of her work. Wasn't the researcher who was trying to understand or looking for a solution, also longing for rain? And if so, didn't she, didn't he have a right, even an obligation, to speak of it? She had wondered if the researchers longed for rain the same way that the Native people were longing for the water to return.

Thoughts crossing her mind, morphing from one random shape to another, not unlike the clouds driven by the same winds, those that crossed the diverted rivers, the dams, the dried up rivers, the end of the natural order. Longing. Reaching back in memory and beyond her own memory to the ways the ones who had lived on the land had spoken to the elementals and had been answered. Her longing for an ancient touch, the familiar tap of rain on bare arms, or a storm strong enough to warrant running out with a small piece of yucca root, or a jar of shampoo you've made from the leaf scrapings to shampoo your hair, watching out for thunder and lightning. Someone had, at one time, successfully drummed to call rain to meet the thirst of the wild plants. Someone had learned to plant crops and hoped the rain would notice and appear. Someone had believed in the myriad relationships that had nurtured the past. Someone had believed life was dialogic.

She would have liked to focus her dissertation with a hypothetical farmer's thoughts and concerns, but she knew this would not be accepted as relevant. How often had she heard a faculty advisor hold out a carrot, "Finish the dissertation then turn it into a book." She had managed to include some of this in her dissertation when she referenced TEK but it was never front and center as Dr. G had indicated was inevitable in that first dissertation conference.

There was a great divide in her, simultaneously a great wound and a great opening. The divide was between the ways she was required to live in the world and the ways she wanted to live, to live within herself, the ways that had been lived once. What does it mean to be a human being? The Native people she had met in Alaska called themselves "real human beings." Feelings that were realizations arose in her. Recollections, but not necessarily her own, of wind and rain, on this land and elsewhere, at this time or of another time, during her lifetime or earlier, stirred not as memory but as concurrent experiences, intermittently sharp and indistinct. She was grateful for their presence, saddened by their inevitable disappearance, like the rain.

Then the phone call returned to her consciousness and preoccupied her. She had spent virtually no time with Dr. Green and now he was familiar. "Sandra, this is Terrence," he had said as if they'd had sufficient conversations for her to recognize his voice, and then, as correcting himself with a little chuckle, added, "Dr. G."

There was snow on the peaks of the highest, furthest mountain. An arrow, a polar bear came floating toward her. She felt an instinct to climb down from the platform, enter the house, lock the doors – she never locked the doors – close the blinds and drapes –she had neither blinds nor drapes – but she forced herself to stay where she was.

"I liked the paper you wrote about Arctic," he had said, his voice warming once he sensed she was willing to enter a conversation with him, awkward though it was.

In the Arctic she had glimpsed other ways of being when her research did not keep her singularly focused in its own terms on the degenerating life systems accompanied by human poverty, violence and hopelessness. When she met the working Inuit carvers and graphic artists, she saw their living relationships to the spirits that came to them in the old ways that almost everyone else had forgotten or set aside. Her observations could have been the entire subject of a paper, but she chose instead to follow the artists' way, to write by stealth and conceal the hidden, invisible as it would be within a carving or a sculpture. A local artist – is that what he was really? Is that how he would have been designated by the tribe before his work became commercial? A local medicine person who carved sacred objects for ceremony showed her a face carved from bone. When she looked through the emptiness that was the eyes, she understood that the figure was looking beyond what the Hubble telescope might see. Now she looked up at the sky, but without the sacred carving, she couldn't see beyond the physical world.

The carving was completely different from and also the same as a recent dream.

She was climbing up a ladder from one earthen floor to another, within a dark structure, a cave probably, or a shaft within the Earth that was invisible to her except for the cylindrical walls that contained her. The ladder was constructed from narrow, continuous tall tree trunks with wooden rungs inserted into the hand carved notches, then lashed with rawhide. The rungs seemed to have been carved out of thick branches, thin enough for the arch of her foot while able to support her weight as she went up and up and up and up, tirelessly. She could not see the base from which she had ascended or the ceiling toward which she climbed. The climb was endless and exhilarating. Intermittently she believed there wasn't a ceiling, but an opening far away as from a kiva leading into light and a new time. Climbing, she dared hope.

Perhaps she wouldn't have remembered the dream then, if she weren't also ruminating on her failure to convince the editors of the journal that the dreams she had collected from the people most affected by climate change were essential to the text. Even when writing about the Arctic where everything had been far less formal, people mixing with each other, depending on each other because of the severity of the weather and the landscape, even though some of the elders still negotiated their lives through their dreaming, she had no permission to do the same.

"What did you like about the paper?" Maybe it hadn't been too broad and too subjective as her colleagues had asserted. She had been lucky to find a journal that pursued the intersection of the humanities and science to publish it. Still, even they had her cut the dreams.

And now this dream was hovering in the background of the interchange between them. What struck her as essential was that the climb, the equivalent of an "uphill struggle" was compelling. As if the dreams were reaching out to her, cheering her on.

"It was challenging to get the paper published," she continued, encouraged. "What did you like about it?"

He chuckled. "I'd rather tell you face to face," he said, which made her wonder even more why he was calling her. She waited.

Why are you calling me? The unspoken question was in the air.

"Antarctica. The Larsen B ice shelf collapsing …" He was referring to something much greater and more tragic than what she had seen in Alaska. There might be some freezing in the south but the ice shelf would not be restored and the global consequences were incalculable. Still, the reference was confusing.

"That was three years ago, in 2002." She covered her confusion by recalling the date. She didn't understand. Nor did it seem she was meant to.

"The tsunami …"

"Last year. But why?"

Why was he calling her? She sensed desperation and her own disequilibrium began to surface as he continued.

"I was just in Montreal. The UN Climate Change Conference." He paused. He hadn't wanted to say anything on the phone. He himself didn't know why he was compelled to meet with her. "The Inuit," he continued. "They filed a petition with the Inter-American Commission on Human

Rights …. Their lives are vanishing with the melting ice …."

Why was he calling her? They had never spoken outside the formality of the department except the brief exchange, if she could call it that, at the conference they'd both attended in 2003.

He must have finally heard her unasked question: "I just read your paper today. You care about what disappears," was his explanation.

It was exactly what she had said to her father.

They arranged to meet.

Terrence Green had always seemed dour to her. Maybe on reflection, he conveyed disappointment. Having accepted his invitation, she reviewed her interactions with him. Realities change strikingly with a clap of thunder rolling forward from a distance. He could not, she finally understood, as a Native man, head the committee when judging a paper that tended to valorize Indigenous knowledge, though he would review her Native references and informants. He would be the last to sign off on her work, which presented the Native analysis of climate change as cogent, compelling and informative, compared, in her view with the extent of scientific ambiguity, the general unwillingness to take an absolute stand on climate change, to accept the judgment of the Anthropocene, to act with certainty on what was evident to any Indigenous or Native observer of the global increase of desertification. Ask the animals, she had wanted to add to fulfill her burden of proof. It stunned and outraged her that she'd had to argue for and prove the fact of climate change in 2002.

Asking the animals was not as challenging as it might seem. "Watch the eagles, they know," Terrence Green often asserted. "The eagles know the catastrophe we are in and are responding. The eagles, like Indigenous people, adapt skillfully. Climate change, global warming? Lay eggs earlier. Lose habitat? Fly further. Adapt. Food in short supply? Find other staples. Salmon will yield to trout. Reproduce. Survive. Except for the question of water. Drought comes. Food supply vanishes. Species death."

Adept readers of the signs understood precisely what was being communicated by those who were bound to be most directly affected. Eagles and other expert readers of the times understood that there would be consequences for everyone and everything. Sandra saw that Terrence Green knew this intuitively through the wisdom of his lineage, and by his training. But he was Chair of the Department and he had to prove all of this in standard ways, perhaps even more convincingly, as he was considered to be biased. Her work and conclusions, by virtue of her great passion, were similarly suspect.

10

Terrence and Sandra

There was a remarkable sunset. "The Gods are good," she teased, accepting his invitation to burrow into him as the wind came up at the moment the sun disappeared.

She was exceedingly still inside herself; they had not spoken for a long time as the light shifted gold and red. She was still but also humming.

He held her and then he felt her knowing in her body, certain of what it was. He could feel where Earth and sky sat in her, light and dark. There were vibrations and emanations that came from elsewhere. She knew that he knew. No one had known before.

"Everything is alive," Sandra said simply.

"That is what we say," he answered. His revelation to her of who he was. The sun had gone down. The clouds flamed and then the sky was suddenly clear. Terrence could feel the warmth seeping out of Sandra and the silver of the moon sliding down her spine as it rose. It was almost full moon. By tomorrow, the moon body would be both platinum and gold at once. But now the sun was just far enough below the horizon, the clouds scudding away and disappearing, the glow fading from the hills, the moon just rising up, Sandra's body registering the distinctions. It was as if everything in their field was alive – in her.

This is how quickly they bonded. His perception, her disclosures were of a piece. An arranged marriage neither of them questioned. It seemed he could speak of the mysteries of the natural world. She thought she could not. He had language; she thought she did not. He could perceive with his hands and his body what was occurring within her. She quivered. He translated.

It would take a long time to get to know each other and they were each indifferent to most of the facts. It would be a matter of coordinating their lives. There were probably decisions to be made but not about their joining.

Suddenly, they had been with each other a thousand years.

Then he could feel that she was afraid. A different trembling now. How could it be otherwise?

He had not even kissed her. It was not that kind of courtship. Dark was coming and he knew that he had to become very large and fold her within him so that the great tear and confusion of being seen and known so quickly and entirely could, like a shadow, slip away from her. He had to become larger than himself and very still as well. He had seen it done, had witnessed that alignment and now it was occurring within him. It was not a matter of will but accepting his willingness to be so fully and heartfully responsible to what was required, accepting the sacrifice of any self he had in order to embody what was coming toward him, toward them, on her behalf and beyond her.

He did not know whether the spirit that he was embodying was male or female, it could be either, so tender and powerful it was. Images flashed through his mind, bear came first, even grizzly, cougar, both too fierce – wind, lake, river – none were right, and there was little time. Then he felt it. He knew it was right. Mountain rose in him, dark green woods, redwood forest, bristlecone pine at the summit, old, old, old, stone and rock. He took her within the mountain; he sheltered the trembling and vibrations, while praying that the Earth on which they were standing would not tremble. He held her thus within him. Neither of them needed to speak, nor could they. What words could there be that wouldn't distract or diminish?

She was crying. It didn't matter. It was a spring; it was the headwaters. He let his shirt and jacket absorb the tears. Her head was in his shoulder and he wrapped her long hair about her and then covered her with his arms, covered all of her somehow. His knowledge, reflexes and responses so precise and exact that it was as if they were generated completely from within her – as they were. Neither of them questioned the movements between them nor did they know how long they would stay there nor what would happen when time resumed.

Most importantly, they were not to speak. He knew this from deep within him. She understood it too without knowing how. Even a gesture as small as wiping her eyes, might break the spell, the deep listening, the joining that had no precedent to it. Blue and fire turned mineral dark into night.

When enough time had passed, he disentangled himself so gently. He took off his jacket, put it on the ground and lowered her onto it. He was not certain she was able to walk. He could lift her and carry her if necessary. It did not seem right to return to the truck and drive. Where would they go when they were already here?

He had blankets in the truck. He had everything with him, everything they would need. A blanket to serve as a pillow. He wrapped her in some others. He kneeled down to put honey on her tongue. It was like feeding a hummingbird. Stealthily he gathered kindling and firewood and supplemented what he found with what he had brought with him. Then there was enough for the night. Smell of pine, tobacco and sage. Water. She would sleep. He would not.

With the sticks he had gathered, and some small tarps he made a lean-to to block the wind but not to obscure the stars. He was grateful that he remembered what his ancestors had taught him. Ursa Major rose above them. He read the sky as the clouds came and went, hiding and revealing, and she dreamed the sky, wide open and full of little points of light. He could see her dreaming as clearly as she could feel the stars traveling across the dark in her body. Without thought, she felt safe. As if she were home. As if she were in her father's house. As if she had had a mother. The wind came up. Mr. Wind. Her old friend. Breath. Her breath. His breath. One breath. No dissembling. No hiding. No separation. Once she stirred and he put one palm on her forehead and one on her heart. Trickles of sand and small creatures. Desert tortoise somewhere close in the underbrush, eighty to one hundred years old. Age was watching over them. Sleep took her again, so gently.

Coyotes howled and jabbered coming close toward the fire. There were no other humans nearby. Had there been, the pack would not have approached. He was comforted by their mammalian presence. And so the night passed and their lives began. Just so.

The sun rose and slowly showed them each other's faces. He traced her features with his finger and she then, as slowly, traced his. In this slow process of becoming familiar with someone who had fully been a stranger, she understood the obvious that she had not understood before – that the light that revealed them to each other came from a great distance in space and time. His people, her people, whoever they were. They were being taken, it felt to both of them, by forces beyond them, into a deep knowing they could not yet begin to imagine.

She closed her eyes so he could kiss her. She could feel the silence in him enter her through the sweetness and gentleness of his lips. The warmth from each to the other and the early warmth of the day brought them to their feet. She was almost as tall as he. She did not know if she could bear the sweetness of his body against hers, of her body pressing into his. She had never known how to love without words.

Maybe it hadn't been tortoise. Maybe it had been the old woman who came walking across the desert from nowhere, going nowhere. She was so tiny, he thought at first it was his grandmother coming from the other side to see what he was up to and whether Sandra was the one he thought her to be.

It was 10 a.m. The sun was fairly high. Sandra was speechless yet again as she beheld the woman's goods, which she was laying out on a red hand-woven cloth. The woman was pretending not to speak English and that suited Sandra and Terrence perfectly. Terrence brought out most of what food he had and offered it to the old woman, careful to withhold only what she was unable to chew. The woman was selling turquoise and other stones. He recognized the lapis from the rare vein in the local mountains. Sandra let him choose. He must have chosen well because the old woman was immediately satisfied and wrapped the rest of her goods and began walking away. He had filled his portable coffee mug and given it to her which she accepted, as he expected, in the right way, as if it was hers being returned to her. Each transaction had to be negotiated between equals. The idea of charity was unacceptable. She had brought gifts and needed to be recognized.

Once the old woman started walking, she kept the same pace that had brought her to their campsite as if she had not ever stopped. She must have seen the smoke, or smelled the fire for they were far from even the small roads.

Sandra turned and turned the bracelet of rough, jagged blue and turquoise beads that he slipped over her right hand. "These are mountains," he said. "Yes," she answered, "I see that." She hadn't seen that but then when he said it, she did. She had so many questions, she knew she must continue to be still.

Finally, she turned to him. "And you?" she asked. Her first words. "And you?" Because he knew so much about her.

"Later," he answered, or, "another time." And so the morning passed. They walked and rested wordlessly. She picked up stones and pebbles, put them in a pouch, stopped, took them out and arranged them on the ground in an order that revealed the history of this particular land. "You pass the test," he teased her, confirming her mastery of the local geology. He had spent the night courting her and this is how she received him.

The plateau they were on dipped down radically at the edge of the protected wilderness and it seemed that the road plunged instantly into malls and gas stations. He pulled his truck over to the side, suggesting she get out here where she could find a place to sit without seeing the commercial world. He would go down to the market and pick up some provisions and then he would drive her, if she wished with her eyes closed, home. That is to his house. That is to the land where his house stood. Or to her house. That is home. That is to her land. She yielded to his home. His land. She wanted to know.

They never even went into the house when they came to his land the first time. He did not go in to check his phone machine for messages or take the mail that was overflowing his mail box at the entrance to the gravel road to the structure despite his receiving most of his mail at the university office. He left the provisions in the truck to be gotten later and walked her up and behind the house to a tent that overlooked trees and chaparral. Inside, a buffalo rug covered a thick mattress. The tent had a moon roof and many windows. Several old camp chairs surrounded the fire pit outside and the wood stove inside. Ragged, wind-worn prayer flags yielding up their praise to the elements wound through the trees that surrounded and hid the tent but were also spaced sufficiently so one could look onto the hills and the mountains in the distance. Prayer sticks marked the entrance. This living space revealed him to her completely.

She walked around on her own, circumventing all sides of the house and the surrounding land.

"You've got your own weather station."

"I love weather," he answered.

"And you love wind," she noted by looking at the tower set back in the field. "Does the station check your observations or do you check its?"

"We've come to be in friendly agreement over the years," he chuckled. "I don't think it's very flexible or willing to negotiate its observations. I recognize that it knows what it knows within its limitations."

"It thinks that is all there is to know."

"Yes," Terrence agreed, "if you call that thinking."

"What doesn't it tell you?"

"It doesn't tell me if the wind is blowing through a pine tree, an alder or a yew. It can't even tell me if it is blowing through a grove of aspen which anyone would recognize."

"But you would know."

"Someday, I hope to perceive at least some of the places from which a wind is blowing. I can't tell yet where it originated and what it landed on, what it touched on the way here."

"I can make you breakfast." He had something of an outdoor kitchen with its back to the northwest from which the wind was blowing even then.

"Coffee? How do you take it?"

"Depends. My father and I are moody. Sometimes black, sometimes cream and sugar. How do you like it?"

"Strong, dark roast, hot, cream and sugar, in a large mug."

"Well, then, I do as well." She dared to come over to him. She dared to put her head on his shoulder. He embraced her so as to confirm everything that had happened and was certain between them.

"I can help so I will learn where everything is." Every simple sentence, every ordinary response, every straightforward offering was also monumental.

"Let me care for you today." He was looking directly at her, into her eyes, knowing what he knew, but not overwhelming her. "You are time traveling now. It takes a lot of energy and concentration."

"The wind is from the northwest, 6 miles an hour. And the land is too dry for an outdoor fire." She had to get her bearings.

"I am sure the anemometer will agree," he agreed.

"And you?" she asked again, meaning everything in the way she had asked earlier.

"I have already yielded to you completely. When my grandmother appeared from nowhere on the road that was no road, bringing you that old bracelet which is a perfect circle of old rough stones but without a clasp, without an opening, I knew."

"What did you know?"

"I knew scrambled eggs with cheese, spinach, red peppers, and with a choice of green or red salsa on the side might please you."

"It does. As will both salsas." He handed her the plate as she sat in one of the chairs. There was a small plate by the stove where he put a tiny portion of everything they would eat and took it out to the edge, offering the food to the ancestors.

Then he sang the prayers he had been taught by his grandfather and grandmother. The food stayed hot. Sandra was crying again. She went to the truck and got the little pail of sand that she had stowed between sleeping bags and a duffel bag. She set it down firmly next to her and between them.

"So you knew," he said. He also knew she would speak about it when it was time. And their life together, or one life as they thought of it from then on, began.

11

History

Sandra stood at the western door of the tent, a little uncomfortable, afraid to cast a shadow over Terrence. He motioned her to come in and lie down next to him, but she shook her head. She was not ready yet to meet him in that way. He lay there smiling at her, satisfied that their intimacy was already profound.

"I understand something about houses now," she said. There isn't anything wrong with our houses, except they are like fortresses that entice us to stay inside. They have a life of their own and impose it upon us."

"You haven't been inside my house yet," he said.

"I know. I am not ready. Every step feels overwhelming. Like a knot being tied but to what? I am going to stay out here for now, though I think I have to add some earth from this land to my pail. It seems it has become part of my world."

"Maybe its not part, maybe it is your world," he answered.

"If I go in the house, I may be taken over entirely," she was trying to be light about it but she was fearful. If the house resembled him – not the Chair of the Department, she could imagine the Chair's house – but this man with whom she seemed to have bonded without knowing him at all – then it would take her over, it would determine her future, everything, it would be like a force of nature. Yes, exactly, if his house emerged from who he seemed to be, or if he had emerged from this house, then this house would be a force of nature. She looked behind her to see it, to see the predatory animal that was gaining on her and would soon devour her, but it was set back behind trees and she could only glimpse what looked like cedar planks ... or flanks.

"Is the house round?" she asked, aware that she had deliberately avoided it when looking around the land.

"No. It is long, and I built it."

He sat up and leaned his bare back against the side of the tent, the buffalo across his hips and legs. She looked at his chest, knowing that soon it would be familiar. The beast that had been behind her was now before her. He did not have the body of a young man or an old man. She could see where the muscles were softening and there was a scar across a rib. It was a safe body. He looked strong but not intent on doing harm. Strong enough to build a house.

"We could go inside," he said tenderly.

In reply, she slipped down on the ground at the opening of the tent, her adamant "No" for the moment.

"We could just go inside, nothing else."

Her "No" was implicit.

"It's just a house. It won't hurt you. It's not a living thing."

"I don't believe that," she countered.

"Neither do I," he was smiling.

"I walked just as you suggested, one hour away from here and one hour back. When the yuccas out there bloom, I will gather the white flowers for a salad," she said. He waited for her to continue. "You parboil them and add a light dressing. They are very delicate."

"How do you know?"

"Hosteen Tseda taught me."

"Who is he?"

"He's my father's best friend."

"Did his wife teach you?"

"No. He did. His wife died. That's why he and my father are friends. They are lonely together. Hosteen lives on the reservation. In the Canyon. Canyon de Chelly. My father goes there a lot."

"Why?"

"He says he feels secure there. That is, at home."

"Did you go there too?"

"Oh yes, Hosteen is my uncle."

"What does that mean to you?"

"It means I walked behind him when we went out on the land and did what he did. It means he never took my hand or told me to be careful. He always knew where I was and he trusted me. When I got tired, he also knew, and put me on his shoulders and showed me where to look to see the hawks, the horses and the deer."

"And now?"

"When I can visit him, I try to cook some food that he will eat and en-joy."

"Is that difficult?"

"For me it is. I have to shop on the reservation and cook what his wife would have cooked but I never met her or her mother. As with every culture, it seems simple but it is very exact. Chili. Communities have chili cook-offs because it is so complex and competitive. My father is no help here. He was a great father but cooking isn't one of his skills – and there was rarely time. I make a lamb stew, buy some steaks and bake potatoes. A compromise. Hosteen eats what he eats and I don't know how to prepare it well. He has no complaints, you understand. Anyway, Hosteen doesn't think about food the way ..." she hesitated as she understood something that had not been articulated before ... "the way we do." Who was this we and where did Terrence Green fit in or around it? Once again, she stumbled over "we."

"So if Hosteen Tseda is your uncle ..." Terrence might have been reading her mind and asking the question as if to suggest a way to think about it.

"It just means he's my uncle. It doesn't mean anything else. It means that neither he nor I nor my father will ever be hungry unless we are all hungry.

"You'll see when you meet him. He will like you. Well, I don't know that. He will certainly want to know who you are. You will like him. I know that. We will bring a leg of lamb. That will help."

"I think you're hungry. You're talking about food a lot."

"No. I'm not hungry. I am happy. But I could make you a cup of coffee. I watched you carefully and can duplicate it quite well, I think."

She looked at him directly as she got up so that he knew he was to stay where he was while she made the coffee. Getting up was not an invitation to him, though telling him about Hosteen was another step toward being devoured.

She brought two cups, put hers down and walked far enough into the tent to give him his so that he did not reveal more of himself. She could tell by his scent that he wanted her but she pulled away.

"And you?" she asked.

"Not yet," he said and she waited.

"Not yet, because you want to know who I am before you let me know who you are? Because you know something of what is occurring here between us and I don't?" She was intrigued and uncomfortable. She wanted to know what he knew but she didn't have the understanding of this moment that it seemed he had. In the past, under such circumstances, she had understood what was occurring first. It had been important to be aware and be able to move accordingly. "You know and I don't know, is that right?"

She was pissed.

"Something like that."

"And you know because you come from a people and I don't come from a people. Is that right?"

"Hosteen Tseda is your uncle." He wanted to ease her.

"Yes, he is. But he is not my people. Or maybe he is. I don't know. Maybe you're my uncle. For all I know, you're my uncle. Or I never had an uncle. My father doesn't know who he is and my mother didn't know or didn't say. I am up for grabs. Will you have me?"

"I will." But he did not try to grab her though the pun would have given him some leverage. She recognized that he understood and his easy statement did not belie the gravity of the implication. Soon she would belong somewhere that was greater than what her father, completely alone, without any resources had been able to give her.

"And you?"

He remembered that she had been very persistent as a graduate student. One might even say, dogged. If she was after something, she was a dog with a bone. She held on to it, she chewed it, she did not let go. No one had been happy with her dissertation topic and everyone wanted him to deny it or accept it. Everyone wanted him to make a decision about it. That is, reject it. He wouldn't accept it or reject it. She persisted. It was an irrefutable paper. It could not be rejected on academic grounds, to do so would be transparently political. It challenged the hardness of hard science. She was granted the degree.

"And you?"

"I can't speak about it here."

"Why not? We are alone. We are alone, aren't we?" There was no point in being alarmed, it didn't seem that there were any houses within a radius of a mile or two.

"Yes, we are alone." The gravity of being completely alone with him destabilized her again. She wanted to know something about him because she wanted to be find a root, and, maybe, to have some power.

He came from an oral tradition. His people lived by story, they sensed when to tell a story and when to be silent, which stories could be told, to whom and when. Telling a story in the right way and the right time implied trust and evoked the sacred.

"Go out of the tent. I will call you back in." Terrence said in a firm voice. When she came in there was a small fire in the wood stove and the fire door was open. He was in the bed under the buffalo robe. A package of tobacco was on the floor by a camping chair.

"When you're ready, Sandra, put some tobacco in the fire and I'll tell you what I can." He was holding a conch shell and had lit some sage.

"About my life, I have an erratic memory. It is not reliable. At this moment I remember a Yakama story called Histo's Narrative from a collection gathered by L.V. McWhorter. That's the professor talking to you now, Sandra, but he is going to leave the tent soon. Here's some of the myth … maybe it is my story.

"'When I was small my mother left me by the water. I heard the wind in the fire and I could see the tops and branches of the trees moving.

"The wind passed through the trees, but the trees were not hurt. The trees talked to me. The trees said, 'Look at us, little boy. You can see us shaken, you can see the wind passing through us but we are not hurt. The wind cannot hurt us. We will give you our power. You will do as we tell you and you be like us. Nothing will hurt you.'"

Sandra could see that Terrence was in a story and she must not disturb him. She watched his breathing. This is what she had asked for without knowing what she had asked for.

"The story goes on, Sandra, and comes to this place. 'Now I have told you how I got my power and it has left me.'"

He was looking ahead of him in her direction but he was looking through her or beyond her. She was certainly not to say anything, hoping the story would resolve itself, would reach its own truthful ending.

"Histo's narrative continues, 'I was telling you a story of when I was young and the Bannocks came and killed people and carried all my playmates away.' Maybe this is my story, Sandra.

"The boy never knew his mother. Or he didn't remember because he had been so young when his father had brought him home to his grandparents and then had left. It was after the Bannocks had come and killed the people and stole their land or it was during that time of killing and stealing. The boy did not know where his father went. He didn't know many things and what he knew kept changing. Maybe his father brought him home or his grandmother retrieved him and brought him home. Which? His father or his grandmother? He never knew. He never knew his mother and he didn't remember his father very well. He remembered his father leaving again and again. Or he didn't remember his father at all. His grandmother and grandfather never questioned whether they wanted to raise him. He was theirs. They didn't know his mother. They knew he was mixed blood and they had to hold on to him fiercely so he could have his people inside of him. The first time his father brought him home, or his grandmother brought him home, they did ceremony for him and installed him in the tribe. The medicine man looked into his eyes and he looked back and so the medicine man gave him a medicine name.

"That's one story or part of it." Terrence was in the story in the old way, as if it were a myth he was singing. "His father left and maybe he came back to visit and maybe he didn't. His father is alive or his father is dead. His father disappeared or he enlisted to fight in Vietnam. The father was in the artillery or the father was a tracker. The father was a tracker who didn't have to cut his hair. He survived the war. The father was a tracker who had to cut his hair and he didn't survive the war. His father took his son away from the mother when he learned she was going to give him up for adoption because he had enlisted in the war. The father learned the child had been taken away from the mother. He stole the boy and gave him to the tribe to raise. He was desolate and enlisted in the war." Terrence did not know his father's story. "I do not know my father's story.

"The mother wanted to give the boy up for adoption because she hadn't wanted to raise a child. The father stole the child and disappeared. Then he brought the child to his own mother and father. The social workers came and took the child away. There were no papers giving the child to the grandparents. The mother had given him up for adoption. The mother had disappeared. The child had been put in a foster home. The mother was alive or she was dead. The father's claim had no validity. The grandparent's claim had no validity. The boy was sent to an orphanage. The boy was sent to a foster home. The boy was sent to a government school. The boy's hair was cut. The boy was forbidden to speak his Native language. The boy remembered it each night as he was falling asleep. When he cried out at night in his Native tongue he was punished horribly. A friend of his had had his mouth stuffed with cactus needles for such a deed. Perhaps the same had happened to the boy.

"The boy was renamed Teddy. There was no way for the grandmother to find the boy. Or the grandmother found the boy and brought him home. The Indian Child Welfare act had not been legislated yet. But the grandmother succeeded. No one cared enough about the boy except the tribe. When the boy was old enough, he left. Trauma erased most of his memories and sapped his strength. He went to college and he went to graduate school. He wanted to know which way the wind blows. He studied wind."

Terrence continued talking but this time to Sandra. "I can't tell you my story, it has been detonated inside me. I remember and then I forget. I dream and the dream has more power than what I remember. But the story I just told you about the boy, that is probably my true story.

"I carry my mother inside of me like a double-bladed knife. I didn't know my mother or my father and I almost didn't know my people."

"You sound bitter."

"Really? Bitter? What do you know?!" His voice crackled with derision. "Instead of my story, maybe I should send you my CV."

She instantly regretted her response, a white woman's response. She hadn't known such misunderstanding was in her. Looking around the tent, she saw that the army tent was in a war zone. Five hundred years of carnage lay around them. In his hand, a shell with an iridescent lining from which a faint plume of sage was twisting up into the air. "I'm sorry. How stupid of me to say that."

"I am bitter, Sandra." As if trying to dismiss all of what had been said, he asked, "And you?"

"I don't want to say now."

"Yes, speak." Was he insisting on hearing from her or closing down what he had said? "Everything is as it is and must be known."

"Not yet, Terrence. Your story hurts. I knew, but I didn't know." They just sat without speaking. It was not the same as being in silence together. When he was ready to listen, he nodded to her.

"I am just sad," she began. "My father was a very good parent. A remarkable parent, but I want to have had a mother. A mother with a history." She didn't want to go on, preferring that she understand him better.

"Will you always be bitter?" She assumed he would answer truthfully. Without an overt agreement, they had committed themselves to speaking truthfully.

"When I get up in the morning and put on a jacket and go to the University to spend my days sitting in board meetings, reading someone's research and writing grants, I find my mother inside of me.

"This is her world growing inside of me. Then I am bitter. My bitterness is a deadly poison."

Not wanting him to get out of the bed, Sandra brought him a glass of water. As much as she wanted to understand it all as he had lived it, she couldn't contain herself. What if she lost him to the inferno that was threatening them. She knew wild fires. How quickly they took off. They only needed some pine needles, dry brush and a spark. There were sparks around. She couldn't dampen hers.

"What about me, then? Maybe I look like your mother. Maybe your mother was my aunt. I didn't know my mother or anything about her. Maybe she had a sister and her sister had a boy. And gave the baby away. How do we know?" She took her hair in each hand and held it out straight past her shoulders so that it looked like wings. Maybe he couldn't feel how hard she was pulling it. She couldn't see, but he could see, how the light fell on her so that her hair looked like water, like light.

His demeanor changed. It had taken him his lifetime to assimilate this story and he hadn't fully succeeded yet. He couldn't expect her to digest it in a day. "Somehow, my grandmother found me and brought me home. And so we are here together." As he said these words he marveled at them and looking at Sandra saw that she was taking them in. The next words he spoke carefully and directly to her. "My heart is open. This is the second time my heart has opened. The first was when I came home to my grand-parents and knew I would be able to stay home until I had to leave. And now when I am home again, with you."

12

Love

Terrence threw back the buffalo rug and stood up quickly, his muscular legs outlined in soft gray cotton pants that fastened with elastic at the waist and ankles. "I will go into the house first and then I will come and get you." Sandra understood that he had made a decision that included her although no discussion would ensue. She would permit it; there was no disagreement. If she were with any other man, a contemporary of hers, this would lead to a power struggle. Between them, although they did not know each other, they were learning to attune to each other and to the circumstances that were enveloping them but were beyond them, were of the beyond. The lapis bracelet slipped around her wrist and reminded her of how perceptive he was. She could feel that he was considering her when speaking as if she were the essence of himself. Her father was like that, or could be like that when he wasn't distracted by his patients and entirely unaware of anything else, of her or even himself. Sandra had not lived in this way with any confidence, but she had always been aware, or made to be aware, that she had the gift to negotiate this territory. Among her peers, her affinity for easily seeing in the dark was a source of humor. But in this moment, it was assumed, again – without anything being said overtly – that this was the way; that this was the Way. She had not thought about it. He had not made a decision. A decision had been made and he was acting upon it. This was beyond their will.

If she had asked, he would have found words to explain it to her. She didn't have any words to explain actions that originated in a field rather than in a person. But neither of them would have felt comfortable speculating on whether the field arose from the essence of the two of them merging, or whether they were yielding to something beyond themselves.

He had laid a bearskin on the bed. He looked at her to see if she was comfortable and went out of the room.

She understood. It was up to her now. He would not force, coerce or influence her. She took off her clothes and examined the bed. She lay down on her back, under the bearskin, and closed her eyes. Then she heard him enter the room so quietly it was as if he weren't there. He would disturb nothing. And felt him slide easily under the skin as well, as if he belonged to this place, this moment, this space and time.

"Some say, the oldest myth in the world," he began as he eased closer to her, aware of her slight but adamant distance, "is The Girl Who Had Married the Bear. In the myth," he murmured, "it took a long time for the girl to shed her human history, her tribe, her family, her village mind, to open herself, voluntarily, out of love, to the bear." He spoke so slowly that even with her eyelids closed, it seemed to Sandra that the room was getting darker, that the curtains of trunks and branches before each window were filtering out the light and the only place they might be was in a den. "It took a long time for the Girl to shed her human history," the truth of the words reverberated in her. She listened, as if in a spell, but still apart.

"In the myth, Sandra, the girl is dallying while her family is picking berries. This is not a fairy tale, this is a sacred story. We have to take it in, Sandra." He moved closer to her and slipped his arm under her neck so that she was turned toward him, her head on his forearm. "The Girl is not blond, kind, sweet and lovely. She is not the fairest in the kingdom nor is she dark, mean, sour and ugly." The cadence of his voice could have hypnotized her if she would allow it. "Sandra, listen, she is not motherless as you are, and she is not the daughter of the stepmother. She is one of the sisters who has gone to pick berries with her human family. It is berry-picking time. It is the right time for picking berries." Now he extended his hand down and around so that he could tip Sandra closer to him and she let him do what he willed, her lips on the smooth curve of his shoulder. "The berries, Sandra, are not for their dessert in a pie or with whipped cream. The berries are a staple of their diet. They will mash and cook the berries, then let them dry on broad leaves to form patties that they will roll and store the sweetness for the winter." His right hand was now on her belly, quite still and firm. He continued, "the girl was not interested in the berries, she was distracted. She did not understand that if the people didn't have berries, they would be hungry. Just as she didn't understand that the bears would be hungry without berries. She didn't understand hunger yet. She was too young and something indefinable was coming for her. She felt that.

"We don't know, Sandra, maybe the Girl was thinking about the moon. But it was because the girl was independent of the others, was outside the circle of family that the Bear came upon her in the briars and was able to take her home." His hand on her belly as he spoke, the sensation blending into the warmth of the story so that words, motion, body were one. "She was averse to being with him at first, but when she saw his beauty, she yielded to him and she married him, she truly loved him and had his cubs in the long winter that they spent together in the dark." Sandra, compelled, moved closer to Terrence as into the dark of him. "Afterwards, however, her loneliness for her own people and her own ways overcame her and, without understanding the consequences of crossing back to her former life, she returned home. 'Only for a visit,' she said. Among her people again, she taught her brothers and sons, as she had been instructed, how to hunt the bear. They became the Bear Clan people. They hunted and killed bear as the Bear expected they would. They ate bear. They took bear into their bodies as she had taken him into her body." Terrence's hand was firm on her belly so that she would not be afraid. "The Bear Clan people and the bears lived in right relationship to each other.

"That is the end of the story but it not the end of the story. At the end of the story," his whispered words were rough and hot on his breath; they had a rasp. "The girl was a woman now, she had married the bear, she'd had cubs, she knew the hunt. One day she waited for her brothers to leave the house. She took the skins her brothers had hunted and then tanned in the right way they had been taught having learned to hunt from the bears themselves, and threw them over herself and her little ones. In a moment, she became a four-legged with cubs. The little ones followed her as she made her way back to the den, obscuring their prints so no one could track them and closing the passage into the cave where they would reside until the brothers ceased looking for them. She and her wild partner lived their lives in such ways that they were never compromised and also so they were never found. It was the force of their love across all boundaries which protected them completely," he whispered.

Then something, a sweet and deep resin flowed as the cave between her legs opened and was sealed just as it had been in the story. Nothing occurring but by natural forces. She thought it was that he was making love to her and not her body. He was in her and he was taking her in. He was making love to her under a bearskin and she felt that he was not making love to her as anyone had before. She didn't know how to explain the difference even to herself except that he was not possessing her, not wanting to conquer her. There was a gentleness and firmness in his touch, in his apparent regard for her in each moment, that made her think he had known land from before the time he had been born and, finally, she was the land.

All was still and convulsing at the same time. The volcanic heat and pressure, the uncontrollable movement upward that seen from space would have been invisible. Two perspectives at once from different worlds existing simultaneously. When she yielded to the event that was taking them both, she could not control the words that were not words but sounds, not animal sounds, but Earth sounds as it shudders apart or closes under the pressure of monumental forces. He could have responded but he didn't, feeling her shock, knowing what she knew, that the energy of space and time was a vessel that held the Earth in place even as it moved along its radius and axis. He let her know without a movement or a word that he was also of the Earth as he embraced her. And he did embrace and steady her because he had been born to this knowing.

Then it began to happen again, the internal trembling, tremors and twirling. It was so gradual and complete, so powerful from within her, as if she had become the black hole spinning at the center, even of the Milky Way, our galaxy, the internal collapse under the force of gravity, while still spinning so that all energy, matter and light were pulled into it.

He reached behind her and held her as she opened to him and then he was as if the arms of sky encircling. He held her again with the same heart that had cared for her so openly and truly in the desert. She knew that he did not forget her, was entirely aware of her, of her every moment while he was in her. When she climaxed, the rough stones of her bracelet pressing into his back, he held her in such a way that she was completely safe within the orbit of time and space. He was as aware of every experience in her body as if it were occurring in his own. Rain and Earth had become one. Then when she withdrew a little, still trembling, he drew her back to him and entered her so deeply he was at the core of her and still as he poured his seed into her, he drew her into him as if once the rain burst, it would continue to rain until it penetrated to the aquifers, the dry land within her and they were both mud and muddied, inseparable.

Under the heavy pelt, she had never felt so naked nor had she ever been with so naked a man. As if he had never worn clothes. As if he had never lied. Never.

"How is this possible?" was all she could ask.

After a time, she sat up, keeping the bear's heavy fur around her breasts, the head of the bear between them. She traced the lines on his face, all the places where time and history had shaped innocence into deep knowing. He was a handsome man, in the way mountains are handsome as they are thrust up and carved. There was nothing smooth about him except where water had known him and that had been, she understood, the way of tears and profound grief. She said nothing and he said nothing but allowed her to know his face as she would need to know it if she were blind though she could see exactly who he was. He felt relief. A weight of centuries, five hundred years, had been removed from him as he experienced her seeing him as he was without any of the dissembling that had been forced on him and his ancestors.

After time, a longer time than she had expected, she looked into his dark eyes asking the same question.

"How is this possible?" meaning the nakedness between them.

"My people don't wear masks," he said simply. And then added, "When we carve masks for ceremony, it's to invite the spirits into the circle."

Then, she began moving and disentangling. He felt the history of shame enter her through the twitch of separation, and the beginning of introspection, self-scrutiny, self-consciousness. He knew immediately what was concerning her. What she was pretending to herself that was concerning her. What she was distracting herself with in order to diminish the moment. His hand on her back, he reached with the other into her purse at his side of the bed and taking out her toiletries pouch, took the eye liner and mascara applicators that he knew would be there because she had used them as he was preparing the house for her, and he traced black lines across her cheekbones and two lines of waves across her forehead. Lines of blue dots down toward her jaw drawn with eye shadow.

"Perfect," he announced and found a small mirror, also in the pouch, and held it up to her. She was not ready, he knew, could not let herself be more fully seen again as she had been in the desert or in this moment of lovemaking.

It was easier for her to return to the conversation they'd had outside and create a little distance between them. "When the bear is walking on two legs among the primates does he think like a bear or like a human?" Sandra asked Terrence, without waiting for him to answer.

"And you," she continued, "are you a bear?" She was dissembling, pretending to want to know something more deeply but diffusing the energy between them.

"What do you think?" she persisted. "Are you a bear?" She put her finger on his lip so that he wouldn't answer. She wanted to be in a conversation and she didn't. Talk could reduce the sacred to love banter and she was afraid of them both.

He gave her the bearskin to sleep under when she was alone in her house in winter so she could keep the windows wide open, which she loved almost as much as sleeping outside. He gave it to her immediately. He did not wait for an occasion. The occasion was this moment. He was taking her back to her house and he took the bearskin as well. He gave it to her so that there would be no breach between his bed and her bed, between this night and the next night, between their unity and her solitariness. He did not wonder what she would give him in return. It was the same as it had been with the old woman, he gave it to her as if it already belonged to her.

Another way of understanding this is, she belonged to him. Somehow she had been given to him. He was responsible for her. This is the way it is in his world. She was not his property, she was not even his beloved, she was beloved to him. All creation emerges from such connections.

"And you?" she asked.

"We belong to each other," he said aloud.

Terrence was not courting her when he whispered the myth into Sandra's ear. He was telling her a sacred story as a confirmation of their bond that would unite them across species. And it was from the beginning as if they had both become Bear at the same time. And under the bearskin later in the tent or his bedroom and on the rare occasions when she returned to her own house each time, under the bearskin, they became Bear again. When she was alone and naked under the bearskin, she wondered what "only skin deep" means and whether she was being permeated by something she couldn't identify or describe. She would wonder if she had grown fur yet. And if it would remain when she stepped out of the bed but retained her real self.

Just as in the story, Sandra had no desire to leave this state of being and as in the story, the world, with all its dangers, called her, called them back into their human forms. The advantage of the bearskin was that they were naked with each other. As bear they could only be bear. There was no possibility of dissembling or hiding; that would be against their nature.

13

Sometimes I Feel Like a Motherless Child

She allowed Terrence to carry the bearskin up the stairs to the deck. He laid it on a white metal table next to a pot of aloe. No further. She carried the little pail of earth. Two small scoops of earth, one from the desert, the other from his land, would be emptied as a thin layer into a glass mason jar and carefully labeled as if the geologic marking of a canyon wall. She would do this before she did anything else, the way someone else might put a bouquet of flowers into a vase and add water before taking off her coat, kicking off her shoes, or checking the phone machine.

Which one had placed his or her finger on the other's lips to say, "Don't speak" as he was leaving? Their silence was true. Language was unreliable. Each of them was afraid that speaking would unravel what had been bound together. It seemed it was his responsibility to find the exact right words in the right form. But in the moment, he didn't dare make a sound. He stepped back from her. He nodded just slightly so that she knew he would wait until she went into the house. She turned, entered the house, closed the door.

A quick glance had revealed to him that Sandra's house faced each of the four directions and the deck encircled it, so that inside or outside, one could observe all weather and every variation of light or sky. He saw that she had added the observation platform on the roof. As his house had introduced him to her, her house revealed her to him.

She did not know how he felt walking down the stairs, getting into his truck, driving back to his own home. They lived relatively close to each other. Half an hour, if he took a highway. An hour, if he took the back route through the hills. He did not take the freeway. He would familiarize himself with the winding roads so that he could, as the saying goes, drive them with his eyes closed.

Would he write or would he call? This turmoil was not familiar. He would have to find the good words to open what would be the good way for the rest of their lives. He would make offerings. He would pray on it so that the way would open in the morning. At dawn, he thought, but was he being too quick? His task was not to decide in advance or satisfy his impulses. His task was to begin their common life in the right way. He did not know if she awakened early or slept late. He would have to intuit it all. But he had the night to listen and to pray and the habit of not needing sleep. In this way, he reassured himself.

He did not turn on music in the truck. She did not turn on music in the house. She heard him drive away again and again, though he had left quietly and quickly. She had never imagined that her house, which had been her sanctuary, could feel empty. Though he had never been in it, it was vacated by his absence.

She walked around the house as one space flowed into another around the central open fireplace that formed the inner wall of each room. It was her habit to set the fire in advance, so that all it needed was a match. She lit it. Fire warmed her but he was still absent. Palpably absent. Or she was inexplicably segmented. The exquisite sensation within of a missing limb.

She went outside. The wind was up, roiling around the trees. For a short time wind and fire were her company. Then she picked up the bearskin and carried it into the house, walked from the kitchen into the living room, then into her bedroom and laid it down on the bed. And lay down on top of it. It was a presence that could uphold her. She got up again, went to the bathroom and saw her face in the mirror. His markings upon her. They were penetrating to her core.

She continued into her study and called her father. "I've met someone," she said simply as if she had spoken such words before. "Now, I need to know everything about everything I don't know. If you hide from me, then I am hidden too. I've met someone," she repeated, accepting that he would understand.

He could hear the gravity in her voice and realized that something he had always expected but had never known how to anticipate was occurring. Upheaval such as he had never experienced and then when it settled, in an instant, he was changed. He felt himself not as the man who had lost his beloved but as a father to this grown woman. The partner, the lover, the mother, all aspects of his lost marriage were far away. So far away he might be able to speak of her.

"I could drive over."

"That would be good," she said and hung up the phone.

Then the phone was in her hand. She glanced at the sheet of paper with Terrence's phone number from the times they had confirmed arrangements. She entered his number. The phone rang. His machine came on to take a message and just as she was going to hang up, he answered. "I just came in."

"I know. My timing had to be right."

She waited and then asked. "The lines on my face?"

"I didn't give them much forethought, but in retrospect, maybe the two wavy lines across your forehead are water. And the lines across your cheeks, nimbus clouds, with the blue drops coming down – well, I guess I repeated myself – they could be rain."

The silence between them was not between them.

He could not wait for prayer or meditation to guide him. "I will call in the morning," he said. "Are you an early ... "

She interrupted him. "Call after dawn but before the golden light turns yellow." Breath.

"My father is coming over. I have questions to ask him."

"Of course," Terrence answered. He wanted to say, "How lucky you are to have him around to ask." But, fortunately, he didn't. He did not want to focus on himself. She had things she needed to know whether or not he had access to similar knowledge. He heard her breath as he knew she heard his. He had run into the house when he heard the phone ring. Breath. He waited for her to hang up the phone. When she did. He did.

"Coffee, Poppa?"

"Let's have it with cream and sugar, it's getting late," John answered. She already had the cream in her hand and the coffee poured into his white mug, identical to hers. "And, I imagine, it will get later." He took the cup and waited for her to begin. As he studied her – she had not washed the markings from her face – he understood immediately that he would have to open his heart to admit another human being into it the way he cared for Sandra. He also understood that the man she had met had a lineage and this had awakened her sense of loss.

He took another sip. He really wanted whiskey. But as much as he had learned to drink in college, he had also learned to do without during the two years on the reservation instead of going to Vietnam. He would not have survived that war. Or whiskey.

There was whiskey in the cabinet. He could have a drink. He felt that he had to be completely steady.

He had almost not survived the desolation on the reservation and the

Native soldiers coming back so broken. More broken then when they had gone, though enlisting had seemed, had been promised, to be a way out. They drank and so he did not. Then there was Hosteen – they kept each other steady. Hosteen was an angry man for all the right reasons and John Birdswell had been a young man although a physician. He had started college in 1955. He went to the reservation in 1966. He was twenty-nine years old. He had medical school and internship and two years of residency in a new specialty, Family Medicine, behind him. He had seen a lot of pain but it wasn't his yet. This was before his loss and before Sandra. If his adoptive parents had been alive, they would have said what they always said, "He is a good kid." When he thought about them, which he rarely did, it was to acknowledge that their straightforward but steadfast devotion had kept him from going to war. For this, he was unequivocally grateful.

She wanted honesty, so he did not look away from her. He was sure he was reading the signs right. The lines on her forehead had to be waves of water. And on her cheeks?

She saw in his eyes that he had interpreted the marking correctly. He began, as she was afraid he would, singing Neil Young's "See the Sky About to Rain."

She waited him out. She knew that whatever they said to each other would be harder for him because for the first time she had someone to lean on and he didn't. But it would be when he got to the line about breaking the silver fiddle that they would be in trouble. He would remember losing her mother and all would be lost.

She said what she had to say firmly, not deferring to his need. "Please, Poppa. Don't sing. No matter what, don't sing."

He looked at her face across the counter. She was standing, leaning against the cabinets. He had his back to the windows. It was dark. The ceiling lights could be interrogation lights. He tried a stool with a wooden back. He was not going to stand for this one.

Everything they had ever said and had not said about her origins and her mother was there as if all crumpled time was between them. John Birdswell was a tall, straight, thin but robust man. She thought of him like a lodge pole pine. When he saw patients, he had to make sure to lean against something at an angle because his tendency was to stand up straight and he could easily overwhelm everyone. When Sandra was young, he would sit down on the floor and then on a stool or a straight chair and she would stand next to him and they would be equals until she was tall enough to meet him eye to eye.

But now as he sat there waiting, his body began to collapse, the emptiness he was discussing becoming real inside him as the internal structures dissolved. In order to meet her, he collapsed onto the chair, his arm on the counter supporting him.

"I told Terrence," she knew she had to begin and so she introduced Terrence as if he had already been introduced, "that you taught me to tell the truth. It seemed right when I began. I told him that you and I were always completely transparent with each other. Like two streams meeting and the light coming through.

"I told him that Hosteen is my uncle. Maybe I told him Uncle taught me to offer tobacco. I don't know what I said. But when I held the tobacco in my hand, I knew that you had lied to me. Something is not right. I can feel it. I can't go further with Terrence unless the lies disappear. There can't be a repeat of your marriage." She did not know what she meant by the last words. She meant: nothing can be concealed.

She didn't know what had taken her over. He saw the change in her. It was not need this time that was pushing her. She was adamant. He had seen this only rarely. A few classmates had stood up and said they wouldn't go to Vietnam and when they couldn't get out of it through the public health service, they made their way out of the country. How could he compare the two, and yet he saw a quality in her that he had not seen before – she was ready to walk out. She would not back down even if she were confronting her father. A father, a country, they could be the same, he thought, for her. Would he have had the courage to leave the country? He had never confronted his father. He had to speak because she wasn't backing away from him, she was waiting to see if she would have to back away, and if necessary, she would flee.

"You want to know?"

"I must know."

"I'll tell you," his voice was hoarse from the years of grief.

"Your mother? She was my naiad, and every time I asked her who she was, she molted, and someone else appeared, until at the end of her pregnancy, I thought I might have a sense of who she was or who she would be becoming. And then … "

He was speaking very slowly or she was listening in another time dimension, checking the validity of each word before taking in the next one. He understood, because he was her father now, that is, he was a father, he was the father, not only the one who raised her, he was the father, that as much as she wanted to hear whatever he could tell her he needed to be trustworthy so she could go on and partner in this life. He had not known this before.

He did deliberately speak slowly, testing each word in the way she was doing in her listening. "My naiad became your mother in the seven or so months that we knew about your existence. That was her final identity and then she died like mayflies do."

Something in his voice, in his hesitation, his tentativeness, as if speaking of a stranger, of someone who was so undefined, alarmed her. "She wasn't your wife?" Her voice broke with disbelief.

"We never married." There was no emotion in his voice. A statement of fact. Cold.

Then he cracked like ice cubes in water. "But even if we had married – which would have been impossible for her – she would never have been my wife. She wasn't able …." His voice kept breaking. He didn't cry. He would have loved to wail. Not because she had died, but because he still longed for her so.

This truth telling, this ordeal. What needed to be said for her that she had a right to hear? What needed to be said for him? Did they need to be distinguished or would Sandra sift through these sands to find what was essential to her, to find all of it as he intended to give it to her, without obfuscating the bare truth, for truth can only be bare, with what memories were rising up in him that were only his.

"You never married?" She didn't think he had said what she thought she heard. "I thought …" She couldn't say more.

"Everyone thought," he cut in as if she had been there at the time.

"But …"

"But what?" Tension crept into his voice. Something she had never heard before. "Why didn't you know? Why didn't I tell you? So you didn't know. It didn't matter. It doesn't matter for you." He wasn't shouting but he sounded like he was. He wasn't looking at Sandra or speaking to her. "It only matters for me. He had never claimed this anguish and his privacy in this way before. "Everyone thought …. Because no one knew her. Your mother wasn't someone who would marry. That would hold her too tight."

He groaned. He got up from the chair. He handed her his cup to fill. He leaned against the sink counter.

Now the story. Story was easier. Story was possible. His voice lowered. He could tell a story.

"She was singing …"

"Slow down," Sandra said. She knew his story telling mode. This was not a story for her. She pulled him up short. He understood they were still on two sides of a great divide. She didn't know what he knew. He had never told this story before to anyone. He had to be careful and forthright so that story didn't spin him away.

"She was singing in a club, the Catnip Club. I used to visit it on the way home from work. I had been in practice about four years. I had just gotten used to being a family physician. I was a loner too. She had long blond hair, like Joni Mitchell. Like yours, but lighter. A great voice, lyric and very light. Like those angel clouds. What are they, Sandra?"

"Cirrus clouds."

"Yeah, angel clouds." He was calm now.

"She was used to seeing me. One night, she smiled when I came in. After her set, I invited her to my table and was surprised when she came over. We had a drink. Only one. I could hold my liquor but didn't count on it. Doctors often become addicts. To keep you going when you're so tired, or to calm you down when the intensity is overwhelming. Mostly drugs, but liquor too. I wasn't going down any of those roads.

"I asked her the usual questions as a way of making conversation. 'Who are you? Where are you from?'

"She didn't have to say. I knew enough even from being a fairly young doc in a small town that she was a runaway and she wouldn't tell me where she was from. Little gestures gave her away. She would lift her hair on the back of her hand and throw it over her shoulder, turning her head, like you do but differently. It engaged me until I realized she was looking around. Fearfully, maybe. Wary. One day she said she was from Greece and the next day that she had been born in Patagonia. She said she was a high school dropout. She said she had studied French literature and written a Master's thesis on Baudelaire. She knew I wouldn't know if she was putting me on or not, speaking of Baudelaire. I only knew one line:

Hypocrite lecteur, – mon semblable, – mon frère!

You – hypocrite reader – my double – my brother!

"She said she had left the program because the chair of her department wanted to fuck her. She said she had been a call girl in Morocco. She did speak French. She said she had sold hats in Paris in the twenties. Her own mother couldn't have been old enough to live in Paris in the twenties – but it didn't disturb her in the least to insist she had lived there then."

Sandra just stared. The story had taken him. Then he saw her face. He was not speaking about a girlfriend. He was telling his daughter about her mother. But he couldn't stop himself.

"She spoke of Paris and then she said she went to Paris to buy jeans.

Then she went on to say that she had been twenty when she modeled Paris jeans for a boutique in Austin, Texas.

"It was always like this. If I asked anything about her, she would confabulate a story. It was like calling a waterfall over the cliff. Watch out you're going to drown. I kept trying, thinking one day, she would tell me. But she never did."

John saw his daughter's face. He had to pull himself together. He was drunk on grief and memory. She wanted to know about her mother, not his love life.

"Here's the truth – I don't know how old she was. I guessed twenty-eight, because she was beautiful, but worn, and that is what it said on her driver's license, but who knows. She could have been twenty-three, a post-war baby."

He continued to speak the way he had spoken. Again, he could not stop himself. It was his history too. Sandra would have to understand that. "She said she had run away from home because her father had split when she was born and her mother's boyfriend was molesting her. She said she had hitchhiked across the US for three years until her parrot died of exposure in Alaska. That is the way she talked, Sandra. She would sing Neil Young's "Married Man" lyrics to me and laugh when she came to 'stop singin' your old song.' "

He couldn't help himself and began singing the song.

"John!" Sandra had never called him by his name before. It was the icy rebuke he needed. He stopped singing mid-line.

"Sorry." He was sorry.

He began again, "She said her father was a Presbyterian minister and her mother was Iroquois but kicked off the reservation when she had your mother. It was a given that nothing she said was true.

"She was probably from somewhere like Missouri, had had an ordinary blue collar childhood and had run away after high school out of boredom, but maybe not. Maybe it had really been a horror. If this was the aftermath, that would make sense. She liked to tell stories and there was nothing ever to hold on to.

"She didn't want to know anything about my life, if I'd had anything to say. We'd talk about the events of our days, but nothing more. If I started to tell her anything, she put her finger on my lips and said 'Sssh.' "

"As if by agreement, we erased our personal history. It seemed natural at the time. I knew so little; she refused to reveal anything. Why not start off fresh? Why not create our lives, then and there together? If I had asked her, I am sure she would have been happy to change her name. She probably thought thinking up a name would have been great fun and was crestfallen that I liked Samantha and that I sometimes called her Crow. When I imagine a woman who would be named Samantha Crow, I see a sturdy person with black hair and black eyes. Tan and athletic. Not your mother. That's when I called her Crow, when she would fade away and I needed to send a large black bird to bring her back.

"I never brought her to the reservation to meet Hosteen. Though she had traveled a lot on her own, she was too delicate, too ethereal for such a trip. But Hosteen teased me when I spoke about her. He said that we had erased ourselves the way so many Indigenous people had been erased by being forbidden their names, history, language and ceremonies. But missionaries hadn't done it to us. We did it ourselves. Those were the times – when independence got us – nowhere.

"We didn't know what we were doing. We thought we were building a life. Or, I thought so. When she got pregnant, we just talked about you. She cried and she laughed and it was the first time I felt like I was holding a real person in my arms.

"Even then, sometimes I'd look at her and think she was just a wraith, that I had been taken by a spirit, that my soul was entangled by something from another universe and that the child that was coming would be equally mysterious and unsubstantial, a shade or jinn. Then she slipped through our fingers and you came in as solid as any child has ever been."

A long silence. Neither of them spoke. Then ....

"Did I ever find out anything about her past? Not a thing."

Then Sandra could not contain herself. She had been turning and turning the very narrow gold ring that he had said had been her mother's and that she wore, as he had said, her mother had worn on her third finger of her left hand. He had never said why. Now, she understood. Third finger, not fourth. Almost married.

"Your ring? Did you have one?"

"Only one permitted. Her rules. I could wear one, or she would wear one. Her hands were lovely, delicate, like the rest of her. The ring on her hand was like light on water. As it is on yours." He reached for her hand but she pulled away. "I didn't need a ring to feel eternally connected to her. And no ring or ceremony would ever convince me we were married."

He stopped talking. He had gotten up from the chair and had stood straight as he was talking until he collapsed again, emptiness overtaking him. He reached out with his hands for another structure to hold him up.

Such stillness. The only sounds were the stripes of blue from the full moon as it moved across the sky above them.

"Tell me something. Give me something," Sandra bellowed suddenly, her arms extended involuntarily, startling both of them.

"You know it all. Her body never came home so I was free to go through all her things. I violated everything. There was no one to stop me. Do you know what there was? Nothing. Nothing. Even her driver's license. She had changed it apparently so that it had our address. Samantha Crow. No social security number. No letters. No old bills scrunched away that might have given me a location. No address book. No check book.

"A few books. No Baudelaire. No Alan Ginsburg, no Anaïs Nin. Nothing underlined. No notes in them. Pristine.

"Her clothes? She had cut the labels out of all her clothes. She said they irritated her skin. The princess who slept on the pea. Yes, she was that delicate. She liked sheer cloth, silk, very fine batiste, chiffon, mousseline, tiffany, tulle, gauze, grenadine, organdy, organza, voile …. I never knew these names. She taught them to me. Everything about her was transparent, translucent, gleaming.

"But when she died … I couldn't forget the story she had told me when we first met. I would say, 'Who are you?' And she would tell me the story. Soon we called it the story and then it became our story."

Sandra knew then what he was going to tell her. It was a myth he used to tell her when she was little. It always made her cry and she didn't know why he told it to her again and again. She would cry and then he would cry too and the story took on a life it was never expected to have between them. She had not known that he had first heard the story from her mother.

Sandra was afraid they would both cry again. It was exactly as it had been when she was young. This terrible story was going to be told and neither of them wanted to hear it and neither of them could live without it.

She was aware, though he could not be, that Terrence had just wooed her with a story and in his way, her father was doing the same. Meeting her lover was not taking her away from her life. It was immersing her in beauty.

He looked around and said, "Let's go in the living room." She followed him dutifully. She was a child now. He sat down on the couch. She lay down and put her head in his lap. Just as it had been. He was stroking her hair as he used to, only she knew his eyes were far away. Thirty-three years away.

"There was a young man who lived at the edge of the world with his mother. When he reached a certain age, he wanted to find a wife, but his mother always dissuaded him. Secretly, he made plans to set out on the journey, gathering provisions and enough coins so he might explore for an entire year. When everything was ready he told his mother, stepped across the threshold and set off.

"The young man wandered from place to place as men do when they are on a journey. Sometimes he was happy and sometimes he was sad. He was frugal and his money lasted him. Then he came upon a young woman whom he could not resist and he brought her home. She was most delicate and most beautiful. He did everything on her behalf so that she would not be a burden to his mother because she was unable to perform even the slightest tasks. But in return for this care, she sang like a nightingale, soothing the hearts of everyone who heard her. Soon the ill and broken came to the home to heal their bodies and their souls. Enchanted by her beauty and kindness, they always left what they could, gold and silver coins to thank her for her gift of music. And so she earned her keep as she could do no chores."

John was stroking her hair as he had when she was a girl and she let him, enjoying the familiar comfort while both of them accepted that this was their ceremony of disengagement.

"One day, the man had to leave their compound and he asked his mother to be gentle with his wife for he feared her anger and jealousy. But he had no choice but to leave. He left provisions for them, including a barrel of white and yellow corn that had been picked that morning. There was enough corn to last them a month though he would only be gone a day or two.

"As soon as he was a few hours away, down the road, and over the hill and across the mountain pass, the mother took out the bushel of corn and asked the girl to grind all the white and yellow corn into flour. The girl was afraid. The girl knew she had no choice but to obey her mother-in-law. She began grinding the corn, slowly and carefully. She began with the yellow and watched it darkening as it became meal. She knew what was inevitable. So fragile was she that she could not help but grind her fingers into meal. The mother stood over her and insisted she continue."

John paused, his hand firm on her forehead. He had to continue but wanted to give her time to prepare for what was coming. Then he began again. "She ground and she ground she ground. Soon all the corn was ground. The corn was ground and the girl had entirely disappeared.

"When her husband came home, instead of his bride, he found the bushel overflowing with corn, no longer white and yellow as he had left it. The corn was shining with a strange light in the many shades of red and also brown, black and blue."

John was crying and Sandra was crying. He was stroking her hair.

"That's an old myth," Sandra said. "She didn't make up the story. She heard it and it sounded like her, so she claimed it."

"Probably so," he agreed. "How do you know?"

"It's a Huichole myth. They're a tribe living around Tepic in Mexico. When I was studying TEK, I heard a lot of stories."

"What else?" he asked. "It's getting late. I don't think I can hold up much longer. Nor can you."

"Tell me one more thing. Anything."

"Anything. OK. She had a 1964 Gibson F 25 acoustic guitar. I used to tease her that she wore white to match the white panels on the guitar. She and the guitar were one. It had a deep, rich tone, and it took her down and one went down with her so that you never wanted her to stop singing, not ever. My naiad. My mayfly. My corn maiden."

He wasn't singing. He was almost singing. But he wasn't singing so she didn't stop him.

"I know the question you are asking. I broke the guitar. I took it outside when you were napping, far behind the house so you wouldn't hear it, and I stomped on it and stomped on it and smashed it until there was nothing left. Nothing left, just like her."

"Her ashes?"

"Her ashes? I followed her damn instructions. Her romantic notions considered no one but herself." He hadn't acknowledged the extent of his fury. "Your mother had a love for the ocean and we would take a weekend and drive to the ocean, to Pt. Arena or Big Sur. When we had time, we went north into Oregon. The craggy coasts, the wild ocean thrilled her. She had said, 'Wait for a stormy day, wait for the wind to come up and go to the ocean and wait for white caps, then hire a motor boat and go out past the breakwater and when that gust comes and the froth that is hungry for me, let me go.'

"And so I did."

"How are you, Poppa?" She lifted her head from his lap and looked at him up close. He was an old man. He was 67. He was not the young father who had carried her around on his back.

"It was a long time ago, Sandra. It was thirty-three years ago. Time to get another life, don't you think?"

"Have you had any thoughts about what that might be?"

"I've got patients. They don't go away, thank god. But to tell you the truth, my dear girl, my heart is hurting now real bad. That's not a bad thing. It's just a fact. So, I'll take off a few days next week and go drink some of Hosteen's lousy coffee. It always makes me appreciate home."

He lifted himself off the couch with some effort. He was an old man. Maybe it wasn't that she had just noticed. Maybe it had just happened.

"Anything else, Poppa?"

Her question required him to tell the truth. He had done so up to this moment, yes, but not what he had withheld.

" 'You protect the perimeter and I will protect the core,' that's what your mother said. Then she died and left the entire territory to me. Left it to me in the United States of America in 1973. The wrong time for such a responsibility. But just like her. Just like the way she had been when I had first met her. I had always known such a desertion was possible; it had been in her cells." It wasn't right to rant this way to Sandra but he was unable to contain himself. "She was so elusive. Face it. That is what drew me to her. That's how she held me – with spider threads.

"Do you want to know more? Here it is, Sandra." He girded himself for her response but could not withhold any longer. His voice was louder than it should have been because the truth was explosive.

"Your mother said, "We'll name her, Spirit." He waited to see Sandra's reaction, but she was standing with her back to him looking out the window to the west where stars were setting. She flinched, her muscles cascading up her back to her shoulders. If not for that motion, he might have thought she hadn't heard him.

"Do you want to know more?" he asked, his voice rising still.

Sandra didn't answer. He proceeded, not knowing what else to do. "She had put my hand on her belly to feel the baby moving. I could feel your head, elbow, knee, rump pushing, making yourself known.

"I asked her, 'A she? How do you know?' "

" 'Because I am carrying wide, not frontal,' she was a bit scornful. 'Didn't they teach you how to tell in medical school?' "

"I remember every word of this exchange between us because I was flustered. I took on a persona to get back at her: 'The latest literature speaks of cultured amniotic fluid cells being suitable for varityping, so we can determine sex and other disorders. Would you like a confirmation?'

"Samantha saw that I was distraught though I didn't know why then. Maybe she knew. 'She's a perfect child, John. You'll see. That's why I want to name her Spirit. The name will adhere to her center and give her ballast.'

" 'I can't imagine Spirit giving anyone ballast,' I answered, petulantly, I guess. 'The name asks a lot of a child.' " John's voice trailed off as he noticed the internal tremors that often occurred when Sandra was with him.

" 'It asks and it gives,' your mother said and then added, 'But if you don't like the name, do whatever is right by your lights at the moment.'

" 'Your premonition again?' I was alarmed.

" 'My knowing.' I can hear your mother's voice right now, Sandra. I didn't press her to say more. I didn't want to admit to myself that I felt her slipping away and the slight thread that connected us, slimmer than the umbilical cord that held the two of you in tow, seemed to thin even more as I thought about it, so that holding on was dangerous, it could tear the delicate cord apart."

He was spent.

"Anything else, Poppa?" She had turned toward him. The light in the room was dim and the darkness bright behind her.

"Nothing else." He clenched his teeth to give himself a sense of his own body after he had revealed the only lie he had ever told his daughter. "She wanted to name you Spirit. I couldn't do it. I needed to have solid ground under me if I was going to father you well."

A blow or redemption? Was she lightheaded or had her feet turned to concrete? She was spinning or she was solid.She couldn't tell which. She could barely speak. "Thank you for that," she managed to whisper as he opened the door as if to make his escape.

He looked back at her. "This Terrence … ? Is he … ?" His question or the cold air entering like a slap or a draught of smelling salts, startled her enough to focus.

"Yes, he was the Chair. I haven't seen him since, except once by chance."

"Who are his people?"

"You know, Poppa, I don't know." It was true. She didn't know. Only now it struck her as strange.

He was standing straight up now, looking at her as she leaned on the open door, her hand on the door knob. "Don't know." She couldn't help herself, she began to sing "See the Sky About To Rain" again.

"Don't go to the end of that, it will break my heart," he said as he was turning away. There was the broken silver fiddle again.

By the time he was at the truck, he was singing another song, as she knew he would. She didn't want to hear it. It was exactly the right song for him to be singing. It was "The Loner."

After her father left, the house seemed even emptier than before. The central fire reassured her but her own central fire didn't seem to catch. Reviewing the last days, she focused on her remark to Terrence that houses seemed designed to keep people from being outside. A barricade rather than a shelter. All the words that came to mind after barricade – barrier, blockade, obstruction, bastion, rampart, fortification – spoke of defense rather than refuge or haven. She wanted to be protected but the price – disconnection – was not what she was willing to pay. What had transpired between Terrence and herself had left her oriented and disoriented at the same time. Then the conversation with her father, even more so. She was not a motherless child any longer. She was a woman who hadn't had a mother, but she had a father-mother and she had an uncle. More than enough to raise a stable human being. She had a lover. She was not alone.

Seeing her father's anguish stripped her of what she had to recognize as obsessive self pity. She was not afraid of self-scrutiny. Having been with Terrence inspired fierceness in her. As for lineage, it occurred to her that she might have used that trope in order to punish her father for what he had been completely unable to control. To punish her father who had never punished her. It was all very tawdry. She could not allow such petulance to continue.

Spirit. She said the name to herself and looked down at her bare feet, her strong ankles, her long legs. Her father had been right not to give her the name. Outside the wind was rising and inside magazine covers and assorted papers were beginning to rustle. The wind didn't like being confined in the house. Nor did she. Outside, she could blow every impediment away.

She often slept outside but not in weather like this. The wind was quite wild. Blustery. March weather to a new power. But she had a sleeping bag, a pad, a bivvy sack, and a bear skin. She didn't need the bivvy. She wanted to let the wind blow across her face.

There is about an hour and half between the beginning of dawn, what is called astronomical twilight and sunrise itself. The slow coming to light would awaken her before he called.

14

When the Wind Blows, Down Come Baby, Cradle and All

Surely, Sandra thought as the gusts awakened her, those are voices in the wind. The winds were much fiercer then they had been earlier. Since she had purchased the house, she'd been able to track the shift without instruments. At this moment, she tried not to burrow into the sleeping bag but to embed herself instead in her memories of Terrence's lectures on wind.

"Take the opportunity to know wind," he had suggested, "rather than know about it." He was no longer her teacher, well, no longer her professor, but she was learning from him again. Outside with the wind, she was not involved in an experiment. She would not make notes. The wind blasted against the windows and rattled the metal gutters. This was not a class assignment. The wind was wild. The wind was blowing through her. It was striking her back, chest, belly as she sat up to see if it would hold her up if she leaned back against it. Then she understood: Terrence had sent the wind.

Terrence had sent the wind and so she spent the night with it. It howled as if it were telling her its story. It sounded like a herd of horses. Wind energy was the current interest. The local windmill converted to an industrial wind farm. I am not to be blindly harnessed, wind said – she thought it said. The word "harnessed" disturbed her just as harnessing horses disturbed her. Hosteen had taught her to ride bareback when she was little and she had ridden no other way, though he himself often rode with a saddle. He rode often. She no longer rode. He lived among horses, she did not. Her mind wandered as the wind did, her thoughts blowing like leaves or like horses stomping through fields, then resting among the trees. The rare horses that were able to wander. On the reservation, yes. The increasingly fewer free mustangs. Horsepower was no longer a measure. That changed everything. Weather was responding accordingly, missing the empty spaces, missing its habitat, blustering.

The wind had had a habitat. The thought stirred her toward wakefulness. Habitat and migration patterns ... the wind suffered them like animals did ... it had to accommodate to all the barriers that were always springing up. The same barriers that inhibited the animals. The wind was blowing through her mind, her thoughts bending to it, like waves moving through prairie grasses, she had to bow to it.

Terrence had brought the wind. The wind brought the horses. The mustangs were endangered, rounded up, penned, under excruciating conditions. Temperatures rising. There was no shade, no way to escape. Every living thing was vulnerable to management. Life yielding to technology. The wild horses rose up kicking at the wooden stalls. Technology was management. Technology led to wind farms. Terrence had brought the wind .... She turned this way and that, sleeping and waking, hoping the wind would blow strongly enough to clear the nightmares, those horses of extinction. Terrence had taught her about wind. In what was left of her restless night, she tried to avoid imagining what she knew he faced every day.

Terrence's task was dealing with the wind, his engineering colleagues would have the task of disposing of, recycling the retired blades. The Earth was becoming a graveyard for dead machines that would never return to the source. The use of wind was being challenged by various Native tribes – they knew what they knew, perhaps from the bald and golden eagles who were falling victim to the blades. The Wampanoag objected to wind farms because the wind turbines would interfere with their sacred ceremony, the wind turbines with their propeller blades slicing the air would be an obstacle to their sacred greeting of the rising sun. Why did energy solutions always threaten the tribal ways – uranium mining, nuclear waste, wind farms? Ultimately, Terrence was ambivalent about any form of harnessing the spirits. He saw what harm was coming to the people and the Earth from such infractions. There was no evidence that the investors, the stake holders – he hated the term, they always used it at the University – had asked permission of the wind. To shift his Western colleagues relationship with the four elements would require more, he feared, than an act of God. He had to keep his own counsel regarding the spirits. One of his original interests had been to understand the interactions of the elemental energies from a Western perspective; it had not been to find economic and material solutions to ameliorate or increase human caused climate change and environmental degradation.

Sandra remained on the deck, offering herself to the mercy of the wind. It was being kind to her, rearranging her mind. What had he said? Different peoples recognized the wind as a spirit. She was glad not to have the name, she wanted to return to who she had been, someone who could hear Spirit without thinking of herself. Perhaps, she mused, it was calling her into an alliance.

Wind. She focused on wind. What did people do against the wind? They put up walls. Wind had to find its way. It had to change its ways to find a way. Climate change came charging through like a conquistador. It was inevitable.

Terrence did or did not sleep that night. Likely, he didn't. He was within his house or outside. In his tent or sitting on a log outside. Beginning to imagine a walking path to her house. He suspected he would not find a continuous corridor. Like the wolf and the mountain lion, he would be stopped by neighborhood fences and roadways. The wily coyotes knew the ways through and they might lead him. Like a wild animal he would have to try, but not tonight. Tonight he had to be home to call her as she had asked before the golden light paled.

Across the hills, Sandra drew the bearskin over her, leaning into the presence of wind. In the distance, a horse whinnied or maybe it was only in her dream that mustangs churned up the soil as they cantered across the fields into stands of red fir and pine. Full moon in the western sky, a luminous presence. She slept and awakened and slept again folded finally into the images of her mother -- crows and mayflies, like the night and the moon cohabiting.

The phone would ring in the morning at exactly the right moment. She did not doubt this. She was thinking, "Terrence is my Mr. Wind."

15

Making a Home on Planet Earth

She awakened as she always did just before dawn and lay quietly in the comfort of her deep knowing, as if weeks, months perhaps had passed in those few hours they had been separated. She knew that the phone would ring at the exact moment of golden light. She answered. She heard his voice, stranger and soul mate at once: She would come to his house. He would come to get her. He would help her pack a few things for the interim. The interim to what? They didn't know or speculate. He said, "the interim," she accepted it. She did not begin before he came, trusting, even depending on the wordless communion that had already guided them.

Rather than begin the mundane task of packing, she had to climb to the roof and greet the surrounding land explaining as if to neighbors that she would be away for awhile. It was then that she was struck by grief. She had thought it was the house that had sustained her here, but she saw it was the land. This should not have been a revelation to her, but it was. She would miss the land and she didn't know if she had the right to leave it. What were the agreements between them? Would the land where he lived receive her? Would she receive it?

So when he came walking up the stairs, tentatively and simultaneously with confidence, she opened the door but not to let him in – that would come later – but to take his hand and walk around the house and up the ladder behind the house to the north and onto the roof so that he would know her by seeing 360 degrees of sky and earth. They conferred on her weather station, some 75 feet away, mounted to a pole in a wide clearing to catch the wind, heat and cold. They went further until they covered every place she walked each day. Then they walked back onto the land encircling the house. Once they had covered the area and had stood before two yuccas he saw the way back and took her hand; it was a slight adjustment, not of power, but of familiarity.

For the rest of the morning, there were only the fewest words spoken;

they were like animals of different species who find their way to each other without a vocabulary or dictionary. Had she tried to find words, she would have said that their common language would have restricted their connection because it was inadequate to their experience. And that would not have said it either.

In a similar manner, she took him through the house, silently opening every door and drawer as they walked as a way of reciprocating for the immediate future when she would be living at his house and have access to everything as if it were her own. She was afraid and she did it anyway. As she opened the drawers, as she signaled to him to help her open the too heavy one with photographs that was stuck, he hesitated until she nodded, confirming her intentions. Their connection, this situation was all so unique, she was adamantly silent. Language creates the opportunity for conditions, she knew this all too well. She was determined to live unconditionally – with him.

There was no reason to assume that their communion would serve them in the material world where things that carry personal history had to be encased in cartons and suitcases. An irrational expectation and they entertained no other. She gathered what she needed of her clothes, papers, jewelry, personal items and work files and closed all the windows – that was the hard part – while he also went through the opened drawers, examining shelves he had not seen before, closing the few closets and cabinets after taking what he sensed she would want, for he would be sure she would need for nothing their first week together or for their common lives. It amused him that he was learning more from her silence than her things.

In the kitchen, he paused before the rows of mason jars that in any other house would hold herbs, rice, pasta, other foods, but which he quickly discerned from the careful labeling were her personal earth history. These he wrapped in colorful linen napkins, earth brown with brush strokes of red, yellow, blue and green, that she used, instead, he guessed, of paper napkins, which he didn't see, nor paper towels. The napkins coordinated with the handmade pottery plates and bowls, a similar rich brown brushed with black that was her dinnerware. He took four plates and eight bowls and a large irregular serving bowl that looked blue until the light hit it and it turned turquoise. He had mugs he thought she would like. He packed a Navajo bear fetish with red arrows along its rump aiming at his heart that made him smile, an old dream catcher hanging over her bed, dating back to pre-tourist years, that she could have easily reached as well as he – they were almost the same height – and two framed black and white photographs of glaciers, one illuminated by sunlight and one against a stormy sky, both clearly from the Arctic. There was an Inuit stone carving of a mantic owl, its great black wings outspread to protect its young and a shapeshifting carving of a bear becoming a whale or the opposite, or both. The bearskin was already in the truck as were several pillows for bed, couch and floor, handy to nestle the two lamps with wood bases carved from small tree trunks she would certainly need, several candleholders and the pottery and photos. He was gathering her up.

"You didn't lock the house," he noted.

"If I did, it would think I'm not coming back. And then the land ...." She didn't finish the sentence. "I didn't turn off the computer either so that it will continue to gather the weather data. Because ..." another sentence unfinished. This one meant – for no reason at all but that the land would want her to know the details its life while she was away. "I'll tell the post office. No one else comes here." Glancing at him, as he left tobacco on her behalf, she assumed he understood.

It was 1:30 p.m. They were done. He wanted to gather her to him formally. From another culture, he might have carried her over the threshold from her house to his truck or from his truck into his house, but neither was appropriate. Alternately, they stood together while he felt her telling the land that they would return. Looking to see what they might have forgotten, he spotted her sun hat in her car, slipped it onto his back seat and opened the passenger door and waited while she sat down. They would come back for her car soon, but today they had to drive out together. She was crying. As the morning progressed, they had spoken less and less. Now they were in full silence again. When she was ready and confident, she would say the first words.

At the half-mile-long dirt road that led from the street to Terrence's land, Sandra put her hand on Terrence's arm and he paused. When they reached the entry, he would turn right to park in front of his house or drive straight to a parking spot before the outdoor kitchen and parallel to the tent.

"Let's go to the tent," her voice quiet, and slightly unsure, in the manner of someone who knows that beginnings imply endings.

"Of course," he agreed assuredly, as if he had thought of it himself, as if he had hoped she would suggest this, as if he knew that everything they did had to be original to who they were becoming because they were together. They were their own future selves meeting here and now by reaching backwards into the present. Not as acts of will, but attuned to what was barely audible and visible. Not stumbling in the dark, but striding with assurance in the dark. And so their first day of living together for the rest of their lives began.

She couldn't go inside his house – that did not surprise her – but she couldn't go into the tent either. An invisible wall prevented it. He made them tomato and cheese sandwiches and they sat on tree stumps looking west, past the kitchen, away from his house. This view of the surrounding savannah was unimpeded, the tips of salt grasses just rising up were golden in the early afternoon light as the wind bent them toward dusty stands of blue-green sage whose azure buds were beginning to emerge. Further away were patches of small trees, oak and manzanita, also blue and white ceanothus coming into bloom on the low rises and hills. Looking across the fields, a pointillist vision of pale colors and textures.

Time changed its nature, it sped and slowed, twisted and turned.

"I'm getting dizzy," she said. "This is a wild ride, Terrence. It's spinning me in one direction then turning me upside down the next."

"Maybe we're in a super collider," he agreed.

"Being reduced to fundamental particles. That sounds right," she answered and steadied herself as she sat down on the stump that he had carved so that it was a seat with a low back. "What tree does this come from?"

"A sycamore down by the stream that has been dry for too many years. No water, no tree. When it fell over in a wind storm, I cut it up. I made these seats and a few butcher block cutting boards from it and gave the rest of the wood to a neighbor."

She had waited so impatiently for her own house, not expecting to find it in her lifetime. The first night she was in it, the former owner's furniture gone, the house carefully cleaned so as to extract the former owner's presence, she had walked round and round and round the central fire open to all the rooms. There was no way to close the fire in for the night, so she circumnavigated it all night long, tending this other living presence in the house.

Incomprehensibly, she didn't want to live in a house now, not hers, not his. Despite her experience in the field, despite her connection with the Earth, she had never questioned living in a house. Now she was repelled by house itself, not his in particular, and was unable to imagine returning to hers, to imagine anything but the two of them living here together, despite cold, rain, occasional snow and extreme heat, in a tent. Perplexing except that it meant a new beginning which meant the unknown and she wanted to be faithful to not knowing, and so wary of imposing management, her will.

A slight smile curved his lips but his gaze was steady and away and what he was thinking was inscrutable to her; she couldn't determine if he was looking across the fields or looking back to another time. Primarily, she assumed, he was letting her take the lead so he could come to know her though she didn't know herself now, her responses were so unfamiliar to her. He was a mystery to her and so was she – both mysteries to which she was bonded for life.

He was himself amused and curious about a path that was opening before him, most certainly, if kindly, likely to undo his current life. He was joshing with himself for it had not occurred to him to live here rather than in the house he had built himself. He had used the tent and the outdoor facilities while he was building the house and then for guests, but not for himself after the house was ready. Then he had brought her here from the desert and not into the house and it had been the right, if entirely idiosyncratic, choice. When he had been so focused on what was occurring between the two of them and occupied only with her well being, ignoring the usual insistent distractions of mail and messages of various sorts, a change overtook him that seemed to have penetrated to the cellular level of consciousness. He had no recent precedents for this moment though it raised memories of his days with his grandparents on the reservation. Days wandering and musing, learning the habits and calls of the four-legged and the winged. As for this moment when he was learning again in these old ways it was fortunate that he was on spring break although this way of being was not going to be over soon, or ever, and spring break would definitely come to an end.

The relative silence between them was puzzling and satisfying. They were both assuming they understood each other and were accessing other ways of knowing, not intuitive so much as primal. Weeks and months from this first day, they would speculate on what their assumptions had been and marvel that they had persisted. She would note that they had managed communicating so accurately, given that they came from different worlds and widely differing life experiences; Sandra attributed the skill to his history. Terrence noted their common longing for each other and the ways that certain fjords merging from different ecologies form one body of water temporarily distinguishable, the blue interweaving with the green.

His house, hidden by foliage, seemed dark and insular to her. It wasn't dark inside, she knew that, as it had glass along the entire east wall while the west wall with fewer windows was shaded by wood panels and trees. He could watch the sunrise from the living room but to see the sunset he had to go outside.

She speculated that she wanted them to become comfortable with each other without the details of housekeeping interfering. The tent was simple. There was the bed, there was the wood stove, there were the two chairs and a few wood boxes that had held firewood that could hold goods or be used as seating. It would be a short jaunt to the connected washrooms and compost toilet just south of the kitchen all of which Terrence had built with cedar planking.

It couldn't have been yesterday that she had been here and then later that he had brought her home to her house and her father had come over and she had gained a mother, elusive as she had been, and a name. It couldn't have been yesterday and yet it had been.

Returning here, but not as a visitor, she didn't want to go into the house, or, unexpectedly, even into the tent, because, because … she didn't want to be confined by stories, his past or hers. So like her father and mother wanting to begin without ties or inhibitions. Could she be repeating their tragic mistake so quickly after learning of it?

This was their first day together as a couple. So quick the transition from colleagues to strangers to … partners … ? It was March, spring, warm and redolent with the scent of buds and new green. It wasn't, she realized, only that she didn't want to be in a house; she didn't want to be inside. Terrence agreed. "Let's begin without any assumptions," were his words. And so they continued sitting outside. Between exchanges, and surveying the land, she or he got up to bring one thing at a time into the tent.

"Every time we say something to each other, our lives are fixed. It's natural to want to tell you everything about my life and to learn every detail of yours. But then we're tied into our histories and spontaneity vanishes." She was suddenly talking like her father's daughter, the one he had wanted to be totally free.

"I don't find my past a restriction. There are the dark parts but also there is the long lineage, the part of history that goes all the way back. Not what was done to us, but how we lived."

"I don't have any of that."

He looked at her quizzically. It was not what he had expected her to say.

"You know as well as I do what they teach us in school. Maybe we went to the same schools only my people put me there without thinking, without any objection, while you had to be kidnapped. There was a kind of different language I spoke before I went to school that I don't remember anymore …." She looked wistful, then shook her head, lifted her hair – her mother's gesture? – and let it fall. She couldn't remember.

"I kept telling my father that school was useless and he should just keep taking me to the office with him where I was learning everything I needed to know." She considered this again and concluded she had been right as a child. "I still believe this. But, he couldn't do it. Home schooling had regulations he couldn't meet and be a full time physician."

She wanted to stop here but one thought led to another. Nothing existed by itself.

"I know nothing about my mother," he said.
"I knew nothing about my mother," she said.

"Here I am telling you about my past when I just said we should forget it." He was listening in the way she remembered from graduate school with great attention. She knew he wouldn't answer impatiently, wouldn't cut her off, wouldn't interrupt. He never did. It gave her solace that he listened in this way. So few did. Her father did but then he would also want to heal whatever was disturbing. It was his nature.

She continued gravely so that she could feel the impact of what she was saying. She wanted to meet his attention with her own seriousness. "My history is the history of wars. Some of the war history is left out – the pain of battle, the consequence to the conquered, what happened to your people – instead we focus on the sequence of victories by my people …." The slowness with which she had been speaking speeded up out of distress, "I can't say 'my people,' Terrence. I can't say 'white people' either. How about 'European'? That certainly creates a great distance. OK. The non-Native people, who seem to be my people – but are they? – think history is conquest and war. And now with …" her eyes filled with tears, "with what they've done to the Earth … I don't have a history to stand on. So, Terrence, who am I coming from such a past? Where's my dowry?" She was staring at him as if it were his fault and not, as she felt, the other way around.

"You're Sandra," he said simply. She leaped up, turned on her heel and sprinted away from him down a path going as far and fast as she could until she felt her heart quicken and came slouching back.

He hadn't known she had a temper. He hadn't known the level of her despair. He didn't know anything about her. A great mystery beyond them both had arranged a marriage and this is what it was like in the beginning. As a man, he wanted to comfort her, but he would not reach out as if he could contain this pain better than she.

They stood arms at their sides, staring at each other eye to eye. The grief for the destruction of the Earth and the Earth-based peoples of the world was between them, the grief that had brought them together. Not a grief to be ameliorated or eased by their joining, but the weight of the enormous sorrow that now they would hold together. A few words had brought the world's concealed, inadmissible anguish into view.

"I don't want us to be caught in history, either personal or cultural," she stated slightly dizzy but standing there determinedly. He reached forward just slightly so she could steady herself by holding onto him – if she wished – but what he said offered no illusion of comfort.

"There's no escape from history." He sat down on a log. "Even when it is stolen from you."

And then she gathered herself together and asked in a more casual voice, "So what do you think history is?" She straddled the log, facing him.

"Well, I think it's a Joshua tree like we saw the other night. It grows fast, has a trunk composed of many fibers and you can't tell how old it is in the usual ways. Its branch system is top heavy and its arms reach to the sky. It carries all of this because it has an extensive root system that goes all the way down. Sometimes it grows from a seed and sometimes extends from the tree as a rhizome. And its leaves are shaped like bayonets and grow to a point. It can stab you."

She put her hand over her mouth to keep from laughing. "You've told this story before, haven't you? It's part of a lecture you've given more than once."

"I have," he started laughing too. It was a warm laugh, inclusive, even as he was laughing at himself, which he did easily. "I didn't think I'd fool you. You certainly know 'the professor'."

Looking at the house again, wondering if they were making a mistake and should go into it, she asked, "Is there a lot of history in your house?"

"Oh yes. How could there not be?"

"I don't know. Most people's houses have no history, or character, or anything that you can't buy at the furniture store."

"Well, it has a lot of history. Deep roots and it'll stab you too. Just like the tree."

"Like you?"

"Not quite me."

"And the tent then?"

"Depends. Now it's pretty empty. But you can't avoid what's hovering around, like pollen that will blow through no matter what. The Joshua tree is pollinated by the yucca moth. It spreads the pollen when it lays its eggs in the flowers. And if it lays too many eggs, the tree expels them." He was enjoying himself, unable to resist playing the role again. "I think the tent will do the same. When we open the tent door and the windows, it will empty and fill, simultaneously."

She waited while he did what he had said, opened the door and the windows.

"Everything is alive out here," she noted. "Maybe everything is alive in your house but I am not taking chances." She softened a little, was less adamant, less afraid, less ashamed, less disheartened. "Let's stay here."

The door to the tent remained wide open with a screen door against bugs and snakes, the windows wide open as well. He must have thinking ahead to this moment because he'd had the tent custom made and the designer used a new technology that allowed for glass windows that slid open and closed.

As the light began to fade she decided to try the tent. She lay down on the mattress, could smell his scent on the sheets and was glad he hadn't changed them, called him to her and burrowed, her back and rump pressing into his naked body. "When I wake up here in an hour, I will be able to arrange the space, because I will have arrived here. I will already belong."

When they awakened together, she asked him to balance her things with his. "What would you like me to bring in?" he asked.

"Books."

He stacked three crates, one each for his books, her books, their books. Over the first year they would fill the crates and lose their distinctions. Trust mattered, not territory.

"What else?"

"Your hiking boots and some clothes. I don't want to feel I am living here alone."

"Clothes? Too bad."

"You don't have to wear them, just fold them on the shelf."

He put the binoculars he was holding down by the books and went to embrace her, looking to see what buttons he could undo, as she was looking out the east door down into the valley. Humor, again. It hadn't taken long for them to begin to tease and laugh with each other.

It was dark, he turned on a lamp and built a fire in the wood stove. She lit a candle as he went to the car and brought in the bear and placed it on the bed next to the buffalo rug. They settled back against the pillows, the fire before them. They had pulled back the moon roof to watch the stars. His heart was pounding so he placed his hand on hers and her heart was pounding as well.

"How do you pray?" No one had ever asked her that before. Momentarily, she was afraid. How did she pray? Perhaps, she didn't. She listened to the elements, that's how she prayed. She wouldn't have thought to call it prayer, but it was her way and there was no way she could speak about it. "Well," he asked, seeing her dilemma on her face, "Do you sing?" A quiet question that didn't want an answer in the usual way, a question to open her heart to him.

No, she didn't sing. Her mother had been the singer. Her mother had died and song died with her. But, that wasn't true. Her father sang and she sang back to him. They had a strange Neil Young conversation always in the background between them. Her mouth opened, he thought she looked like a bird who had raised her beak after drinking, the water trickling down the extended throat, red feathers against dusky ones, and then. as if she didn't dare, as if the lines had hidden between them, she began, startled, to sing a few lines from Neil Young's "Out of Control."

She wanted to stop, but she was out of control. The song wouldn't let her, the way her father hadn't been able to stop singing when she had begged him to stop, because it was singing her more than she was singing it. It was wispy, her voice. It was smoke curling out of a pipe, it was stillness articulated more than sound, it was an audible mirror to the white mist that was this moment padding down between the dark hills to the east, fog approaching. She began again, braving the moment, the words she hadn't expected, her daring, her calling out to him, a gift from her mother and her father, this song, her prayer, ending with "If I can hold on to you."

Everything between them was so new, fresh, tentative, delicate, he had to reach for her carefully, he could not startle or overwhelm her, as he lay back and drew her to him, reaching to turn off the light, letting the candle glow soften the room so she would allow this moment to become real even if enacted in whispers.

The tent could be secured against almost any weather. Precarious and unstable as a tent might be, this one had the strength of cocoons and nests, fragile and resilient. The two of them were quickly becoming adept in the ways of birds and caterpillars, open to and secured against the weather. What was occurring between Sandra and Terrence was not anything they could have imagined or expected and it needed seclusion for the alembic to occur. They established a secret life.

Within a week Terrence had carefully placed shelves against a portion of the south wall of the tent to hold her mason jars of earth, her history of the mother, confirming this was her home. He carved the stripped supporting branches, above and below the shelves – a bear reaching down toward a whale breaching. She especially enjoyed looking at them in the morning and at sunset as the light gleamed on the glass and at night when the fire or candlelight struck them. The outer and inner, the eye and the heart. They were no longer personal but present in the room, not like paintings on a wall, sometimes forgotten, but as icons of living history, they belonged to both of them. The common history of their connection being created from the stories they told. "Tell me the story of this jar," he asked frequently and she would check the labels and find the index cards that elaborated on the time she had taken this line of earth: "June 14, 2004. Yakutat, Alaska. Hubbard Glacier surges."

Every story required a location. Every story was a location. Where it took place, the land, its story was the foundation of the human story; this had always been true for Sandra but she had not been able to articulate it. When she put soil into her pail, she was taking the story home. The story embedded in soil, the soil linked to place, and the developing strata of different soils, became Sandra's evolving story, like the Grand Canyon is the story of the Earth itself in this place. Terrence understood this, now she could also. This story of their connection, their alignment, their growing unity was happening here, in this tent, on this land, woodland, chaparral, wind coming up the canyon below, cougar and bobcat, owl, raven, fog, then sun, unremitting heat, sometimes heavy winter storms, and snow in the wind, the hint of it further north at the higher elevations. This place.

"Our neighbors?

"Bear, supposedly, but I haven't seen any."

"What have you seen, Terrence?"

"Coyotes. Always coyotes."

"They seem to be everywhere."

"Survivors. That's why. Maybe they are survivalists."

She went running. Daily explorations. Soon she traded her running shoes for moccasins that Terrence made for her. His hands had to be busy. She normally raced, but had to slow down now or she would twist her ankle, had to run lightly, not so heavy a tread, then feeling each step and the ball of her foot rolling over the dirt, reading an earthen Braille manuscript, letter by letter, line by line. Under her an alphabet of soils, stones, leaves, twigs, creatures too small to avoid. The composite of the Earth, this Earth signaling its nature. Sensations, particular and exact. She stopped and ran her toes through the rippled soil, following a water line or wind furrows. She closed her eyes to see with her bare foot. Rolled a round pebble with her toes on the shale surface. A single letter in motion, becoming and dissolving and a history of the universe, both at once.

She had watched her father tap his fingers along patients' skin, bones and muscles until he could say what was healthy and what was ill. The words he used were for the sake of the patient before him, the one who lived in that body but didn't know it. Otherwise, John Birdswell made a wordless alliance between what he felt and what wanted to be received, augmented or deleted in order for healing to occur.

She transferred this skill to the Earth body, explored its particular intelligence, the Earth's willingness to be known on its own terms, in its own language so as to avoid errors and misinterpretations. Sandra's early statement to Dr. G, Chair of the Department, "I want to know," translated. Knowledge through intimacy. Reciprocity. The intention behind the moccasins, almost bare feet. Sometimes bare feet. Naked to the Earth. Sandra willing to be known herself. To be known, reciprocally, without invading. Without probing.

How to discover, explore, investigate without prying? This had been Sandra's essential question although she hadn't verbalized it. Now that she had, she understood that formulating a question implied a direction of investigation within a particular body of knowledge and field of understanding. If the question simply led to an answer, it wasn't a good question. The question led beyond any answers. The question provided essential focus. The question mattered; the answer hardly mattered at all.

One night Sandra asked Terrence to teach her how to make a fire in the good way in the tent. Spring break was over and Terrence was at the university again three or four days a week. She was also teaching again and traveling to building sites, trying to create a relationship between the land and its fate and those who thought they could do anything.

They had been in the tent for a month and the nights were still cold. The good way meant sacred not expedient. Hosteen spoke this way and so did Terrence. She felt that she was ready to meet fire and so she asked him to instruct her. She was adept at setting the logs and tinder and had always prided herself on making "one match" fires. She'd been making fires since she was very young. But Terrence knew something because he came from a different culture. Knew things John Birdswell did not know.

Terrence was sitting before the wood stove, his face ruddy in the flames. They had taken a long walk together. It had pleased her that she was learning the trails, could anticipate the few oaks that came up and disappeared into chaparral. They had walked like one entity, like two hawks gliding in tandem in the thermals. When they had come into the tent, he had gone to the wood stove immediately and gathered the kindling into a pyramid, balancing one dry twig against another. Leaving a doorway between, he placed pinecones and pine needles in the center. Every gesture took him further into the process until it seemed, now that the fire was roaring, that it could easily consume him. That he would allow it without flinching if it wished. She did not dare speak, would not startle him, but felt her own pining for what she didn't know. Then he returned to their intimacy, closed the glass and iron door as if closing off the past. His eyes met hers and he saw that she recognized that he had been elsewhere.

When she inquired, he indicated that the old rituals were the ways he stayed connected to the Earth. She understood he meant something greater and beyond that couldn't be expressed in English. There were words but they weren't equivalent. The language his grandparents had spoken is inspirited but such recognition of the reality of the world is absent from English and that difference could not be breached. She learned by watching him; his gestures and actions were quiet and yet eloquent. She loved this about him. Love. The word had not been spoken yet to each other.

Terrence showed her how to build a fire on a sprinkling of tobacco from the materials on the ground. He taught her the fire song. When the fire was hard to start, she sang it and sometimes it helped. When he sang, the fire started. It wasn't technology but the singing that made the difference. She had acquired the song, but it wasn't in her yet.

Sandra asked Terrence: "Is it good to be naked or clothed before the fire?"

He said, "It doesn't matter. Fire sees right through you when it burns away all your impediments. To fire, you are a breath that will bring it to light."

They were in the tent as in a den. Not hibernating, but secluded. It was so quiet, she began to feel the global tremors. More and more, she felt tides and the sun's energy. Sometimes she thought she felt the stretch of the moonrise, its drift cross the night sky and the yoga of setting. The new moon was a ping like an egg leaving her ovary. She was a stringed instrument the wind played, the Earth vibrated in her. What had been intermittent became frequent. She had never had words for these sensations. She had not understood their meanings.

"If the Earth is alive," she began tentatively. Hosteen spoke of the Earth in this way.

Terrence put his hand on the small of her back. Gentle. Holding her up. Listening. Terrence's added slightly, almost indiscernible pressure on her back, meeting her exactly, responding to the increase in equally indiscernible tremors so that his touch continued to be consoling, if imperceptible.

Earth's pulse. Or the Earth's swirl on its axis. Or the suction and slide of the magnetic poles shifting. A windstorm. A tornado. A series of multiple sensations, as if she were in weather itself. All of it. He held her so she let herself sink into the center of it. She was the axis and everything turning around her.

But then she was taken by a stab of nausea followed by dizziness and the fear that the Earth was buckling under her. Earthquake, landslide or tsunami somewhere. These were common enough, any might be occurring and so she was perceiving them within her. Or an aerial bombardment, a pipeline exploding, a nuclear plant leaking. Drilling, taking out the life blood. Mining causing huge abscesses. Iridescent pains, knives jabbing in sequence. Or the sensations of thorns growing into her flesh, and then fevers taking her, her skin blackening under her soft shirt until she shook with sudden cold. In contact with her, he felt it all as well, his hand burning then turning to ice. He could not flinch or withdraw. Dread. Then woe. Still, as she was willing to experience it all on behalf of the mother, so was he. Alongside the pain, the wonder of the continuity.

"If the Earth is alive ..." she was going to dare to go further ... "if Earth is alive ...if Earth is our ... *Mother!* ...."

Sandra's thoughts, jagged and breathless as they were, continued. Sandra was in the space between breaths where everything is and nothing moves. Awe. Suddenly, despite or through the pain, it was clear — Earth was alive and Earth was The Mother.

Sandra had a mother! She stood up. She stood up straight to contain the quivering that was overtaking her. She had a mother. The Mother was alive!

Then came the avalanche of bereavement. Devastation. She moaned. Her eyes rolled back into her head as she shook and wailed. Tearing, stabbing, explosive burning pain as all the ways the Earth was being violated were enacted inside her.

The great weight of knowing without being able to mitigate, to save, to change, overwhelmed her. Almost greater than the agony of knowing, of seeing clearly, was the anguish of being helpless. She was living a myth. She knew this myth. This was the story of Cassandra. The one who saw the devastation coming and her warnings went unheard. The one who knew. The raped one.

She groaned, "Cassandra." So, her name had been prescient! What she had tried to set aside, obscure, evade was now central. Cassandra was her core. Her father had known. He could not protect her, he could only name it, so, in time, she would know.

She wept and Terrence wept as they collapsed onto the floor. They had both wanted to begin their lives together in nakedness, and down they had gone, as if they were being skinned. Everything they knew about the burning, melting, injured, poisoned world was here between them. His breath in her ear, his sobs and then words, words she didn't understand. He was praying. His instinct. Praying to the mother. Praying to the injured mother. That she might hold them. That the mother might hold Cassandra. The name, an explosive. He softened it, "Sandra, Sandra, Sandra." His gentle hands stroking her hair. He was praying without even knowing he was praying in the way one speaks to the mother as if speaking to oneself, as if there is no division. After a time, he felt Sandra's body relax slightly, her posture ease. She had met the mother. The broken, besieged, agonized mother was holding her up.

16

Love Between Strangers

They were trying to find their way. There were no known paths. The more they knew, the deeper and darker the unknown loomed. Climate change was not merely a subject to be studied, while one's life continued in conventional ways. Climate change meant living in the whirl or threat of ongoing rain storm, fire storm, hail and lightning, flood and drought. Risk was constant. The entire world and all the interconnected events were their focus. In such a short time in human history, it was becoming clear to everyone that no walls, barriers or borders could keep them separate from others. Drones and satellites above, hungry, thirsty coyotes, bears, even mountain lions coming down into urban areas. No wall or shelter between any nation states would prevent the wind or water from sweeping in where it willed. They examined each other's faces for clues: Is this the end or are we beginning again?

Sandra, like others, had had to know climate change – in her bones – before she grasped the magnitude of what was occurring. As soon as Sandra entered graduate school, she no longer doubted her calling. She wanted, as she had wanted as a girl, to doctor the Earth. Sometimes she thought of it as her assignment.

Sitting with Terrence, Sandra traced the idiosyncratic route she was taking regarding work.

"Your work now?"

"I don't care about it much. But I don't think it does much harm. What I hate about it is that I have to use a cell phone a lot, which interferes with the bees and birds. All those road kills are birds who have lost their direction.

"So now, I'm an environmental consultant to a large housing development that's a mixture of private and government funding. It's an experiment. It's not so different from what you do. You have to create the budget and everything that goes along with that, all the limitations. Not opportunities, limitations. Whatever I suggest has to conform to the budget first, then to government regulations and investment considerations. But still, I'm there to bring everything into the picture so they can choose: wind energy and solar, thermal heating, green spaces and corridors. I get to dream about balance: condors, kit foxes, cougars, migrating birds, butterflies, local farming, community gardens, permaculture, water conservation …. What's going to be interesting is considering the relationship of the project to the original landscape, the history of the local Indigenous people, the original fauna and flora and then the potential dangers of pollutants upstream, our polluting downstream … all of it. I'm the environmentalist, archeologist, anthropologist, engineer …. They brought in one consultant – I'm it. The argument for wilderness engages me. Not more manicured green spaces and golf courses; I want to preserve the wild. We'll see. The developers want to overview me. I'm going to give them an overview from an eagle's perspective."

"And here you are living …"

"Living in a tent. It's my R and R.

"Sometimes I take a job because it pays and the work I really want to do can't pay." She shrugged. He was aware of the moving graceful line of the silky ivory fabric of her blouse rippling from her shoulders across her breasts. Like water, he thought.

"A friend was involved in a long research project and she wanted to travel. So I took it on and when she returned …"

"…you went back up north to consult with some of the tribes. And they paid you in …"

"Stories."

"Which ones?"

She laughed and waved her index finger at him, "Can't tell unless the time is right and the purpose clear and I have their permission. You know that."

"And so what good are they if they remain secret." He was challenging her and she appreciated this combat. It confirmed that they were peers.

"What good are they, Terrence?" She pretended to contemplate this question. And then she answered as if contemplation had revealed something she hadn't known. "They are activated each time they are told or remembered." She spoke slowly but with increasing assurance. "They work on my mind. I begin to think differently and respond differently. Hmm. Maybe I respond like a fisherman might respond, not a city girl." This was interesting to her as she began to realize the truth of it. The stories had been working on her, changing her mind since she had been up there.

A smile lit up her face just as the sun emerged from a cloud and met her light. They both twinkled from the coincidence. "The stories have prepared me for this. For you, Terrence."

"For us?"

"Yes, for us."

"And how is that, Sandra?" He wasn't intending to trick her. The professor's habit of nudging the student forward to insight. He couldn't always leave himself behind.

"When the stories are in me, I know that every step I take up there, and maybe even here, because of who I am and where I was born and how I was educated, every step melts a little bit of snow in their region.

"Slush," she continued. "You know what it looks like. Snow sliding into water, mixing with the soil and the dirt from the shoes, the imprint of the sole on the snow, gray ice crystals melting. We are slush makers, that's who we are. Now do you want to know the stories, Terrence?"

"Of course, I do but not to make slush. But I will probably absorb enough of them from being with you, Sandra. In the meantime ..." he raised her hands to his mouth and kissed them. He had the quality of every large mammal she had ever seen — enormous strength and power blended with the most exquisite tenderness. The carving of the mantic owl, her wings outspread to protect her fledglings. And so she could say what was true for her.

"I want to doctor the Earth. Yes, hands-on healing. I can see injury everywhere. Just like you do; you taught me well. The patient is right here in front of us, Terrence, and we are sharing our doctoring with several billion people who are also making her sick.

"So where do I put my hands, Terrence?"

He took her hands in his. Many lines, many stories, crossed her palms. He wanted to know them all. She took her left hand back and ran it down his arm. He watched while her eyes were closed. When he closed his eyes as well, he could discern when she was investigating, when she was sending energy. Then she withdrew more suddenly than he had expected. He was a human. She wanted to bring relief to the soil.

Given the causes of climate change, he was thinking, it was ludicrous to expect that the same perpetrators would want to employ people at significant salaries to work more than forty hours a week to remedy that which would mean change. He had been counseling his students with limited confidence in regard to their future work. The too familiar goal of making a standard living to support a standard life style continued as if the right to it was carved in stone, notwithstanding that it was entirely contradictory to the evidence in the field that the intensifying winds would reduce that rock to sand far sooner than anticipated. Finding a stable livelihood wasn't how he had been trained to think by his grandparents but he managed it for his position. What had he expected of Sandra? It had been ten years. She had been unusual, he had probably imagined she would carve out a route no one else could follow. And he had been right.

"Does it matter that I didn't pursue a prestigious appointment?" she asked.

"Not at all," he answered.

The coffee they were drinking was strong, creamy and sweet. They agreed they both liked it that way. They were finding they liked many of the same things, and that they didn't disagree very much – that mattered to Sandra. It alleviated the ongoing surprise, astonishment actually, that they were living together and partnered. He brought her his black sweatshirt. The afternoon breeze was coming up as the sun began to dip. She would feel chilled soon and he was amused that she liked to wear his things. When she wasn't sleeping naked, she slept in one of his shirts. It was, she said, like entering into his very center, covering herself with his essence.

"I never found the ongoing work that could meet the situation. That could meet ..." she gestured with her hands 180 degrees.

It wasn't easier to hold tragedy together. Alone, they might compartmentalize, meeting the moment, reading what was required, working hard enough to fall asleep quickly when they came home from work, or only considering the research that related to a particular area or focus. But together, the globe, its beauty and its suffering was always and entirely between them. Each other's presence, however, the fact of their alliance and concern, supported them in meeting what was coming toward them and everyone else: The glaciers were melting, the sea level was rising, 146 dead zones in the ocean had been counted, one covering 27,000 miles and one species after another was going extinct because of hunting, urban development, agriculture, loss of habitat, pesticides ... the golden toad, the Zanzibar leopard, the Javan tiger, the Pyrenean ibex, the black rhinoceros... bats and bees endangered worldwide and so, potentially, the food supply, increasingly threatened by drought, fire and flood.

"What do you tell your students, these days," she asked.

"Simple. Everything we are doing and the way we are doing it must change. I know they can't face everything, so I have them examine, at the least, what they would alter or transform in their own specialty, and what radical shifts their particular specialty demands – if they are honest. I do suggest they consider what, from their perspective, might stabilize the environment. What's their particular role?" He was thinking aloud, reflecting on what, in fact, he was doing.

"It all sounds so simple," he continued, "when I first ask them to consider it. But when they get into it, overwhelm enters. But I can't spare them what is happening and it is going to be in their hands."

"And that paper on paper, in fact, do you assign it still?" she asked.

"Yeah. They don't have to do any original thinking, just calculations: How much paper are they going to use in their academic or professional life and how many trees will it require? Do you remember? You had to imagine the books you might write, the number of pages in each, the numbers of each book published, as well as articles in professional journals, and the books and periodicals you might buy."

"I think you stopped short of toilet paper."

"Well, the university now contributes money to plant trees for each ream of paper we use in the offices. 16.67 reams of paper from one tree. 480 to 450 pages in a ream. Of course we use recycled paper, but as this doesn't account for all the paper uses, they have gone along with it. I put one of the student papers in with my proposal. It had been submitted in a small typeface, 10 pt font, printed single-spaced, with narrow margins and double-sided. One just assumed, he hadn't printed out an extra copy. He made a few corrections by hand. The young man had not only calculated the amount of paper he might use, but slipped in the various "costs" of conflict minerals in lives, arms and pollution, that were used in the university's computers. The Dean passed the paper around at our next meeting and now we literally replant forests. I call it writer offset instead of carbon offset. It's a miniscule offering."

One night she asked him, "How do you bear it?

"I can't." He answered in the kind and steady voice he used with students. "Sometimes, the simple task of assigning a paper and reading twenty of them, or giving a lecture, no matter how dire the material, or going to a meeting, even the tedious, or especially the tedious task of preparing a budget, distracts me enough to feel I have survived the day. Sometimes it's reassuring. It deludes me into thinking we will somehow go on and on and on."

She had awakened the agitation that was buried in routine. The familiar and regular nature of a teaching position was sometimes insanely reassuring or numbing, thus bringing some relief, like the intermittent drizzles that falsely convey an end of the drought, to the inherent loneliness and desolation he experienced otherwise.

"And you know, Sandra, the view from my air-conditioned office is completely beautiful. And when I look out, I am not in the part of the country likely to see the dark churning of a tornado sucking everything in its path into the black furnace of its belly." He leaped up and kicked the base of the nearby oak, hard.

Now the tornado was in the space between Sandra and Terrence. That's what their partnering was accomplishing. What they had previously compartmentalized, what they had neutralized or suppressed, arose between them, dangerous and real. Everything was with them and they were sucked into it.

"Let's go inside," he said, as he turned abruptly to wash the rest of the dishes from their evening meal.

"Can I help?" she asked.

"No one can help," he was firm and clear.

"Are you sure?"

"Oh yes." He was.

They engaged in their separate bedtime rituals. She went to the outer bathroom and then he followed. "Why not go in the house and take a hot shower?" she asked.

"The equivalent of a cold shower, to cool down?"

"Maybe, just for the pleasure of it."

"It's not part of our agreement."

"If I said, I needed a hot shower, what would you say?"

"I'd say, wouldn't you like to take a hot bath? I'll run the water for you and wash your back."

"And so?"

"And so, it still isn't part of our agreement."

She had thought it would be best for each of them to be in their own silence. But when he came to the bed, she put down her book and reached her arms out to him. "I don't think I can," he said so quietly she thought he might be suppressing tears. "When I hold you, there are no barriers between me and the Earth. I can feel all the suffering of the Earth — here at my fingertips, through your body."

And he was right. She was trembling. And so what was he to do? He took her in his arms.

Yes, everything was with them and in response they had the morning fire and the evening fire and the moon in the moon roof and the windows opened wide to the winds and then the tent sealed, all the wind and rain protections, rain fly, double seamed flaps, vents, windows, doors, in place and closed. Still, everything, and no safety offered in the path of a cyclone or a mudslide such as they experienced internally. Their inner worlds were in states of violent flux like the weather. They had become for each other the forces of upheaval and creation.

The next morning she asked him, "Those papers we were talking about that you assign at the end of the four years, do you ever read them?"

"Every word," he said.

"Why?"

"To see if the students took the assignment seriously, if they did the work as diligently as they would for an academic journal, if they wrote it themselves or just read a few articles and rolled them into one."

"You could get a teaching assistant to check all of that."

"Yes, but I wouldn't know if anyone discovered anything, if anyone set themselves the task to do the assignment because they wanted to know as badly as I do."

"Want to know if there's hope?"

"Something like that."

"I don't think they will find hope that way."

"It's why they came to study, so they may as well try."

It was close to the end of the semester. She had cooked dinner though he had refused ribs. "Cows fart too much," he said. "Methane. Between the cows and the melting permafrost in Siberia and Alaska … ?" He had started off jocular but the real danger overtook him.

"Soon there won't be anything left for us to eat," he stated somberly.

"Maybe that's the best solution." Quick with the quip, Sandra was trying to keep the conversation light although real.

Probably Terrence hadn't found a lot of hope or integrity in the student papers as he was unusually gloomy. "Maybe you could teach them other things than what is in the curriculum," she continued.

"Sandra, are you thinking of TEK again?"

"Yes, but not teaching about TEK but living it. You're TEK, you know."

"Might have been. But no, I'm not. You may be better at it than I am."

She swatted him but he caught her arm. "I think I know what Hosteen might say. And maybe you are thinking the same thing. You're not sure, Terrence, that your people should speak of what they know."

"Because no one cares, Sandra. Nothing will come of it."

"I once asked a friend why he was studying the old fishing rituals?" said Sandra. "He said that he had promised the salmon he would help to unwind the curse that was poisoning their water."

"Was he working in my territory?"

"On the Columbia River. He always ate fish. They were his friends, he said. I guess that's the way a taboo works, you either don't eat your kin or you eat your kin. Like the Bear clan, they eat bear. He said, he made it a point to eat the salmon no matter the danger."

Terrence understood immediately. "When you go up and down the river at night, you might see the fish hanging on a line by the house to dry for winter food. How do you see them? Because they glow. They're radioactive. Did your friend talk about this, Sandra?"

"No."

"What did he talk about?"

"Just about trying to learn the rituals. He was trying to figure out what they had been before the dams were built. Looking at some of the myths. Asking around."

"Did anyone tell him?"

"Oh no, Terrence. You know they wouldn't. I didn't see what good would come for the waters from his knowing the rituals. I didn't say anything to him."

"I suppose," Terrence said, "that those who still know the old ways won't speak about them. The anthropologists claim everything will be gone unless they find out and save them in books or museums. But I'm not convinced. I hope the people won't speak but will preserve everything themselves, but many Native people are so devastated, we don't know if they will resist. And the white man's desire to know and help is so seductive," Terrence paused, "and, sometimes, seemingly lucrative."

Sandra didn't know absolutely, if Terrence was talking to one of his own or to a white woman when he spoke of white men. She didn't want to ask and tried to intuit his intention. She looked at him directly, his expression was benign. There were no barriers between them. She could recognize the changes that had occurred since they had first encountered each other. Hadn't she also come to him wanting to know?

"Despite my studies, Terrence, or because of my studies, despite Hosteen, I didn't understand until you and I met."

"What do you understand now?" He didn't know where she was leading.

The conversation had, as it so often did, led to something she hadn't considered even though she thought she had. Her response was tentative.

"There are things you will never let me know." As she spoke these words, she felt the weight of their reality. She was not a Native woman and could not become one by marriage or alliance. This would be an ongoing challenge; she must never try to learn what was prohibited to her. Held in the wrong container, the wisdom or ritual might be damaged. In order to honor Terrence and his people, actually, to help protect the rituals, she had to keep her distance.

Terrence had that expression on his face that appeared when he was thinking deeply about something. He would not answer at all if he weren't certain about his response. They had both assumed they would find their way to each other without impediment, even or especially the impediment of coming from different peoples.

Maybe she wanted him to praise her for understanding and caution. Knowing it was right to step away from what might be most significant for him also bonded her to him. He stepped back a little to study her face, wondering how she could know this? At moments like this he thought she might be both a sister and a lover. Flesh of his flesh. Then he saw that trap. She was speaking heart knowledge; there was a space between them they should never traverse. He must not dissuade her. He had been away from his ritual heritage for a long time and, accordingly, there were teachings he would never receive even if he began to walk the path. The same with her. Despite his growing love, despite their sense of destiny, there were situations he couldn't spare her, conditions from which he could not protect her. The world would never be set right, even between them.

Sorrowfully, he tried to redirect the conversation: "What else do you understand now?"

"That you can't learn everything in a day or a year or from a book or even from observation and experience or from asking an elder to teach them to you. That's another reason they didn't tell my friend the stories or teach him the rituals. You learn over centuries. Hosteen teases my father about the 'efficacy' of a thirty-year trial of a medication – and you can't get that these days. Hosteen says, a hundred years or thirty hundred years in one location will tell you something. Maybe, he says, if you are reliably skilled you will learn what you need from a dream. My father laments testing that is reduced to a year or two. Ten years is considered a run long enough to trust. Thirty years? Three hundred years? Without that kind of time learning them, the rituals aren't going to work. That's what you think, isn't it?

"Sometimes, that's what I think."

"So that's why you don't teach TEK, because it takes lifetimes."

"Something like that. But sometimes … time expands. We've been together how long?

"About sixty days."

"And as many lifetimes."

She sat down on the ground and leaned back against him. "So you can't teach me anything, is that right? I mean," she sighed, "you can't teach me anything important." She meant the sacred. "Is that right?"

"Yes, but not quite. You are learning a lot by yourself. Also the ancestors are teaching you. Between us, we create the conditions for understanding. For both of us. So much comes through you …"

They were sitting around the metal fire pit outside the tent. An unexpected late spring drizzle had dampened the ground and they relished the particular fresh scent of wet earth, rosemary and sage, and the pepper of wood smoke. Each morning, when they could, when weather and schedules allowed, they met in this way. Terrence had offered tobacco.

"This is how the Bushmen start the day," Sandra said, "Only they smoke cigarettes."

"Still?" Terrence asked, meaning the morning fire ritual.

"Still. Yeah, they still smoke, Terrence, but everything is endangered. For the few that still live in the bush. Sometimes they can call rain, even if they haven't been able to close down the diamond mines and keep their land.

"Did they teach you?" he asked.

"You can't learn it. You have to live it." They fell into their own thoughts.

"You have to live it." She repeated the words he had said to her earlier, "But you know that, Terrence."

"I once did." He always allowed spaces between his thoughts for something else to emerge. "Ironic, isn't it, that I'm in a teaching profession. My grandfather taught me a lot, but not through formal schooling or lecturing."

"Did my dissertation help you 'out' yourself?" Sandra teased.

"What do you mean?" He was puzzled.

"Well, it was received and I got the degree while you virtually recused yourself. Maybe you had foreknowledge of our current connection and couldn't support or challenge my dissertation choice if we were going to be partners. So my 'very independent' research may have given some legitimacy to TEK."

"And TEK to me?"

"Maybe." She paused, "Why not?"

"It isn't called TEK anymore, you know. TEKW – probably sounds the same. Some sympathetic scholars have added Wisdom.

"You've really changed," she noted. "And you're still the professor."

"I never had the option of being mediocre so the professor had to en-grain itself in my bones. Sorry, sometimes I forget and start pontificating. A really bad habit. With your help I'll keep edging toward myself."

Rain on the canvas roof had awakened her. An intimate way to be with the elements. Terrence jumped out of bed and quickly started the fire in the stove. He always set it the night before so that it would only require a match as she had done in her house. How easy it is, she thought, to live in this way. She was holding the quilt and bearskin open for him; how easy it is when it isn't necessary to talk. How much more was said without words.

She hadn't expected it to be easy with a man who'd had a plastic liner for ink pens in his shirt pocket. Without words, memory looped in images. The way the wind had come up that first evening in the desert when he wrapped her within his jacket, the way he had slid under the bear skin the first night and wrapped her into him, the way he slipped toward her now and drew her to him in one gesture. That he folded himself around her so she was at the core.

"You hold no bitterness to me," she noted. It wasn't a question or a challenge. A statement. "You could, as a man, be wary of me as a woman." But that is not what she meant. There was nothing in his way of being that indicated any fear or anxiety about women. Well, she thought, maybe those are cultural responses. "You hold no bitterness to me as a white woman." It was necessary to be blunt.

"Our ancestors will have to work it out," he said. She understood that five hundred years of history might never be erased. It had been inscribed onto his flesh, grandfather, father, Terrence, in turn, sometimes literally with a whip. Such scars handed down over the generations remain scars. He did not perceive bitterness in her either. She wasn't wary of him as a Native man.

As if reading his mind, she said, "I feel entirely safe and protected with you."

"Entirely, Sandra?" It wasn't a question so much as a consideration.

She braced. Didn't he believe her?

She saw that he believed her. It was something else. "You don't trust yourself, is that it?" she asked. There was something in the tent that wasn't there before, that had slipped in as a snake might, through an infinitesimally small opening. It moved like a snake might, but in the air, an eddy of energy, like a whip flicking. He had felt its bite sometime in the past, this she knew in this moment.

She had almost fallen into a trance when he went out into the rain as the light was inching toward day and came back with his dark hair loosened from his braid, falling straight past his shoulders. She was startled and for the first time, she felt afraid. He was letting something loose, she hadn't seen before. Suddenly, he was a stranger. Unpredictable. Now his past entered the room. Now history. Not only his personal history, but history itself. And so her history. He had only a towel around his waist. "You're afraid," he said facing her directly.

"Yes." They were past any possibility of dissembling with each other.

Something she didn't know or recognize was released in the room. "The scar by your ribs?" she asked though she had seen it every night since they were together.

"A knife," he said.

Seeing her fear, understanding its origins, he approached her directly. He tore the bearskin away, pulled off the quilt. He didn't make love to her, he fucked her; he kept himself separate. There was a space between their chests. She kept her eyes open, on alert, and so did he, challenging her. She put her arms back on the pillows, held on to nothing, the gesture was simultaneously submissive and daunting. There was no permission given, there was no withholding. He was riding her. If they had not been facing each other, she might have thought of them as horses, but she didn't feel the congruity of the mating between stallion and mare. He can kill me, she thought but did not bring down her hands to cover herself. Maybe she raised her chin a little, then more, her neck exposed, and arched her back, testing or taunting him. It was when the orgasm began and she let it take her without holding on to anything, that he demanded, "Trust me. Give yourself to me." She didn't know if it was age or culture which gave him the authority. It pissed her off. Then came the convulsions and her determination to allow them without comfort. Her way of retrieving herself. She would not capitulate to him. She would not name this pleasure. She could only call it earthquake as there was nothing to be done. And he, straddling her, seated as on the mare she imagined, heard her insist through clenched teeth, "Trust me!" as he convulsed without gathering her to him. His eyes still locked into hers so she did not look away. So they assessed each other's mettle, each other's strength.

And in this way, it was done.

And then it wasn't done yet.

17

This Is How Dark It Is

"I dreamed the Earth." They were in the tent. In the last weeks they had gone down to bare bones with each other. She wanted to know the history of his body. He shrugged his shoulders, and she decided not to probe though he wanted to know her body in the same way. She didn't have scars. Life had been kind to her. What she had thought was a permanent scar of loneliness was fading away.

"No injuries?" he asked.

"A few ankle sprains running down hill. I'm not a competitive runner so when I hurt, I just stop or slow down. My father didn't care. He didn't need to get anywhere. We could run around in a circle for an hour if that were the only possibility, he wouldn't mind. You could say he prepared me to run in the moccasins you made me."

She had to decide if she was going to let the conversation veer away from the dream that was really disturbing her. Meanwhile, he was quick to observe her mood and her terse statement had alerted him. Something important was going to be said.

"You remember Stevenson's thought experiment, where he speculated about blasting his way to the Earth's core. He had a sense of humor. He called it "A Modest Proposal," after Jonathan Swift mocking harsh British policies in Ireland by suggesting that the Irish alleviate their poverty by selling their children as meat to the English ….

"Stevenson said it was a 'thought experiment,' but you know, these days, there is no thoughtful process that distinguishes between a harebrained idea and its inception, so who knows …. Stevenson started out imagining a thermonuclear explosion to blast a crack several hundred meters deep and then pour 100,000 tons, probably more, of molten iron into the crack to propagate the crack downwards to the core, with a probe at the bottom of it all being pushed down by the iron sealing above it and sending information back. If I say it feels like being raped with a laser while molten metal is being poured in to seal the wound, I am only getting close to the pain of it."

She couldn't stop talking. It was as if she was digging down with a jack-hammer, trying to get to a place where she could stop. "I never stop thinking about it, glad I didn't specialize in geology, as I never would have survived all the digging and probing. I prefer seismographs. They are a parallel record of the Earth's trembling and I can feel the vibrations pretty accurately myself when they aren't too faint and far away."

"You always feel the strong ones as I've come to know," he said as he began listening to her again.

"Yes," she admitted, "the Earth quakes, the machine quakes, and I quake. I like the parallel."

"Last night in the dream," her voice was strong, "I was journeying into the Earth as far as one could go. It seems it was possible, maybe for anyone, even any tourist, to go to the place where the molten core of the Earth had broken through into the crust, where some human action or experiment had breached what should have always remained an inviolable separation. Science has no council of elders to decide what might or might not be explored. So anyone can do anything, if he gets the money. Clearly, neither he nor the money lenders have to be wise.

"I learned that there was a place where the very different atmosphere of below was entering our environment above. Someone had created the breach. We were sinking down into it as well. I went to the place where we were able to descend to witness what we have done. There was probably a fee so someone could make money from the peep show of what might end everything. There had been a terrible rupture as a result of certain experiments. All the consequences were still unknown, but, you know, people, scientists, Europeans, Americans, some first world nations were responsible.

"I had to go. I had to bear witness.

"I followed a dirt path down into a mountain. It then became a paved walkway that led to a black door that opened into a familiar commercial enterprise as one would find in a train terminal, but everything on a slant, descending. There were bathroom facilities and anterooms with vending machines and meeting rooms emptying downward into other raked meeting rooms with tables or desks in concentric circles. Naturally, it was all windowless and brightly lit by tubular ceiling lights. Everything was very hygienic and neat. Perhaps even cheerful in the way of plastic, Formica and chrome.

"I sat down next to a man who seemed knowledgeable but he would not answer any of my questions though his refusal was not initially apparent. He was responding as if he were cordial, as if we might even know each other, might be colleagues, and yet he would tell me nothing of what had happened or what I might expect. This room was slightly darker than the others, not because the lights had been dimmer, but because the dark was more intense due to the descent. Those of us who had come this far were closer to what we were seeking, to where we were determined to go. Our desire to see this, to bear witness was not what was causing the disturbance to the core. But maybe it was.

"We were seated at one of many slightly curved, bean shaped school desks in one of several concentric semicircles. It became apparent that he was not another tourist but an official whose job it was to say nothing. Even though the room was darker than the others above it, it was still too bright, fluorescent. The floor was tiled with squares of gray linoleum. The chairs and tables were molded plastic. I vaguely remember them in pale shades of blue, pink, gray. Very faint. They were in concentric rows. It was not how I had ever imagined it, but I realized I was descending through the rings of hell.

"I got up, like someone who is fulfilling a sentence of hard labor, and went further down. I came upon a platform designed for entertainment at the base of a room. Completely ordinary, it felt final. A local band had just played a set and another would soon replace them. A thin, worn yellow cotton curtain was pulled across the stage. It was makeshift and tawdry; I became alarmed. Then I saw an exit behind the stage. The entertainment had been designed to distract those who had come so far from going further. But I had come to see this to the end.

"I opened a door to the right of the stage and found myself outdoors in a dark woods on an incline going down and down and further down. Natural paths meandered in between the trees and underbrush. It was dark, but neither day nor night. There were no stars. There was no light, natural or artificial. The darkness was. Except that lines of fire emerged from the Earth in different places. Perhaps these enabled us – I assumed there were others here – to see. The trees and brush did not seem to be burning despite the fires that were emerging in lines, as from inside the roof of various berms that were also aligned in concentric circles, but far more unruly than the furniture in the building where I had been. The fire in the center of Earth had broken through. This eruption was not volcanic. These fires were from a deeper core, far beyond lava. They came toward us like froth from a wave. The eruption had been deliberately released. This was ominous. I don't know who released it or if it had determinedly released itself. The Earth was so dark we have to say the dark Earth. Then we can say there were fires lapping at the edges, as from a lava field, but without lava. The fire was rising up, a fire such as I had never seen, wave after wave, animate, then slipping back into its angled crevice, like an animal into its hole.

"But awful as this was, it was not what I had come to see and witness. Something else, even more horrific, unimaginable, not quite visible, perhaps invisible, had occurred. Something we might not comprehend if we came upon it, so extreme was it. These fires might have been a consequence but the breach, the violation, was further away. Down, down, down.

"Perhaps it was not possible to see what has occurred. Perhaps, it was not visible. There was a place where some destructive environmental change has taken place at the border, twenty, fifty, a hundred, maybe five hundred, a thousand miles down between the inner core and the crust where we live. Perhaps so far down it was where the fire of the Earth is said to be the same temperature as the sun. We have never gone beyond 7.6 miles – the Russian Kola hole – it took twenty-two years – and they stopped. Now this ….

"I stopped and stood still. The dark and the heat – were disorienting. There were paths but they didn't lead anywhere. Fire was coming to my feet. Still there was something even more awful, the place of violation …. But I didn't know how to get to it. If I stayed here, I would soon be consumed. And that place that was calling me was hotter still, was beyond heat. A vaporizing presence that had its own inexplicable form and power. The planet had been changed irrevocably. There would be consequences we could not imagine.

"I woke up.
"What have we done, Terrence? What are we doing?""

PART III

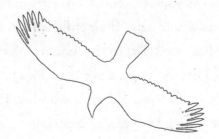

STONE HEAPS OF THE nCHE-WANA

Long time ago, Indian boys were sent to the mountains by their
father, or next of kin. Maybe it is an old man, a good hunter, a great
warrior or medicine, who sent the boy. The boy stays two or three
nights in a lonely place. He must not drink water he must not eat
food. He must pray and call on the Ruling Spirit. He must not sleep,
but after a time he will fall down and sleep. He then sleeps; hears
strange things. The boy piles up stones so that his people will know
that he has been there. Perhaps such are the stone heaps you saw on
the summit of the boulders along the nChe-wana.

Heard from Joe Tuckaho, Nez Perce, on July 5th, 1922

THOSE STONE HEAPS

Those stone heaps you ask about! They are made this way. Years
ago, the old Indians would send their children, their little boys when
about ten and twelve years old, to the mountains to stay seven days
and seven nights. The boy made a pile of stones ….

Sometimes there is an old man who has lost all his people.
He feels lonely; he is sad. He goes up and down the mountain somewhere. He builds up stones. He sits there and cries for he is alone in
the world. In this way were many of those stone-heaps made. The
white man should not tear them down.

Heard from Tom Hill, warrior of the Nez Perce War of 1877 on July 5th, 1911

156

18

IPCC and Mt. Hood

Autumn 2007. Terrence Green was at the foot of a mountain, of Wy'east, Mt. Hood. He was approaching the trail his ancestors had used for hundreds, perhaps thousands of years to pray, make offerings and do ceremony. He had not understood when he set out running from the office and jumping into his truck, taking off without a suitcase, what was driving him. He had his wallet, boots, moccasins, down vest, sweater, jacket, sunglasses. He did not take his computer. He had a pen and paper. He had his cell phone but turned it off. He had wanted to leave it behind but he didn't have absolute confidence in his vehicle. He was not naked but close enough by contemporary standards. He had an early copy of the IPCC report that had disturbed him so.

The 2007 IPPC report. The United Nations International Panel on Climate Change. The last one had been submitted in 2001. This international assessment of the reality of climate change is the most important official document of this time, he thought. Conservative and compromised as it was, it had been written by contributors from across the globe. It declared climate change as real. The Anthropocene as real. He knew what a courageous step it had been to confirm that the use of fossil fuels is responsible for the dangerous rise of carbon emissions in the atmosphere.

He had begun to read the report at home and then continued in his office. He came to a small paragraph among the more than 2,000 pages of the report and he stopped reading for a while and then continued to the end – altered. But it was not sufficient; he had to read that paragraph away from his office, away from brick, glass and steel. He had to read it on the land in order to absorb its implications. The content was not surprising, its inclusion was.

He read, "**9.6.2 Indigenous knowledge systems.** The term 'indigenous knowledge' is used to describe the knowledge systems developed by a community as opposed to the scientific knowledge that is generally referred to as 'modern' knowledge (Ajibade, 2003). Indigenous knowledge is the basis for local level decision making in many rural communities. It has value not only for the culture in which it evolves, but also for scientists and planners striving to improve conditions in rural localities. Incorporating Indigenous knowledge into climate change policies can lead to the development of effective adaptation strategies that are cost-effective, participatory and sustainable. (Robinson and Herbert, 2001)."

He had to read it as an Indigenous man, not as a scientist. He had never expected to find these references in an IPPC Assessment Report. Two worlds, the one into which he had been born, and the one that opposed it, but had kidnapped him, slammed into each other. He stood very still for a long time and then he began running, but not as a man running away, though he was running from his office, from the building, from a way of thinking and acting that he'd had to take on and fit into, from a mind and a style that had penetrated into his core like a poison, the way its poisoned breath, acid rain, penetrated into the leaves and roots of living beings who, unable to escape, tried to open to it even more in order to take in and separate its elements, in order to return it to its formerly neutral elements.

He was moving fast and steadily, as he had learned as a child. Running was memory. It was so steady, it could go on for hours or even days. The Earth turned and the people ran on it, turning with it.

He almost ran past his truck, which he chose to park in the furthest outside lot avoiding the fumes of the parking structures. If he were not in an urban area, he might have deluded himself that it was possible to run from where he was to where he needed to go now. Then he was on the road, driving as if he were running. He did not call anyone to say he would be gone. He did not call Sandra from the road. He just went.

At home, Sandra had watched him carefully as he was first reading the report. He paled, his eyes filled, he bit his lip. They had both known what would be in it, as well as how extremely it would be tempered to make it acceptable, having several colleagues who were working on various United Nations committees: Climate change is real and humans are responsible. Beneath the neutral and formal scientific language was another message that he and Sandra and certainly many others recognized. Our situation is grave. The damage is most probably irreversible. Unless … all life is doomed.

The goal of the report was to confirm what was obvious in order to inform those, particularly in government, who needed such confirmation to enact change, and those who would not encompass the new reality without such evidence, and to challenge the willfully ignorant but powerful who were devoted only to pursuing their own financial goals. At the same time it was necessary to prevent worldwide panic.

Terrence's people were familiar with meeting the worst contingencies in council and so with awareness. He did not find this resilience outside Indigenous communities in part, he thought, because non-Indigenous people were no longer living in vital and interdependent communities. The global transition from we to I was almost complete. The world to which he had been exiled was based on maintaining a state of fear and its members were constrained from acting together on their own behalf. He understood that despite being marginalized, Indigenous people had the ability and willingness to assess the world situation precisely – they were also the ones no one heeded. Instead, they would learn from the news that what they had long known was happening had been confirmed by science. Despite having been ignored, they would still retreat to the long house, pray through the night, and sit in council in the day. What new role might open to them on behalf of the Earth?

Terrence imagined trying to call such a council at the university. The dean would have to consider a budget. Why did he need a budget and administrative approval to take an action on behalf of the planet? It was all hopeless. Hopeless, Terrence realized, should not be in his vocabulary. Hopeless was not a word his grandfather would use. Hopeless does not coexist with the spirits. Nor does hopeful. Hope in any form turns us toward ourselves. "You do what you are called to do," his grandfather had instructed him. "Those other folk are always thinking about what they are going to get out of it."

Not hopeless, but still aware the world could end. Terrence struggled against the vortex of emptiness that was threatening to draw him down into parallel dimensions of subterranean oceans and fires. He could drown or burn. He preferred the exquisite pain of the auto-da-fé. He did not intend to privilege his own death. If the Earth was going to burn, he would burn with her.

Glancing over at Sandra, he saw the set of her jaw, her fingers trembling slightly as she turned the pages. They were a council of two. It would have to be sufficient.

Terrence had to read every word in order to fulfill his academic responsibilities and between every line to know what he had to know. Sandra was freer to choose which of the various panels she would read. They sat down to their tasks while each knew that the abstract filter of scientific language would not be sufficient to remove the implicit anguish and horror of knowing they were, humanity was, bringing the great and wild beauty that is planet Earth to an end. There had never been an evil as great as that which has been attacking all the living beings of Earth, and the two knew, that if only by the lives they lived, they were complicit. Their eyes continued to meet over the texts, then they lowered them and turned the pages.

He read as long as he could. Toward dawn he sat down in the north, hoping the ancestors would speak to him. They didn't. Then he got up and went to the office. He stood still looking out the window. This was not unusual for him, except he was standing there a very long time. Then he ran. Then he fled. Then he went forward.

In his tradition, in the past, one did not have to "telephone" and say one was going on a journey. The community would have known when the person knew. One did not need to send a runner. One did not need to send out emails. One did not need to leave a vacation message on a phone machine. He would be gone and the community would understand that he had left to find what could only be found alone and they would wait patiently for his return, praying for him. Recognizing he had to leave was a simultaneous event for the person and the community. That is just the way it was. Not fleeing. No foul play. A mission. Going on one's way. Halfway to his destination, he understood what he was doing differently. He was running away from the world he had inhabited and he was running toward.

He did not turn on the radio as he drove. Words repeated in his head and he couldn't clear them.

"Traditional Indigenous Knowledge.

"Traditional Indigenous Knowledge and Wisdom.

"Traditional Indigenous Knowledge.

"Traditional Indigenous Knowledge and Wisdom.

"Traditional Indigenous …."

They repeated, a chant, until he could no longer understand the words or how the world was vanishing, was going extinct. And so much beauty and wisdom with it.

And so he went on. Miles and miles. Light fell and night rose and light rose and night fell. As he had been trained, he went without sleep. Then he was at the river. Then he turned south again and east.

"Volcano," he murmured at the very first glimpse of the mountain from the twisting road, as if he could erase the feelings that were rising in him, churning the way the concealed molten rock was churning under the Earth, and replace them with facts and information, as if lecturing to undergraduate students in Geology 101. He had taught such a course several times even though it was not his field, filling in for another professor. But the words defining and describing a volcano that would have followed in a class didn't follow.

Reducing it as science does would be a violation. He came to the place he intended to leave his truck. The truck would be visible but not prominent. He could disappear without vanishing entirely.

Then he walked. He did not allow himself to describe the path even to himself. His steps had to be invisible so there would be no chance of the way being known by anyone except his Grandfather and Grand Uncle who were on the other side.

Finally, he was at the foot of the mountain having come here like a man on fire, exploring. Then, like a man emerging from a fog, remembering.

He came to the place of vision that he recognized, that he had known as a young boy, and so he stopped.

"Snow" and "Fire," he whispered to himself as he looked at the mountain he was remembering from childhood. "Mountain." He corrected himself, "**M**ountain." Yes, he had come here as a boy with his grandfather and his father's uncle. His grandfather had not spoken of Terrence's father, had not spoken of his own son then. Too many young Native men had died young or disappeared or suffered unbearable distortions of body and soul in the dark times. Still, the line of fathers behind Terrence, straight as the cedars from which they carved the guardian spirits of the land, was coming into focus. And, maybe, his own father, so long on the other side, was standing with them.

"Never forget this," his father's uncle had said, but his grandfather had said nothing, knowing the boy would have to forget because he would be sent away on behalf of the people. Would this moment come back to him at a critical point in his life? Whether Terrence would recognize it and remember would matter.

Only the **M**ountain itself, its presence on the landscape, that moment with Grandfather and Uncle on the mountain, the living imprint of ceremony performed upon Wy'east for thousands of years, was given to him to treasure and protect. Had he remembered? He had repressed it. It had slipped out of sight and was buried under the field of rubble formed by the debris and preoccupations of the dominant culture that had been claiming him.

If he were fortunate, if he had, wittingly or unwittingly prepared for this moment, if he was remembering, then it was like the sharpened bone with which a man would pierce his own flesh so that he could hang from the tree of the world and gain … what would he gain? Gain was not the issue. What would be the offering? In his mind, he thrust the bone of memory through his chest wall and wisdom and despair poured through him like blood.

His grandfather had known that they were entering into the darkest time of forgetting, erasure and eradication. Genocide of body, mind and soul. His grandfather had known the great pain. Foreknowledge did not prevent disaster. Understanding did not diminish the agony. They had fought for their land and lost. Losing was not the tragedy, losing to the ways of the white men was the tragedy. Had they lost the land to another tribe, it would not have destroyed their ways of life, would not have damaged the Earth. But having to fight the white men for the land was defeat from the beginning. Having to use weapons that were not their own, that were not coordinated with their sacred lives, undermined them and damaged the Earth beyond redemption. Having to fight, having to fight in the way they were required to fight, for the reasons they had to fight, being forced by war to think of land as property that could be stolen or conquered, was an anathema, but they fought anyway because they had to stand for the land.

"I left my land on my own," he told **M**ountain as he stood at its feet. "They didn't have to come and get me by force. I went on my own.

"'I was asked to go, it was assumed it would be of benefit, and I agreed. My acquiescence became my agreement, my choice."

He lowered his eyes, but truth required him to look forward.

He wanted to speak truthfully aloud. Without planning, he had come to this **M**ountain. Because it was a sacred place. Because he would know what had to be known here. An urgency such as he had never known had brought him.

He had his braid. He still had that, though he had been accused of sentimentality or display for keeping it. It had become his silent mnemonic. Once Sandra had offered to braid it for him and the chill of the forbidden went through him though her intentions were only loving. She had not understood the grimace of violation or loathing that had transformed his face beyond his own recognition. He had turned away from her, gone outside, relocated himself in his own heart and slowly, carefully, twisted red cloth into so tight a braid that he was aware of the pull on his scalp each time he moved his head.

He and she understood afterwards that like so many Indigenous peoples, he lived within a system of holy taboos that provided order in a chaotic world. For some members of Western culture, breaking taboos was exhilarating. He felt the wisdom of acquiescing.

"**M**ountain," he repeated, not in English, but in his original language. He spoke the sacred name as if he had never seen such a phenomenon before and also as if he remembered every detail of the time he had been brought here. Then he was on his knees, the lifeblood pounding heatedly in his body as his legs chilled from the frozen earth. He was on his knees, he was prone, his head was on the ground, he was weeping. Then he stood up as he had been taught, barefoot now. He looked around him and found stones and piled them up so he would remember that he had been here. As he remembered what his elders had known, he straightened up and looked **M**ountain in the eye. Steady. Steady ....

He had left all his identification in the truck. It would not be appropriate to come to this place with the dog tags of the alien world in which he lived. He had been recruited to live among the enemy on behalf of the land. Coming home to the **M**ountain, he had to return as himself. With every step, he had stripped himself of the acquired identity. What his Grandfather had thought might come to be; Terrence knew this as he revealed his face before the **M**ountain.

Afternoon. Sunset. Night. Moon rise. Starlight reflecting off the snowy peak. The **M**ountain saw him and he continued standing, looking at the **M**ountain.

He was in sacred time and sacred space. Even history ceased to exist. Everyone and everything vanished from his sight. Finally, he had arrived.

Sandra stirred restlessly in the tent when Terrence did not return from the University. His teaching assistant checked and saw Terrence's truck was not in its usual space and a parking attendant searched the area and attested that it was not in the lot or anywhere on campus.

They had both been reading the IPCC report and he had taken his volume with him when he went to the University. She could imagine that he had gone off to mourn and to pray. To honor that possibility, she stayed in the tent and read the report in more detail than she might have otherwise. She needed to share his ordeal. His ordeal? She was embarrassed to have thought she wasn't completely responsible. Let the ordeal be her form of prayer.

After two days, she lost the connection with him. Then she was a stranger in the tent, an intruder.

She was of the people who had created the Anthropocene, which some dated from the Industrial Revolution, and others calculated it from the Holocene, the Neolithic, the start of agriculture. Agriculture meant stores and property. Stores and property created power. Power meant fortification. Fortifications meant hierarchy. Property, power, fortification, hierarchy, conquest, war – the present.

Or it was dated differently: to the end of the eighteenth century and the beginning of the Industrial Revolution, the moment of James Watt's newly invented steam engine and the enormous expansion in the use of fossil fuels. No matter the cause or the time. It was here with its consequences.

She knew her people were culpable while his people and the Earth were among the victims. Now he had bonded with her, the other. He was carrying her within him, the way, inevitably, he carried his mother inside. He could not refuse them though it might also be a betrayal of history and his entire life to be one with them. Terrence and Sandra carried the same grief for the Earth and these times; they were both reeling from it. And they each carried different grief. The first had bonded them until this moment and now it seemed it was tearing them apart.

She couldn't stay here a moment longer. Looking around at her things so carefully placed in the space, she shuddered as if they had been strewn. Her thoughts stormed in her mind, the winds of doubt blasted her. She gathered up as much as she could in her arms and fled also.

When she arrived at her house, she brought everything inside, including her pail of earth, as if she would settle down here again, to fit into an old life as if she had never left. She opened all the windows. She still owned the house. She had not prepared it for sale. It had been their intention to sell – certainly they did not need so many houses, though they were concerned that the land would fall victim to developers. They were considering the options, how to restore the land to its own autonomy but neither she nor he had wanted to be preoccupied with real estate when they were just beginning to know each other. So as it was still hers, she could slip in as if returning from an assignment, from the Arctic or Africa. Or something more casual, a site visit to the development where she was consulting.

But she no longer belonged in this house. She was in limbo. It was not that she had been away, it was that she had entered another life. The house did not belong to her anymore or, rather, she did not belong to it. She was from somewhere else that was disappearing too. She paced the circular deck looking in the windows. Then she came into the house and circumambulated it similarly from within. It wasn't as if she hadn't been here recently, she had, but like a sojourner to an outpost. Now, supposedly, she was home again. The furniture was unfamiliar. She examined the curved andirons that were still in the fireplace, the fireplace tools that seemed ornate now, the bellows, the carved box that held firewood. They had been created with fashion in mind, with appearance. She had wanted a house that looked simple, not a simple dwelling.

Terrence had used a wood bench when he sat and stared into the fire. Terrence had thrown a blanket across a wood box so she could sit down next to him and stare into the fire. That had become natural and comfortable while the artifacts, the appliances that furnished her house, all seemed alien. They seemed to have a will of their own, calling attention to themselves. The house was declaring itself to her as worthy of a magazine display on simplicity. Four dimensions folded into two. She was being pressed into a given shape by the corners and angles of her possessions. Possessions. In the last months, the idea of possessions had left her. The spaces in between took her attention, as if she could see both time and space without concern for the events or objects that might occupy them. Earth had been her element, but Terrence had introduced her to motion, the elements of wind, water and fire. She had once wanted a solid house, a well-built house, dependable. A signature house. A house with things. Not many things, but things nevertheless. Signature things.

That was before she met Terrence. Thoughts of him began to assault her and she forced them away. She was not to fix him, to capture him, even in her mind. Now she was in the dissolve, the way one dimension morphs into another. Terrence had disappeared. Maybe he had shapeshifted. Maybe he had become wind. Maybe he had never been anything else. A storm had come and blown away her life. She turned and turned in the circle, but when she realized she was spiraling down into dread and fear, she stopped in her office, picked up the phone and called her father. It would not take him long to join her; he'd had no need to ask any questions over the phone.

While waiting for him to join her, Sandra went onto the roof and then onto the land. There, finally, among the trees, she settled down. Walking, well, not really walking, but pacing and then slowing down, then sliding down against a tree looking north because she felt he had gone in the direction of his people, land and ancestors, she found calm within herself. There was still a thread between them, thin though it was. She imagined what it might feel like for a spider to spin silk from the spinnerets on her abdomen and to let the thread waft in the faintest breeze, just a hint of wind, to attach where it must, there, wherever he was.

The palms of her hands flat on the Earth, looking up at the trees she had known so well, she was filled with the mystery of here and there. Had she abandoned this land in her rush to be with a human? This land and the land where she had been with Terrence, and Terrence, wherever he was, the thin silk of being emerging from her, honing in and attaching to him so the web could be woven that connected them. Crows flew into the pine and cawed. She had forgotten them. Her neighbors. She had been confused by notions of roads, miles, boundaries, highway markers, zones and designations, houses, property, real estate, but the true connections had never been interrupted or severed. The crows did not live in the bounded world. Her connection was with a terrain not a parcel and she shared that terrain with others. Then a raven entered the field uttering the round sound and hollow mating call that assured her that there would be others. The land enhanced and maintained by the presence of all the others; it could not exist without them.

Threads emerged from her abdomen and fluttered in the currents as they connected here and there, the web illuminated by the sun, flickered in and out of visibility as it stretched from a sycamore in the streambed by their tent to the branches above Sandra's head to Terrence wherever he was now. The tires from John's car crunched over the gravel in front of the house. Sandra got up so carefully not to impair the weaving that had gathered her in.

Dawn.
Terrence Green turned around to walk the seven miles back to his truck.

Terrence walked back from the **M**ountain with the same care with which he had approached the place of ceremony. His steps were heavy; he was carrying the **M**ountain with him. Until this moment, he had been a man of wind. It had allowed him to move the way he had, to leave one place for another. To be fleet footed. But now he, as others before him, would have to carry more than one spirit. Sometimes when his people were being initiated, they would be asked to carry the world. When one is asked, one cannot refuse. He remembered that **M**ountain had come when he was caring for Sandra. She and **M**ountain joined in his mind. He was weary. Her presence assisted him.

One slow, deliberate step after another. It was hard to stay erect, to keep from falling and tumbling down. A ponderous descent.

He was almost at the trailhead, not far from where he had hidden his truck, when he collapsed.

When her father arrived they repeated the pattern of standing and circling. First they stood helplessly in her house, then began moving from room to room, window to window, not knowing what to do, repeating the pattern. Sandra wanted to pace outside but she began to be afraid when night fell. She was not afraid of what might be in the dark. She was afraid of the inside of the house that was completely transparent to her from the outside.

Sandra answered the phone on the first ring. The woman said, "He told me to call you at this number, your home number. Yes, he was clear about it. He said, you would be home. He said, your father would be with you. He said, 'Drive.' He was adamant about this though speaking was difficult. He said, 'Set out going north.' He said, 'Tell her, no matter what, go north.' He asked us to call you again on your cell phone when we know where he will be taken. He said, he knew it would take you many hours. He said, you will have enough time. He made sure I understood. Again, he was certain but I am not sure I understand what he means."

"Anything else, did Terrence say anything else?" Sandra asked.

"No, but I think this is serious. He isn't conscious now."

When John Birdswell's wife, her mother, Samantha Crow, had died in the hospital, there had been no lack of enforced activities and then there was the baby to hold who was suddenly his entirely. As if from one belly to another, the child had disappeared into his great arms folded around her tiny body that immediately became the stake upon which he rested the rest of his life. Now he had to hold her up, but he had never seen her lean on anyone or anything but herself.

"We're cursed!" he bellowed as if the extent of his pain would be a sign of strength.

Unexpectedly, Sandra rebuked him but without knowing the source of her optimism, only its necessity. "He will be OK. That's what his message says." She had not expected such certainty to emerge from her. But in the moment, she was recognizing that "He will be OK," was part of holding a field of possibility within which recovery lived.

"You believe in possibility, don't you?" she dared him, certain that her faith was necessary and that their interaction could also make a difference.

"Yes," John murmured. "I believe in possibility." He said it quietly, a throwback to the years he'd had to modify his behavior on behalf of a child who was often asleep in his arms, slung across his shoulder, her mouth slightly open, fully, completely, absolutely, unconditionally trusting him. Now, as if compensating for the quiet days, he often bellowed around her, if not around his patients. His bedside manner was exuberant. His patients were reassured by his confidence in the medicine he offered and his simple love for anyone that came to him for treatment.

This was different. He recognized this immediately from Sandra's response. The tables were turned and he would have to follow her lead. He stepped back to look at her as she leaned on the counter. This was not a time for reflexive behavior. He took in her stance, her long, confident body so like his own. This was his daughter. He knew her as well as he knew anyone in this life. But at this moment, he didn't know her at all.

"He will be OK." These were not the words he had expected to hear. He echoed the words, reaching to copy the exact inflection so that he could incorporate its precise and profound meaning. More than understanding in its usual sense was implied though he had never considered understanding outside of language. He had to slow the phrase down because the words were like a moving car that were taking him somewhere he had never been, where, it seemed, his daughter, unbeknownst to him, had started to live. Not only new territory, distinct territory.

He stopped reviewing the few details that passed for medical information. He was not to consider worst and best scenarios. He was not to review the literature now or later. He was traveling, traveling down, descending into a terrain he had never traversed before. There was an enormous stillness around and within him. As if the entrance of any habitual thought would demolish this experience. Everything he was experiencing was wordless and he was required to keep it so. Thank God for meditation; he could do that, and realizing this, was quieted.

He had expected her to continue to pace wildly as she began to do for the first minutes after the phone call; such had always been her way when she was upset but then she stopped abruptly and meticulously filled her suitcase. Now she was still, a different person. Considering. Did she have what they needed? He did not recognize the stillness that was in her. In the hospital, no one was ever still during an emergency and there were always emergencies. The hospital was a field of frantic energies. Because she was not frenetic, he was not frenetic. It was as if she was filled with a power he did not recognize and it was ballast. He was contemplating his daughter as if she were a new patient, assembling signs without interpreting them. The aggregate simply was. A presence. There were no words for this in English. He wasn't sure there were words in any language. He was reminded of the posture Hosteen sometimes assumed in urgent situations, but not with intention. It came over him without his awareness. As if he were an eagle, a bear, a horse – that confident. It was a way of standing that was motionless despite others' external frenzy and chaos so it seemed that movement and gravity were creating a single arena of infinite being and Hosteen was of it. Now Sandra was subsumed in it and maybe, he, John, was entering it as well. For Hosteen, his dear friend, it was an energy that could be used. For Sandra, he didn't know, but she was, he thought, inhabiting another understanding. While for himself? He was only at the very edge of recognizing where he was. He could feel it but it was a foreign country still.

"He will be OK." Recognition not reassurance.

He didn't know how close his perceptions were to what was occurring within his daughter. Curiosity, his faithful ally, a family quality, led him to look more closely at her. He trusted himself not to be intrusive or manipulative. Unlike so many, their relationship was dependable as, he thought, such relationships should be. What he saw, what he thought he saw, astounded him. Like a wooden post, that armature within her … was Terrence Green. Terrence was present with them even if he was also on his way to a hospital bed somewhere in Oregon or Washington. Sandra was leaning on Terrence as he, though perhaps unconscious, was holding her up. Inexplicable. Terrence was present here even though he was outside a language and a territory either of them knew.

Terrence would be OK because he knew things they couldn't know, might never know. He knew why he was called to live and so he knew what this illness or injury meant and what might have caused it, or contributed to this dangerous condition. He knew where the breakdown would take him and why he had to suffer it. He was at a threshold; he could only cross it on his knees. He had been found by two hikers who had, inexplicably, gone off trail. They never did that, they asserted. Something impelled them, they tried to explain. The man went speedily to get help and the woman stayed with Terrence.

"My husband is a runner," the woman had said on the phone.

"So is my daughter," John Birdswell added quickly as if the declaration would support the only runner who mattered in the moment. As if they were at a support site, waiting for him with ice, drinks and ace bandages.

There was a pause on the phone. "Terrence? Is that his name? He has no ID on him. We put in a call for help, but Grayson decided to run to the ranger station. He gave us his car keys. And your phone number. We're not quite sure where we are. He will bring help back. Grayson agreed your friend would be safe with me."

John Birdswell thought he was seeing the two of them. Terrence on the ground. The woman seated next to him, her legs folded to the side, holding his hand. Khaki pants. A brown blouse. A black down jacket. Her hand was square, soft and warm. Comforting.

"What's your name?" he asked, meaning somehow to buttress her. As soon as he asked, he knew it wasn't necessary. She had already crossed the line from stranger to friend and the usual exchanges unnecessary. Though he knew she was holding her phone, that isn't what he saw. He saw her focused on Terrence, the intimacy of her narrow feet in white socks, her boots by the tree that shaded the two of them, her broad, freckled hand very still on Terrence's arm. The jacket now folded under his head.

"Charity," the woman said. "It's a silly name to have for a moment like this. But it is my name."

The response was obvious and so he said nothing. John said, "Thank you, Charity. We will finish packing and you can reach us as we drive." She hung up.

When the helicopter arrived, circling and coming in lower and circling and descending until a landing was possible, they were already in the car. Sandra answered the second call as she had the first. Terrence had come back to consciousness, circling up one vortex calling forth another, if only for a moment. "I am going to be OK," he had said, using the phone belonging to the medic. "It will take a while. I don't know where they are taking me. It is a bleed. An aneurism." There were long spaces between sentences filled with his jagged breath.

John Birdswell and Sandra had the phone on speaker and were listening intently.

"Anything else?"

"I'm very cold. Like the mountain. We're kin."

"Why do you think it is a bleed?" John asked.

"I can taste the blood coming through the roof of my mouth."

"You wouldn't taste …"

"I know," Terrence said, "and John, I know."

Once again, John Birdswell understood all his particular knowledge, training and experience, was irrelevant. As if he was a doc on the reservation again, he didn't have the last word. He looked at Sandra in the dark car. Terrence was going in and out of consciousness and Sandra was going in and out of stillness. It was night and they were speeding north on US 5.

The Medic took his phone back and said he'd call them from Portland or wherever he would finally take him. "Be ready to travel," he said.

"We're in the car," she said. "I packed quickly. And my father always has a suitcase with a change of clothes in the car. He's a country doc."

Then the medic gave the phone to Terrence again. "Be very brief," he said.

Terrence was broken. But all the pieces were laid out, as they might be, if an old pot or body was to be reconstructed from shards.

"I will be OK," Terrence repeated as if he were giving an order.

"I am here, Terrence," she said, meaning so many different things.

Then the medic disconnected the phone, or Terrence lost connection, or both.

19

The Tunnel of Dark

Two people hurtled down a dark highway, passing through impersonal clusters of stores and malls that pass for human settlements and which stop abruptly before intermittent orchards, vineyards, dry fields. Redwood forests had been decimated to build the towns. There was no logic for the terrain except human willfulness. The dark was protective, allowing only the sensation of landscape, of generic trees and long shallow curves of obscured hills leading to mountains. Lights sped toward them and passed beyond. Strange lights that eclipsed the stars. The punctured moon fell down and further down.

Twelve hours, John calculated, plus two hours for refueling, food and bathroom stops. He ran around the gas station and sprinted to the furthest fast food place to bring back provisions that Sandra wouldn't eat. Sandra waited in the car when he went to buy food; she did not want to leave the dark. Terrence was in the dark so she must be in the dark too. She reached out to him through the liquid medium of night. When she had to relieve herself, she put on dark glasses and squinted her eyes behind them to further diminish the input from the outside world that felt as if she was embedded in a continuous, insistent commercial, too loud and obscenely glittering. She stayed in the shadows, spoke to no one. John continued to drive, allowing her to slip away from the assaults at the gas stations and convenience stores even if it meant she would be separated from him – and even from herself – as she slid out on a line of electrons speeding toward a target, Terrence, to confirm that he would survive because he was not alone.

She searched for him, the infrared ray of her being inquiring, reaching for heat, for heart to locate him, to assert his existence through gathering a scattershot of particles that would cohere into the familiar shape of her beloved. She had a goal: identify, contact, track, fuse and … protect.

Sandra turned to John who was gripping the wheel with both hands as if holding himself up with his intention, "Do you think this is a repeat, Poppa?"

He didn't know what she meant, but he gripped the wheel even tighter, afraid he did. Afraid that a thought uttered had gained the possibility of becoming real that it had not had when it was unthought. He was fearing thought as manifestation.

"What do you mean?" Neutrality was fighting for dominance over fear.

"I mean, am I going to lose Terrence the way you lost your lover?" They both recognized the strange construction. She couldn't say, "The way you lost my mother," because she hadn't had a mother to lose.

She was unsure of her capacity of bringing healing to Terrence. She hadn't learned the fierce mother energy that can defeat any danger to her child; she knew the calm, thoughtful, paternal medical intelligence that could find an appropriate treatment. She didn't feel helpless so much as inadequate. A subtle difference which gave her a bit of an edge but not enough to feel confident about Terrence's recovery. Then her mood shifted and she felt "He will be OK," again.

John slipped a disc into the CD player. A perfect lament. The violin was haunting. She couldn't place it at first and then, against the tone of the music, she had to laugh quietly. "Where did you find that?"

"I took the instrumental and looped it until I had it for thirty minutes without the words and burned it onto a CD. I often need the company of grief like you do now." It was Neil Young, of course. It was the bridge from "Running Dry, Requiem for the Rockets." She didn't need words. No words could hold the sorrow in the music, in her heart. Her father was a better physician than she had known.

The car hurtled into the dark, the helicopter hurtled through the night.

20

Bow Down

The moment he fell, Terrence accepted the blow. He bowed down to receive it. He called it in. He was speaking aloud though didn't know to whom he was speaking, or whether he was speaking, or in a dream of speaking, or in a spirit realm to which he had been transported by what appeared to be injury, but was also something else. He was no longer in time or place. There were a thousand different ways he had accepted that spirits are real although Western mind was a miasma of denial that entered through the cracks and fissures of his being, like water seeping through rock, undermining the original structure of all things.

He could focus on his body, the pain in his head and his back and hips from his fall. He had fallen and broken, or he had broken and fallen. He could worry about dying but it seemed irrelevant. The Earth was dying, that was the death he was considering. He was a single particle that would survive in one form or another, if the universe survived. But the Earth, orbiting as an unburied corpse …. Perhaps the sun would blow before its end and vaporize the evidence of human failures? He was wild with the pain of reality. All volcanoes erupting at once. Unprecedented storms and searing heat in an avalanche of melting snow. Explosions in his head. Supernovas. One after another. It was his body and it wasn't.

Transport. He had been invited here or it was insisted that he come here to the sacred place, The **M**ountain. For thousands of years, so many had been transported here, though transport was not the word he was being given, rather it was, rescue. He was being rescued. In this place, perception, experience and language were one.

"My mother," he said, as if emerging from a war. He was going back through the mother line to the origin of the bloodletting that had become an incessant flood. He sought the origin of the hemorrhage of this time. He wanted to bleed his mother out of him. He had stood at the snow line that was turning red. His own brain was following suit in a minor key. He had to understand that it was also within him as it was without. Was it in him as an alien or was it now part of his Indigenous – not Indigenous – but still intrinsic, nature?

He had to do a scan. He had to know before the bleeding stopped. It wasn't injury; it was knowledge. The bleed was memory. He had to taste it in this form. The bleed from his brain that contained his experiences, and his ancestors and their experiences, encoded outside of language but translating now into thought, which was the way he knew things. In sharp contrast, the doctors would inevitably make understanding out of alien figures, chemistries, test results, computations that for them, somewhat, but no longer for him, translated into information. Information is not knowledge, nor is mathematics he argued in himself, and then realized he did not have time for the argument, a distraction. He pulled himself together, creating an inner tourniquet, pressure on the tear.

What could blood tell him and what did blood want him to know? His mother …. Not what she had been but what she had rejected. Had forsaken. And before her, her own long unknown history that had, this much was known, catapulted from one violence, one brutality to another. He came from this, from her brokenness, though he had not chosen it or her. Nor had she chosen, he heard. What had he chosen? He was choosing now.

When he felt himself weakening, the inner stain like a scent or taste in his mouth, he shifted away from the mother line and red, the Red path, took on another meaning and he could rest without being threatened with imminent death. Or he took on another shape and stanched the flow. He didn't know how it happened.

He'd had to know if he was a hybrid or a battlefield. From the point he had reached on Mt. Hood, he couldn't see the Hanford Nuclear Reservation that had taken his sacred Rattlesnake Mountain, Laliik, into its maw. Though it was about 150 miles as the crow flies, he could smell Hanford, the way his people had been trained to smell the death force as it came west over the mountains from across the eastern sea. Not that awareness had enabled them to successfully resist, overcome or escape. It had turned the entire continent into a marsh. It smelled of sorrow. Broken sorrow. Salt sorrow. Poison sorrow. Radiant sorrow. The way that rivers and oceans smell when all the fish die in them at once.

Whatever was in him that had contributed in any way to the murder of the land, he had to find and expunge. He would have to cut it out. He was cutting it out. That was the bleed. Purification. Out with the bad blood.

He felt the ripping pain again. Wild explosions. No, no longer explosions. No longer supernovas, no longer volcanoes. Although, later, the young resident in the ER would find such metaphors appropriate. When the body is exhibiting an injury, the resident is used to identifying violence.

Still now, no blasts. No more outbursts. No detonations. Something else. Something far more subtle. Nothing broken, but rather the delicate, as in careful, removal of barriers, obstacles, boundaries, casings, walls. Each entity within or without remained itself and yet it was no longer distinctly partitioned off from another entity. As if the banks of a river that had been reinforced with concrete had become porous and then earthen banks again, tangles of stalks, trunks, roots and stones that allowed the structure to remain while the water penetrated the soil unimpeded. Even so, the hurt in his body was experienced also as the agony of the Earth, with no distinction, except that he could bear his own suffering while he knew that her pain was unbearable. Still he was to experience her without complaint. They had become cognates of each other. The particularity of anguish, even intermittent hints of agony, dissolved, as he dissolved into everything around him – earth, tree, bramble, trampled snow, lava flow. His own pain was inconsequential as he felt the enormity of Earth's injuries. The two were not distinct and yet they were and his willingness, ability, or fate, to take in her unremitting torment, her bellow, sustained him so he could modulate his own response in order to know hers.

Here was Terrence. If he began to think in English, he would be gone, his injuries would deepen. In the English language, he was mortally wounded and had to get to a hospital quickly: only Western medicine could save him. But if he forbid himself English, its fears and alarms, and entered an Indigenous language, even if he had only shards of it, or a child's vocabulary, he would gain another understanding. Here he was in the dynamic interchange, in the unceasing whirl, the ever present stillness, which was encompassed in the ten thousand years of his almost, but only almost, extinct language. Here he was in his language, the deeper knowing.

Enabled by his language, a greater agony was coursing through him, melting him into the hidden fire at the molten core of the mountain, and into the air around him, Hanford Nuclear Reservation, that abomination violating the rivers, the poisoned Columbia river, her veins and arteries pumping plutonium, strontium-90, phosphorus-32, zinc-65, arsenic-76, neptunium-239 and sodium-24, radionuclides, radiation into the aquifer, the torque of mutation, a reflex of survival, water, earth, blood clotting the streams, seeping into the terrain, his body, the earth, the winds, the fire and the water, a dynamic, yet unmoving exchange, interpenetration, the blood then that he tasted, was not a tear, but a dissolve.

Mind succumbed to heart. Before he spun into unconsciousness, he managed to scrape some earth into his mouth. To stanch the bleeding, he explained to himself. It was dank, sweet and cold. A poultice that eased his grief. He gave his body up to the dark vultures and carrion eaters who would gather should he die in that spot. He heard the unlikely sound of an owl in daylight and he blessed whatever his future might be. He blessed Sandra and the **M**ountain.

"I'm sorry," were his last words before the dark entered like a landslide of ice and snow.

21

Help Me

Quietly, Sandra began singing, as did John: "Oh please help me. Oh please help me," which both of them knew from Neil Young's "Running Dry."

She didn't know where Terrence was now, but she knew where he had been from Charity. It was possible to pray aloud if she did it by singing someone else's lyrics. Though she didn't know anything, she sensed that Terrence had been on the mountain praying, trying to apologize, to make amends. She didn't know what his mountain looked like, she had never been there, but she prayed to it nevertheless. She didn't know if it was a male spirit or a female spirit. But the mountain was earth, and Earth, she knew was the mother. The mother she had always had even if she hadn't had a mother.

"I'm sorry. I'm sorry, I'm sorry, I'm sorry, I'm sorry," she wailed to the mountain and to the Earth. Everything she had read, studied, observed of devastation rose up in her like lava and fire. She closed her eyes and stood at the fire line in the dream where she had gone to see the worst violation that humans had committed against the Earth but hadn't gotten close enough to know exactly what we had done. What we had done this time. What we had done beyond everything she knew we had done, were doing. What would never be remedied or healed. What did the unthinkable imply?

She began to sense that Terrence knew something that was beyond the IPCC report. Though she could not think of anything worse in this moment. The report spoke soberly of what interventions might save the planet but everyone knew the goals would not be reached. Something dire and sinister was at work undermining all life.

"I'm sorry. I'm sorry, I'm sorry, I'm sorry, I'm sorry," she howled. She could not contain it and it was, also, her prayer on behalf of Terrence. It was not that he was a good man and she was asking for his life. It was that he was able to remember the winds, the cloud people and the rain. He knew that the **M**ountain was a spirit, a living being. The **M**ountain needed such a man.

Her father drove fast and steady as she keened. She had to reach to the **M**ountain with her knowing. Though the distance between them was diminishing, she still had to use all her energy to project herself and make contact with its cold and rough peaks.

The **M**ountain had to know the extent of her grief, of Terrence's grief. For the **M**ountain's sake. So that Her outrage, the **M**ountain's outrage, could be eased.

The resident was waiting in the ER. The helicopter would arrive momentarily. The resident was beginning his shift. Miraculously, he had slept and showered. There were no other patients to attend at this moment. Another miracle. He was ready, intrigued by the case that was being flown in. The patient seemed to have made a self-diagnosis convincingly enough to divert the helicopter, a diagnosis that could well be correct. If so, the situation could be dire. The people who had found him and called 911 had hinted that he was an unusual man but they couldn't explain why, that he was probably very intelligent and intermittently uncooperative or contradictory. He has a presence. That is all they could explain. His family was driving up from the south. Maybe he was a foreigner. He spoke English. It was as if a diplomat was going to arrive.

The resident called several attending physicians. There was much to consider: disease, injury, exhaustion, exposure, hypothermia. Diagnosis, then treatment would follow. Terrence would no longer be the authority on his own condition though he had been flown to the State Aneurism Center based on his own evaluation. From the resident's perspective, Terrence was not coherent enough or conscious long enough, nor sufficiently educated in medical matters to confirm or deny anything. It was necessary for the resident and the attending to do something and do it quickly and skillfully. Terrence was no longer in his own hands. His understanding, coherent as it was to him in his moments of consciousness, was of no significance to the medical team that took over except as among several possibilities to be ruled out.

Terrence went in and out of consciousness. When he was awake he was fearful, as the people did not make him feel safe; he went under again. The environment was strange. There were more machines than people. He was among strangers who moved quickly and efficiently like machines themselves. He couldn't tell the difference sometimes. They asked him the same silly questions again and again. What was his name? How old was he? Where did he live? Who was President? They confused him.

Mostly he became afraid they would give him blood, someone else's blood. He was afraid that he would no longer be who he had been and he would not be able to trust his own judgment. The fears ran rampant inside him. Who was afraid? Who was thinking these thoughts? What percentage of himself would remain himself? Which part of himself had bled out? If he got one transfusion, $\frac{7}{8}$ of himself would remain pure, would remain what he had been, after he received the transfusion. But what if he had only been $\frac{5}{10}$ pure before. What is $\frac{7}{8}$ of $\frac{5}{10}$? He couldn't quite do the mathematics in his head. He got close and then was scrambled. He might remain 3.8888, he calculated. How would he access this portion? Would it be sufficient? He was overwhelmed. He didn't believe that blood mattered in a fundamental way, and yet it seemed he did. Whose blood would he get? Culture mattered. But he hadn't been raised entirely on the reservation. Values mattered, but they sat differently in different people. Even now, who was calculating? His essential 3.888? It was said his tribe required $\frac{1}{4}$, so he was safe even with a transfusion. They would test his blood type but not his blood quantum. His blood was beginning to boil. His ancestry might escape in the vapors. His people didn't, hadn't, calculated in this way until the white people came with their disembodied math. He had engaged such calculations as a scientist. He was losing himself in more ways than he could count.

Sandra and he …. Yet she was different. Did he trust … ? He didn't let himself finish the sentence even inside his own mind. "You have to know the land and the ancestors who are here," his grandfather had said. He had to know the land that he was and the ancestors who were within him.

Someone else's blood could enter him unimpeded by any barriers of personal history, race, culture, time and place. Someone would have unconditionally offered such a gift to save his life. The stranger's generosity had to be considered even while he feared the gift might disappear him. He had friends who had received body parts from others and they had been changed by it. He had to take care of himself. He had to protect himself. He had to protect the red. He had to be sure it pumped through his veins. He searched for a drum beat to assist the heartbeat. Later the doctors would claim to have saved his life. It was true, he was alive and out of danger. In ICU, yes, but not for long.

While they are operating in their world, Terrence was doing his own work sustaining his essence.

John and Sandra came to the hospital in bright sunshine. The white cube of a building was covered in sharp white light bouncing off its walls. Everything was straight and angular, meant to be bracing, to exude confidence and authority. It was intended to be reassuring as the IHS hospital had been to John so many years before, but it was cutting to Sandra who took off her sunglasses for the full impact. John said nothing. He was not in his territory yet, though he would normally take charge here. He was still the driver, a humble but necessary designation. He did it well. It was high noon and though the day was filled only with September light, it was still as bright as it could be. John hoped everything would become clear. He would like the privilege of ordering tests, conducting the exams, picking up the unblemished, disinfected stainless steel instruments in gloved hands, prescribing, but such would not be granted. He was from another state, another system. He had not been tested here. Sandra strode toward the entrance, her glasses in her hand, reeling slightly from fatigue and the glare. She did not want her glasses to disguise where she was. He steadied her. This he could do.

Terrence was unrecognizable in the white bed in the white room. A dark form on white sheets. Tubes. Machines. Whirrs and clicks. Serum in transparent tubes. Pulses not his own. Monitors. He spoke a simple sentence: "Get me out of here. There is no healing of the Earth here." He was asking John to get him released, to John's care or custody, if required. Sandra was being called to release his soul from the trap. Body and soul were gravely wounded.

When he fell asleep, even though the two had just arrived to assist him, he believed, through his fitful but precise dreaming, that his life was threatened. From the medical perspective, that was exactly why he had to stay in the hospital. From his understanding, he would die if he had to remain longer. He had no choice but to recover quickly. Asleep, as attentive as he would be in a lucid dream, and then waking, he gathered intense meditative strength and focus and willed himself to mend, even risking that it might draw attention to himself, which would undermine his purpose. The best he could do would be to impersonate a man who was healing himself. This could convince the staff, though no healer would buy it. Still it was the best cover he could imagine and so he wrapped himself in the disguise so he could begin working.

He gathered all his strength so that he was more like wood than clay but like the wood of a flute, vibrating. He began chanting in a low vibrato, a hum that seemed to invite whoever entered the room to stop and hum with him. Reflexive alliances. Beneath it was an imperceptible drumbeat driving the chant back into his bloodline.

John flinched, momentarily afraid the subsonic sound would interfere with the monitors. His fear, reflexive as when one trips and is falling, was responding to the sudden change in the room. A penetrating calm. Was a storm coming? Terrence seemed more a presence than a person who was activating this state.

Later John would quip, in the manner of the tall tale, that the machines healed themselves, slowly reverting to normal for each monitor. John's fear that the vibration would disturb the repair in Terrence's brain morphed into a belief that the wound and machines were responding, returning to their default position. Later John would wonder if he was also acted upon, was also being calmed. His anxieties and protests diminished.

Terrence had understood that Earth required healing attention and the very nature of the building and institution designed to heal undermined it. Terrence couldn't locate the harmony and balance in the environment which were crucial to restoration, his and Earth's. He was thinking, "one body." He was thinking "one body, his and Earth's, while he was divided within himself. As long as he was here in the hospital, he would remain shredded no matter what an MRI said or his vital signs indicated about his recovery. Even when enacting the moment of healing theater, he was aware of where he was and calculating the forces he had to balance. Though he had to give himself completely to the energetic field that would ease all and everything in its sphere, he also had to maintain a portion of worldly alertness or risk being confined indefinitely. He could only keep this up so long. The energetic toll was great and he was exhausted by the entire ordeal, his drive up north, the climb up to Wy'east, the hours on his feet, the difficult descent, his injury, whatever it was, and collapse. Also medical treatment itself is traumatic, whether one is sedated or not, the body knows. Then there was the effort of retaining consciousness though he had been invaded, not unlike the challenge his people had faced since the conquest. And, in addition, there was the enormous effort required to initiate and maintain the healing stance that he was resurrecting from his DNA seeds of memory. Epigenetics. Science was verifying what his people had always known, that trauma can be passed on generation to generation, also that we remember back into history and forward into the future. So healing can be remembered in the way that the ancestors, awakening in Terrence's system, were asserting and demonstrating. But, again he could only maintain this awakening for so long before he would certainly collapse again. It was up to John to get him released.

John understood this somehow. His own version, he thought later, of shapeshifting, though he didn't think of it consciously. He was suddenly

John Birdswell, MD, the first responder and last resort, who had presided over hundreds of emergencies over the years. He stood up, aligned his tall body exactly, straightened the clean and pressed shirt he had just put on in the men's room, checked his tie, straightened his sleeves, adjusted his cuffs, read the chart tucked into the holder on the door, thought a second and tucked it under his arms as he strode to the nurses' station to set about contacting the attending physician and the resident. They met in the resident's office. They went for coffee. The attending physician paid the cashier for the three of them. The discharge was arranged.

During all this, Sandra stood still, her hands on Terrence's arm and shoulder or his forehead. Her eyes were open. Her eyes were closed. They had sat together in such composure before the fire. She withdrew herself from having any influence. Somehow she knew that this hospital drama had to be played out between Terrence and her father, Terrence in one world, her father in his. And while the two men differed extremely, especially now, they would find a common bond, as of two diverse but intersecting systems which had, each, to attune to coexist.

Sandra's medicine at this moment was to meet all the divisions and hold them in relationship to each other. When she needed to renew her focus, she silently sang the Bear song he had taught her, invoking the long hibernation in which, nevertheless, birth often occurs. If birth, then healing. Her father had had a colleague who worked with spinal injuries after discovering that the body could remember and reinstate necessary versions of the primal embryonic processes of creating life through certain continuous motions. As Sandra had never learned the technique, she called to the Bear instead. She had to conjure and sustain the world in which all animate beings, spirit and manifestation, coexisted as companions to confirm a world undivided though distinct in its parts and attributes. Everything in vibrant relationship to everything else. The foundation from which his chant was emerging. She invoked Bear and **M**ountain to ground his meditation and her father's activity. She brought what she could together into a still point. She didn't know what she was doing. As long as there were no sudden local earthquakes or tornadoes in her body, she had confidence in what was occurring. She let the stillness in her seep into Terrence as he had received her knowing in the past. In this way, they would spend the last hours in the hospital. And in this quiet way, they would depart.

When John returned to the room with the discharge papers in hand, Terrence let the chant diminish. A nurse came in and disconnected him from the medical apparatus. It was hard to move but he managed to sit up, step onto the floor, and walk, if unsteadily at first, to the bathroom where he put on the clean clothes Sandra had brought. When he emerged, he grinned faintly and lopsidedly, for she had read his mind in advance and brought the formal informal outfit of a Native professor of science. Pressed dark jeans, denim shirt with the plastic pocket; she wanted to make him laugh. A bolo tie with a rectangular silver and turquoise slide and silver tips on the ford. A perfect disguise for shapeshifting into a healthy persona who has the organizational capacities of the Chair of the Department of Earth and Environmental Studies, which is how he has been identified by the hospital. He needed to assure the staff that he was well enough to leave.

"Where did you get these?"

"I ran out of the tent when you didn't come back, feeling like an intruder, but … still, I stopped in your house and rummaged through your drawers in case we were still connected and you might need something."

They both smiled, relieved to be together.

He expressed his gratitude to physicians and staff alike, he made arrangements to pay his bill, he clasped arms with Sandra and held on tightly, but no one could see who was holding up whom, and walked out of the hospital into the brilliant oranges and reds of a fiery sunset.

22

Recovery

Terrence couldn't go back to work. He couldn't lie to his students. A light tan deer hide tobacco pouch was in his shirt pocket now. To feel its presence fortified him and he had to be completely honest. The very nature of the various curricula within the architectural construct of the university buildings assured everyone who entered that they would find answers to check the unimaginable that was slowly engulfing them, a slow moving lava flow. Though the university claimed to be dedicated to inquiry, it exuded certainty and confidence, and when expedient, a little denial, a window trim. Terrence could see through the brick walls and polished floors. With Sandra as his medium, he could feel the earth tremors. Wind movement he had understood, the Earth's movement was another matter but their existence was the basis of his knowledge.

He doubted that most of his students would be able or willing to devote their time after graduation to seek out the complex of underlying causes of the planet's certain progression toward annihilation. Having an acronym, AGW, Anthropogenic Global Warming theory guaranteed that the wound of those words would scab over and be forgotten.

Given the diagnosis, it was not difficult for Terrence to take sick leave and when it terminated, perhaps a leave of absence from the university. They stayed in Sandra's house to be near John who was charged with following Terrence's recovery. Taking full responsibility, John was also leaning back into his experience on the reservation. He was far more skilled at carrying the two worlds than he had been in the beginning although years in private practice and working at the local hospital had erased his sensitivity to the issues that Hosteen had raised initially. When he went to the reservation he remembered, but his Native patient was here, now, in his daughter's house and he owed him his own ways. John had never transferred what he had learned at the reservation directly to his medical practice but Terrence was his patient and a one man hands-on residency in Indigenous medicine.

However John phrased the medical questions: What were the causes? What circumstances led up to the break? What prior conditions had not been attended? Terrence translated the medical questions into another language with different meanings. John was seeking physiological, biological answers; Terrence was looking to history and the state of the Earth and all beings. He could answer John with a look. The two realities could coexist as long as the one, longing to be dominant, the one considering domination its destiny, yielded to the wisdom of the other. It was Terrence's instinct to align himself with his experiences outside of his scientific training. As if one half of himself was immersing itself in his other half. As his mother had once yielded to his father and let him enter her. As she had taken his father in.

Terrence had never thought to consider his mother's nature or what longings she'd had. She had always been a cipher, a statistic, a dysfunctional person, as the Lakota and Dakota called such, a *washichu*. Had his father paid her or had they mutually coupled? Why had she taken him in? Terrence looked over at Sandra. She sometimes insinuated that she could be related to him, not a kinship he had wanted to imagine, not as an enemy.

They were living in her house. Sandra had literally taken him in. Her father, his physician, was doctoring him, was his medicine person. Before they had lived in his tent, before they had thrown off the walls between them, she had spoken of this house as her body and he had stalked her heart, had tracked the fire in her, the way she circumambulated the central fire in the house, around and around. He needed her fire now. There was a fire burning in the house, just as there was a fire in her. Hers, he was discovering, was an eternal flame. He was quite weak; despite his preferences he had to stay largely indoors. He walked around the fire inside, but preferred to be outside. Around the house or up on the roof. Round and round. He would not have partnered with her if she didn't know the sacred wheel.

Rest, the doctors had said and he capitulated but without believing it was the way. He would have liked to resist the doctors forcibly, by mustering all his strength and going out to meet the wind. Lying down when weakened was not his way of recovery. Rallying was a better response to exhaustion. To recover was to reenact health. Bed rest was a white man's response to illness; it puzzled him, as white men were so violent. He was back to *washichu* and his mother. His new obsession.

Sandra came into the living room from the roof deck like a tree falling. "There've been a series of earth tremors," she paused for breath, "what are you doing?"

They looked at each other, both startled by her words.

"I don't know anything," he said without accounting for the trembling that was overtaking him. It was internal not external. How had she known? The one she was or had become knew. That was who she was. She knew when it was they were in him and when they were in the Earth.

"Why do you say that you could be related to me through my mother?"

"Remember, we had this conversation? I don't know anything about my mother," she said plainly, the tension she had felt the first time she said this to him, no longer current. "My mother was, without question, a white woman. She was a wanderer. Maybe she had an older sister who was your mother. Maybe you're a cousin. I don't want to have to be 'understanding' when you wake up next to me one day and think you have been sleeping with your ancestral enemy." She held on to her midsection as tremors went through her. His fear? Her fear? He didn't know and she would not say.

The ghost of his mother was in the room and Sandra saw her face and how the woman had etched her imprint on Terrence though until that moment, Sandra had assumed that only his father's family lived in his body because his body was a manifestation of his soul. Until this moment, his mother had been a young girl, an eternal teenager. Now she was old, as old a woman as she might be if she were alive, with tightly curled white hair like a rough wool winter cap around her round face that had once been sweet and now was vinegar lined with disappointment and wrong choices.

"No more bloodletting." Sandra's words were barely audible. He had to hear it; she didn't want him to hear it. He had to meet the ghost as she could not, torn as she was between understanding a young woman who was more likely to make mistakes than not, and her fury with where all these mistakes had led, not only for people, but for the Mother, herself. Sandra reached out to the world with the balm of heartbreak. She would not differentiate Terrence's distress from Earth's distress. But without the woman and her mistakes, Terrence wouldn't exist.

Terrence did not see a ghost. He did not think he had spirit sickness in that way. He knew he was making the right choices though they meant cutting himself in two. Being with Sandra had restored his Indigenous ways. Every step he had taken since was toward his grandparents, including this moment and the last months he and Sandra had been together in the tent and speeding to Wy'east after he sat down with the IPCC report, and the time on Wy'east, itself, the wisdom in his collapse, the moment he called into the department, sick, and left his work, every moment since … fortified him.

A major shift and commitment. He wavered.

"Leukemia," he said as if such an illness could attack suddenly like a virus. "No surprise that so many of us fall prey to leukemia. "Too many white cells. I can't heal," he insisted but so weakly, Sandra had to catch him before he collapsed. Vertigo was informing her of his condition.

"You don't have leukemia," she said between clenched teeth.

He reached away from her to a chair. He was not, she understood, going to lie down.

"What do I have, Sandra?"

"Terrence, you have heartbreak with complications that have manifested as a glitch in your brain, in your thinking."

"Is that an official diagnosis?" he asked glowering.

"It is for some people."

"Like whom, Sandra?"

"Like me, Terrence, like me."

"What are the complications?"

"Do you want to go over them again?"

"I do."

"OK. Exposure. Hypothermia. And an aneurism they are going to watch."

"Where?"

Was he taunting her? She didn't know but she was getting exasperated and afraid for him, for them. "Where? Anywhere. Your heart, your stomach, your brain, Terrence. You're going to blow if you don't release some pressure."

"Like a volcano?"

"Yes, like a damn volcano."

"Looks like you're going to blow too, Sandra."

Yes, she was going to blow. She didn't know what was overtaking her. All the tension for so long and now, yes, hot magma moving inside her also, from very deep inside her, the tectonic plates shifting, and a long shrill sound, almost a scream, of the grind of rock and earth within, emerged from her. After all, she had seen the ghost.

"I'm sorry. It's my fault. It's the fault of the *bilagáana*. It's not the fault only of the *bilagáana*. There is no fault, only tragedy. Yes, we are destroying the Earth. We are the only ones … we are not the only ones … there is good in everyone … there is no good here … the devil … there is no devil … we can heal it … nothing will heal it … I am sorry … so so sorry … yes, condemn … forget … no, you can't forget, must not forget … so punish …

withdraw … begin again … understand … there is no understanding … forgive … don't forgive … you can't forgive … you have no right to forgive … forgiveness doesn't matter … forgive, you must, can't, mustn't, please forgive me …."

Either the individual disconnected words poured out of her or they were an internal cacophony. This was babble, the Tower of Babel, every word in argument with the next word – chaos, destruction, melee.

Finally, she sat down instead of towering over him. "I don't know what to do." Confession. But not to another authority who could absolve her. Not with the hope of any comfort. Then silence as of ash settling everywhere, a dark, heavy snow that could block out the sun.

She took a breath. "You were on Mt. Hood," she said, question and statement, what they both knew the other knew, but needing to be between them.

"Yes."

"Did you read the report?"

"Yes."

"Did you read it on Mt. Hood?"

"Yes."

"All of it?"

"Yes." Pause. "Did you read it, Sandra?"

"Yes," she nodded.

"Could you see Hanford, Terrence?" One question led directly to the other.

"No."

"But?" as if she knew something.

He shrugged and stood up, shuffled a little so he could steady himself with his right hand on the back of his chair. She knew she had to remain seated.

She had to see where he had been without asking him. It was difficult and she didn't want to project her own thoughts upon him.

Perhaps he felt her need to share his suffering as he had held her in his mind the first night they were together in the desert and she had yielded to another way of being, trusting him. He had enough stability to recognize remnants of the sometimes worded, sometimes wordless exchange that they had been refining between them. Something in him relaxed enough for her to ask.

"But you saw something?"

There was nothing he could say that would convey his experience, but he had a story.

"There are stories about the five sisters who lived at the Cascades building a dam for themselves at Celilo Falls. The salmon couldn't get to the upper waters and the people had no fish to eat," Terrence droned in a monotonous voice. "Coyote broke the dam and my people lived and fished on the *nChe-wana* for 15,000 years."

He was back again on the south side of Wy'east, looking around it or through it to the Dalles, like the Winnemem Wintu of Northern California wanting to create a swim way for the salmon around Mt. Shasta to the McCloud River to spawn.

NChe-wana, which he had not said for years, the Columbia river's name for itself, came up in him like the threat of a dam exploding at once without regard for the sediment that had accumulated for all the years of the dam, or the speed and breadth and extent of flood waters suddenly released.

He closed his eyes as he had closed his eyes then at the **M**ountain, when he felt himself near the river. Terrence was a climatologist but he wasn't thinking like a climatologist. The story he was remembering hadn't happened at the time it originated. It had been a future story, a precognitive myth. Where was Coyote to break the dam, all the dams?

There is a cosmic law that his people had recognized, established at the time of creation: Salmon and other fish should not be dammed but allowed free access to swim up rivers to spawn … He couldn't tell if the violation he was feeling in his body, was the *nChe-wana* or the salmon, or the dam itself, all which were in him now because he was remembering. All the concrete, steel, wire, metal were in him. The dam which stretches more than eight thousand feet across the river was in him and the radiant fish who couldn't go up river or down to the sea were in him, thrashing. Was the river the same river if it was dammed, damned by the violation of the first laws? If he had been dammed up for years, since he was a child, almost for his entire life? The process of dismantling a dam was long and required caution. The sediment that collected from upriver all the years of the dam had to be released slowly so it could find its way, restoring the rightful curves and turns of the river, remaking the banks and the beaches, providing spawning places and habitat for the water creatures, even to the oysters in the ocean at the mouth of the river. That far and that slowly over years.

But it took enormous strength and will to contain the flood that was wanting to exit from him, and he could sense the weak places, the beginnings of cracks and fissures, where it seemed the weight of water and history were pushing such a dam to thin and so balloon out imperceptibly. And so he began to understand the aneurism yet again in another way that he had never perceived.

So he was the dam, and also the river, and the salmon, gleaming with the poison of different radioactive particles. He had memorized the list so he would not forget, ever, a litany: strontium-90, cesium-137, phosphorus-32, zinc-65, arsenic-76, neptunium-239 and sodium-24. Plutonium! Struggling with his deadly sheen, he tried to make it upriver, up over the dam to spawn and experience that natural death in the life process. But he couldn't. Death would be too easy. He had to see this, this portion of time, this less than a gasp of air moment in his history and his people's history. He could not die; he had to bear witness. He knew. The **M**ountain was teaching him.

He was staring ahead of him as if he were in a trance. It was as if he were seeing through the mountain, Wy'east again. Through the mountain back to 1957, to the establishment of the Dalles dam, three years before he was born, through the Nike Ajax Missile Base established 1956 on Laliik, Rattlesnake Mountain, through the time when the Mountain was appropriated for Hanover in 1943 and back through the entire history of his people who could not stop the colonizers from ravaging the Earth.

"Did I see something, Sandra? I saw everything. I saw through everything. And I remembered everything. Did I tell you this? My uncle — on the reservation everyone is a cousin or an uncle, that's how it is — my uncle was in prison and the feds offered him a deal. He would get out if he agreed to an experiment. They injected strontium-90 into his testicles and let him out. In two weeks, he was dead."

"That's not true."

"It is true. There are no words in our language for what is coming next. We cannot imagine it. Your people are creating it."

He saw her flinch.

She sat as still as she could, relieved. The moment had been inevitable and now it had appeared. How could she or any white person escape the lash of this pain. Knowing it was also her pain was the antidote.

She proceeded to seek connection as the only medicine possible for each of them. "You took the dream I had with you. When you were on the mountain, you were living in my dream too, weren't you?"

"Were?"

His voice cracked, tears choking him. He looked at Sandra in a new way. He hadn't realized how much she had been with him, that he wouldn't be understanding this without her. She had gifted him the terrible dream to tie them to each other. The IPPC report had taken him down but the dream had held him up. It held him up because Sandra had dreamed it. Because it had been given to her and she had taken it in to guide her. This meant he was not alone. He was glad, in this instance, that she was a white woman. A white woman who was not an enemy. A part of himself now. A necessary union at this time.

Sandra couldn't read the thoughts ricocheting in his brain, but she could feel vertigo inside her and she had her own references for it though she was trying to read his delirium. Strange how the personal still had the immediate impact while the knowledge he carried of Hanford, of *nChe-wana*, all the creatures, the people had a far longer and more tragic half-life. Yes, he had to wrestle with the fact that his mother had taken his father in. Money? He asked himself again. Rape? Drunkenness? Seduction? Affection? Love? He didn't dare consider the latter. Love? He was dizzy and tried to steady himself. His mother, guilty or innocent? Or both? It didn't matter. Sandra put her hand on his arm. She was here. Maybe they were kin. They were kin. She loved him. He loved her. That he was suffering the consequences of his mother's life was not of concern now. Perhaps the past didn't matter. But the future did. The future mattered.

As dramatically and swiftly as its appearance, the ghost of Terrence's mother vanished. Sandra saw her flee. The future mattered. His mother was not important in this moment.

What he was suffering in his own body and mind did not matter. What he was suffering in the Earth's body was another matter. Not because he embodied it. The Earth mattered. Sandra didn't matter and he didn't matter or both of them mattered and so the Earth mattered. The future of the Earth mattered.

"We don't know anything," they agreed.

They heard John's car pull up. He would take all the packages out of the car and line them up on the stairs. He would close the door loudly. Then he would wait five minutes or so before he lumbered up the stairs, to allow them time to receive another person. Watching them the last few days, he knew that they met in a realm he did not yet know. They had extended invitations in their way, started conversations, repeated something they had been thinking about, Terrence had offered tobacco in his presence, had told a story John had not expected to hear, still John did not know yet how to meet Terrence and Sandra when they were together. He was used to jostling with Hosteen, but the two lovers seemed to want something else, camaraderie, perhaps. So now he gave them warning. He did not want to insert himself in their territory without wearing moccasins he had made himself. He knew that much.

How was Sandra doing it? She seemed to have moved into Terrence's territory, like a bride taken to the patriarchal landholding. She wasn't talking much about work. The project that had engaged her as a consultant was interesting, at least to John, but she was barely involved. He suspected she would have quit if that weren't more complicated than to finish her part in it.

"About the aneurism?" John had turned to Sandra earlier when Terrence was sleeping. He wanted the little girl who had gone on rounds with him, who had "consulted" on various cases, who had advised him on what he couldn't understand but she did, to speak to him about Terrence.

She said nothing. Because it was Terrence, he had to meet him on his own. He was struggling and she could not help him

Though John wasn't able to think the way Terrence thought, he accepted that Terrence believed conventional medicine reduced critical events to mere physical functions. Illness and symptoms, Terrence maintained, on the rare occasions he was willing to spend time discussing his body with "his doctor," were markers of breaks in complex relationships that occurred when right relations were askew.

Terrence was not willing to discuss high blood pressure, arteriosclerosis or diet except in the ways he understood them as limited metaphors for the dynamic between an individual, the culture and the land. As for genetic factors – implying his family, his line or his people carried a fatal flaw – such suggestions did make his pressure rise and he didn't need a blood pressure cuff to measure it. When pressed, he responded bitterly, "I never knew my mother – so I'm not saying anything about her. My relationship with her is difficult enough without looking to see if she did me intrinsic harm." He marveled that he saw it this way; the pressure was easing, his mother fading to an ordinary woman he had never known.

Terrence could not and would not make a differential diagnosis, in the way John was required to do. Rather the opposite, everything was interrelated, and no factors, not even the genes, nor especially who his mother was or wasn't, could or should be singled out as central when what was germane was the dynamic that caused such pain. How wrong it seemed that his health seemed to require that he focus upon a set of physical symptoms instead of the root cause. His mother's genetic makeup was minutia in the vastness of the mystery of his pain although he begrudgingly admitted to himself that the fact that he did not know his mother had been one under-lying condition.

"We always blame the mother." The words exploded from John startling him as much as it did the other two. By giving voice to what was unspoken, he entered their field of understanding. Without elaborating, all knew it was true and each was culpable and no one of them was a mother.

"It's because …" Sandra began and then caught herself continuing the reproach and so stopped. They were each distinctly torn between their own pain and the common vision of the injured and agonized Earth mother, whose suffering they, each, experienced in their own way. Terrence knew the Mother as a fact without indulging symbol or metaphor. He knew it the way he would have agonized for the pain his own mother had suffered, if he had known her, if she had mothered him, if she had walked a path of primary connection to Earth herself.

John was not trained to address the vast morass of the underlying con-ditions that Terrence insisted on identifying and Terrence was not interested in addressing anything else. Not addressing the underlying conditions was a cause, if there wasn't only one cause. Terrence was clear about that. Clear that his own failures were blueprinted by the symptoms in order for him to read them and make a structure of meaning.

"We learn best from our own failures." Terrence's internal investigations were rigorous and required a high pain threshold. He had always chosen to be cognizant rather than comfortable.

"Your way, our way," Terrence hesitated and became even more ashen as he spoke, "is to break down, divide, isolate the parts in order to understand an issue. It was my way too." He turned his back to John and stared out the window and then he opened the glass doors. Maybe he called the wind be-cause it came whistling and shrill through the trees. He sprang outside and he let the wind batter him as twilight descended.

Still, Terrence was John's patient, so John was compelled to bring what-ever he knew or could research to bear on the situation – "the best available medical treatment." As he witnessed his inner activity, skimming the latest research, consulting with trusted colleagues, seeking referrals – the best hospitals, the best doctors, the best procedures – he became aware of the thought processes Terrence was challenging in this debate that Terrence wouldn't allow to be a debate if it ended in any version of a winner. How often he'd had to assure the patient before him that she or he would be getting "the best available." He remembered Sandra's belated ironic self-criticism of the time she had been in the Arctic studying ice: "I had wanted to be part of "the best available science." The reflex in their civilized – "colonized," Hosteen called it – minds that sought out hierarchy, being on top, getting or being "the best."

This was not Terrence's way. Certainly not now. The best for Terrence was the most collaborative and complex. Inclusive, not efficient. Conceptual, not procedural. John was overwhelmed with the sweet feelings he had for this man who was and was not his patient and who was his instructor in matters he had not ever considered before. Yes, he was coming to love Terrence in a way he had not loved or considered a man before, as if he was his kin, a brother, or his own son. Meanwhile he was struggling to understand that they were residing in entirely different worlds. Although Terrence's work, like Sandra's, like his own, required "the best available science," they both seemed skeptical of that standard which he had not questioned – until perhaps now. Terrence, and yes, now Sandra since she had met him and had allowed her original self (it seemed to him) to emerge, were thinking differently about everything. Everything! Was that possible?

John was in his daughter's house. A house he, himself, would never have purchased when they had lived together. A house open to the elements, far too exposed to protect a little girl who had lost her mother. And yet, she claimed she felt safer here because of the proximity of the elements. One night, she said, she had felt threatened by the presence of many locks and walls, implying permanent danger, implying that something must always be kept out. Hadn't her father taught her about Mr. Wind? A friend. Was she to keep him out?

His daughter was longing for the tent that she and Terrence had lived in for the last months, despite the two houses they owned. He, John Birdswell, MD, the medical authority, was keeping them encased in what they insisted was an artificial shell. There was no real argument. He could not have kept them against their will. Not even for Terrence's "own good." And yet they were here by his authority. The situation did not serve any one of them.

Suddenly, he knew what to do and he felt a childlike glee at being the one to suggest the treatment. Whistling "See the Sky About to Rain," was his way of confirming what he knew. His self satisfaction was obvious as he emptied the groceries he had purchased. Wild Alaska salmon, greens, salad, potatoes and apples. She thought his obvious delight was because he had bought the ingredients for a meal he could make quickly and skillfully. He was insisting on cooking for them. "To make up for years of top ramen and eating out?" Sandra had teased him when he announced this plan. "My best doctoring," he asserted.

It was when he was putting the salmon in the iron skillet, everything else having been prepared and laid out, that he turned to both of them sitting at the counter, and said with more authority than he had ever used with them, singly or together: "We're going to the reservation. It's time to introduce Terrence to Hosteen." He did not need to say more. There was so much that could be said that would remain unspoken but that summed up both John's defeat as a medical doctor and his recovery as a healer.

Sandra stood up and went to him. "You're a real doc, Poppa," she said, her eyes filled with tears.

PART IV

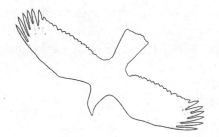

In the landscape lay powers for the mind and spirit especially on nights slashed by lightning, when medicine makers sought it face-to-face.

Where the Lightning Strikes, Peter Nabokov

You have people there who say they know the earth, plants and animals. Well, I wonder if they really know these things. I have seen things. I have seen things they have never seen. I have heard things they have never heard. I have spoken to these things, and I have heard their words and stories.

Andrew George, Palouse Elder and Traditionalist.

Some even call it a stereotype of Indigenous life, but today an Apache girl dances on the grass beyond the ball field, talking to the wind and when recess is over her teacher asks her, what she was doing. "Talking to the wind," she says smiling, matter-of-fact.

Going to Water, The Journal of Beginning Rain, Stan Rushworth

Sometime after the emergence to the Glittering World, a few women gave birth to monsters, as a result of transgressions that had occurred in the previous world. As the monsters matured they began to prey upon the people, causing the death of children and creating a climate of fear. When the monsters had killed off most of the young children, several events occurred which eventually resulted in the placing of the earth back into harmony.

Changing Woman became impregnated by the Sun. She gave birth to twin sons, later called Monster Slayer (Naaee' Neezghani) and Born for Water (Tobdjishchini).... As the twin boys grew up, they became curious about who their father was. Very reluctantly Changing Woman told them that their father was the Sun. Aided by spiritual beings like Spider Woman, the boys traveled to the home of the Sun. There they went through a series of endurance tests to prove that they truly were sons of the Sun. After they passed all the tests devised by the Sun, they were offered many material goods; but they refused the goods, saying they only wanted the spiritual weapons of lightning (Atsiniltl'ish K'aa'—male zigzag lightning arrow and Hatsoo'alghal K'aa'—female straight lightning arrow) to kill the monsters (naaee') on Earth. When the twins returned to Earth they used their weapons and killed the monsters, beginning with the giant Ye'iitsoh La'i Naaghai, thus making the Earth safe again for human beings.

23

As If On A Trail

The IPCC report was the dark thread running through each day. Terrence felt that his collapse was detracting from the seriousness the times required rather than helping him focus on the essentials. He had seen it happen with his students who predictably turned away from their larger interests when they suffered a physical or emotional setback. His own people took themselves in another direction. How could they possibly be well, if the Earth was afflicted? Suffering turned them to the world, looking to heal the larger circle in order to heal the circle that was themselves.

He scrutinized John warily – John was a physician and so pledged to heal individuals. He had not been trained or called to heal community wounds or Earth wounds as a way of healing the patients that came in the room – even though he probably knew that whatever results he achieved, he would be sending them out to be re-infected. 99% of the time, the individual hadn't caused his or her own illness, though conventional thinking implied one did.

And yet Terrence felt he was responsible … conundrum. His situation was bringing them closer together and further apart. Crisis exposes the cracks, the tensions, the disagreements. What did he want? He wanted to be standing on the Mountain. He wanted to be in a vision pit. He wanted to smoke his pipe alone on the land. He wanted to be with Sandra.

He couldn't find her. He could see her but the closer he came to her the more apart they seemed. She was far away. Where was Sandra? First he disappeared from her and now she was absent from him. While she tended to him, his condition was separating them. They were each increasingly in their own private worlds, exacerbated by his need to be cared for by John – so there was a third with them and a third undermines a two.

Terrence's heart clenched. It surprised him how much it mattered that Sandra was gone or it seemed so. He had quietly criticized his students and colleagues for the attention they gave to themselves and he had fallen into the same trap. His own story had overwhelmed him and he had lost sight of Sandra. He had thought he was impervious to loss – he read about it each day and though he tried to hold the necessity of the complex net of beings vibrant in his mind, he was aware that many species fell through the gaps in his awareness and memory. There were less than a dozen northern white rhinos and no Sandra. They would not reproduce themselves enough to save their species, nor would she.

He called out to her but heard no response. She was probably off somewhere with John or on a run. She knew that healing was primarily in his hands and she absented herself so that he could do what was required. The classic Western healing journey – he had to go off to find the way of healing in order to return to the woman. Not a story he would have been proud to invent. But maybe it was the story he was in.

And so now with the same meticulous awareness with which he had approached Wy'east, he reviewed the thoughts and observations that had taken him up the Mountain to see which were accompanying him on this lingering descent.

The IPCC report. Not what was in it. He had known it all. So had Sandra. But those two small references to Indigenous wisdom. Brave references, he acknowledged, bitterly. He didn't know how the authors had gotten them through the long process of submission and scrutiny leading to a final accord of all persons and institutions concerned: Climate change? Yes. Grave? Yes? Human causation? Yes!

Could there be remedies? There were many suggestions, which seemed increasingly unlikely to be implemented rigorously and in time.

Why not consult with the people who lived there, who had always lived there, the people of the land? Terrence had his own answers. A clan brother, a medicine man, had bemoaned his difficulty in healing the *washichu* illnesses. In order to heal he had to go deep into the mind of the affliction. He could bring healing to those diseases that were endemic to the land and to the people. But the alien disturbances —the mind of he *washichu* was so convoluted he couldn't find its logic. But when the alien illnesses affected his people, he couldn't bring himself to accept the standard medical treatments that were designed in a laboratory where a stranger who would never meet his patient and would likely never encounter the illness in the flesh, still created an exact potion designed to cure. Why assume the stranger in a laboratory would know more than someone who had been born on the land, exposed to the elements, who was fluent in the languages of the other creatures?

Did a stranger really know more about the atmosphere from his instruments and research than his grandfather had known about wind?

Climate change! Why not go back to the old ways, the ways his people had practiced, that had not caused harm? There was something so intractably stupid and stubborn that refused the necessary 180 degree turn to save all life. Could he find his way back? All the protestations assumed that humans would not survive if they went back, but, increasingly, the reality seemed to him that nothing would survive going forward. He had no idea how the many species including the human would survive the future.

It had been a difficult trek up the mountain. He had wanted to run, but he'd had to walk slowly, to consider and be still simultaneously with each step so that when he had reached his destination, whatever that would turn out to be, he was prepared to do and be what was required.

To recognize that other ways of knowing, that the old ways that had been warred against, did still exist and might be useful, even essential, was to concede that the five hundred year war was still being waged … and … climate change, the euphemism for the end of all life, for extinction by human hands, was the final *victory* of the *washichu*. So small an entry in such a long document he could have missed it. But he didn't. Not a reference to his own people but to farmers in Nigeria and Burkina Faso. They could predict the weather. His field. Kinship.

He brought the acknowledgement of Indigenous knowledge to the Mountain. He made an offering. And his life was changing.

Standing at the foot of the **M**ountain, the sun setting and turning the snow red, he had been no longer on a mountain, but at a river bank at Fallen Timbers, Ohio on August 20th, 1794, with the story his grandfather had told him. They had told him the story so he would know how important it was to remember even though he would forget:

"The moccasins trickled blood in the sand and the water was red in the river." History had been passing through him like a jet stream and he traveled on it back to the armies that George Washington had sent to fight Blue Jacket the Shawnee war chief leading the Northwest Confederacy. Blue Jacket was trying to protect the lands east of the Mississippi and south of the Great Lakes which the British had ceded to the US as if they owned them by right of war. Two hundred and thirteen years earlier and concurrently present he was seeing the armies to the present day. The past enfolded itself into the future that cocooned it. The beginning of this nation state and the end linked through the simultaneity of time and blood.

On the other side of the Mountain, Hanford, another culmination of the dark longing, "looking for a stone" as Sweet Medicine, one of the chiefs of the Cheyenne, had put it, "that would take the white men across the continent in every direction," including here, where Terrence was standing. "They will tear up the Earth, and at last you will do it with them. When you do you will become crazy and will forget all that I am teaching you. The white people will be all over the land and at last you will disappear."

"You will do it with them and when you do you will become crazy." Yes, he had become crazy. He had known this for a long time. Sandra and he joked that everyone living now was mad. And then, he had collapsed. Of course, he had collapsed. His internal structure had collapsed. The internal structure that sustained all life was collapsing. The five hundred year war against his people and similar wars against the people of the earth, all across the earth, were culminating in extinction.

He roused himself from under the blanket of night. Wind, his mentor, was slipping through the needles of the pines. If it could blow through him, he believed it would relieve his unease and teach him something. John had said they were going to Canyon de Chelly. He had never been there. He didn't want to stay where he was and he didn't want to go inside. He went to the deck and started circling the way Sandra often did. He liked perimeters. He liked the consolation of a circle.

24

A White Crow

Sandra had not disappeared. She had retreated into her own world. She was torn, even more than Terrence was between her father's world and ways of healing and other ways she was just glimpsing. Maybe they weren't ways of healing so much as forms of diagnosis. How did one know what was really wrong when the great pain did not reside in a human, but in place? What she had once picked up in her father's patients, and related to similar intensities in the earth, she now felt directly. Her pain, Terrence's anguish, the Earth's howl and trembling, she could not, would not distinguish them. Terrence's condition was an earthquake or a tsunami, a tornado, a category 4 tropical typhoon, a volcanic explosion and lava flow, an X category Solar Flare, a dam over a great river giving way, in her life.

Sandra was up on the roof, pacing. Terrence was on the deck, pacing. A similar restlessness afflicted both of them. The woman who had built the house had had the same need to get outside and away. John Birdswell was in the kitchen to the east, washing the dishes, singing, whistling, his private conversation with the wraith that he still loved and communed with exactly as he had, if shyly, when she was alive.

Sandra heard the musical breath and then his silences as if he was engaged in a back and forth, call and response. She listened too, without realizing she had done this all her life, not ever expecting that anyone would respond from the emptiness.

It had never occurred to Sandra to invoke Samantha Crow as an ancestor. That is, to call to her mother on the other side for direction and insight. What her father had finally told her months before had given her an image where before she'd had nothingness. Now she wondered what pain had driven her mother to take on the role of a stateless woman, belonging nowhere, passport or not. A passport that allowed her a range of exits and entrances, but not agency or power.

That her mother had suffered was not a thought she had ever had. Nor that Samantha Crow had endured long enough to bring Sandra into life and then had left. That her mother's romantic stories had not been bravado or an overactive imagination but, perhaps, camouflage for an unbearable life. Maybe her grief hadn't been as personal as John had imagined or maybe it had been and John had not been sufficient, though he was the kindest man Samantha could ever meet to help her stay alive. Not even the child had been sufficient for her to live past the birth. What had she suffered that had made her so sure she would not live? Sandra would never know except that she felt unexpected empathy with a wound she would never know herself. And who was this man, her father, who had secretly kept the connection alive for Sandra's entire life?

Her father must have finished the dishes as she couldn't hear the water running. It was so still, she could hear her father's whistle and then a pause and the whistle again.

Terrence had stopped pacing and was leaning silently against a tree.

"Ma," she tried. "Ma … Ma…." She couldn't say Mom or Mommy. That hadn't ever been in her vocabulary. She couldn't utter the most basic sound in the world.

"CrowMa," she heard herself calling soundlessly. "CrowMa! Do you know we are dying down here?"

Her mother had known. This was Sandra's realization.

She remembered the European myth that maintained that crows were originally white but had been burned black when a guardian crow had not interceded when Apollo's lover was dallying with a man. The Shawnee have a similar myth, where Crow had been thrown into the fire for warning Buffalo that the hunters were coming. Sandra preferred the Shawnee myth as the burned crow had been saved from death by the littlest hunter who noted that Crow was warning its brother Buffalo of danger. The Shawnee recognized the sacred connection when it was shown to them. And through this understanding all had become related – Crow, Buffalo and the Shawnee. "Everything is connected to everything else," Terrence insisted that under-standing this made good science. He could not speak of any element without tracing its relationship to everything in its field. He had pushed his students to seek out connections that weren't obvious or commonly stated, arguing for the ways in which global warming drives the arctic cold to the Midwest.

Her father had described his lover as a young woman who always dressed in white, a white crow, and so an ancient crow, from the time before crows were black, before humans had enacted their power over them. From the time that humans could imagine being kin to other beings. From the time before extinction.

What did a white crow symbolize? Was it like the birth of a white buffalo, an omen of hope? Sandra could feel hope rise in her. What if she came from an old line despite an entire life believing that she had no lineage whatsoever? What if her mother bird had been waiting for her to call? She could feel her head rising, her mouth puckering into a yellow beak. Birdswell. Her surname gave her the shivers.

A wave of benevolence, like a west wind, engulfed her, scented with pine pollen. She had not even noticed, so preoccupied was she with her own pain and confusion, the sweet yellow dust that was everywhere, harbinger of new growth, unlike the yellow dirt of the reservation. When you open the door, everything can enter. This time, luckily, it was the west wind. Benevolence and sorrow had the same tone. One engaged the other.

It happened so quickly, it startled her. She had a mother, a spirit, an energy to address on the other side. White CrowMa. The source of the benevolence that even until this instance, she had assumed emerged from her own heart. And the wind had come up. Maybe the pine pollen hadn't been there before.

25

Massacre Cave Overview

"They're killing us," Hosteen grinned, poking John in the ribs with his left hand as he faced Terrence and welcomed him, "and we're supposed to heal each other from their illnesses."

"*Ya'at'eeh!*" Hosteen greeted Terrence.

"*Áay,*" Terrence responded. It was not awkward for the two to simply stand in each other's presence and find it good.

"I guess, Hosteen," John said, "this is the first time we've had a patient to work on that isn't from the Res."

"Except for you," Hosteen responded.

John grinned. "Terrence, I put you in Hosteen's hands. Sometime after Sandra's mother died, I came out and Hosteen did ceremony for me. I guess we were working together on me because I really wanted to heal." He paused and looked around. His words were not said lightly. "Hosteen did ceremony and … here we are."

"Who is he?" Hosteen seemed to ask Sandra. She was standing by the tall juniper outside his house, too singular to ever be shade, looking west, watching the sky configure itself into a praise poem that mirrored the land in shape and color. Spider Rock, a spine of sandstone reaching skyward, was some miles behind them; she felt it had her back. He had come up next to her.

The best she could offer was, "We are bonded."

"Shall I give him the hogan to sleep in?"

"That would be a good thing, Uncle. Poppa thinks he might heal here."

"Do you want to stay with him"

"If it's OK with you."

"Not mine to decide."

"You know, Uncle, I wouldn't be with him if not for you."

He nodded.

Then as if it were an idea that had just occurred to him, though she knew he had been waiting to say it to her, he said, "If you stay in the hogan together, it will be good to do ceremony while you're here."

"We know that," she said in appreciation of the inevitable.

Smells, onions, garlic, meat searing came from the house. That first sharp scent which indicates that flesh will become food. Terrence had begun to prepare the leg of lamb they had brought after John had poked it skillfully with a knife to insert garlic. Now Terrence had John cutting potatoes and was amused, again, to see that a knife in his hand placed John in a surgical theater where every movement was exact and careful. John would not let the irregular shape of the russets daunt him. They would end up as a mound of potatoes each piece almost the same exact size and shape.

"How long are you going to be at that?" Terrence was entertained.

"As long as it takes."

"I hear you're living in a tent," Hosteen continued the conversation with Sandra.

"When you come to visit, we will give you the house, Uncle."

"What did you buy to drink?"

"Dr. Pepper and Mountain Dew."

"You didn't."

"We didn't. Ice tea and lots of coffee and cream and, ok, sugar."

"What else?"

Sandra took the red package of tobacco out of her purse. She never knew if she should offer it in a formal manner as he had taught her when she was very little. The back and forth before he took the package or she was allowed to take it, always made her laugh.

What was the way of respect? She held the package out, offering it simply and he took it, his acknowledgement so subtle, she could have missed it except that he had also taught her to be observant.

"You know Reynolds bought Natural American Spirits. They also own Camels, Newport and Pall Mall," Sandra said as if she knew something he might not know.

"Indians never owned American Spirits. Started by some white guys in Santa Fe." He set the record straight.

"But they're still organic," she couldn't stop her too earnest self from countering.

He chuckled. "Our tobacco always was."

They had found their way to each other.

Wanting to be alone and satisfied that Terrence needed to be with Hosteen and her father, Sandra took the truck and drove to the north side of the canyon to Massacre Cave. The Navajo name, *Adah Aho'doo'nili,* Two Fell Off, referred to the woman who, when the Federal armies invaded, jumped on to one of Kit Carson's soldiers and the two fell down to their death.

The distance that Terrence had felt between him and Sandra was not an aberration. There was a divide, each carrying what they had been given – by fate? – alone. But on the planet, the great divides are rooted in beauty. One might not be able to descend easily to the common green river that snaked down the amber sandstone riverbed, but it could be seen and courage drawn from it. How else had the people who had lived here before the conquest survived? They had become adept at clambering up and down the sheer cliffs to drink in beauty and be sustained. She had driven west to the end of the National Monument and up the other side and where the Canyon yawned open, driving along Canyon del Muerto until she came to the outlook she was seeking. It was not the most beautiful of the ten outlooks in her eyes. There were seven outlooks on the south rim and three here where she was. Neither she, Terrence nor her father could descend to the bottom except in one place designated for tourists willing to walk up and down more than two miles – a canny way to limit foot traffic. But with Hosteen they would be able to walk, ride or even drive the 45 miles at the bottom of the great stone walls, wind shaped into great wings from the dark body of the earth.

She wanted to blindfold Terrence so the first time he saw the unparalleled beauty, he would be facing Spider Rock where Grandmother Spider lives. For wasn't the Grandmother weaving them all into a web that would protect them no matter what they would have to face? For herself, Sandra had to make this pilgrimage first and alone as she did almost every year to the place that marked the great violence done by the Federal government to the Navajo. She never wanted anyone to go with her and Terrence was not ready in his body and soul to encounter another place of grief although he knew as well as anyone that entering onto any Native or Indigenous reservation anywhere in the world was to enter into yet another particular story of appropriation, ongoing war and colonization.

They each had their work to do though she was nonplussed that the IPCC report had set them in motion. It wasn't, she consoled herself, that she needed confirmation from an authority, but once the United Nations had testified to the reality of Climate Change, there was no way to diminish the tragedy that was enfolding them. "The North pole is shifting," an Inuit elder had told her as he tried to communicate the extent of the harm that he perceived as a result of his tribe's observation that the magnetic core was moving, throwing human instruments and non-human homing instincts awry. How long would it take for non-Natives to see it? What did the statistic "moving 40 miles a year" mean in addition to the confusion of the sea mammals and the birds? Was there any way to set the world right if north were no longer north? Would the ancestors' spirit homes move too? She'd had no answers for anyone, not for the non-Natives and not for the ancestors.

It was a relief to be by herself at the North Rim outlook. She knew this land well and for so many years that sometimes she dared say to herself that she belonged to it. She went off the trail and settled into a nook among the piñon pines, speaking her heart to the earth. She had chosen this outlook as it would break her heart for its iron twist of violent history against great beauty. At various intersections of the many colors of water in the Canyon particularly at White House Ruins, copper streaks of blue, green, turquoise ran down from the top of the cliffs into the sandy colors of dawn – mauve, taupe, amaranth. How could these not be sky weeping, blood flowing for what had passed and what was coming?

The Navajo, and before them the Anasazi, had lived here, built their homes in the rock, believed in a weave of paradise and sanctuary. Well, not paradise, that was the concept of the killers, but a relationship and harmony between the people and the spirits who lived here so that all might be secure. The Indigenous had known cruelty and violence between themselves, but not ever such as this which had come in the form of armies of mountain men like Kit Carson on killing sprees of humans and animals across the lacerated belly of the earth. Kit Carson had been a murderous killer, particularly of Indians. "May his name be blackened," Sandra thought, taking his actions personally.

Adah Aho'doo'nili – Two Fell Off. A Navajo man with his two young children arrived at the outlook and Sandra backed away to give them privacy to experience their own land. She thought she had pulled far enough away, though maybe she hadn't, and so was alternatively dismayed and yet appreciative to hear the father tell the young ones, the boy, probably nine and the girl more like seven, that the Spanish had given them the name Navajo, "which means *enemy*. "But," he said, "our true name is Diné which means the People." Here Sandra's designation was *bilagáana*, which, she was assured meant white person, but she had determined that it implied, enemy, in the same way as Navajo, or maybe it had become so obvious that the white people had been and often continued to be enemies, and anyone might be assumed such, until proven otherwise. And how could you prove innocence and alliance except by the way you lived your life to the end?

The man and his children left and she waited until she no longer felt their presence and hoped she would not disturb their spirits for whatever time they remained there in this story that had preceded the tragic, forced Long Walk of 1864. Three hundred brutal miles, at a pace most couldn't maintain, often without basic supplies, food and water, without any mercy for children or the elderly. Pregnant women, even one in labor – who died after giving birth – were forced on the excruciating march to exile from their own land in eastern and western Arizona to imprisonment in a forbidding climate and without the barest necessities at Fort Sumner in Bosque Redondo, New Mexico.

Sandra went to the railing and glanced down the one thousand foot painted sandstone cliffs to the bottom where Russian olive trees followed the narrow snaking river through the canyon.

Adah Aho'doo'nili. Was that the alternative? Knowing there was no hope, but to leap onto one of the soldiers massacring the old men, old women, children trying to hide in the canyon walls, and take him down, the woman, clinging to him, also falling to her death. Because, the younger men were out hunting, believing a place so sacred, had to be safe. Sandra found herself leaning far out, as far out as she could while still holding onto the iron handrail burning into her palms with the heat of the sun, wondering who or what she might take down in a desperate leap to avenge the massacre of the earth.

211

26

What She Didn't Say

Even at the edge of the Canyon, holding on for her life, the old story burning into her hands from the place where the Diné father had stamped it into the metal with his grief and his pride of being from the people who came out of such a land, Sandra didn't want to acknowledge what was buried deep within her. She was feeling one with the young girl who had stood between her father and her brother, momentarily comforted by both their presences, while grasping that it had been a woman who, without guns or arrows, would spontaneously throw herself upon a soldier scaling the cliff to take them both down. The girl was involved in the leap. The boy stepped back to comprehend what his father was saying while reading the sign in front of him, a young man who would be called to be a warrior. The boy didn't know what he would be called to confront, but he knew that he would be called and so he stepped back to take it in without seeking comfort.

The boy's father probably no longer lived here. Maybe he had never lived here. But it looked to Sandra that the children understood that this was their land. She had overheard the father speak of touring Dinétah, from one of the four corners to the others. Not the four corners designated by the government on maps but the original four corners of holy land held in place by the four sacred mountains.

The family had unnerved her. She had seen them before, in the market in Chinle, in the Thunderbird Lodge where John preferred to stay because it wasn't a Western chain but a hotel on the reservation itself. There they could eat simply in the cafeteria surrounded by an array of Navajo rugs. Tourists and community members all ate here and so in the course of a week, John would inevitably meet Native people he had come to know over the years so he could inquire about their health, their children and grand-children.

This family had a magnetic presence and yet was unapproachable. The strong bond between them seemed a way of protecting themselves from the tourists, Sandra included, who were everywhere. They were a solitary unit and she was a crowd of questions and concerns and feeling so alone, though solitude is what she had been seeking.

She had deliberately left the three men together to facilitate Terrence's healing but now she felt separate from them, another cultural divide had asserted itself. She was the woman outside the unspoken camaraderie of men. She could be daughter, niece, lover, friend, but she could not be buddy. In that first moment of meeting, when Terrence had held Sandra wordlessly as she trembled, they had crossed a boundary of separation dictated to them by their academic studies through the shibboleth of objectivity that rejects engagement. But that startling intimacy was not present between them now. At night, around a fire, in the dark, all preoccupations might dissolve and the divide she was sensing, as much in her as in the others, might disappear. But now she was unaccompanied in what else she had confront.

She might have been able to dismiss or bury what was agitating her if she hadn't overheard the father talking with his children about visiting the sacred mountain, Tsoodzil, Mt. Taylor. All her studies of uranium poisoning across the country, but particularly on Native land, came rushing through like the toxic flood at Church Rock when over 1,000 tons of solid radioactive mill waste and 93 million gallons of acidic, radioactive tailings solution had flowed into the Puerco River, the contaminants traveling downstream to Navajo County in Arizona and onto Dinétah itself. A spill whose consequences were worse than Three Mile Island which had occurred four months earlier than Church Rock in 1979.

Sandra had only been three years old at the time of Church Rock so she hadn't been aware of it, but ultimately as she had been born in the West, it had entered her consciousness, in the ways that her Eastern colleagues were always talking about Three Mile Island. Though only eleven, Terrence, as a Native boy, had quickly become aware that tribal land was being rendered toxic again. How and why this was happening continuously on Native land was the ongoing mystery that his people confronted on a daily basis. Many of the people living down water of the project didn't know exactly what had occurred but a shudder had gone through all tribal people everywhere; they knew an ill wind when it blew toward them.

Tsoodzil, where, according to the Diné, Turquoise Girl lived, had been a major site of uranium mining, greatly poisoning the land around it, but despite this, various companies were still agitating to reopen the mine. It was to be seen what the blue mountain would do to protect herself.

The clouds were coming in. Behind them rain. In a few days, she would take Terrence to Spider Rock and then back a short distance to Face Outlook to have the long view to the west down the canyon of earth and sky. Soon the weather beings would gather around the rims, the rain descending at sunset, as if intentionally, to be bathed in fire, punctuated by lightning again and again, held taut by the dark wires of vultures and ravens in flight. When she sat in the dining room at the Lodge within the circle of Navajo rugs, she could feel the weavers' intentions to praise the energy of the gray hills, the rivers, rain, corn and the *Yeis*, the medicine spirits. This was one of the very few places she felt at home because of the ways the land seemed to be both outside and inside her at once.

Now she was looking east toward the sculpted bare cliffs that approached each other, great mammals seeking company for the night. What remained of the river was lined with long ruffs of Russian olive trees that should never have been planted here by the US government, taking up water rather than controlling erosion. The government violated the sacred wisdom of the sovereign nation it had conquered and limited to small parcels of land, as it had violated the river itself, and in the aftermath, the bears had gotten to like and depend on the olives, and so restoring the land wasn't easy, as it never is.

And still, so delicate, the sandstone feminine cleft opening to juniper green, maiden and lover entwined, and then the rains coming down amid the celebration of sky and sunset. Opening to the beauty that rendered her so helpless before its presence, Sandra could not prevent a fearful memory from rising in her.

Two years earlier, before she had connected with Terrence, Sandra had come to the reservation to support a colleague's environmental work on the reservation.

Tired from driving for over eight hours, she had pulled her car over to the side of the road and parked. The Cameron Trading Post had been closed since 9 pm and most of the lights were out in the hotel. It was dark enough to see the stars although she had failed in her promise to herself to learn the constellations. Hosteen had shown her the configurations he saw and following his custom had, but only in fall and winter, told her the stories in the sky. Her father pointed out the ones he knew, sometimes overlapping with Hosteen's. John showed her Cassiopeia while Hosteen pointed to *Náhookos ba'áadii,* the Woman reclining near the Central Fire and *Náhookòs Bikò* which John called the North Star.

It was a short drive from Cameron to Tuba City where she would spend a few nights before going on to Canyon de Chelly. She and John always stopped here; it was just inside the border of the reservation and was, for her, the first long look into the vastness of this land. When she looked around and could see far in every direction, it was the equivalent of taking a long drink of water from a safe mountain stream that eased her of all her urban ills.

She leaned back against the passenger seat door, breathing in the frosty air. Cold, distance, night, stillness, stars conspired to remind her of the quiet life that mostly eluded her and almost everyone she knew. She came here and stopped because she could think here. She needed a lot of space around her to think about weather and climate. Work was crowded. Crowded rooms full of machines, people, sounds, screens, pinging. It was no place to learn about the state of the earth or to receive any information that would reliably tell anyone what to do. Over the years she accompanied her father to the hospital where mechanical and technological soundscapes are organized for healing. John believed in hospitals, participated wholeheartedly on behalf of his patients, and so Sandra, as a child, believed too. But she didn't believe in the climate hospital where the patient, Climate, was diagnosed, treated and met with emergency procedures – Code orange, bells and whistles. Seemingly everyone was stopping what they were doing to minister to the one who was dying and had to be brought back to life. But then … what ongoing care was offered to prevent relapse and assure health for the one or the community?

Sandra did not fully believe that her workplace, one of many emergency centers of offices, conference spaces, labs, classrooms, rooms filled with computers and instruments competing for space and place, were successfully designed to change the current trajectory of life on the planet. She was afraid of actions she might take. She feared long-term repercussions of discoveries that led to harm. It was unavoidable because there was little time to evaluate consequences. Calculating the long-term side-effects, collateral damage of any discovery, project or technology did not seem to be front and center.

The colleague she was visiting was wrestling with the complexities of developing appropriate tribal energy policies consistent with Indigenous people's right to self determination, their sovereign authority to develop their energy reserves, while respecting obligations to other communities, to the earth and to the future. Annie Blakeddy was like Sandra, obsessed with climate change, sustainability and globalization but she was caught, as everyone was, in the conflict between energy and environment. Still, Sandra envied her. As an Indigenous woman aligned with her tribe, she probably did not have to fear being conscripted to working on climate engineering, climate and weather modification, solar radiation management, artificial weather programs or even weather warring – all the possibilities that Sandra feared her work might, inadvertently support. The dangers had dizzied her and she was grateful for a comparatively benign way to make a living by juggling the environmental costs of a new human development while advising housing developments.

All of this was on her mind when she arrived in Cameron. After driving for so long, it was good to stand. Alone in the car, she had yielded to her father's passion as if he were there and had been listening to Neil Young's "Goin' Home" as soon as she'd crossed into Arizona.

She didn't want to hear a human voice, preferably not even her own voice or thoughts. She looked in all directions – this *was* the long view. The wind came up. It wasn't a sign or a message, it was just the wind coming up. Still she was inclined to integrate the sudden gust into everything that concerned her. She wasn't in an office with the windows sealed and the temperature regulated. Climate change, climate control, one invoked the other. Sandra and her fellow researchers could be impervious to the wind's rising if they wished. She could consciously choose to include the wind in her prognostications or she could keep the wind out of her calculations. But then it likely would happen that the wind would come up, not come up in her thinking, but come up in the world and demand attention. There was no direct or discernible connection between her lean computations and a later storm five thousand miles away, but … something she didn't understand might be at work. She couldn't prove it, but she could feel the consequences of not taking everything into consideration.

The gift of coming to the reservation was that the emptiness and spaciousness helped her think. There was nothing in the way of the horizon, nothing as far as she could see except for the skimpy power lines, occasional houses, and a few business establishments in the very small towns. The relatively flat earth was dry, broken, dusty, stony and rough. Various scrubby dull green plants, dusty green chamisa, skeleton weed, barbwire Russian thistle were scattered among patches of sand. Empty plastic bottles, tin cans, some crushed, some not, casually strewn.

It was twenty miles to Tuba City. It would be an hour before she was in her room. She opened the car door to arrange the items on the passenger seat before she got in to drive and her cell phone fell out on the ground. Tired as she was, when she bent down to pick it up she tripped and caught herself, palms on the earth. The sands were hot.

It was 12:30 a.m. Confused and disoriented, she tried to think logically: there had been enough time for the earth to have cooled after a hot day. Only it hadn't been a hot day. It was March. March, just before the Equinox. It was after midnight and the sands were hot. It was March and the night air was a few degrees above freezing. She could hear the tiny chink of a thin layer of frost as it formed a covering over a puddle, not yet extended to the edges. Everything has its music.

She bent down again, picked up handfuls of sand and dribbled them onto her palms. Then she walked away from the car, a few feet, then further. She stood her ground. The wind was fiercer now and she could feel the cold on her face but the sand in her hands was very warm.

Of course, she could, anyone could, predict the temperature of sand at night. Perhaps, she hoped, her hands were cold and the contrast was deceiving her. She took another handful and poured it over her head, so that it rippled down slowly. It was very warm. It was warmer than body temperature. You could say it was hot. She was feeling a little crazy. She half expected to be able to see by a fire in them. It made no sense. Heat. Radiation. If it were plutonium that was at issue, it could be hot. But there was no plutonium here. And she had no understanding that could, according to her best knowledge, explain heat and uranium. Uranium-238 has a half life of 4.5 billion years so it was not likely to give off a lot of heat. Uranium-235 has a half life of 700 million years. But … the sands were very warm.

Her mind whirled. The hot sand was warming her hand. Maybe the heat increased with her agitation. Death in the palm of her hands. Cameron had been a major uranium mining and storage site. Jack Daniels open pit mine #1 produced more uranium than any other pit in the area. The mine was not named after the Diné men who had discovered the uranium as was the custom, but after a discarded whiskey bottle. No substantial precautions had been taken. The water holes were poisoned. The animals, the vegetation and the people were dying. The required cleanup and compensation had not occurred. Knowledge had been withheld from the people. Illnesses were denied. Sandra's middle of the night conclusion: The sands were radiant. The sands were hot because … she didn't know why but knew it was a fearful situation.

September, 2007, Canyon de Chelly. It was just weeks since Terrence had collapsed. As they drove in the long about way she and her father favored through Cameron, Tuba City, Kayenta, Many Farms to Chinle, Sandra's thoughts inevitably flitted to the earlier trip. She had never gained an understanding of the hot sands. She couldn't set it entirely aside because she believed that Terrence had buckled when he penetrated, with his piercing eyes, the history that led to the contamination of sacred land at Hanford Nuclear Reservation. He had looked through Wy'east to see it, in the way he had looked at the IPPC report through the wide-angle multidimensional lens of his mind.

Alone at Massacre Cave Outlook, the sands dribbled back into her consciousness. Terrence's precarious condition had seemingly allowed her to set aside the entire spectrum of ills from the Anthropocene – from war to the poisoned earth – to focus on him. And also his condition had raised her alarm to orange alert. Worried about him, she turned away from the hot sands, but she could not forget them when standing at Adah Aho'doo'nili.

She could see into the earth to its fiery core and as far as the sun, as he could see forward and back seven generations and widely to the origin of the wind, its destination and return, to the swirl of currents, rising and falling, emerging and diminishing, an unending circle encompassing the globe.

Now she – so much had they become one – had to hold alongside Terrence's collapse looking at Hanford, the inescapable fact, though she did not understand it, that the sands at Cameron had been hot at midnight on a cold March night, 2005, just before the advent of the spring equinox.

27

Three Turkey Ruins

Sandra came back to the house around 1 p.m. and saw that the three men were still inside, together. As the sun was overhead, they had probably gone in to keep cool. September was often the hottest month, and there was always a great difference in temperature between sun and shade, like black and white. Through the screen door, their voices were lyric and easy, one phrase edging slowly into another, a lilt and a drone, a comfort pattern. In the short time they had been on the homesite, they had bonded, as she hoped they would, and she had become an outsider. The energetic configuration was a triangle, the strongest form. To enter and require that two, John and Terrence, detach from each other, so that she could fill the space between them, would undermine what was occurring. Maybe the cube of the four of them could smooth itself into a circle with the energy flowing unimpeded, but she was too jagged to accomplish this. She was broken pieces and edges. She was shattered glass. Knowing the ring was essential and that she had, they had, come here to re-establish a flow in which Terrence could heal, she started circling, as she did at home. She had to find her own center before she met with them again.

When Hosteen came out, the screen door twanging behind him as it shut, she had gone around the house several times. He stood there watching until she came round again and nearly walked into him.

He didn't speak. Whoever spoke would set the tone for what needed to be said, what silence was calling in.

Hosteen was a patient man. He somehow settled into his posture without moving to lean against the side of the house or against the half-maintained fence around half of the house that was never completed, as if the thought of a fence had been a mistake from the beginning. Whatever had needed restraint, sheep or goats, was being sheltered elsewhere. Nothing else was to be confined. The government strategy of dividing sacred land held by the tribe into individual lots, that turned earth into property, had worked to alienate the people from their history and lives, increasing poverty and despair. "You can't fence in wind, light and rain." Hosteen had told John that he was waiting for the Bureau of Indian Affairs to understand this.

Startled by Hosteen's appearance, Sandra adjusted to stabilize herself. Hosteen's balance was subtle, precise and easy. The earth was holding him up. Sandra had no such steadiness, she leaned against the back of his turquoise blue pickup.

"I need to run."

"How many laps around the house?"

"It's not working." Perhaps he knew that already for he had been rock still a moment before and now he was moving toward the pickup, throwing the passenger door open for her to scramble in. She picked up her water bottles and waist pack and sat down.

"Three Turkey Ruins?" his question was a statement.

"You can drop me off at the junction and I'll run back."

"Can't. You're *bilagáana*."

"You're my uncle."

"Can't." His answer seemed curt, but he was studying her while driving.

"*Bilagáana* always want to be the exception," he was smiling somewhat, then became more sober. "You're hurting hard in your heart," he said. "I can't let you go alone. You might get lost."

"I'm already lost," she said.

"Exactly," he said.

"Terrence is going to be OK," Hosteen said in the event she had been afraid of going into the house and feeling gloom. Then added, "You were on the North rim," a statement that invited elaboration but didn't insist upon it.

"I was at Massacre Cave. There was a Diné man there with his two children. He was teaching them."

"Are you after more history or more ruins?"

"Aren't they the same, Uncle? I want my feet on the ground."

They didn't speak for the next miles, the roadway became an unpaved road when they left the National Monument and soon they came to the barely visible, unmarked turnoff. Rather than a Do Not Enter sign, which would be enticing to tourists, the entry was hidden by what appeared to be impenetrable brush. Hosteen made the sharp turn and entered, riding the truck as if on horseback. Sandra smiled. Slippery seat, saddle, the same. If one imagined the truck was animate, driving was a form of communication – human and vehicle one unit. If she were running, she would have made a similar gesture, turning suddenly, racing fast into the brush, not to be seen, not to be giving away her position, not to reveal this opening.

The truck shimmied, sheared, sped up one path and then another. The ways, just large enough for a single vehicle, divided, then divided into two, into three, veered off to the right and/or left, sometimes straightening, sometimes turning. Hosteen drove fast and steadily despite the dry ruts and stones in the path, as if his momentum was his map and if he lost one, he would lose the other.

Here and there, they passed someone on horseback. There were home sites here too as there were in the Canyon. But not the kind the government was building in the towns, erecting housing projects with one house next to another, when the Diné, unlike the Anasazi who had lived here before them, had always lived far from each other. Each Diné family had been a unit living on the land with its animals, out of the others' sight. Strong clan and tribal bonds, which did not depend on proximity, maintained intrinsic interdependence distinct from relying on shops, gas stations and government buildings for survival and connection. On paper, the government had benign intentions regarding housing – and the *bilagáana* believed their ways were the right ways and so imposed them. Chinle, other towns were beginning to change, developing small shopping malls and housing developments and all the urban ills that went with them.

An old man on a dark stallion watched them with an open gaze, neither welcoming nor disapproving, but an acknowledgement passed between him and Hosteen who increased his pressure on the gas pedal enough to show he knew the road and then slowed to indicate he was responsible. Turning back, Sandra could see the man was nodding. It was then that the encounter she'd had with some mustangs in the morning cantered into her awareness, the early morning dream riding with them.

After the turn to Massacre Cave Outlook, several horses had sauntered across the road, occupying the entire width. So coordinated with her passing by, their action seemed deliberate. A traffic guard. Had she been going too fast? She stopped, quickly, as if heeding a yellow light turning red. They continued facing her so she turned off the engine. This was their territory; she heeded their instructions. She was in the middle of the road, blocking any cars from behind that might spook the horses. Sandra got out, wanting to talk with them. If they stopped you on the road, they had a mission.

She looked directly at the horses. One brown mare stared back, taking her measure. The brown mare, two stippled horses, and two frisky colts, all thin and supple, had been feeding on what the dry land offered.

"I dreamed that I was walking in the rain last night," she told the mare who approached her. "Is it going to rain?"

They continued to look at each other. Sandra wanted to stroke the length of the long bone in her face, but what she, Sandra, wanted was irrelevant. This was the horse's land. The mare had stopped her. The horses had autonomy. Their relationship with the people who lived here was outside Sandra's understanding; she had to yield to the unknown, to the people's way and to the horses.

The mare stood there listening and Sandra continued. "In the dream, I was on open land somewhere. I had decided to take a walk that had no goal but to be outside for as long as I could be outside. I was not going somewhere. I was not exercising. I was walking and the walk had the quality of breathing." It seemed the mare was listening intensely so Sandra continued. "This was not unusual, this is how I live, unless," she paused, "I'm at work. At work, we walk differently. Fortunately, you will never know as long as you live here."

There was no doubt in Sandra's mind that the mare had stopped her on the road in order to hear the dream, or – this seemed closer to the reality – in order for Sandra to hear the dream herself.

"I was walking on the land and it was raining. It was raining hard. And … yes, that was the point; I didn't slow down. The rain added to my pleasure. Yes the pleasure of the walk was that it didn't matter that it was raining. You understand that, you don't always seek cover when it rains."

The memory was so strong, she was back in it, oblivious to the turmoil of Hosteen's driving on such a road.

Sandra had stood there talking to the mare who also just stood there. The colts had left the road with the other horses and were frisking under the trees, engaged with each other and the scent of leaves and bark. "It wasn't only a drizzle. It wasn't a female rain. It was raining hard, storming. I didn't stop walking nor did I look for shelter. There were several tall trees in the area but none had a large canopy. The branches were sparse and vertical. That was where horses would go when it rained. I fell down into the mud. So what!

"That's the whole dream. What do you think?" Sometimes, it seemed to Sandra, that animals smiled, appreciated humor. Otherwise they found humans tiresome. "Do you think it is going to rain?" She thought the mare agreed: it was going to rain and Sandra had needed to know.

Much, much later, she would tell Terrence, "It was as if the mare nodded to me when she turned and walked back into the brush and juniper from which she had entered the road." Sandra was thinking that if she were an animal, she would be a mare.

Re-running the dream, she stepped back into the rain. Water. Her water jar fell out of her hand. Startled, Sandra was back in the truck: the road they were on was nothing like water.

They had driven several miles from the road on sand, stone and gravel almost to the top until the way was blocked by a fallen tree. It had been there last time she was here, positioned to block the road. Hosteen got out of the truck, pointed the way even though she knew the path and indicated he would wait. Yes, he knew that she wanted to be alone; he did as well. He nodded, she ran up a steep rise, turned another half mile to the overlook, picked up some soda cans and beer bottles and placed them in the cloth bag she had brought for this reason and hid it behind a piñon pine with low branches. After turning in a circle, recognizing all the familiar landmarks, she lay down at the cliff edge and looked down at the ancient dwellings wedged under slabs of sandstone. The Anasazi had been a Pueblo people, unlike the Diné.

Her chin on her crossed arm, her toes pointing down on the sandy soil, a few stones and twigs removed from under her. Everything that grew here – juniper, piñon pine – was scratchy and straggly, and well it should be as the sun beat down, the rain pounded when it came, the lightning struck. The sky was close to the ground here and wide, the earth, she was an old drum, hammered, bang, bang, bang.

Time fused. Sandra wasn't with the Anasazi *then*, but here *now* with the Anasazi and Hosteen, his people and, simultaneously with Terrence and his people. A meeting ground. Her people. Who were her people? As everything gathered into the moment, linear time yielded to the simultaneity of presence. Where had the Anasazi gone and why? Had the climate changed and they'd accommodated to it, turning up again as the ancestors of the Pueblo people? Or had there been some disregard of the natural conditions that had done them in? Under the sandstone slab, the old buildings were left, the people gone – as if a kind of neutron bomb had been exploded. There were signs of other ills not unknown to modern times: mass migrations, drought, deforestation, human conflict. What was left? For those willing to read the alphabet of weather, minerals and desertion on the walls, it could be a cautionary tale for these times. Then and now, the same present moment.

The sands were not very hot here, a relief, though they might be with the sun beating down. She tried to lay still and listen but heard nothing. She

223

wanted to speak of Cameron to Hosteen but couldn't. She had spoken to him the day after she had fallen onto the hot sands. It seemed to her his eyes filled and then, immediately, his face was transformed into a mask that could be labeled "Endurance." It wasn't for her, a white woman, a climatologist to come into his world to tell him about the harm being done to his land, as if he didn't know who was suffering from cancer and who had died, who had worked in the mines, whose house had been built from contaminated materials, whose livestock was ill and bleating and who and what was responsible. The dire ramifications of uranium mining were not secret nor were the economic, energy and health needs of the tribe and the people. And it wasn't only uranium that was the problem. She could flip a switch in her home or office, one of a half million homes, and thank the coal burning plant for the light. She could also thank the APS (Arizona Public Service Electric Company) who leased the land and bought the coal from the Tribe who were forced to trade survival for income, extreme pollution and climate change. This was what her friend had been working on two years before. The reservations that had been delegated before the colonizers knew the value of the minerals that were there, were being exploited while her people were sending probes into the earth everywhere, and even up into the sky, looking for more territory. A space experiment had sent bacteria out of our orbit to see what would survive beyond. "Twenty-first century pestilence blankets," Terrence had noted.

Hosteen knew all this. She envisioned he might even know what to do, how to heal it, but – letting her imagination fly – would have to gain assurance that the reservation would be closed to anyone, including Sandra and John, closed indefinitely to all but the native people, for the land to have its own, continuous healing lodge ceremony. Maybe forever. Her head was spinning as she dreamed the scenario. But the Anasazi Pueblo had not been able to heal the climate dilemmas. Or had they?

As much as Westerners thought they knew, they didn't know what the old ones had known. Her knowing was hurting her. She wasn't happy with what she knew, what she had studied, the fundamental assumptions of her profession. Her professional advice was that she should have checked her computer to learn whether it was going to rain, rather than ask the horses or even her own body, as a storm might come up suddenly, might without visual warning, darken a blue sky, cause flash floods. How were the horses going to know and if they did, how were they going to communicate that to her precisely? Satellites and the complex system of weather balloons, and the ongoing constant, precise feeding of data into computers, could predict what might be coming. That was Weather 101, a course she had taught as a graduate student. Yet lying here on the ground, the sun seeping into her body, as if each photon were articulate, she felt she might be given understanding and vision if she stayed still enough and listened in what she thought might have been the old ways. Terrence's people and Hosteen's people had known them, and still might though they were suffering the pain of silencing. They were taken down by the machines that came at them in the hands of men who were increasingly like the machines themselves – her own lineage. Those men had come on horses. She had to reckon with that.

She closed her eyes, then opened them to the beauty around her. The ones who had lived here had feasted on the sight of this land. The light was sharp and blunt simultaneously, a direct hit and then a sidelong glance as they were approaching the autumn equinox. She was imagining scaling the walls of the canyon, hand on handprint, to the sanctuary of the houses tucked into, carved out of the womb of stone. To emerge from there into the light of day must have shaped their minds differently than the mind Sandra was experiencing She placed herself in a ledge and looked back across the chasm to where she was lying. It felt like a great distance and she was taken by vertigo. She tried to look steadily and make a link back to the past on the other side, but she couldn't make the bridge she hoped to construct out of longing and tall grasses.

A vortex. Like being in the vortex of a tornado about to be swept up and around in its dark flailing. So much was revolving inside her, the Anasazi, Cameron, the hot sands, plutonium and other poisons at Hanford, the aberrant weather patterns, the elementals raging in drought, fire and convulsive rains. The ancestors had said nothing in particular. They had left but where were their descendants? Lying on the ground had only given her a momentary reprieve. She rose as if startled, picked up her things, and sprinted down to the truck, opened the door, threw in the garbage, took out another water canister, tucking it in her belt. The way Hosteen lowered his eyelids indicated he understood her desperation. "I'll follow you and meet you at the highway," he said, rising from the boulder where he had been sitting in the light and the dark, the sun to the west striking his profile as he faced the dusty iron rose quartz path she had just descended.

When he met her at the highway, where she was dutifully waiting, he turned and pulled over to the side of the road. She started running again as it seemed at first that he was going to lag behind. Maybe he became impatient and wanted to leave her to her own fate, for within ten minutes, he pulled ahead of her as if to leave her to the ten or so miles home. Four or five miles down the road, red-faced, feeling the heat, sufficiently spent, she came upon him outside the truck talking to other mustangs.

"They said I should wait for you," he chortled. He had left the passenger door open so there would be no shame. She climbed in and threw her head back on the seat.

"Thank you." She was grateful.

28

Fire Circle

Coming night. Fire circle. The far field of sky was intermittently illuminated by lightning flashes, distant fireflies. John was tending the fire, an honor that Hosteen bestowed on him. This small home site, a sanctuary within sanctuary, Canyon de Chelly a world apart.

Terrence and John had made the meal, Sandra and Terrence had washed the dishes, Hosteen brought out the coffee he had brewed in an old aluminum pot and poured into white ceramic mugs. Sandra followed with sugar and cream. The rhythm eased her. Preparing the meal was a ritual activity. Eating it another. Washing the dishes, a third. All related to each other and each mattered.

Sandra had been waiting until Hosteen sat down, expecting him to take the elder's place. But then she was so tired, and the youngest, she just sat herself down on the ground with her back against a log in the east, stretching her bare feet toward the fire. The east, dawn, new beginnings, the younger one, was certainly her place, like it or not. It was a small fire, so that they could sit close to it, see each other across the flames and be frugal with the wood. A circle was inevitable and a direction, its wisdom and perspective. Hosteen took his place, as elder, in the north, on a short, thick trunk, turned on its side.

Hosteen was both her support and her scrutiny. She would not want to sit across from him even though they would not make eye contact. Better he view her with a sidelong glance. With his eyes closed and from a great distance, she knew he could penetrate her core and yet – she puzzled this – without intruding. He had no need to know anything for his own gain, he considered her only on her behalf. She couldn't anticipate his thoughts though she believed he understood hers. He thought in a different way, she edged toward his mind and met a barrier she could not cross. He was not keeping her out of his mind, he was not being inscrutable. The only way she could account for it was that she was meeting a singularity. Across the line was another world where thoughts, if she reduced the process of his mind to thinking, were broad and all encompassing, were of a world in and of themselves that reached out to the world she inhabited. His thoughts were approaches, one being to another, embracing. Words failed her, the familiar inability to language what she was perceiving. Her words, thoughts, felt like constructs, devices, like the weather balloons, like the variety of scientific probes and instruments essential to her profession, without being on behalf of earth, wind, water, or light itself. Was it as simple as his tools of understanding were alive and hers were not? She was dizzied.

She withdrew from thinking, like moving from land into water. Not a word needed to be said for understanding to occur. Then Terrence sat down on her left, in the south; she felt his presence in her heart. She leaned toward him without a muscle moving. Her father was across from her, in the west, which some designated as the place of kinship. How right for the man who had brought this little family together. Understanding this, she looked at John differently. As if she hadn't known him before. How could a man who was born into such loneliness forge these bonds? And Hosteen – wasn't he lonely too? His daughters had not returned to the reservation. Sandra didn't ask Hosteen about them. He would say what he thought necessary and appropriate.

John lifted the end of a log with a poker and balanced it on another log closer in to the fire. The sparks left a trace in the night and were extinguished. The fire surged. A small wind came up, just enough to stir the flames. Terrence smiled to himself and Sandra noticing, felt a great sense of relief. He was at home here. At home meant he was healing. At home here, meant he would not die soon, would not die of this affliction. If Terrence and the wind were in alliance then … then he could heal … because something entirely enigmatic … might come to be.

Terrence had been watching Sandra. This was the first time he had been able to observe her calmly, to respond to her since he had run toward Wy'east. They had driven in the same truck, intermittently shared physical space, exchanged words, they had slept next to each other but they had remained cultures and lifetimes apart. The great suffering of the earth and each of their different histories, and then his injury, had taken them both down into the bone pits of time. She looked weary and restless, jumpy; she couldn't find a place to land.

Sandra had felt like an outsider when she returned from the Massacre Cave and even more so after being at Three Turkey Ruins. She had no understanding of what had occurred between the three men and they did not know what was preoccupying her. But now, mysteriously, the four were settling, without any conversation, into a sacred pattern, and it was having its effect, even on her. Sandra could feel a gentle vortex that was binding them to each other so that what could not have been imagined was coming to be. A deep kinship that neither she nor Terrence had ever known was kindled. Nothing in her father's demeanor indicated what he was thinking or feeling except that he was particularly attentive to the nuance of fire, neither acting hastily nor letting it die down. If fire could ever be presumed to be steady, it was so in John's hands. John had never been a fire keeper in Hosteen's lodge; he'd always been a guest. The last hours had positively altered the pattern so carefully established over more than thirty-five years of friendship. John, not Terrence, had been asked to tend the fire but both men seemed completely at ease. Origins were not an issue. She looked for her own settling in.

Hosteen had the gift to recreate the essential harmony of the world whenever it was damaged, when someone who was suffering came to him or when the broken pieces were before him asking to be reset. Illness didn't break the harmony; illness was a sign that it was ruptured and needed to be attended. Terrence's injury corroborated this.

Such a slight wind. A branch bowing in it, as if a bird were landing and taking off, shifting the balance. So it was for Sandra swaying between the great disturbance of Cameron and the unexpected peace she felt here. Balance was not to find a midway point between the two or to consider that Cameron and peace were two extremes of a single trajectory. Cameron was a disturbance that emerged from a damaged world and this small fire was a still center in another sphere altogether.

She rested. She allowed herself to sink into the unexpected amity of the circle. She was not separate; she disentangled from whatever kept her apart, though sadly, Cameron would not/could not disappear so her grave concerns would remain. But in this moment, she could also yield to Hosteen's medicine. Her decision must have been palpable because Terrence reached out and took her hand.

Here was something she had never known, deep intimacy and exquisite privacy within a circle. The field of connection which had arisen among the men took her in.

Later she would confirm that it had been the wind that had revealed the realignment of the broken. She could not have explained it otherwise, even to Terrence, except to say, "It was the wind." It was because the wind came in his way to the circle, and to Terrence, she interpreted what had been taught to her by her uncle when she was very young: one of the Holy People was present. The winds, corn, rivers, rain, mountains, earth, the Holy People, they were different faces of the same presences, always had been known this way by Indigenous people, except the *bilagáana* didn't know this and felt no remorse when burdening the wind and the other Holy People with all their poisons. Was there any part of the planet they hadn't damaged in some critical way? But then it became somewhat clearer to her that if the wind was present in their circle, then so was earth and fire. Maybe the rains were coming as the clouds had been building their great white, gray, black towers during the afternoons and moving across the sky.

She turned to Hosteen. "Uncle," she said. She could tell by his attention, he was listening. But she had no words. Or that was the one necessary word. "Uncle," she repeated, her voice dropping, so that it became a statement not a call. He stood and carefully sprinkled corn pollen in a circle that contained them and the fire.

Quickly, Sandra sprang to her feet and ran to the truck. She could not be without her pail of earth. She put it on the ground next to her.

Hosteen had seen it before, but asked where the earth was from.

"This land, Massacre Cave, Three Turkey Canyon, Alaska, Kenya, Joshua Tree, Terrence's house, my house, our old house, where Poppa and I lived. Maybe my mother is in it, I don't know." Her father's wince propelled her to add, "Cameron," and relieve herself of some of the pain she was carrying, then turned to him immediately to indicate that she was sorry for bringing up Samantha Crow. Yet, it was true that she had always hoped that her mother's ashes were dispersed in the back yard; she had, as a child, rolled in the dirt and on the grass in the hope of attaching something of the maternal to herself.

Although John always asserted that he had scattered Samantha's ashes to the winds and the sea, she had a memory of him sitting in the back yard, his hands rising from a box on his lap, white with ashes. He had looked like a ghost himself. Logically, it couldn't have happened as she had been born as her mother died and she believed him when he said he had dispersed the ashes within weeks of her death. Samantha had been like a moth, fleeting by nature. She would not have wanted to reside in a box. Had her mother lived with them in the house, Sandra would have known. She would not have been oblivious to the presence of that spirit.

There was a long silence. No one felt inclined to comment. They were not in a conversation. They were in silence and sometimes words broke through like the fire crackling.

"I never knew my parents. I spent so little time with my grandparents, if that is who they were. So I wasn't immersed in the ways of my people. And the schools, you know, they try to beat your history out of you." Terrence spoke as if to the fire rather than the others. If he were addressing anyone directly, it would be Hosteen. Or he was speaking to Hosteen, so that Sandra would understand what he could never explain to her because of the five hundred year rift. She had just been in the Canyon struggling to leap from one time to another and ultimately failing. He didn't know where she had been but she was his other soul and her hand was in his. He would not be speaking of this great wound if she had not brought him to this place that was more than a geographical location. They were in the sacred and he knew it, in the mystery of what can transpire in its presence. What a strange configuration they were in, he thought. A sphere of coexistence that they were all inhabiting even as it was manifesting from within them. Hosteen, John, Sandra and himself.

Sandra's hand twitched. Cameron was dominating her thoughts again and Terrence was flooded with grief about Hanford and *nChe-wana*. Beauty and poison, Sandra had been thinking. Terrence felt great peace here, finally, but also coincident deadly disturbances.

What if he let science go altogether? A radical thought for the Chair of a respectable science department entirely devoted to bringing some wisdom to the most pressing issues that had ever confronted humans. Issues that most of the world had been led to believe could only be solved by science. A few thinkers allowed themselves to be influenced by TEKW, a grace note in a larger composition, but no one was suggesting it become the dominant response to climate change, to agriculture, to environmental devastation, to … to, well almost everything. To science itself. In the years he had been teaching, his field had changed radically in its understanding and its ways of coming to knowledge. In another life he might have trained and become a hurricane hunter. That would have meant flying a machine with all its instruments into the eye of a hurricane but, he would be in the storm with his body and insights. What his people had known had come to them after years and years of devoted observations. Their bodies and souls were their instruments and these had been more than sufficient.

He was talking to Hosteen, but to Hosteen within himself. Or, it was as if he was speaking to Hosteen within himself but hoping perhaps that a spirit who could guide him was listening. Hosteen said illness came when things were out of balance. Terrence was out of balance and the world was out of balance with everything within and without itself. Maybe the Holy People, as Hosteen spoke of them, would begin to guide him.

His great-grandfather on his father's side, whoever he had been, and others like him, confronted by today's issues would have spoken to storm or wind itself, also to eagle, and the spirits would have taught the old man because they would have been in relationship with each other. Yes, this was myth, but it didn't mean it didn't happen. This was myth and myth was a story form of the transmitted teachings and experiences from which, over centuries, his people had built their informed cultures and their lives.

"I never knew my people," was how he had begun and then remained silent. What did his personal history matter? It was a variation on thousands, millions of stories that were his people's story. Anguished or wise they held him fast. And now, whatever he had suffered and lost, he was sitting in Canyon de Chelly, his vision brightened by a small fire and occasional flares of heat lightning, and he had arrived by mysterious means.

John Birdswell had brought him here. Sandra's father, who was so responsible as a father and a physician and yet curiously boyish. Sometimes John felt like a younger brother. He was not younger than Terrence but he seemed so. Was it because John did not have lineage? If you don't have ancestors then you may remain interminably young because you are not carrying what they learned over millennia. Without ancestors you are carrying only what you have learned yourself. Earlier in the day, Hosteen had said that if one is of Deer clan, even if Deer is your only ancestor, you carry that wisdom. This awakened a memory of his grandfather telling him that Creator had asked the animals, the First People, to sustain the human beings that were going to be made, their lives, their bodies, their hearts. The first to speak up was the fish, the Salmon. He thought back to the first night with Sandra when he was certain that tortoise, the old one, had come near them to give them the blessings of his age.

Terrence looked away from Sandra to John. The boyish aspect was a mask. He saw the lines of grief and the years of meeting pain and illness on a daily basis. They had this in common, didn't they? What was it that was so confusing about John? He carried the gravity of a man who had raised a daughter, but he did not carry the gravity of a man who had cared for a wife. Was that it? Terrence pondered, thinking also about himself. Having been so young and American when Samantha Crow died, having had no marriage time with her, no house holding, John was in some aspects still a young man, perpetually a young man pining for his lost love.

John didn't know his own people either, neither who his parents had been or his tribe, clan or ancestors. That was the part of him that couldn't fully develop because he had been uprooted from the place which had birthed him. He had been taken from it and no stories had come with him. And yet Sandra was so exquisitely tuned to the earth as if she had born, as Hosteen had, to the place where her ancestors had lived as long as their stories remembered. Terrence admitted he wasn't trying to understand John so much as he was trying to understand himself.

He turned his gaze back to Sandra and pressed her hand. Startled, she met his eyes, then looked away. He had deserted her when it was his task to take care of her as she was persistently caring for him. It was an important lesson for him that personal pain could have cocooned him so. He had been arrogant about such responses and so had not been aware when pain had taken him over.

He pressed her hand again, insisting that she look at him and when she did, he locked his gaze with the sadness that was in her eyes. They had opened each other to grief, but he had not helped her carry it. He stroked her hand and nodded to her to indicate that he understood. Her eyes filled with tears and so did his, both of them knowing they were being observed. Then he took her other hand. She took the pail of the earth from where it had been and put it between them, then she held his hands tightly. They were both aware of each other. He knew what he had to do though it was not something that could be taught nor could he imagine it. He looked toward Hosteen and addressed him: "Uncle." A world of kinship and relationship fell into place.

Hosteen got up and came over to the two of them. Ceremony. He blessed them with corn pollen and then he blessed John. John began weeping. Terrence and Sandra held tightly to each other as a storm of fear and wonder shook them. All the time Hosteen was in ceremony he was singing. The trees were trembling with the wind rising. Terrence closed his eyes and let himself dissolve into the night and the circle. When he opened them, he turned to Sandra, noticing pollen between her brows and understanding that he had some also.

"We are married," he said. "We are married in the right way." The tremors he felt in her were not in response to earthquakes or solar flares or tsunamis. She was tremulous with their common life. As was he.

Despite his history of loss, he had acquired a wife, a father-in-law and an uncle. He didn't really know if he'd had blood kin near him as a child. His grandparents might have been his grandparents, his uncle might have been his uncle, or not. Or perhaps, his grandmother had simply found a way to save another child for the tribe by claiming him. But then they had let him go or sent him away. It had never been clear and his memory was faulty. Trauma erased memory. He was resigned to never knowing.

But this moment had given him a wife, a father-in-law and an uncle. He had gone to Wy'east and now he was on tribal land and he had found sanctuary. He had a history and maybe he had a future.

At midnight, they went into the hogan. They had not slept in the hogan before. An Elders Circle of Life, Pendleton blanket, with its sun divided into four quadrants, red, yellow, white and black, was hanging on the north wall. The community must have given it to Hosteen. Terrence and Sandra edged their sleeping pads against the wall and covered them with the sheepskins and blankets that had been left for them. A hand drum and two rattles were to the side. Nothing more than what they needed. Healing requires the sacred. John understood this but could not provide it – and the hospital and his medical practice were oblivious. It was Hosteen's sphere and intrinsic to who he was. Sandra slipped under the blankets and held them open for Terrence who suddenly bolted out the door. He came back moments later, the bear rug in his arms.

"You brought it?" a quizzical inquiry. How many times a gift can be a gift. He covered her with the bear and entered the den. Everything proceeded with the greatest care. Observed, their motions would have seemed so slow. He turned on his side and carefully lifted her toward him in the most tender gesture that would assure them both of his utter devotion. And she, in turn, took him into her arms. Her devotion equal to his. The slow, exact sliding of one tectonic plate under or over the other, without explosion or disruption. A quiet and perfect realignment of the energies that had, inevitably, been disconnected by time and history. Not the erotic but the embrace. With stillness, she took him in, he entered her. When they did make love, it was as the first dawn of their married life opened the sky with light.

29

A Night of Thunder and Birds

Four is a sacred number. It creates perfect balance. It is complete. It is the earth. When they met again in the next days, they continued in the configuration of four. The circle they had become remained intact, each member distinct and intrinsic to the whole. Their places in relationship to each other, not fixed, but in motion. Terrence had brought her pail of earth to the hogan from the fire circle where she had left it. Her personal story had become an icon for the circle, earth was present with them.

As if they had each chosen the burdens they would carry, Sandra was increasingly agitated by the earlier experience in Cameron. It burned in her as heatedly as if she had just stopped at Cameron with Terrence and her father on the way to Canyon de Chelly. Nothing eased her; ceremony and marriage had not extinguished it, Terrence's gradual but steady recovery had not eased her. Contrarily, it was inevitable that the burn would increase now that she was married, not only to a man but to a people and to a history. These were inseparable; this was the marriage basket.

What was spoken and what was unspoken were part of the circle. The terrible kinship of injury was shared among them, especially the great damage done to the Columbia Gorge, to *nChe-wana*, and the Native land including the Yakama Reservation, through the Manhattan Project, which had similarly laid waste to so much of the Four Corners Reservation.

Terrence's father was among them as was – because Sandra had invoked her – Samantha Crow. For Sandra who had not had family in any conventional way, this silent acknowledgement of relationship was destabilizing even as the truth of relationship offered her a unique solidity. She was wordless and grateful. It was so much like understanding weather – so many factors, visible and invisible, current and historic, had to be considered in order to comprehend the shifting whole of it. She understood, as she watched both John and Hosteen gather around Terrence, the actuality that an injury to one was an injury to the circle; she was learning this in her own body. Terrence's body, her body, the same. And the earth body, as always, echoing deeply within her.

Several days later Sandra could not restrain her need to return to Cameron, nor did she want to speak about it. She took the pickup in the morning, saying she was visiting Annie Blakeddy at Tuba City, the same one she had been working with two and a half years ago. It was a meeting, she said, they had agreed would take place when she arrived back in Arizona. As it would be a 2½ hour drive (and another forty-five minutes or so for the 25 miles between Tuba City and Cameron), she said that she preferred to stay overnight and return the next day – they had so much to discuss.

When she came to the exit from the canyon to Chinle, she found herself taking the U-turn that led to the north rim. She was on her way to Massacre Cave even if she didn't know why.

Unexpectedly, the Diné father was there again with his two children. The first flutter of recognition among them all, before they each looked down or away, confirmed their former awareness of each other. They were surprised at the other's reappearance, as if they were all after something, perhaps the same thing, they couldn't explain to themselves.

Sandra dared to greet them and spoke what had been in her heart without remedy since their former meeting. "I'm sorry," she began, pulling away to emphasize her sincerity. "I should have left the three of you completely alone at this viewpoint. I am sorry. I tried to leave but I wanted to hear what you were teaching the children; I wanted to learn myself. My curiosity overwhelmed my manners. Forgive me," she looked down and shuffled back a little further, unsure whether she should simply leave or give him the opportunity to reply. How could she withdraw or stay without increasing the awkwardness of the encounter?

It was the young girl who asked with the straightforwardness of a child who had not been diminished because of her age or gender, "Why did you come back?"

Sandra was disconcerted by the child as she had been by her own action and answered openly. "I don't know," she faltered. "But, I think it was to see you. This doesn't make sense, because I'm surprised to see you here. And surprised to find me here too." She hesitated; surely she should step away, but she didn't. "I've been thinking about all of you. It must be hard to be here and mourn your ancestors and what was done," she wavered and plunged on, awkwardly, "I feel there is something …." She was talking too much, caught herself mid-sentence. There was nothing else she could say without intruding further. She wondered if she was being patronizing, so she waited to see if the girl would reply, readjusted her khaki sun hat as a way of wiping the tears from her eyes, and nodded, hoping it was a neutral goodbye, preparing to withdraw.

The girl, her brother and the father turned away to look down the canyon to the east, and Sandra began to follow the paved path to the west where there was a loop that would take her to the parking lot without encountering them again, unless they willed it.

But she wasn't far away at all, when the girl turned and called after her in a remarkably reassured voice, "Are you a history teacher?"

"No, Sandra answered carefully and slowly so the girl would understand. "I am a climatologist."

The girl seemed to take it in and followed with a sweep of her hand along the canyon, "Then you know the olive trees and salt cedar aren't good for us." Her tone was slightly accusatory. "The birds don't like them. And if the birds don't," her voice drifted off, she was not going to explain all the complications that would ensue.

"I know," Sandra hoped she sounded in agreement and sufficiently regretful. The girl had clearly understood what a climatologist is. She reflected that the girl would not have asked her what she did for a living if she had been a Native woman. Sandra felt diminished and pigeonholed. There wasn't time to consider the exchange; the three had gathered themselves into a single unit allowing no entry. Her agreement had not freed her from culpability. How could Sandra pretend that she was not responsible even if she'd had no hand in the misguided decision to plant the river's edge?

Sandra continued around, up and to the truck. The girl's statement had been an indictment. Had Sandra's opening words sounded arrogant, or privileged, or, worse, condescending, as if she thought she knew something the girl, perhaps even the three, did not? The trees, birds, lizards, all life forms around her, were absent from her awareness as she focused on the invasive species below.

She might have argued that the plants weren't in the realm of climatology, and so she was innocent of harm, but such a separation of knowledge into discrete units would certainly have brought scorn. Or she could have argued that she didn't do it, nor did her father, or that she didn't know why white people had brought such invasive species to someone else's land; futile and shameful responses, these would have been. There was the family cluster looking over the cliffs, surveying their losses by the hands of people whose background was, most probably, the same as Sandra's.

Terrence's Toyota was in the parking lot. For a moment, she forgot she had taken it. He wasn't here. He was at the home site, healing the wound of his disconnection with his history, John as a witness. She was here alone. Alone, in a red 2006 Toyota Tacoma, 4-wheel drive pickup, with, thankfully, plenty of dust and mud to cover the shine. A great tragedy had happened here. A people, *the* people, the Diné, as they had known themselves, had lived here once on what was now a parking lot. What were the ancestors thinking, those who had been forced on the long walk to Bosque Redondo, as they viewed the iron guard rails, the concrete walkways, the clutch of descendants selling turquoise and silver jewelry, pottery with images of pictographs, stone bear and wood antelope carvings? After their march from hell how did they view the many cars and tour buses filled with the progeny of Kit Carson and the like? She'd better leave. Tourism was a terrible compromise for survival. She was a party to it. She wanted to be locked in the truck before she dismissed one more person with her *warm* "No, thank you." Marriage did not redeem her. She had to make her own amends. Though a runner, she couldn't imagine that she would have survived the march. The sky was darkening like her mood. She got into the truck and sped toward the weather coming in, as the horses had confirmed, from the southwest.

Two and a half hours alone on a quiet road gave Sandra time to think or not, as she chose. She was quite aware that she had just lied to the people who meant most to her in the world after having been married in a ceremony that was based upon truth telling. She had violated the holy of holies. If she called Annie to schedule a visit, which she could do, that wouldn't change the essential, if small, falsehood that she had introduced into their relationship. Mostly, she concentrated on the two lane road, passing, being passed.

She thought of the reservation as another nation occupied by the Federal government that demanded that the Diné conform to government laws, even when they violated, as they too often did, the spiritual and cultural values of the Diné. The same on any reservation. Unlike the Feds, she recognized she was on the land of another nation and should follow its laws. She had just married a Native man and within hours, it seemed, had violated his ways. She was, herself, opposed to lying, was always looking for truth in a situation, not "her" truth. There was truth and truthfulness; it was not personal. There were Federal laws about perjury and sworn testimony, but it seemed most people, even, or especially, those in government, lied all the time. She had come to the reservation to escape such practices and she had indulged them.

Why had she dissembled? No one was stopping her from going. They hadn't even pointed out the coming monsoon. She was driving into a squall; there was no doubt about this. They had not discouraged her. Still, she had lied.

She went into the hotel in Tuba City, took a room, emptied the truck, ate dinner in the restaurant and walked slowly back to her truck and started driving again. There was a hotel in Cameron but she was afraid to stay there. Whatever she discovered, she wanted to be able to leave. She did not know why she was going to Cameron. The sands were hot, she repeated to herself, trying to understand. There was no explanation. Uranium. Uranium, she had told herself, even though she knew uranium was not hot. But she had no other explanation. Even if it had been uranium, so what? Was this her great discovery like Columbus discovering America that had been there all the time and quite familiar to its inhabitants? The Diné and Hopi certainly knew that uranium had been mined, that the uranium tailings were poorly stored and scattered, that the water and land were toxic, that the people and animals were ill, had cancers of various types, and were dying of the poison. What they didn't know was how to clean it up and how to get the government to clean it up as promised so many times. They didn't know, no one did, how to survive it. They didn't know how to restore the earth to its original balanced nature. They didn't know how to get back to the lives they had lived before 1864 when they were marched to Fort Sumner in Bosque Redondo. They could reimagine, even reinstall their lives, but not if the *bilagáana* were present and in control, and they were ever-present. The Native people didn't need Sandra to "enlighten" them.

Between Terrence and Hosteen, science and TEKW, she could certainly puzzle out the dilemma of the hot sands without having to make a great discovery. But she couldn't ask them to come with her any more than Terrence could have asked her to go to Wy'east to read the IPCC report with him. When she wasn't thinking like a scientist, her relationship with the Earth was entirely intimate. She was making a pilgrimage to other beings and she needed to come as she had said she would, alone and unarmed.

It was getting dark. Not nightfall dark yet, but a pre-storm dark formed of boiling clouds and intermittent cloud cover. In the far distance, a trunk of azure rain was falling from a gray cloud tree. A few nighthawks were swooping into billows of gathering insects awakened by the hint of rain.

The earth would not hold on to the day's heat for very long even if this was late summer.

Maybe she was not to understand in scientific terms. Maybe there were other ways of knowing and this was an opportunity or a challenge. Maybe different ways of knowing emerged from different ways of perception. She had recognized sun flares when there was no way she should have known sun flares, but she had. There had been her father's patients, whose illnesses she could diagnose as a child, even before she knew the names of their afflictions.

Understanding came to her suddenly and simply as it had when she was young. The earth had a fever. It had been violated. It was trying to heal itself with its own immune response. Yes, a fever.

This was followed by another thought that plagued her. If the sands were hot, what effect was this having on weather? Heated seas changed weather patterns drastically. What about heated earth? She was thinking in simple sentences: Weather responds to temperature. Winds, storm, rain are all influenced by the temperature of the land and the sea. If the warm seas create certain conditions – even a few tenths of a degree can make a great difference, then what consequences from the heating of the body of the earth herself?

What effects were there that she, others, *science* hadn't noticed? Mining radioactive materials and dispersing them across the sacred lands, violating everything sacred, must have consequences whether or not the perpetrators had calculated them. No such act can remain neutral. Her mind was teetering. She had to steady herself. It was easier to think about her own transgressions than to consider that the materials that made the bombs that had been detonated on Hiroshima and Nagasaki and the enormous stockpile of weaponry from uranium mined here, were exploding in other forms everywhere on the planet. That the war that had been started with Little Boy was ongoing – another kind of chain reaction – that every bomb that was exploded afterwards was the same bomb still exploding, that all people were living within its field, that was, like radiation, invisible and deadly, with an eternal half-life.

She turned on the radio and turned it off. Then turned it on again. Listening to Navajo when she could not even understand the inflection distracted her from the understanding that was flooding in.

Swirling like a cyclone. Sweeping up the debris of odd thoughts along her path. Every new thought cancelled an older one. Her mind was no longer her mind and she offered it up to whatever was entraining her.

The earth had a fever. The thought shifted everything in her from alarm to maternal concern. Uranium may have been the original and continuing contaminant that caused this illness. The deadly poison that was spread over holy land. There was something reassuring about a fever in this moment – maybe reassuring because fevers can often be reduced. There are medicines for fevers. Cold baths. Rain. Maybe the fever called down the rains.

She was wandering through the Cameron market and gallery, waiting for closing time, for people to leave, so she could return to the place she had originally stopped when entering the reservation to be alone there. The place where she had fallen more than two years before. It was still fairly hot outside and her thoughts seemed to raise the temperature. Night and the chance of some showers would cool the sands, as if their knowing the medicine was coming would ease them. There was no logic, there was no clear field to explore, there was no cause and effect, there was no linear progression, there was no "therefore," no "ergo." She was in another mind.

Surely she should go out and watch the sunset. The great artistry of color and light, particularly when a storm was bending the beams of light into a wild spectrum always engaged her. But she couldn't go outside yet. When the dark came, she would be more comfortable. There would be less to see and less to try to understand. She would wrap herself in the dark to find the mystery of the hot sands. She knew they would be hot. She knew there would be a fever. Could she ease it by putting her cool hands on the fevered brow of the Mother?

The restaurant and the Trading Post closed. It had started to rain, the tourists were safely tucked away from the weather. Sandra was alone. She started up the truck. She needed to drive off the reservation, turn around, and come back and enter just as she had that night. She did this listening for the voice saying, "Here, stop here." A little way past the hotel, it was clear; she stopped. She put on a light rain jacket. It was raining harder and the wind was up. Sandra opened the door of the truck, stepped out and walked south onto the land, a thermal imaging device seeking the shape of heat.

There was very little traffic behind her because of the approaching storm. She went into the bush a short distance until she felt invisible, was being led more than determining her direction. The wind was even fiercer, was whipping the small knee high bushes and she kneeled down to them. She had forgotten why she was there; she was simply there with the wind and the brush, holding the expectation that the earth would keep her warm.

A pilgrim depending upon the benevolence of the natural world. And the opposite: A woman who wanted to ease the suffering. On her knees. She put her hands on the warm sands to ease them and she wailed.

The storm she had not expected, hit. Perhaps she had called it forth, had become its magnetic center. As if she had found or been led to this place where warm moist air of the feverish ground was meeting the much cooler clouds in the atmosphere above, and all were beginning to whirl. The wind was wild. Thunder boomed and blasted. Rationally, she knew that she needed to head back to the truck, but she couldn't retreat. The storm was not circumstantial. She was to be here whatever that meant. The storm was a great bird swooping down. These were not careful considerations except that she did hunker down in fear and out of respect, making herself as small as possible, hoping not to be a target. There were flashes of light from the black bird's beak and rain poured down its wings. With her head bowed, her forehead and then crown, on the earth in grief, the sand seemed to light up. She was lost in it or she was no more and the storm was, or the elementals were showing their faces to her. A gross violation requires extreme action to set it right. The storm screaming. Thunderbirds screeching. Wind, rain, thunder, lightning and hail pummeling her. She was crying, she was wailing, no longer with her head in the sand, but trying to come up, to get a foothold, to see the great dark wings above her more clearly when out of the great bird's eye, the lightning flared, hit a nearby power pole and streamed across the land, riveting her to the spot.

It did not come to her in a blinding flash. It had not struck her down. It hit the earth some distance away and crept across the ground in stealth, and rose up like sap rises in a tree, to fill her with its strange blue light. For seconds before she fell back onto the ground, her face open to the rain and all that was around her, she saw herself in a blue glow and wondered if a true self was being revealed.

There is a geography between consciousness and unconsciousness, between knowing and not knowing, a place and a passageway, a location and a world. She lay face up in the rain, wondering if the blue light would come again or if it had only been a momentary visitation. She knew that rain was beating down upon her and that there was nothing to be done but to welcome it. She was weeping under the weeping sky. The sand had been warm and now it was no longer there. It wasn't cold. It just wasn't.

Then she heard something, not the under current of lightning, but a hum that translated into voices, coming and going like an electromagnetic tide. It was a buzz of language she couldn't understand, like an ebb and flow of code talkers, men and women, or maybe animals, or birds, rain birds, she couldn't distinguish the species, but they were speaking at once and to each other, while the simultaneity of the sound did not diminish the certainty of coherence among them. It seemed she was comprehending what was said through her cells so that she was being altered by the sounds that she was hearing even without understanding, without translating them into the particularity of her own language.

The bird sound traveled from the southwest to the east and back again, like a tide. Then the sound became form and an idea entered her mind that these were beings and they were the dead, what Terrence called, the ancestors, marching across or through the latitude under her.

And the light, streaking above, was of them as well. She didn't pretend to understand. She had no cosmology for this. She was cold. The ground was wet. The earth was warm as a sentient being. She was not alone.

Were they always there? Had they always been there? When she could structure a coherent thought, she entertained an idea, but then lost it. It was not strange to her that she heard the bird voices here and now. Earlier, she had been a woman without ancestors and maybe this was remedied now. Or was it simply that whatever knocked her down had sensitized her to what she had been too dull to perceive before? At this moment, she was in a replenished world, an aquifer filling through a heavy rain, entirely foundational in its vibrant presence. Oh, her thinking was not so coherent.

The voices were not speaking to her. They were speaking to each other, maintaining a continuous underground river of sound that sustained the world. This is what they wanted her to understand. Once this was revealed, she was not afraid. She was grateful. Grateful for the company. Grateful for their company in the universe. A new meaning arose from the words she had heard so many times, from Hosteen and Terrence: *Everything is alive, even the stones.*

Sandra fell into unconsciousness and rose up again into the physical reality of her circumstances without being able to do anything about them, without being able to move, and not caring either. Fleeting moments of awareness spiked into half finished thoughts. You ought to…. You will get ill…. You could die…. Get up! But she couldn't do anything and so didn't struggle. Facts began to cascade haphazardly through her thoughts. Two thousand thunder storms occurring at any given moment. Five million lightning strikes a day on the planet. The sky lit up and darkened.

Rain yes. Lightning yes. Thunderbirds. Any minute, she could be burned at the stake of a shaft of light. Thunder crashed. She counted the seconds between the lightning strike and the roar to calculate the distance of the storm. Count the seconds, divide by five, count the seconds, divide by five, lightning can strike from ten miles away ... she forgot what she was doing, then started again, then forgot and lay back into the mud and the water pooling around her, as if she were dissolving.

Then seeing a steady shimmering light spreading into the sky from behind a cloud bank staked to the length of the horizon, she settled down even deeper into her sodden circumstances, because light was entering her, the quiet but persistent light of understanding. She was *in* the weather whereas until this moment she had been trying to know it from outside itself. She was *within* what she loved, porous to it, and at its mercy. It was merciful! She was within a formerly unrecognized, and therefore alien, consciousness that had suddenly been revealed as sentient and compassionate. And the two, sentience and compassion, were aspects of each other. She offered herself into their care as the hush of voices rocked her to sleep.

Sandra never learned why the Tribal Police stopped to investigate her truck. Maybe she had left the lights on. Maybe she hadn't closed the door behind her. The key was in the ignition and they began to look for the suicide or the drunk who was mad enough to be out in such weather. When they found her, it was easy to lift her, like lifting the trunk of a small tree that had fallen down into the mud. One officer drove her to the hospital in Tuba City while the other drove the truck. She was not able to talk or identify herself, nor did she want to. But they found the registration and called Terrence with the number on her cell phone. Terrence, John and Hosteen could not be with her until the next afternoon. The freak storm, not predicted in its intensity, had made the roads from Chinle to Tuba City impassable.

Thunder is good, thunder is impressive; but it is lightning that does the work.

Mark Twain

30

The Blue Glow

The hospital room was spare, but Sandra marveled at the faint blue glow that illuminated it whenever she came to consciousness and fell back intermittently, into the dark. She didn't wonder how she got there no more than she had considered where she was as she lay on the increasingly muddy earth, under the rain. She was still listening. Fortunately the tribal police hadn't seen the glow, or they would have hesitated to pick her up for fear of receiving the charge themselves, nor was it evident to the nurses who came in when Sandra asked for the window to be opened. Sandra's words and gestures garbled together and the nurse put her cool hand on her forehead to ease her agitation.

Sandra vaguely noticed that she had an IV in her arm. A doctor must have seen her. A kind woman had gazed down upon her; maybe she had been the doc. Someone had cut what was left of her clothes from her. Memory faded and returned. She remembered scissors and the satisfying grind of one blade scraping against the other through fabric. She could hear every sound in the hospital. Every sensation, so many she might have ignored in her usual life, was exquisitely sharp. The sheets were white. They had probably washed the mud from her. She was in a hospital gown. Dozens of miniature bears marched toward her head. Good, she needed their healing energy.

Her arm burned, so did her back and her chest, the heat as intense as sunset, and she felt a visceral longing to increase the blue around her, for sky and water to ease the heat. She was in a delirium of blue, of cobalt blue glass, delphinium, hydrangeas and irises. Then the blue burn of a hot flame overwhelmed her and she needed to douse herself in the ocean, to live underwater. She wanted blue salvia and morning glories, banks of blue. Blue, the afternoon sky before the storm had overtaken it. Finally, she rested on ice blue, and crawled in her mind into a blue cave in a glacier she had seen years ago and cooled her burning body there.

In the moments of icy lucidity, which alternated with feverish confusion, she was grateful for the experience and had been grateful, she admitted to herself, even when she was in the midst of the extreme ordeal. Yes, it could have been avoided but instead she had gone toward it. Maybe she had brought it on, though she didn't know how. She fell into a pattern of waking and sleeping almost as rapid as breathing, thankful and tormented. She had been foolish. Had she been foolish? Had she placed herself in grave danger that she of all people, given her profession, knew how to avoid? But she had been called. She had not been foolish. She had been responsible. The sands were hot and the night birds were the medicine. She was consoled by accepting that she had been responsible, had been attentive to an inner calling, linked to a mysterious force that she had never encountered before nor had dared to imagine or recognize. There had been voices. Voices, she understood, as real and present as the emanations from the sun or the earth's trembling. They had wanted her to hear them, had tested her, had dared her to do what was required, to see if she could be faithful. There was meaning to this, and purpose, even if she didn't understand and might never know. They had called and she had gone and heard their bird voices. That would have to be sufficient.

When she awakened, Terrence was leaning over to kiss her on the forehead, between her eyebrows, above the bridge of her nose, on that shallow crater. His eyes were filled with tears. She struggled to take his hands in hers but she could still barely move. Imperceptible gestures overtook both of them. A slight shaking of the head from side to side, a faint "no" which indicated not knowing. A slight raising of the shoulders to indicate wonder. Nodding that indicated awe. None of the gestures were purposeful. The two of them were both trembling. Lightning was in the room.

She could dimly see Hosteen standing in a corner and then her father at the foot of her bed. Terrence was gazing at her arm and from an inch or two above her skin lightly tracing the outline, as if in henna, of a long bough of a tree or vine, its graceful branches cascading from shoulder to wrist. "Could also be feathers," he whispered. "They've marked you."

"A Lichtenberg figure." John named it as a way of steadying himself, wishing there had been more of a ground to receive the charge. "Lichtenberg figure," he repeated, meaning this has happened before, was frequent enough to be named, named after someone who had noticed it, not for itself, meaning, please let her survive without great damage.

She could see her arm below the elbow, the drawing, or so it seemed to be, was beautiful. "Paisley," she managed, pulling the word from far recesses of memory. Like a child learning speech and priorities simultaneously, she tried, "Poppa," attempted, "Uncle" … then, "Hosteen." Reassured, she focused her eyes on Terrence, and finally said his name.

A nurse came in with a medication she was to add to the IV, and showed it first to John, who had, at the desk introduced himself as a physician who had worked in this hospital in the past. Hosteen standing behind him had gesticulated that it was true. Then, because she was very familiar with wary patients though she knew Sandra couldn't make decisions, she showed it to Sandra who just looked alarmed, confronted by her helplessness in knowing what was wrong and what was being prescribed. John nodded his head, the nurse added it.

In a moment, she returned with a cup and whispered to Hosteen. This time, it was for him to approve it. He took the cup and she left the room, not willing to be responsible. "We don't know how well you can swallow," he said, "take very tiny sips. It's a tea made to heal lightning strikes. Go slow. It is a medicine. You only need a hint of it."

Terrence dipped his finger into the brew and put it in her mouth. To begin with, she took it in this way, and then she dared to sip some of it when he raised the bed so she was sitting and offered the cup to her lips. She could swallow, but she couldn't hold the cup yet. The tree on her arm was on fire whenever she moved.

The nurse returned to announce that only two visitors were allowed at a time, surveyed the three men and determined that they would not only stay all together in the room, but would stay the night. The nights. She went to order three sleeping pads for the floor. John was arguing that she be moved to Flagstaff, but Sandra was dogged about staying to the extent that she could express any force or insistence. "You may not recover this way," her father argued. Knowing Terrence and Hosteen would both go with him to Flagstaff, he wanted the best of both worlds. But, she refused.

"Can you tell me why you won't go to Flagstaff? We will go with you. Why do you think it's right to stay here?"

"Blue," she said, trying to point to the cup of tea she would only get here.

A day later, it was still raining intermittently. Whenever the rain started, she wanted to be outside and did whatever she could to remove the suffocating comforts of bed, sheets, of any warmth. The longing was overwhelming and her nerves were afire from the light that had grazed and singed them as it entered her body from below. She could not bear the walls, the lights, the confinement of an inner space. She could not bear the discrepancy between inside and outside. Inside, where everything was static, outside where everything was alive. She would have tried to jump out of the window, if she could free herself from the tangle of wires and tubes, if she could navigate herself, if she wasn't in pain, if she wasn't at each moment with at least one of the three guardians.

The tension that arose around the best ways to treat her condition seemed to strengthen Sandra. While before, she could barely move, now she was resolute and focused. "I don't want to recover. I want to go where I am being propelled." She had overheard the police speculating that she had been thrown some feet to the east and that became an internal metaphor. She had, in her mind, been moved further away from the mind that had been cultivated in her.

And while no one berated her: "What were you thinking? You're a climatologist …?" The question was in the room. She heard it.

Terrence and John leaned upon the old post and rail fence outside of the reservation hospital. John needed a break and Terrence knew John wanted a cigarette and that's why he wouldn't go to the cafeteria. He rarely smoked but now he seemed to want to light one cigarette with the last of the other.

"Would you like a burrito?" Terrence asked.

"Not hungry."

"What about a cup of coffee, John?"

"You smoke like an Injun," Terrence said. John couldn't tell if it was self-mockery or – he didn't know what – irritation? He attributed it to tension. Neither of them made any motion to do anything but continue staring out toward the hills in the far distance.

"I'll stop as soon as she gets out," John said.

"It'll be soon," Terrence spoke quietly. "When the rain stops completely."

"Rain did enough harm," John was bitter or rather he was frightened, but bitter was an easier stance. They were in the misty border between wet and dry.

"We can go inside and have lunch. It'll get you out of the rain."

John shook his head, perplexed by his own stubbornness. As if the rain would explain Sandra's behavior to him.

Terrence could feel John's confusion. "Lightning came. She survived. When the rains stop, the circle will close."

"How do you know?"

"Don't you know?"

"I don't know anything anymore."

"I wonder," as if Terrence was pursuing something but John didn't know what it was. So John lit another cigarette.

John took the cigarette out of his mouth and examined the end, brushing a piece of tobacco from his lip. "Rolled it myself. As I am going to be here for a while, I thought I should try to pass."

"John," Terrence's voice changed as if he could console John with his tone alone. "John, how long do you know Hosteen? I mean, how long have you been coming here?"

Terrence saw that John had to calculate, that he was surprised by his answer. "Almost forty years." John paused, "Is that possible?"

"You don't need to pass." Terrence was serious and John was wary. "You're a good man," Terrence added. Were the two men trying to meet each other? John wondered. Who was this man whose father-in-law he had just become and what did kinship mean?

The sky and earth were turning redder as the late afternoon dark entered. Clumps of grasses rustled in the rising twilight breeze. Both men stared off into the distance as if the past lay there. When he had first come to the reservation, he had thought there was nothing to be seen between the road outside the hospital and the sandstone hills in the distance, but Hosteen had taught him the subtleties that appeared when one regarded the land as home.

"Did you see… ?" John Birdswell knew that Terrence had no intention of finishing the sentence.

"Did I see? Did I see? Did I see what, Terrence?"

"Did you see the blue glow that is still there, hovering around Sandra's arm and her head?"

"No, I didn't see it!" John paused irritably as he had heard them talking about it in the room though it had remained invisible to him. "Such phenomena aren't described in the PDR." Anger was a new experience for one who once had the ability to cordially meet whatever came to him. His Aikido reflex, Sandra would tease him. Now he was uncomfortable in every way he could imagine.

"Maybe the glow isn't a symptom that needs treatment. No treatment, no need for a reference." Terrence was unrelenting though John was clearly uncomfortable. Everything was awry; John was being interrogated by the man who had recently become his son-in-law.

Terrence had adopted a rhythm of statement and silence that enhanced what he was trying to say, so he took his time, and then he asked,

"Why do you spend so much time on the reservation, John?"

Silence again and then Terrence persisted. "You're the one who brought Sandra here. And now me."

John looked at him quizzically. He couldn't breach the rift that was, he felt, increasing.

Terrence caught himself. What was he getting at? He looked hard at John. It hadn't ever occurred to him he might be wanting a father. The possibility took him by surprise and he put it away quickly.

"Maybe I am expressing gratitude. Just saying, you're a good man. I am glad for the family I have married into."

John had no idea how to respond. Stepping back, he dropped his cigarette on the ground and assessed Terrence. Sandra, if she were present, and it seemed she was, would have said, "Intimacy, Poppa. It takes so many different forms."

"Question still is, did you, John, see the blue glow around Sandra's body that is fading but hasn't disappeared yet, or not? Did you see it or won't you say?" Terrence was asking the question sincerely and he was also trying to recover his equilibrium. He admitted to himself that he wanted John to have seen it.

The two men fell even more deeply into silence. John was trying to integrate the fact that Terrence was his son-in-law. What did that mean? His history had not prepared him for whatever this was or would be as he sensed that the Native ways inserted them into a continuum within a natural and incontrovertible order. He could not challenge the relationship any more than a tree could argue with the existence of a leaf.

His daughter was injured after doing something stupid, quite unlike her. She was in a hospital that he had to respect or his medical life would be suspect to him. She was in pain but didn't seem to care. Whether or not he could see a blue emanation round her was suddenly crucial to her well-being and maybe his. She had just married in a ceremony that the courts would not recognize and yet he had been a critical witness to its authenticity. Maybe he was supposed to father the man who had married his daughter, but in this moment, Terrence was, without argument, definitely his son and Terrence was also, at this moment, his elder. It was a relief, John recognized, startled, to be cared for in his soul.

"I didn't see the blue glow. And I didn't see the red flare she saw either. But I believe you and I believed her. Inept as I am, Terrence," the words were difficult and he had to be strong and open to say them, a daunting combo, "I'm going to try to be a good father to the two of you."

The words startled Terrence. Was that what he had wanted?

John assessed the situation. "Let's get a burrito," he said, stooping to pick up the cigarette butts, "You're hungry and tired. And so am I."

Recovery came rapidly it seemed, hour by hour. Slight movements, then larger ones. Language returned, but she didn't want to speak. Several days later in the afternoon, when they were all in her hospital room, her father, seeing that she was recovering, looked into her eyes, "You didn't have an appointment with a colleague." A statement. "If you had, she would be here now. She would have called you and not getting an answer, she would have tracked you down."

Sandra nodded.

If she apologized, he might assume it was for walking into the storm. She would have to mend her breach of trust at another time

But he didn't allow the postponement. "Why?" He continued, the question shaped by confusion, anger, perplexity, betrayal. And then, looking at Hosteen and Terrence, he realized that he was being tested by circumstances and that his question betrayed as much as her dissemblance.

She had thought she had betrayed Hosteen and Terrence with her white lie, but she had betrayed her father. Confronted again, she did not hesitate. She had searched her soul. She was aware now of the dangers and consequences. And though she did not have the words that Terrence might have had, she said, looking directly back at him and then Terrence, "I was compelled."

"I should have just gone, like you did, Terrence. I couldn't tell you and then work it out reasonably with all of you. I was crazed and I should have let you see me that way. I should not have lied. But what I had to do, I had to do alone. For whatever reason, I had to do it alone. If we had consulted, we would have considered it reasonably. That's how people act when they are together. I had to relinquish everything I thought I understood."

Her voice quavered. She was afraid to say what she would never have understood if they were together.

"The earth has a fever. I don't mean climate change. I mean Earth herself. She may die of it.

Some days later, she was released. John was given medications to administer, but the discharge nurse was speaking her last instructions to Hosteen. The two men, John and Hosteen, more like brothers than ever, had done this before so many times over the years. Anyone might have assumed their grins were relief, and they were, but they were also camaraderie. Years of practice together, each confident in his own way, had led to this moment of alliance in their medicines. Sandra walked slowly, refusing a wheel chair, as Terrence had refused his, but balanced on Terrence's arm, toward the wide hospital doors that would open for her.

At Hosteen's home site, the two men settled into a routine caring for Terrence and now Sandra, each a little crazed, but compliant. The ground had dried from the storm that had inundated this area as well and so they weren't alarmed each time Sandra escaped, as she put it, to the outside or refused to come in at night. When the wind came up, she needed to meet it. She wanted to be cold. If a cloud appeared in the sky, she wanted to address it. Each night she sat near Hosteen asking him to teach her the constellations again as he saw them, trying to remember their names and configurations, remembering playing cat's cradle with Terrence. Failing, but starting again.

"Why do you want to learn these?"

"I want to incorporate different patterns. I want to see if it is possible for me to do this now.

"That's the secret, isn't it?" she asked Terrence. "Learning to see differently." He held her as she put her head on his shoulder. They were sitting on the log. It healed his mind to hold her just as it healed her to allow herself to rest against him. Their fierce independence was softening. Affliction and marriage did that. For both John and Hosteen, it was their time to assist from a distance. The role of the elder brought its own losses.

She marked the healing by the changing intensity of the burns. Soon it seemed to her that the pain had become specific to the design. She could trace the outlines in her mind as if the blueprint was being engraved on her skin again with a fiery knife. The pattern on her body, the words she had heard, the same code she couldn't translate into words, they were present in her.

There was a smooth slab of sandstone behind Hosteen's house. Except that it was angled, it could have served as a dance floor. Despite Terrence's objections, she insisted on lying out on the stone, taking in the sun. She refused sunscreen and wouldn't cover the burns. It was impossible for her to consider that the sun would do her harm.

"Respect," Terrence argued futilely and lay down next to her, facing into the sun.

"I want to be as dark as you are," she tried to coax him into indulging her. He let her move closer to him and then raised himself onto his side, sitting in the wrong direction to cast any shadow, yet sitting there so she would have to face away from the sun to talk with him.

"There are many ways to look at the sun," he began. "It is not only the benevolent light."

"Let's look at everything from different perspectives," she imitated his professorial voice.

He was remembering a sacred story that had always puzzled him. Now was the time to tell it.

"According to the Chumash, the Sun and Coyote play a gambling game each night. On the winter solstice, the Moon tallies their games to see who has won. If Coyote wins it will be a rainy year and food will be abundant. If the Sun wins, he is paid in human lives and will continue his southward journey, picking up his bounty of the dead. The Sun's sack of dead is always heavy upon him. Each year, the Chumash hope that Coyote will win and the relentless drought will ease."

"It's a real Coyote story, isn't it, Terrence? It's upside down, unmaking the trickster Coyote by having him be the rainmaker. So it is still a trickster story.

"I don't understand anything that happened. You know that, don't you, Terrence?"

"I don't know anything. Just like you." He took his denim shirt off, rolled down the sleeves and covered her with it, relieved when she didn't refuse it.

"Terrence, why do you think the Sun, not Coyote carries the dead?"

"I don't know what the storytellers think, but for me, today, the sun is light and it is also radiation. It's entirely radioactive. An atom bomb is a little sun. You went to the radiation. It drew you like a magnet."

"The sands were hot."

"I hear you, Sandra."

"There is no way to explain it."

"I agree."

"And then it rained, Terrence."

"That's Coyote."

"And then I was struck down by the light. I don't understand anything."

"Nor do I." When he lay back, the stone was hot from the sun beating down upon it.

Healing, whatever that would ultimately mean, was slow. She remained unsteady. Terrence could see, even if John couldn't, that the blue glow still surrounded her. The henna burns were gradually fading, becoming more a root system now than a tree or vine. She was marked by energies that were beyond him, and beyond her, he recognized. As if she had offered herself as a sacrifice.

31

What They Come To In the Rain

Under the rain of night birds, under the dark cloud, a rainbow slipped, handhold after handhold, down the ruddy curved stone body of the canyon to the sands below and then tipped up in another arch to a distant perch in the east where dusk was being born. The palette of creation. The tools of beauty. A covenant.

They sat down facing each other on the stone floor of Face Overlook, watching the elementals assembling, taking in signs and symbols. To the west, the elementals were gathering in a procession. More than thirty miles away, the entire length of the canyon and beyond, lightning was striking in long shafts and broken arches, illuminating the black clouds, which swept in and away like so many black birds, wings spread, soaring.

She watched the light hit the surrounding cliffs without flinching. She felt safe as it would not strike her again, or it would. The ravens were there and vultures, cloud and birds hovering together and speeding away. The thunder was steady as the heartbeat of the sky. Water gathered in shallow pools on the stones, reflecting the sky or inscribing it onto stone. Sometimes the setting sun broke through to catch a low cloud, which burst into red and orange flame. Then the sheer dusty pink and taupe walls of the canyon blazed too and dulled in the oncoming shadow.

"Can you read the lightning yet?" Terrence asked.

"No. Not yet. Can you?"

"No."

It was raining but they sat on the stones as if they were dry.

"You know," he said, "that when thunder approaches and lightning is visible, actually, even before lightning is visible, you are advised to go indoors immediately. At the least to seek shelter that won't focus the lightning on you. Best to get back in the car but be careful not to touch any metal in the car. It is not advised to be near metal," he continued in a mock rendition of his professorial tone, nodding at the metal railings set in the low stone walls.

"I know," she said simply. "I also know that one can be struck twice. Of the small number of people who are ever struck by lightning, a goodly number are struck twice." She said this while sitting as still as the stones in the guard wall which seemed far more solid than the walls of the canyon, which flowed like water does in graceful curves. Below them the formerly dry river gleamed with water as it snaked through the narrows.

He saw the faint blue glow along her arms that had faded but not disappeared completely. He didn't know if she saw it too. The lightning was far away; the indigo glimmer was from the past. It had remained upon her as the wisdom had remained with her.

"What did you learn?" he asked. "What did they teach you?"

"We can't go back to our old lives," she said. "That much is clear."

The lightning struck somewhat closer, this time in the canyon but near the first entrance while they were seated at the last. The wind rustled through the olive trees at the sandy bottom so it seemed that they were running with the water.

"I have to choose. The life I was living or listening to the voices. They can't coexist." She looked at him so deliberately that he would understand how committed she was to what she was saying. "We can't be hybrids anymore."

He understood that she was not using hybrid as a metaphor. He hadn't known how deeply he had carried his mother inside him, fighting her with every breath but still yielding to her ways and so letting her divide him.

He had one more thing to do. He had to admit his attraction to whatever it was that called him toward the life that has set its claws on this continent. He did not have to make a list – any recognition would link to all the others in a round world. He just had to admit his attraction to the life he had reluctantly but fully lived.

And so he did. Then he felt the rain come closer filling the space his mother had vacated. She had always been gone. She had deserted him. But he had held on to her ghost. Had held on to her *chindi*, Hosteen, might have said. "When someone dies in the hogan, it has to be broken open so the *chindi*, can escape. It's best to die outdoors." Hosteen had explained this to John and John, in turn, had told Sandra.

Maybe, Terrence was trying to understand, the elders hadn't wanted him to find out what the white men were doing. Maybe the elders knew more than they needed to know. Maybe they wanted to see what would happen once he found out. Once he knew everything he could learn, would know everything he needed or wanted to learn, what would he do?

"It began when you left the hospital," she was speaking as if in a trance. He had heard elders speak that way in a Lodge, their voices coming from elsewhere, from the stones, from the earth under the stones. Maybe the way she had heard them after the lightning struck. "I knew that you had reached another understanding on the mountain and you were being asked to live accordingly. I didn't know it in words until this minute and I don't think you knew it in words either, but you knew. I watched you pace and wrestle with the most ordinary needs as if you were literally shedding a skin."

"What will you choose?" he asked, opening a place for her to speak whatever was most truthful for her.

"I choose to sit here in the rain with you and listen to the lightning." She took long breaths and looked around at the display that was everywhere. She had not known that Beauty could be so alive, so active.

"And you, Terrence, what will you choose?"

"I chose a long time ago, but I didn't know it."

"I thought the spirits would speak differently. I seemed to think they would speak directly and clearly," she was embarrassed but knew she had to admit this.

"As if they were writing to you in an academic paper?" He was amused.

"Yeah, as if I were listening to them in the lecture hall. Taking notes. Waiting to feed it back in order to pass the exam. But I was still going to get a degree from the University. This course was extra credit."

She grinned. Laughing at herself erased the shame. "Yes. I wanted precise instructions: Do this. Then do this." Water was running down her face.

"We'll sit here until it is too dark for me to see your face glistening in the rain," he said, wanting to wipe it as if there were tears, but holding back. He did not want to alter anything. He realized he was also wet.

Lightning struck down and then rose up as it sometimes does, illuminating the dark clouds behind it. A clap of thunder burst down at Tunnel Overlook and reverberated up the entire length of the canyon until it reached them. The canyon was resonating with it, had become its drum and he could feel the vibrations in the stone floor begin to rise up in her as she began to tremble with the tremors of the earth. He knew they had her now. He dared to put his hand on her knee and he could feel the buzz. She was a hive. The spirits were making honey in her.

The clouds were developing red flanks that turned colors, orange and purple, as if on a spit. It was getting darker. The dark was coming down on the wings of the raven soughing overhead. The sun was a red fire bent out of shape by the far mountain.

They heard a horse neigh down below. Everyone was happy for the on-going gentle rain. The horse did not worry about the monsoons or that they were increasing in strength if not in frequency. The horse would meet what he had to meet. He was glad for the rain and the mud around his hooves. He would stand under a juniper tree and watch the rain running down the rippling flanks of his brown mare. He would nuzzle her wet mane and she would shudder to loosen the raindrops, and from pleasure.

"Your dream," Terrence began. "It didn't matter what it was that we needed to see. It didn't matter what the horror was that surpassed all the other horrors. It mattered only that we, humans, had done it." Then he also smiled or grinned, his expression a blend of love and knowing, also shame, regret and sorrow.

"There doesn't have to be a hierarchy of torture and devastation. We have already done the unthinkable so many times. Let us not look for some-thing worse, Sandra. That itself is an unspeakable crime. It matters only that you, Sandra, knew that something unspeakable, unfathomable, had been done. A great evil to the earth. It matters that you knew that we had done it.

"It matters that you knew that the source of such devastation was the world to which you had given your life. We have done it. We needed to know that." The rhythm of lament was in his voice.

"I can't say it elegantly," she said, "so I will say it plainly. I didn't know I couldn't be a climatologist and also listen to the voices. I want to sit outside and watch the weather rather than sit inside and watch the instruments. I want to be in the weather so I will learn what to do.

"I had thought," she continued, almost trance-like, "if I used what I knew for the common good ... even if ... the means often do harm. If I chose the lesser ... if I measured it against the greater ... if I sometimes looked away .... But I can't continue that way. I can't continue to live by nu-clear light. I must defer to the voices. I have to learn their languages. I don't know. It's really raining. I am very wet again. It eases the blue fire. This is good."

The sky lit, candle after candle, lit and extinguished. Crack of lightning. Across the canyon on the highest mountain where the trees have been logged, a few trees remained. The tallest pine was struck. Flames engulfed the tree. The tree would burn for hours. Flames shot straight up blazing with sap sputtering from the trunk. From the black cloud that loosed the charge, rain began to fall. The tree would burn, then smolder, but it would not collapse, it would not set anything else on fire. Its candle would burn on its own and go out on its own. The fire was dull, murky, smoke laden. In the distance, an alarm of coyotes. Ravens were flying westward, seeking white hail on black feathers. The thundercloud was reshaping itself, a funnel was forming as the rains descended.

She reached up and undid her chignon and let her hair flow down like water upon them.

The thunder came up sharp and loud, insistent and reverberating, flapping its dark wings. A horse whinnied. Terrence remembered the horses living free on the reservation when he was a boy. Memory opening like a break in the clouds, blue. "I will have to tell you about the wild horses I knew as a child," he said.

REFERENCES

When I first read the two references to Indigenous knowledge in the ICCP report of 2007, I was as unnerved as Terrence Green. I was exceedingly grateful to read them and disturbed that such essential wisdom is not consistently respected and included in all climate and environmental discussions.

9.6.2 Indigenous knowledge systems

The term 'indigenous knowledge' is used to describe the knowledge systems developed by a community as opposed to the scientific knowledge that is generally referred to as 'modern' knowledge (Ajibade, 2003). Indigenous knowledge is the basis for local-level decision-making in many rural communities. It has value not only for the culture in which it evolves, but also for scientists and planners striving to improve conditions in rural localities. Incorporating indigenous knowledge into climate-change policies can lead to the development of effective adaptation strategies that are cost-effective, participatory and sustainable (Robinson and Herbert, 2001).

9.6.2.1 Indigenous knowledge in weather forecasting

Local communities and farmers in Africa have developed intricate systems of gathering, predicting,interpreting and decision-making in relation to weather. A study in Nigeria, for example, shows that farmers are able to use knowledge of weather systems such as rainfall, thunderstorms, windstorms, harmattan (a dry dusty wind that blows along the north-west coast of Africa) and sunshine to prepare for future weather (Ajibade and Shokemi, 2003). Indigenous methods of weather forecasting are known to complement farmers' planning activities in Nigeria. A similar study in Burkina Faso showed that farmers' forecasting knowledge encompasses shared and selective experiences. Elderly male farmers formulate hypotheses about seasonal rainfall by observing natural phenomena, while cultural and ritual specialists draw predictions from divination, visions or dreams (Roncoli et al., 2001). The most widely relied-upon indicators are the timing, intensity and duration of cold temperatures during the early part of the dry season (November to January). Other forecasting indicators include the timing of fruiting by certain local trees, the water level in streams and ponds, the nesting behaviour of small quail-like birds, and insect behaviour in rubbish heaps outside compound walls (Roncoli et al., 2001).

Indigenous peoples

No internationally accepted definition of indigenous peoples exists. Common characteristics often applied under international law, and by United Nations agencies to distinguish indigenous peoples include: residence within or attachment to geographically distinct traditional habitats, ancestral territories, and their natural resources; maintenance of cultural and social identities, and social, economic, cultural and political institutions separate from mainstream or dominant societies and cultures; descent from population groups present in a given area, most frequently before modern states or territories were created and current borders defined; and self-identification as being part of a distinct indigenous cultural group, and the desire to preserve that cultural identity.

http://www.ipcc.ch/publications_and_data/publications_and_data_reports.htm

At the time that I was reading the 2007 ICCP report, I came across a seminal essay, "Indigenous Knowledge and Science Revisited," Glen S. Aikenhead and Masakata Ogawa, published the same year, in <u>Cultural Studies of Science Education Journal</u>. I understood then the recognition of value and importance of Indigenous wisdom had finally begun.

I wish to acknowledge the prodigious studies of Native American history by Clifford E. Trafzer, including but not limited to the history of Northwest Indians, with particular gratitude for: <u>Death Stalks the Yakama: Epidemiological Transitions and Mortality on the Yakama Indian Reservation, 1888-1964</u>, 1997 and <u>Grandmother, Grandfather an Old Wolf</u>, Michigan State University Press, 1998.

Thank you also to Donald M. Hines for his treasure, <u>Magic in the Mountains, The Yakima Shaman, Power and Practice</u>, Great Eagle Publishing, 1993.

And thank you Peter Nabokov for the extraordinary texts, <u>Where the Lightning Strikes: The Lives of American Indian Sacred Places</u>, and <u>Indian Running: Native American History and Tradition</u>

And finally gratitude for the richness and heartbreak of bearing witness in <u>Sweet Medicine: Sites of Indian Massacres, Battlefields, and Treaties</u>, Photographs by Drew Books, Essay by Patricia Nelson Limerick, Foreword by James Welch, University of New Mexico Press, Albuquerque, NM, Copyright © 1995.

ABOUT THE AUTHOR

Deena Metzger is a writer and healer living at the end of the road in Topanga, California. Her books include the novels *La Negra y Blanca*, (winner of the 2012 Oakland Pen Award); *Feral; Doors: A Fiction for Jazz Horn; The Other Hand; What Dinah Thought; Skin: Shadows/Silence, A Love Letter in the Form of a Novel* and *The Woman Who Slept With Men to Take the War Out of Them* - a novel in the form of a play. The latter is included *Tree: Essays and Pieces*, which features her celebrated Warrior Poster on its cover testifying to a woman's triumph over breast cancer.

Ruin and Beauty: New and Collected Poems is her most recent book of poetry. Earlier books of poetry are *A Sabbath Among The Ruins, Looking for the Faces of God, The Axis Mundi Poems* and *Dark Milk*.

Writing For Your Life: A Guide and Companion to the Inner Worlds is her classic text on writing and the imagination. Two plays *Not As Sleepwalkers* and *Dreams Against the State* have been produced in theaters and various venues. She co-edited the anthology, *Intimate Nature: The Bond Between Women and Animals*, one of the first testimonies to the reality and nature of animal intelligence. *Entering the Ghost River: Meditations on the Theory and Practice of Healing*, and *From Grief Into Vision: A Council* examine the tragic failure of contemporary culture and provide guidance for personal, political, environmental and spiritual healing.

Deena is a radical thinker on behalf of the natural world and planetary survival, a teacher of writing and healing practices for 50 years and a writer and activist profoundly concerned with peacemaking, restoration and sanctuary for a beleaguered world. She has been convening ReVisioning Medicine – bringing Indigenous medicine ways to heal the medical world – since 2004, and is imagining a Literature of Restoration as foundations of a new viable culture. She, with writer Michael Ortiz Hill, introduced Daré to North America in 1999. Daré and the 19 Ways Training for the 5th World, are unique forms of individual, community and environmental healing based on Indigenous and contemporary medicine and wisdom traditions.

Cheyenne is her current four-legged companion.